MY DARLING ROGUE

A WICKED ROGUES ROMANCE BOOK I

APRIL MORAN

MY DARLING ROGUE

A Wicked Rogues Romance
Book I

By April Moran

Editing by: Kendra's Editing and Book Services

www.kendragaither.com

Cover Design by: Dragonfly Ink Graphic Design Services

For James, always.
For every person who supported me when I said I would write romance books.
And for every person who did not—you only made me more determined to follow that dream.

CHAPTER 1

1 *841*
Beaumont
The country estate of the Earl and Countess of Ravenswood

GABRIEL ROSE CURSED THE SKY. The earth. The moon and sun. God and gods. It did not matter. He cursed them all for the hand Fate just dealt him.

"Lady Celia Buchanan and her mother will soon arrive," Sebastian Cain, the Earl of Ravenswood, said with a grin. "Can you control yourself with the object of your obsession in such close proximity?"

"What do you mean by that?" Gabriel's response was almost a snarl.

Sebastian chuckled. "Do you think I've not noticed how you stare at her? How you have trailed in her wake around the edges of every social gathering this past year? I know full well your interest in her. What I don't understand is why you've not acted upon it."

As the earl's man in all things requiring assistance, and as one of his closest friends, Gabriel knew it was useless hiding the truth. Sebastian was incredibly astute, which was to Gabriel's detriment on this subject. But Sebastian was also discreet. Any knowledge regarding Gabriel Rose and his interest in a certain young lady would never become fodder for the gossip mills.

But Sebastian's insistence on discussing the matter was problematic. Gabriel realized he'd failed in concealing the unfortunate attraction he carried for Lady Celia Buchanan.

"You may forget my humble origins, Seb, but I cannot. Any interest I have in Lady Celia, or any lady for that matter, must remain unspoken. Her father would never allow it, and I daresay her brother would muster an attempt on my life because of it."

"Nonsense. Tristan Buchanan is far too enamored with his new wife to pay heed to his sister's activities, or her admirers. This is your chance, my friend. Do something about your Lady Celia. Something other than lurking in the corners and admiring her from afar."

Gabriel tamped down his rising irritation. This was a conversation he never envisioned having with Sebastian, but little dissuaded the earl when his mind was set on something he deemed important.

"I know women seek your company," Sebastian pointed out. "From all social standings."

"Perhaps. But this particular one would not welcome the attention of a bastard. You know this." Gabriel crossed one leg over the other as he settled back in the leather-tufted chair. In one hand he held a glass containing a splash of Ravenswood's finest brandy.

"Oh, stop acting as though you carry the plague. You know as well as I that the matter of your birth does not hold the same weight as it might have in the past. There are plenty of bastards in society. Some even wind up with pretty wives, if not wealthy ones." Sebastian held his glass up and toasted Gabriel. "Catch Lady Celia and you'll have secured two in one."

"Those bastards are at least acknowledged by their fathers," Gabriel shot back. "Mine provided an education and the most basic of care when I was a lad, but that was the extent of his willingness to claim me as his son."

Sebastian regarded Gabriel with piercing scrutiny. "While true your father is unknown, the fact he was a nobleman counts for something. You've far more standing than you realize. And if you are indeed interested in Lady Celia, you should pursue her. Before she is wrangled into marriage with someone unworthy."

"I am *someone unworthy*, Sebastian." Gabriel took a sip of the brandy, savoring its rich flavor. "Your persistence in elevating me beyond my station is a noble endeavor. Useless, but noble. And you know I've no wish to wed. I can only hope you will not pursue the matter. Or, God forbid, set Lady Ravenswood to the task."

Sebastian laughed at that somber declaration.

"Ivy will be heartbroken. After all, Her Ladyship is an excellent matchmaker. Gabriel, you will not lurk in the shadows during this event. I insist you join the festivities the same as my other guests. And instead of pining after Lady Celia with moonstruck eyes, you will press your suit as the other gentlemen most assuredly will. She's certainly a challenge, but I'm confident you'll capture her attention."

Gabriel considered the earl. He was a most stubborn man. Annoyingly so. And also his closest friend. After Sebastian saved his life they'd become family. Gabriel was devoted both to him and Ivy, the Countess of Ravenswood. He'd sworn he would serve them for as long as he was needed.

It was the unique situation he'd been born into. As the bastard son of a nobleman and an actress of the opera, Gabriel straddled both worlds. He blended just as easily in a ballroom full of pompous lords and silk-clad ladies as he did in a whore-house populated by murderers and thieves.

"Ah, Gabriel. From the moment I fought alongside you behind that French brothel, I've known you as a man of honor, honesty, and fortitude." Sebastian smiled, his tone gentle but stern. "These characteristics are far more valuable than titles or land holdings. I challenge anyone to dispute your worth." He sighed heavily. "I feel our friendship holds you hostage. The vow you made has held you here longer than I ever expected. You should not spend a lifetime tied to me. It's time you sought a wife. Time you put aside your oath and find happiness within your own home. Find contentment with a family you may call yours. Everyone deserves that. I dare say bastards deserve such gifts far more than the average man. And if Lady Celia is not the woman you see spending a lifetime with, then you must find someone who *does* make you happy."

Gabriel found it difficult admitting Celia Buchanan was precisely the woman he wished to claim for his own.

If only she wasn't so far out of reach.

"You are quite mad, my friend." Gabriel sighed. "Does Lady Ravenswood realize how mad her husband truly is?"

"Of course, she does. Who else would demand I speak with you on this subject?" Sebastian replied cheerfully. "She and I share the same affliction, apparently, because she first pointed out how your eyes never stray far from Lady Celia. And that the lady's gaze seeks you out as well when she believes no one watches."

"Now, that, I know is a lie." Gabriel laughed heartily. "The lady in question has no interest in me. True, I've aided her a few times in past months, but we've hardly said two words to one another. She views me as little more than a servant. Perhaps even less."

Although he laughed at the possibility of Celia Buchanan ever accepting him as a suitor, Gabriel admitted the idea filled him with a longing he could not ignore. He'd give his soul to have all obstacles of class and background erased between them. To be seen as an equal, one fit to pursue the lady he desired, accepted based on his character and deeds.

"Who knows what will occur?" Sebastian shrugged. "Give it a chance and see where it goes, my friend. I vow the lady will not resist if you exert even a tiny bit of the charm you possess."

"You truly are mad as a hatter, Ravenswood."

Sebastian only grinned. "You may be right, but I'm also rarely wrong. Now, drink up and gather your courage, for when the lady arrives, you will find yourself quite busy with the task of proving yourself worthy."

CELIA TRAILED behind her mother as they stepped into the grand, barrel-vaulted foyer of Beaumont, the Ravenswood ancestral home.

"Ah, there you are! At last!" The Countess of Ravenswood swept forward, embracing Lady Darby and Celia in turn. "I do hope your journey was a pleasant one?"

"Not a single raincloud marred the skies during our trip," Lady Darby replied. "I wish Lord Darby could have accompanied us, but with his health, it just was not wise to venture so far from the estate."

Celia remained silent as the conversation carried on without her. Glancing around, she recognized a few guests who'd come to greet them. She smiled at Lady Sara Bentley, then stiffened when she saw the huge form of the man she'd studiously avoided over the past few months.

Gabriel Rose shouldered his way through the small crowd and positioned himself in a doorway, leaning against the door-jamb as if he owned it and the world. His eyes caught hers, and although she blushed at the scrutiny of his gaze, Celia did not look away. Instead, her chin lifted, and she glared back, her cheeks heating to a faint pink.

The last time she'd seen this man, he'd non-too gently rescued her from a precarious situation, marching her to safety in silence. The scowl on his face that night had suggested he found her slightly distasteful.

It was a thoroughly humiliating experience. Made more so by the fact she had required his help and been grateful for it. Only to have that gratitude snubbed when he unceremoniously left her outside Lady Sutter's ballroom. He stalked away without even so much as a glance over his shoulder.

Ivy's turquoise eyes rounded with sympathy. "Oh, my dear Lady Darby. I hope the earl is not unwell."

Lady Darby waved her hand. "No need to fret. He's much better since our son's marriage. Longleigh and Violet send their gratitude for your attendance at the wedding."

"We are so happy for the couple. Violet is such a lovely girl. Celia? I heard you recently visited the new couple. How are they?"

"Disgustingly happy and content with one another."

Lady Darby frowned at her daughter's flippant reply while Ivy laughed with delight. "How wonderful for them! I know you are most relieved, seeing how close you and Violet are as friends."

"Much like yourself and the earl, Lady Ravenswood, my dear brother and his new wife are perfect examples of a successful union." Celia sighed as if troubled with the heaviest burdens. "I can only hope I am similarly blessed one day. But it appears one must wade through a veritable sea of frogs before finding a prince, and so far, my luck has proved abysmal."

Celia could see Gabriel Rose's reaction to her rash declaration. The man's lips twitched with something that might have been the beginnings of a grin. Hard, golden-brown eyes assessed her, searching for a chink in her armor.

Celia's jaw tilted higher. He could look, but he would not find one. She would not allow it.

"Celia," Lady Darby warned under her breath. "It is most unseemly to refer to your suitors in such a manner." She flashed a helpless smile as Ivy choked back her own giggle. "Excuse my daughter, Lady Ravenswood. You are friends, so I know you are accustomed to how she speaks her mind even when it is not proper."

Ivy leaned in, breaking off the connection between Celia and the impossibly arrogant Gabriel Rose. She hugged Celia tighter this time, her voice low with sympathy and understanding for the trials all young ladies endured in their search for a suitable husband.

"Perhaps you should adjust your hunting techniques, sweet friend. And look for a frog among princes."

CHAPTER 2

"Shall I tighten these ribbons, miss?"

Celia turned so her maid could lace the corset up a bit tighter. "Thank you, Katie. My dress is there on the bed when you are ready."

"I'm glad you are wearing the blue silk," Lady Darby said from her perch at a walnut wood vanity table. She attached a pair of teardrop-shaped diamond earrings to her earlobes. "It is lovely with your coloring. A gentleman shall find it difficult looking away once he sees you."

Celia lifted her arms so the dress could be lowered over her head. She waited until the fabric was settled around her before addressing her mother. "I'll have none of your matchmaking, Mother. Promise you will refrain from negotiations, deal makings, and comments regarding the size of a man's estate. Or lack thereof."

Lady Darby smiled. "There are no men in attendance lacking qualifications as husband material. But I shall refrain from remarking on any particular one. As with your brother, I hope you find your happiness in your own manner. But I would be remiss in my parental duties if I did not guide you."

Celia bent and kissed her mother's cheek. "You hide your schemes well, but I realize how you push us into making the correct decisions." Her tone held a note of exasperated affection. "It worked with Tristan and Violet. You dangled her before him like a ripe apple until he could not help but notice her."

Lady Darby's eyes twinkled with mischief. "I admit a tiny bit of matchmaking, but your brother's decision was his own. And it was the correct one to make. I only endeavor to do the same for my dearest daughter."

"Well, do not endeavor too hard," Celia smiled.

Her mother reached up, patting Celia's cheek in a show of affection. "Of course not, darling. We both know you will make your own choices. With or without my interference."

CELIA FELT his presence before she saw him. Gabriel Rose had a way of filling a space without saying a word. Oh, the man carefully lurked in the shadows, but it was difficult ignoring how the air shifted and changed when he was in the vicinity.

"May I help you with that, my lady?" His low rumble of a voice, beautiful in its purity and yet intricately masculine, sent a quiver down her spine.

Celia glanced over her shoulder as he approached. She'd just exited the library with an armload of books stacked as high as her chin. The volumes contained plays by Shakespeare and had been gathered for an afternoon of entertainment. She, along with a group of other guests would reenact a few favorite scenes.

"No need. I have it under control," she insisted just as one book on top of the stack slid sideways. It defeated the pressure of her chin holding everything together and tumbled with a clatter onto the gleaming hardwood floor.

"So it appears." A hint of amusement danced in Gabriel's words.

Celia grit her teeth in annoyance. She bent at the knees, maintaining the balanced books while attempting to retrieve the one she'd dropped. A rather graceful maneuver, if she thought so herself.

The remaining books wobbled and began giving way.

"Oh, blast it!" Celia exclaimed.

She tried containing the spill, but that proved useless. The books splayed across the marble floor in a haphazard pile of leather and gilt covers, spines, and exposed pages.

"Now, see what you've done." Dropping to her hands and knees, she began pulling the books back into a heap. It was wrong directing her annoyance at this man, but it was his fault he'd broken her concentration.

Gabriel obviously heard the words muttered beneath her breath and the irritation they contained. Biting back a grin, he stepped forward, although Celia raised a hand to ward him off.

The glint of interest in his eyes could not be dismissed. Celia knew she was susceptible when it came to gaining the attention of inappropriate men. Why she found rough and tumble males so much more attractive than the titled gentlemen of her world was an inconvenient tragedy.

With a sigh, her hand lowered, and she gazed up at him as he came closer.

"If I am to blame, then at least accept my assistance." He knelt beside her, his body large and intimidating, and Celia's breath caught in her throat. Large hands with squared-off, clean nails and blunt fingertips quickly arranged the books into a manageable stack.

Celia could not stop staring at those hands of his. Couldn't help seeing how strong they were. How capable. And she couldn't stop remembering the heat of his palm when he escorted her to safety the last time they'd been together.

That night at the Sutter's Ball.

"This is not necessary, Mister Rose," Celia protested weakly, but it was too late. Gabriel already had the books tucked under his arm and was rising to his feet. His free hand wedged beneath her elbow as he dragged her up along with his momentum. His scent, clean and sharp with a swirling combination of leather, spice, and evergreens, tickled her nostrils.

Damn him. He smelled delicious.

"Where are you taking these?" He murmured, "I will carry them for you."

Celia could not form an immediate response. For a moment, she simply stood in the shadow of his body and basked in the comfort his presence created. There was something ridiculously intimate about the way he knelt and gathered her books. How he spoke in that husky dulcet voice of his as if intent on gaining her trust. Yes. There was something exhilarating about it all. Something horribly… perfect.

"Lady Celia?" Gabriel's head tilted at her silence, his eyes glittering like gold dust in the brightly lit corridor. "If you will lead the way, I shall follow."

His voice dropped into little more than a coaxing whisper. It did strange things to Celia's insides. Made her tingle in the most surprising places and ache in others. She didn't understand how he possessed such power, but it was alarming. And it was certainly inappropriate she should feel anything at all for this man when no meaningful connection existed between them.

"Um, the rear terrace. The others await me there," she finally stuttered, cheeks flushing with embarrassment. She was behaving like a complete half-wit who'd never been in the presence of a handsome man before.

"Very well." Gabriel released her arm and Celia felt the loss immediately. It was as though the sun had gone behind a cloud.

Did he know how he affected her? She suspected he did. The beginnings of a smile made his lips twitch. Lips that looked firm and irrationally plush at the same time. Everything about Gabriel Rose was an annoying, mysterious contradiction. She was foolishly fascinated by the paradox this man presented to the world.

A nod of his head was a deferential invitation that she begin walking ahead of him. "My lady."

Taking a deep breath, Celia started down the corridor. A cloak of politeness settled over her, tamping down the attraction she was experiencing. She was the daughter of an earl, for goodness sakes. And being unnerved by someone outside her social circle was unacceptable. And dangerous. "Thank you for your assistance, Mister Rose."

Gabriel chuckled, his amusement setting her teeth on edge yet again.

Blast the man.

"Think nothing of it, Lady Celia. It appears I have a habit of coming to your aid when you are in need."

CHAPTER 3

Gabriel Rose clenched his teeth.

The whisperings from inside Ravenswood's library began low, but the tone was climbing higher. He could hear the anger in their voices, although thick oak doors muffled the sound.

He knew who was inside that room. Awareness sent an unfamiliar noise rising in his throat. It was almost a growl. A tiny sound constructed of annoyance and foreboding. Certainly, nothing good would come of this situation.

It was two o'clock in the morning. If anyone should stumble across either him or the couple whispering furiously behind those library doors, there would be hell to pay.

"Ow!"

"Serves you right, you miscreant—Oh! How dare you? Stop that! Stop this very instant!"

Gabriel's fists tightened. Obviously, the owner of that very feminine voice required assistance. He'd been reluctant to intercede before now, but this development most definitely changed things. The thought of rescuing her again sent a twinge of anticipation singing through his veins. And the possibility of collecting on her gratitude was even more intriguing.

He unfurled himself from the uncomfortable chair where he'd spent a quarter hour patiently waiting for the rendezvous to end. He stretched, tilting his neck side to side and popping the knotted kinks out.

A crash came from inside the library, and Gabriel immediately straightened, alarm rippling throughout his body. Before he could react, the doors flung open.

"Damnation, woman! You've split my chin!" Lord Robert Harvey exclaimed, backing out of the room. Dotting at the blood on his chin, he did not notice Gabriel standing just steps away.

Gabriel carefully retreated into the shadows. He'd rather his presence remain unknown as it appeared the incident might resolve without his interference.

"If you ever attempt that again, I shall do much more," Lady Celia Buchanan threatened. She followed Robert's retreat until she stood inside the doorway.

She wore only nightclothes, a billowy, muslin wrap the color of soft butter molding along her curves. Her feet were bare, toes curling against the chill of the hardwood floor. Dark waves of hair were only slightly tamed by a thick braid that hung nearly to the middle of her back. Little tendrils escaped the braid's confines and curled around her face.

Gabriel swallowed hard at the sight of such decadence and retreated another step so the corridor's deep shadows enveloped him even more.

Robert muttered beneath his breath. It appeared he might approach Celia, but instead, he glared at her, indecisive and angry before turning on his heel and abruptly stalking away.

"Oaf," Celia muttered in a loud whisper. She watched Robert disappear into the darkness before glancing down at the broken end of the candlestick clutched in her hand. "Oh, blast it."

Gabriel waited until the man rounded the corner. Then, his jaw set at a grim angle, he materialized from the shadows.

Celia squeaked in alarm at his sudden appearance, her dark brown eyes wide. "Mister Rose!" She sputtered. "Whatever are you doing here?"

"Back inside the library. Quickly. Unless you wish to find yourself locked into marriage to that buffoon," Gabriel growled, moving past Celia while simultaneously grabbing her arm.

He dragged her into the library's interior, shutting the door behind him. Only the low burning fire in the grate and a single lamp provided light in the spacious room.

"What the Devil are you talking about?" Celia asked with breathless annoyance. She trotted to match Gabriel's pace, then bumped into him when he stopped in front of an ornately carved wall panel.

He grunted when he felt her breasts against his arm and heard her little exhale of surprise.

Focus, Gabriel, on the problem at hand. And forget how soft she is. How warm her arm is within your grip. Forget all of that.

He needed a good place to hide her. Not a single divan in this room was high enough to crawl beneath and a quick search would mean discovery.

"Here." Gabriel pushed on a wall panel. It swung open with a slight groan, revealing a space just large enough for a person to stand. A secret passage led from there to an opening just beyond the kitchens. It was a holdover from Beaumont's long and storied past, with only a select few aware of its existence.

"My goodness. What a clever thing," Celia marveled before her brow creased in a frown. She stared at Gabriel with frank suspicion, then back at the space. "Hide? In there? Whatever for?"

"Because, unless I miss my guess, Lord Harvey will return soon with witnesses to your ruination. Now, either you go in there, or I do. Make your choice, Lady Celia, but know should I go into that space, they will find only you here. And while I'm aware of your behavior of granting men the honor of kissing you, you must admit the dangers of your current situation."

Celia's chin lifted in a challenging manner. "A woman should not be forced into marriage simply because she allowed a few harmless kisses, Mister Rose."

Gabriel inclined his head in mocking deference. "That is true, but in your case, it will hardly matter. At this late hour, dressed as you are and alone with that man, there will be no talking your way out of this misadventure." He barely suppressed a groan when she began worrying her bottom lip between her teeth. Bloody hell if he wasn't dying for a taste of the same kisses she granted other men caught in her orbit. "A hasty trip to the altar with a groom ecstatic to have caught you is your future if you don't do as I say. Make your choice, my lady."

An expression of dread crossed Celia's lovely features at the mention of a groom. Her skin paled until it glowed like cream in the firelight. Indignation quickly faded as the dire situation impressed upon her. "Yes-yes, of course. You are right, but sir, you see, I am rather uncomfortable in dark places. I don't think I can possibly—"

"Lady Celia, this is the second time I have rescued you from this particular gentleman. Both occasions have taken place at night so I find your discomfort suspect. I don't believe I'm remiss in thinking you'll be damnably more uncomfortable wedded to that boor. Or, perhaps you prefer being caught alone with myself?" Gabriel's brow raised in question as Celia hastily shook her head in contradiction. "I thought not," he said in grim satisfaction while shoving Celia into the space. "Now, be quiet. I'll let you out once I deem it safe."

Celia's chin tilted as she handed Gabriel the broken candlestick. "You may use that on Lord Harvey should you find it necessary, Mister Rose."

"I doubt there will be further bloodshed," Gabriel replied in a dry tone. "Remember, not a peep out of you."

The door pulled closed, the light receding until he could no longer see her face.

Crossing over to a divan, Gabriel saw the other end of the candlestick alongside a pile of books scattered across the floor. A nearly empty bottle of brandy sat on a table beside the divan. Picking up the other half of the candlestick, Gabriel quickly devised a plausible story as footsteps neared the library.

The doors swung open with a bang.

"She's in here, all right," Lord Harvey addressed someone Gabriel could not immediately see. His voice held a smug note of triumph. "How else do you think I obtained this damnable cut on my chin? Lady Celia plays rough, but the game is at its end. I'll claim her as my bride with you serving as witnesses to her downfall."

CHAPTER 4

Celia smothered a panicked whimper.

Remember. Breathe through the nose.

Carefully, she exhaled through her nostrils. Slowly, deliberately, until the wave of panic enveloping her was staved off using techniques she'd learned over the years.

This space behind the hidden panel was horribly dark. And the air was dank. Musty. A thin sliver of light penetrated where the false panel met the wall. It wasn't much, but it was enough that she wasn't left standing in complete darkness.

What a god-awful tangle she'd gotten herself into this time. Robert, that twit, was completely to blame.

How could she have known he was up at this hour? Roaming the hallways during a break from an all-night card game, he'd followed when Celia slipped into the library. He'd shut the door against her protests, taking the books she'd selected and setting them beside the divan. Then he tugged her into his arms.

Oh, what a fool she had been agreeing to a game of Kiss the Candlestick with him some months ago. That unfortunate incident resulted in a very precarious situation she'd barely escaped before. And today, during a reenactment of *The Taming of the*

Shrew, he'd taken even further advantage. Pressing her against his body, forcefully claiming her mouth for one scene, then refusing to release her at its end.

She'd played along for the sake of the others gathered in the rose garden, accepting their applause when it was over, but Celia realized the trouble she'd fallen into. Lord Robert Harvey had it in his rather thick skull that he'd gained a spot on her list of potential husbands.

Was the man worthy of kissing? Yes. Robert was handsome, charming, and smelled pleasant enough. In fact, he was only one of a handful of men she actually *enjoyed* kissing.

But marriage? That was taking things a bit too far. She'd yet to find a man suitable for that. Suitable for *her.*

Taking another deep breath, Celia leaned her forehead against the panel wall. She could not make out what was being said. The voices were muffled, but she recognized Gabriel Rose's controlled rumble.

It made her stomach flip over itself.

And Celia found it annoying she should recognize the man's voice at all.

She supposed she should be grateful for his quick action in saving her again. That is *if* he managed pulling this off. A hysterical giggle almost escaped her at the thought of Robert squaring off against the other brawny, well-muscled man. And if Gabriel's own size and personal countenance did not give one reason to pause, the influential friends he carried in his pockets certainly would. It was madness crossing a man so well connected with both the upper echelons of society and the criminals in the darkest corners of England.

Celia's palms grew damp. Gabriel Rose was truly fearsome. The man was built like a mountain. Darkly brooding, but with a surprising twinkle in his eye when amused. And the scar slicing like a lightning bolt through his left eyebrow only enhanced his mysteriousness. With a ruthless reputation backing up the frightening appearance, he was not someone a sane person would dare trifle with.

Celia vividly recalled the night he rescued her from that dimly lit garden path just three months before. She remembered how he stared at her. Furious and with a glint of helpless attraction in his darkly golden brown eyes. He helped her escape Robert's drunken pursuit by taking her arm and navigating the path's twists and turns. Returned her to the safety of Lady Sutter's ballroom without a single word.

Then he'd disappeared into the shadows along the crowd's fringes before she could stutter out her gratitude.

Gabriel came to her aid then and he did the same now. Like an angel swooping down. Wings spread wide in a muscled shield of protection.

The voices drew closer. Despite the fear of discovery, Celia pressed her ear against the wall, straining to hear the conversation. She must see what was happening. Perhaps if she squinted hard enough with one eye while looking through the tiny crack in the wood...

She could see the divan in the pool of lamplight, but nothing else.

"When I entered, I saw no one. Only this broken candlestick and a bottle of brandy. And it is nearly empty, as you can see," Gabriel said in the calmest of manners. He moved into Celia's line of vision.

Her heart gave an odd little jump of exhilaration.

"How do you explain my injury, sir?" Robert bit out.

Gabriel chuckled in a tone so melodic and soothing that even Celia believed his assertion. "I imagine, Lord Harvey, you tumbled from the divan and landed on the candlestick. It is rather late, after all. A bit too much brandy, and well, accidents are likely. I say, you might want to have that wound seen to. Speaking as someone with experience, you could end up with a scar."

"He's right, Harvey. It is rather nasty," another voice piped up. Celia squinted harder to identify it, but the gentleman remained on the periphery.

"Lady Celia could not have slipped past me. There is nowhere else she could be other than this room," Robert insisted. Ducking down, he searched under the piece of furniture.

"Unless she's the size of a barn cat, she couldn't fit under there, Harvey." This came from a fourth man in the room. Possibly Lord Anniston, but Celia wasn't sure. "Perhaps Rose is right. You left our card game some time ago. Maybe after too much of Ravenswood's excellent brandy, you found a cozy spot here by the fire and dozed off. Maybe you dreamed Lady Celia was here."

"I did not dream it. She was here. I can smell her perfume." Robert's voice was terse.

"I smell nothing, my lord," Gabriel said calmly.

Celia watched with one eye as Robert moved toward the floor-to-ceiling windows just beyond the divan. He shook the heavy drapes as though Celia might tumble out of the fabric's folds. "I did not imagine kissing her, nor how she filled my hands—"

"Careful, my lord." Gabriel's low growl was a warning of such violence it cut Robert off in mid-sentence. "It's unwise maligning a guest of Lord Ravenswood. You risk offending our host, as well as the Earl of Darby and the lady's brother."

The man Celia thought was Anniston spoke up. "Come along now, Harvey. Let's get you cleaned up and see the damage in better light. I believe you will require a stitch or two if you are to keep that pretty face of yours intact."

"Tiny stitches are best, provided there is someone skilled with a needle up and about at this hour. Your valet, perhaps?" Gabriel's voice grew distant as the men's receding footsteps indicated their departure. "You certainly do not wish to end up with a scar like mine."

Letting out a sigh of relief, Celia leaned away from the sliver of light. She rubbed her eyes, easing the strain she'd placed on them.

There was the slight swish of the library doors closing, men's rumbling voices, then nothing.

Complete silence.

Celia's breath hung in her throat while the eerie stillness stretched on. Now that the danger of discovery was over, the darkness around her was growing. But as her heart pounded like exploding cannons in her ears, and her lungs expanded and deflated with increasingly shallow pants for oxygen, she heard glass touching glass followed by a sigh of satisfaction.

Once again, she placed one eye to the panel's crack. Her mouth formed an incredulous "oh!"

Gabriel refilled the abandoned glass tumbler with a healthy splash of brandy and downed it.

The insufferable cad! Has he forgotten he locked me in this space the size of a broom closet? How dare he—

"I've not forgotten about you," Gabriel stated calmly as though he could plainly hear her innermost thoughts. He poured yet another glass of brandy and took a more deliberate sip.

Celia sucked in another deep, shallow breath. Did his tone carry a thread of amusement? And was it her imagination, or was the space around her becoming steadily darker?

Gabriel continued speaking, oblivious that Celia's panic was increasing by the second. "Lord Harvey might return, and I'll not risk being discovered here with you. My efforts in concealing your presence would be for naught. So, my lady, you shall remain where you are until I am certain they will not come back."

Several seconds of silence passed.

"Very foolhardy of you to meet with the man like this," Gabriel remarked in a strangely lowered voice. "Here in Ravenswood's home, I mean. Somewhat dangerous as well, with all manner of guests roaming about. Is your mother aware of your nocturnal adventures? I cannot imagine she condones such behavior. You would do well to stick with hasty kisses in alcoves and along deserted garden paths."

Celia's stomach dropped as Gabriel's insinuations sunk in. Did he actually think she'd sought Robert out for a clandestine affair?

Indignation battled her fear of darkness in a war of emotions.

"Ah, well. No matter." Gabriel let out a long-suffering sigh. "The incident resolved itself rather nicely. Do not fret over repayment for my assistance. A simple thank-you will suffice, as well as your pledge this will not happen again whilst a guest at Beaumont."

The fear rippling through Celia blotted out Gabriel's words. She heard him as if from a distance. As though she stood at the end of a long tunnel while he occupied the other end.

Oh, God. Did something just brush against her foot?

It happened again. Something warm. Something furry. Something *small.*

Her mouth opened with a demand for release from the coffin-like space, but all that escaped her lips was a pitiful whisper. She blindly lashed out, a fist connecting against the wall with a dull thump.

Somehow, she managed a reedy gasp.

"Please."

CHAPTER 5

Gabriel shoved the panel open just in time, catching Celia as she slumped forward. Her eyes were wide, her face ghostly white, and where he gripped her forearms, her skin was cool and clammy.

"What the hell," he muttered as she filled his arms. "You're shivering, Lady Celia."

Celia clung to him, snuggling closer than was proper.

Damnation, there wasn't a single thing proper about any of this.

Walking her toward the divan, Gabriel refilled the crystal tumbler with a healthy dose of brandy, then sank onto the cushioned seat beside her.

"Here. Drink this," he urged, placing the glass against her pale lips.

Celia's huge brown eyes fixated on Gabriel's face as she automatically sipped the liquor. A tiny grimace crossed her features but her hand clutched the tumbler, her fingers closing over his until they both gripped the glass.

Gabriel's jaw tightened as she drank.

The brandy would help Celia regain her composure and,

hopefully, quell the tiny quivers in the tips of her fingers as they pressed against his own.

Gabriel knew he shouldn't, but it was impossible not to stare. His gaze raked her form, clad so sumptuously in all that billowy, yellow muslin. A pang of desire stabbed his insides.

He ruthlessly shoved it away. And pulled the glass away from her mouth.

Lady Celia Buchanan is not meant for the likes of you.

Her shivering was slowly subsiding, her skin tone returning to its usual creamy shade. Licking her lips, she moved her hands in a slight motion that let Gabriel know she wanted more brandy.

"One more sip," he murmured as she closed her eyes and drank again from the glass. "It won't do to have you intoxicated as well as compromised."

Celia's eyes flew open at that, the chocolaty brown depths darkening with his statement.

"I've had brandy before, Mister Rose." She did not turn her gaze away as he considered her.

"Of that, I have no doubt, Lady Celia. But best not to complicate matters further, don't you agree?" Gabriel set the glass down.

"Yes." She sighed, her brow creasing with a tiny frown.

Silence fell between them once more, with Celia seemingly uncaring they sat indecently close on the cranberry-hued settee.

"Thank you for rescuing me." Her voice was tiny, but just a shade resentful.

"You are welcome." Gabriel used the same gentle tone used when digging out information from people reluctant to give up any secrets. "May I ask what frightened you before? When you were inside the passage?"

Celia's eyes cast downward, the thick eyelashes casting shadows on her skin. "It is silly, of course."

"I will not laugh."

"I-I thought a mouse ran across my foot," she muttered.

After years of interrogating people, learning the secrets of the underworlds, and dealing with every sort of criminal, Gabriel knew when someone was lying.

And Celia was lying. Glancing down at her lovely, bare feet, he saw a smudge of dirt across the top of one. His hands itched to take it into his palm, to wipe the offending bit of dust away from the creamy skin. He would be so careful with such a delicate creature.

"Ah, I see. Regardless, I wish it had not come to the point you required concealment."

Her lips tightened with faint irritation. "I agree. Harvey had no right following me here."

Gabriel knew a moment of scorching jealousy. Robert Harvey had every right to be in the library with this girl. "It's not unusual that a man might get certain ideas in his head once he's been granted liberties."

Celia half-turned toward him, eyes flashing with defiance. "I have not granted him anything beyond a few kisses."

"Those kisses were enough, as evidenced by his behavior. I must insist you give your promise you will avoid such predicaments while you and your mother are guests of Lord Ravenswood."

"Who are you to dictate my actions, Mister Rose?" she demanded angrily.

Gabriel leaned closer, his voice lowering to a whisper. "Why, Lady Celia, I am the enforcer of the rules set by the earl."

He'd lied before, claiming he could not smell Celia's perfume. It was a beacon for any man interested in her, and Gabriel was far from immune. It drifted over him. A soft layering of roses, the scent richly delicate and complimented by the essence of tart lemons he decided emanated from her glossy hair.

His gaze gravitated until it landed on her full mouth. A hint of brandy existed in her breath, sweet and heady. Desire washed over Gabriel like a typhoon set on a dangerous course. Kissing Celia would likely result in his complete obliteration. His utter ruin.

"And I will not tolerate disobedience. Do you understand?"

"Kisses mean nothing," she flung back at him, ignoring his subtle threat. "Should I kiss you, Mister Rose, and prove their worthlessness?"

Gabriel's eyebrow rose. "I'm not sure, Lady Celia. Should you?"

The cynical dismissal seemed to infuriate her. With a huff, she replied, "Yes. I think I will. If only to prove I am right. It means *nothing.*"

True, he goaded her, but gentleman or not, he would not deny Celia the opportunity of proving her point. After all, he was simply a man. And wicked enough to anticipate the thrill of her mouth touching his.

He smiled at her and nodded his head.

"Then, by all means, Lady Celia. Do your worst."

Gabriel nearly held his breath when she leaned in closer. They now faced one another in the library's dimness. The crackling of the fire and their soft breathing were the only sounds in the room. Celia hesitated as if reconsidering her brashness, then suddenly, her mouth was on his.

It was a tentative brush of a kiss. Barely even a kiss at all, if the truth was known. And yet, it was as though the air around them was sucked into a vortex of flames. Gabriel's heart thundered with awareness. With heat. With overwhelming want and need—all completely foreign.

And over far too quickly.

Celia eased back until space once again existed between their bodies. Her eyes were wide, confusion flitting in the dark depths. She appeared so lost that Gabriel suspected she'd experienced the same jolt of electricity.

Then she said in a less than triumphant voice, "There, Mister Rose. Do you see? Meaningless."

Gabriel's eyes narrowed. "You are not trying hard enough, Lady Celia." His voice dropped to a silky purr as he deliberately licked his lips, tasting the lingering sweetness of her mouth. "Pretend I am one of your many suitors you've stolen away with for a quiet moment. Pretend we are behind closed doors with others standing just outside. Or that we've hidden behind the tallest hedge of a maze garden. Maybe the corner of a terrace at twilight. Pretend for a moment and kiss me in the same manner you have so many others."

A flare of comprehension spread across Celia's features. "You've been watching me."

Ah, if she only knew how often he watched her.

"A good deal of my position with Ravenswood requires observation from the shadows. It just so happens you frequently appear in those same shadows. And I know you do not kiss the men huddled with you in those dim corners in the same manner you just kissed me."

"How dare you spy on me. I shall have you tossed from this house," Celia vowed in a shaky voice. "Banned from all events and polite society."

"I've never cared much for polite society." Gabriel reached up, brushing away a dark curl that had fallen into her eyes. "But I am curious how you will accomplish your mission. What reasons shall you give for my banishment?"

It was madness, this desire to prod and poke at her with his knowledge of her clandestine activities. He shouldn't give a pauper's half-penny about her affairs, but he couldn't help himself. Over the past year and a half, he'd discovered a disturbing fascination for hellions—this one in particular. He could not stop searching her out whenever they appeared at the same social functions. And while he was hopelessly aware of her every move, Celia danced and kissed her way through the Season and her admirers without a care of his own existence.

It was quite brutal, actually, watching her emerge from secret corners with lips flushed scarlet from stolen kisses and a man close on her heels eager for more of her affection.

Moving on the outer fringes of the same social circles, Gabriel's position proved advantageous. He watched, but never interfered with Celia's actions other than that one nearly disastrous occasion.

That was almost three months ago and happened during one of the last parties of the London Season. He'd seen her to safety, and she acknowledged his help with a slight lift of her chin. After aiding her, he'd blended into the background as was expected.

Yes, he stayed to the shadows, but right now, every shred of self-preservation he possessed was burning into cinders. Right now, he wanted to shake this girl in frustration for her disregard for her own safety. Gabriel realized the danger in his actions in pursuing this. Like a moth incinerated by the very flame enticing it closer, he might never recover from this encounter with Celia.

"Tonight is an excellent example of why you should refrain from such reckless behavior," he said almost gently. He should at least make an attempt at resisting the flame sitting beside him. "You cannot comprehend the danger you repeatedly place yourself in."

Celia's spine straightened as she glared at him. "I shall do as I please, and when I please, sir. I do not require a lecture from someone like you on my personal business."

Gabriel let her words sink in, telling himself he should not accept her brash challenge. However, it was her quickened breath and the failure to place some distance between their bodies that decided matters.

His grin turned lethal. "Ah, it is to be a lesson, then. One I'll happily teach you."

CHAPTER 6

*B*efore Celia could interpret his statement, Gabriel's arms swept around her. She was crushed against a wall of muscle. Surprise stole her breath. She did not even think of fighting his embrace.

He smiled, a lion's smile that hid his true thoughts. It sent a shiver coursing through Celia's veins.

"I hope you learn it well."

"And what is it I am supposed to learn?" Celia asked through clenched teeth. How could he be so devilishly handsome with that dark stubble shadowing his jaw? A gentleman should be either clean-shaven or sport a well-maintained beard. It was unseemly to appear as though one had abandoned the effort of grooming halfway through their toilette.

"Danger lurks around every corner for a beautiful woman. Especially young, wealthy, beautiful women. There is always someone eager to take advantage. For example, I can do with you whatever I please and no one will stop me."

"After surviving the *ton* for the past two years, I've learned to deal with such despicable behavior. In this instance, I would begin by demanding Ravenswood hold you accountable and fully punished for these insults." Celia's voice trembled the slightest bit. "My family would see to it, have no doubt. You would face their wrath. My brother, for example, would make you sorry you even knew my name."

"Not withstanding your brother's ability in defending your honor." Gabriel laughed softly, his perfect white teeth flashing in the darkness. "Do you really think they would find me if I did not wish it? Now, regardless of your threats, let us address something else arousing my curiosity."

"What might that be, Mister Rose?"

"Why does the thought of kissing me frighten you so terribly?"

The question he asked rumbled against her chest. It was impossible not to feel Gabriel's every breath and utterance when he had her pressed so tightly against his larger form. She was nothing more than a hapless bit of prey caught between a predator's paws.

Sweet Jesus, the man's arms were hard as tree trunks. His cologne, a scent of spices and evergreens mingled with the bittersweet tang of the brandy he'd sipped earlier, was making her dizzy. Tilting her head enabled her to better stare at his face. A lock of rich, russet-hued hair concealed the scar's path on his forehead before it sliced through his eyebrow. His eyes were the color of aged whiskey, swirling with bright, gilt-edged embers. Long, thick lashes cast smudgy shadows on his skin, leaving him with an endearingly vulnerable air.

She'd always thought him striking in appearance, but now Celia realized he was more than that. He was brutally handsome.

He moved, shifting quickly until he reclined on the settee; one leg propped up on the cushion, the other braced on the floor. Celia now lay caught between his thighs, her feet curling somewhere around his knees, one hip resting in the junction of his legs, and her upper body twisted so her chest was flush with his own wide expanse. His shirt gaped open, giving her an unobstructed view of his bare chest. It was warm and bronzed, the flesh lightly dusted with a swirl of dark hair. For the oddest reason, Celia wanted to twine her fingers in that smattering of hair. To learn its texture and see how far down his body it actually traveled.

Oh, bloody hell! What the Devil is wrong with me?

Gabriel's large hands settled in the hollow of her spine, and for a fleeting second, Celia felt his fingers flexing as if intent on reaching bare skin before they stilled.

"Well?" he prodded in a low growl.

"I'm not afraid of anything," she swore in a faint whisper.

Beneath the layers of her nightrail and robe, Celia's breasts tingled. It seemed possible her nipples were actually catching fire, if the intense sensations were any indication. Taking a deep, shuddering breath sent her bosom sliding against his skin in a sensuous caress.

Celia abruptly froze in place.

Gabriel bit out a muttered curse.

Heavens, was it possible she might swoon? She'd never done so before in her entire life, but a strange feeling of weightlessness was overtaking her. Staring at Gabriel's firm mouth, in particular the surprising Cupid's bow shape of his upper lip, she dreamily wondered what he might taste of. Brandy? Or something equally dangerous?

"Prove it. Show me how unafraid you are. Kiss me, Lady Celia, and make me believe it."

The challenge and the taunting manner in which Gabriel issued it sent a ripple of defiant anger through the fog Celia floated in. She took another breath, this one a cleansing inhalation that cleared away the cobwebs.

He believed she was afraid of him? That he could lecture her and dictate whom she kissed and where she kissed them? Oh! She did *not* care what this arrogant beast thought. She did not care he correctly guessed Robert's intentions tonight, saving her from certain ruin a second time. Most of all, Celia did not care that deep down inside, in a place where she hid her true feelings from the world, she knew Gabriel Rose was absolutely right about her.

About everything.

Furious with herself and her own reaction to his softly spoken command, she looped her arms around his neck.

"Such bravery," Gabriel murmured.

The mocking statement ignited a fiery need to wipe his smugness away. Celia's lips tightened. She would teach the man a much-needed lesson. She would kiss him and leave him floundering in her wake as she'd done so many others before him.

Just before her mouth touched his, she saw a faint, glittering spark of satisfaction in his tawny gaze. It flitted through her consciousness how very dangerous this behavior was. Perhaps she should reconsider the impetuousness of her actions.

And then it was too late.

Gabriel immediately took control, one hand clamping on the nape of her neck. Holding her at the precise angle he preferred, he kissed Celia.

It was more than a kiss. It was a ravaging. A claiming. A declaration of mastery and possession. Gabriel's tongue battled hers and claimed victory. The kiss deepened. Swirling, dancing, and collecting all resistance. Coaxing her into a state of such wildness, Celia barely comprehended his other hand, still riding low on her back, pushing her pelvis against his own.

The force he exerted, the pressure of their hips grinding in unison, sent shocking waves of pleasure singing through Celia's veins. She melted into him, too caught up in the mystery of sensations to question why it felt amazing and... different. He held her so tightly, kissed her so unapologetically that Celia did not possess the willpower to demand that he release her.

Something was happening. A spark between her thighs. An

igniting of flames. The impending explosion of the universe. All of it uncharted territory and the journey was orchestrated by Gabriel. The ridge of flesh beneath his trousers was made of stone, and with his encouragement, Celia moved helplessly against him.

"By God, you taste sweet as sugarplums," Gabriel muttered, tearing his mouth from hers. He still held the back of her neck in his hand, but his grip shifted. Adjusted until the palm of his hand was under her chin, his thumb rubbing the sensitive spot just behind her earlobe. His fingers splayed out down the other side of her throat, following the vein thumping there with erratic desperation. "Go ahead, my lady. Take your pleasure, but do not forget I am the one giving you this."

The grip on her throat tightened a fraction. His other hand remained locked on her back, directing her movements with breathtaking, unrelenting brutality. Celia was lost in a hazy world of intense desire as she rode him with layers of clothes between their bodies. Her pelvis ground against his with mysterious purpose, searching and desperate, climbing higher and higher until she was thrown over into an abyss where there was no bottom.

The world faded into gray, then burst into every imaginable color. Pleasure, unimaginable and pure, flooded her veins. She may have cried out, sobbing his name, but whatever sound emerged was swallowed by Gabriel's mouth. He kissed her with the fierceness of a lion ripping apart a helpless lamb. While she shuddered atop him in complete surrender, Gabriel finally gentled the assault of his kiss. It melded into a series of soft nibbles on her bottom lip, his tongue engaged in leisurely sweeps of her mouth.

His grip loosened when Celia slumped against him. Even then, Gabriel did not release her. His fingers skated along the line of her throat in a soothing caress. The heavy weight of his palm on the base of her spine slowly eased up.

He did not utter a word, recognizing perhaps that she was a trembling mess of contradicting emotions. Between her legs, his erection still throbbed as the silence stretched on. Together, their breathing slowed until it was measured and even.

Celia blinked, gathering her senses with horrified awareness.

What had he done to her? Worse, why had she allowed it?

Shame crept along her insides until it bloomed red on her cheeks. She had used his body with his encouragement. And loved every second of it. Loved the feel of his cock pressing against her softness. Loved the force he yielded in bending her to his will. She even loved the fact he'd been silently watching her for months.

How could I want that? Why did I not stop him?

Celia swallowed a moan of sudden despair, recognizing the truth inside herself, even if she did not completely understand it. This was something to fear. To hide from. To avoid until a future husband made it his business to control.

"Let me go, Mister Rose."

Her directive wedged between them like an iceberg. Chilling. Cold. Impersonal. A lady speaking to a servant.

"Of course, sugarplum."

Gabriel's arms immediately opened. He watched her scramble off him, his lips twisted in faint mockery.

"Don't—don't call me that," she whispered from behind clenched teeth as she stood beside the settee.

Gabriel did not move from his sprawled position. He merely gazed up at her, the bulge in his trousers unmistakable.

A quivering spasm of bewildering need streaked through Celia. Gabriel had not found the same release she experienced. He was still hard. And he wanted her achingly aware of his current state as the firelight danced in shifting shadows across his features.

Light and dark.

Good and bad.

Merciless and tender.

The voice of an angel residing in the very Devil himself.

A wicked rogue she should stay far away from.

A slow grin of awareness spread across Gabriel's face. He knew exactly what she was thinking. This was a terrible mistake. And she wouldn't stop him from doing it again.

"I wish to return to my room now." Her voice shook.

"I've no doubt that you do. After all, what if your mother should wake and find you missing?" He spoke with such calmness that Celia shivered in foreboding. She must escape, and quickly.

"You are no better than Lord Harvey," she bit out, embarrassment making her words hot and uncharacteristically cruel. "Brutish louts, the pair of you. Rogues willing to take whatever you want from a lady. Worse still, you are nobody. A commoner with no social standing or station, regardless of Ravenswood's support. I shouldn't acknowledge your presence, and you should never think so highly of yourself to approach me for any reason. You will keep your distance from here on out. Now, I bid you goodnight, sir."

During this dressing down, Gabriel merely listened, his manner serene, although his brow lowered at the comparison with the other man. When it became apparent Celia would make her escape, he rose to his feet. His movements were fluid, as smoothly confident as that of any high seated lord in Parliament.

Celia blinked, still taken by surprise when witnessing the innate elegance of his mannerisms.

Taking her elbow into the palm of his large hand, Gabriel rumbled, "You will permit my escort."

"That is unnecessary." Celia froze with the warmth of his hand, her anger arrested by a sudden, distressing realization. Only moments before, that same hand had been wrapped around her throat. "I don't require nor need your aid."

"I know Beaumont better than anyone. Maybe even better than Lord Ravenswood himself. I'll return you to your room without detection, and you will remember your promise of avoiding empty gardens and deserted libraries in the dark of night."

Celia was sorely tempted to snatch herself away from his grip. Promising this man anything left a bitter taste in her mouth. More than anything, she wanted to tell him to go to the Devil. How dare he ignore her demand to stay away? And how dare he not be affected by the insults she'd just hurled at him?

"I am waiting, my lady." Gabriel's unmarred eyebrow rose slightly.

Not a shred of regret existed in his darkly golden brown eyes. No remorse for forcing her to writhe on his lap as though she were a seasoned harlot. She hated him for that. Hated him for exposing that side of her. That side which had led her into trouble once before so many years ago.

The side of herself that could not help but seek out trouble.

Resentment nearly choked Celia, but she managed a terse nod.

"You have my word, Mister Rose. No more nocturnal library visits while I'm here at Beaumont. Especially if there is a chance of finding myself forced to tolerate your attentions a second time."

CHAPTER 7

"You look tired, my dear." Lady Darby poured Celia a cup of tea, handing it to her from across the table set up in their rooms.

"I did not sleep well last night." Celia took a steadying sip of the fragrant brew. "I'm fine, Mother. Do not worry."

"I confess I never stirred during the night. I've slept so deeply these past few weeks. Your father's condition has much improved since your brother and Violet's wedding, and that certainly has helped matters. Their marriage has eased the earl's mind." Lady Darby winked at her daughter and teased, "Now, his only worry is seeing your future secured. With the right gentleman, of course."

Celia ignored the tightening of her stomach and smiled brightly. "Of course. Although the selection is hardly noteworthy. It's a rather bland, uninspiring lot, don't you think?"

A tiny frown creased her mother's brow. "You rarely give one the chance to prove otherwise, my dear. Perhaps a choice will become clearer now that so many of your friends have found their own husbands. Oh, I'm not saying you must rush about on a husband-searching mission, but you are reaching a certain age that will make things more difficult."

"I've only just turned one and twenty, Mother. Surely, I'm not quite ready for a walking cane and help getting up and down the stairs."

"The years fly by quickly when you are young, my love. Besides, the earl and I want nothing more than for you to find happiness and contentment, no matter the man you decided upon. But you will think upon it, won't you, Celia? Surely, there is a worthy suitor with whom you might consider marriage."

"I am trying, Mother. Truly."

Lady Darby gently patted Celia's hand. "I know, my darling. It is all we can ask of you. To try. To give a gentleman a chance before casting him aside. I think you are searching for something that perhaps doesn't exist. The mythical knight on a white horse. That sort of thing."

Celia said nothing. If only her mother knew the truth of what she needed from any man offering for her hand. The requirements far exceeded the usual listing of a good family name, the means to provide, and shared affection and respect. She needed a husband whose adoration was unquestionable. A husband who would understand and forgive her anything. A husband who would willingly ignore certain matters, or perhaps not care at all.

She'd been searching for ages, hoping to find such a man.

Celia sighed, her thoughts drifting again to Gabriel Rose and the things she'd done with his encouragement. Why she should think of him at all was most vexing. And her reactions to him were stomach-wrenching. Why she ever thought him attractive —or honorable—was an awful error in judgment. The man was a complete scoundrel. She must do her best to avoid him during the rest of their visit.

"Lady Ravenswood is a lovely hostess and Beaumont is the perfect place to spend these last few days of summer." Lady

Darby's attention focused on the scenery outside their bedchamber's window. "She spoke of plans to visit Richeforte and Grace before the Season begins. Since Ravenswood and the duke reestablished their friendship, they apparently visit frequently with one another. Especially now that Grace is with child. It's heartwarming how close the four of them have become."

"We should visit Grace before the baby arrives. When last we spoke, she said she had no desire to give birth in London." Celia nibbled on a piece of toast, which only reminded her how Gabriel had feasted on her lips. Blast him for invading her thoughts, and for looking through her with such intensity she wondered if he didn't already know all her secrets.

"What a lovely idea! Your father will understand if we should take a detour when we do head for home. I shall send the necessary letters today to Oakleigh and inform the Duke and Duchess of our plans."

Hopefully, her mother's attention would now focus on their new travel itinerary rather than what Celia herself was doing. Because she could not be certain Gabriel would not cause trouble for her.

She must be extra vigilant in avoiding Gabriel during their remaining time at Beaumont. The man did not possess any scruples, as evidenced by his scandalous behavior last night. Even if she had kissed him first, he'd taken advantage of her unexpected weakness.

He could not be trusted not to do it again. And if he dared try, she would not make it easy for him a second time.

THE NEXT DAY, Celia entered the solarium where a few of the young women had gathered.

An outing into the neighboring village was planned for the

ladies' activity, and Celia welcomed the opportunity to escape the house. She'd spent the day before skirting Gabriel's path and ignoring his confident smirk. Even Robert's sulky demeanor was preferable, but he seemed mysteriously hellbent on avoiding Celia.

"Good morning, Celia." Ivy motioned to join her and Lady Sara Bentley where they stood at a bank of windows.

Celia had become fast friends with the two countesses over the course of the past year. This enviable circle included Grace, the Duchess of Richeforte, and Celia's closet friend and new sister-in-law, Violet, the Viscountess Longleigh.

"Good morning, ladies. Is something amiss?" Celia asked, puzzled because the two women wore matching somber expressions. She did not miss the quick exchange of glances Ivy and Sara shared.

"I'm not sure," Ivy replied, sliding an arm around Celia's waist and squeezing it with affection. "A most unusual conversation occurred this morning between Ravenswood and Gabriel Rose. They were in the antechamber of our room. So I could not help but overhear."

Celia's heart thumped faster. Surely, Gabriel would not boast of the incident in the library.

"It was a very hushed conversation but involved keeping a close eye on Lord Harvey." Ivy frowned as she continued the story. "Ravenswood mumbled something about the man's audacity, and Gabriel mentioned your name as they moved into the hall. I could hear nothing at that point. When Ravenswood returned, I asked what had occurred. He would say nothing on the subject other than that it would be handled by himself or Gabriel. He would not say anymore, even when I pressed for details." Ivy scowled in disgust. "He simply kissed me on the forehead and bid me a pleasant day with our guests. The man can be extremely vexing sometimes."

"I do hope Lord Harvey has not been overly zealous in his

pursuit, Celia," Sara said with a concerned smile. "We all know how single-minded some gentlemen can be."

Ivy gave a good-natured roll of her eyes. "I should know better than anyone. Sebastian was most persistent when convincing me I should marry him. He could not be dissuaded, although I fought him at every turn. Thank goodness he succeeded in his endeavors. I cannot imagine life without that stubborn man. But let us return to the problem. Why should Gabriel concern himself with Lord Harvey? More importantly, how does Celia factor into their conversation?"

Both women turned to Celia, waiting for some manner of explanation.

"I know as much as the two of you. Harvey has been no more of a pest than usual," Celia smiled calmly as she appeased their curiosity. "As for Mister Rose, I've scarcely had the opportunity to converse with him during our time here. Indeed, I hardly know the man, so I cannot fathom any interest he might have taken in me."

But somehow, I found the opportunity to use the hardness of his body for my personal pleasure.

The unbidden thought flashing through her mind sent a guilty flush of remembered satisfaction throughout Celia's body. Laying a hand to the warmth of her cheek, she stepped back from the windows. "Goodness, isn't it rather warm in here?"

Ivy's turquoise gaze hardened with understanding. Reaching for Celia's hand, she gave it a quick squeeze. "If Harvey has overstepped, I swear to you, Celia, I will see that it doesn't occur again. That is, if Ravenswood doesn't handle the matter first. I'll not have my dearest friends harassed and hunted by unscrupulous gentlemen at my house party. No matter how well connected they might be."

Celia gave a soft laugh, intent on steering her two friends away from such a dangerous subject. "I assure you, dearest, the man has done nothing so terrible as to merit your wrath. Or Sara's. Set this aside and let us continue with our plans for a pleasant afternoon in the village."

～

CELIA SWUNG her pretty bonnet by its ribbons as she and the other women walked along the road leading away from the village. It was a lovely day. The sun flitted between a few puffy clouds and the air was warm and sweet with the aroma of wild-flowers.

Some ladies lamented not making use of the Ravenswood stables and their comfortable carriages, but Celia did not mind the physical exercise. She relished the opportunity to stretch her legs. Turning her face toward the sun's rays, she squinted, wondering if one of the darker clouds might hold a sudden afternoon storm. While she admitted a love of walking in the rain, it was an activity best undertaken with the proper outerwear.

"Aren't you worried you'll become hopelessly freckled, Lady Celia?" Lady Lydia West inquired. "A lady should always protect her skin when in the sun. An application of Olympian Dew can only accomplish so much."

"Not worried at all," Celia replied, giving her hat a few extra twirls. "A few freckles should hardly be considered flaws. I honestly don't understand why they are."

"Says the girl without a single freckle," Ivy laughed. "Knowing your habit of going without hat or parasol, I find it vexing you do not possess a single spot on that perfect complexion of yours."

"You are too kind, Lady Ivy." Celia grinned at her friend. "And you know very well your freckles are enchanting."

"Ravenswood certainly thinks so." A dreamy expression crossed Ivy's face when speaking of her husband.

"Celia, I overheard Sir Beeson declare your skin to be the exact likeliness of thistle weed milk," Sara teased.

"A compliment I could live the rest of my life without hearing ever again," Celia said dryly.

"He once compared the shade of my hair to that of a dying primrose." Lydia examined a lock of her pale blonde hair with a frown. "Perhaps he means to be poetic, but rarely do his words come out that way."

"He means no harm, truly." Ivy smiled at the group of ladies and linked her arm with Celia's. "I believe his earnestness is genuine."

"What of Mister Rose?" Lydia asked Ivy with a tilt of her head. "He is a most interesting person, for all his scowling and habit of ducking into the shadows when a lady approaches. Is it true Lord Ravenswood saved him during a drunken brawl behind a Paris brothel after which he promised your husband eternal gratitude as repayment?"

The sudden resentment rising in Celia's throat was surprising, her muscles tensing with some unknown emotion. Why would Lady Lydia inquire of the man when he was hardly one of their social standing? Worse, why should Celia even care?

"Mister Rose's story is not mine to tell, and I'll not betray his loyalty to my husband or myself by gossiping of his past." Ivy glanced at Celia, her brow knitting the tiniest bit. "True, he is one of our closest friends and a valued, although unconventional, member of our family, but he is also an extremely private man."

Celia forced her body to relax as they continued along the graveled path leading back to Beaumont. But she felt like growling at Lydia when the girl blithely continued.

"It has been said he is the illegitimate son of an English lord. Or maybe it was a French count. It's all so mysterious and fascinating. The man is quite handsome, and reportedly rich as Midas to boot." A dreamy expression passed over Lydia's face.

"I've never seen him actually take part in any social events, but the man is hardly a peasant. Would it be beyond the pale if he took a lady's hand for a waltz or two? I mean, Lady Elise married a commoner and she's the daughter of a marquess."

"The daughter of a penniless marquess," Ivy clarified. "There are many reasons Stalling accepted that offer for his daughter's hand in marriage."

"And all counted out in pounds," another lady said with a giggle. "But it's said the marriage is agreeable to all parties. Indeed, it's rumored Lady Elise's husband is quite in love with his new bride and she with him."

"I wonder if Mister Rose has ever shown an interest in a woman of the upper class?" Lydia mused aloud.

"You could ask Mister Rose these questions yourself, Lady Lydia," Sara invited with an amused chuckle. "In fact, here is your chance, for I believe he rides toward us along with Lord Bentley and Lord Ravenswood."

"No, thank you!" Lydia waved her hand so quickly it loosened a few tendrils of hair. The wisps flew around her pretty face as she dramatically declared, "I would fear for my reputation and perhaps my personal safety if I spoke so boldly. Mister Rose does not appear he would invite prying into his affairs in any form, even if for the sake of harmless curiosity. I merely speculated aloud. My father would never approve of such a man, even if his coffers are deep."

"Wealth does make it easier to excuse a lack of title," Lady Caroline Robertson remarked with a sly smile. "But perhaps Mister Rose is better suited as a lover, rather than as a husband."

"That scar of his nearly frightens me half to death," one lady commented with a shudder of distaste. "Although the rest of his form quite makes up for that one flaw."

Ivy shot the women a quelling glance. "Remember we do have a few unmarried ladies among us, please."

Lydia smoothed the front of her gown and straightened her

elaborate bonnet. "Anyway, one must admit he is handsome, even with the scar."

"Yes," Caroline agreed in a sultry voice. "We can all agree on that point, at least."

More than a few of the ladies craned their necks for a better view of the men advancing across the meadow.

Celia's annoyance increased as the three horses galloped closer. She'd always believed her own interest in Gabriel Rose to be a singular thing. After more than a year of watching the man from beneath lowered lashes, she never considered someone else might also find him attractive. Nor had she thought another might seek his attention.

He sat atop his horse as if born to the saddle, his size suited to the massiveness of the dark gold gelding. While Ravenswood and Bentley were large men, Gabriel surpassed them. Taller and heavier, he possessed a brawny elegance, comfortable in his skin and unashamed of the muscles bunching beneath the dark brown breeches he wore.

Yes, Celia grudgingly admitted, a strange twinge of desire rattling her composure. *He is certainly handsome.*

Sebastian Cain, the Earl of Ravenswood, reached the group first, swinging off his black stud horse with a flourish. Ivy barely had time to slide her arm from Celia's waist before the earl was sweeping his wife up against him. He planted a quick, open-mouth kiss on Ivy's lips while the other women twittered behind gloved hands.

All three men were dressed for a casual ride across the estate's rough terrain, not a single one wearing a coat or hat. In fact, crisp white shirts were open at the throat, the material revealing far more than was proper.

Several of the women appeared fascinated by the blatant display of such masculine virility. Celia heard their excited whispering as she attempted blending into their midst.

"My lord, behave yourself," Ivy gasped in mock outrage

while attempting to conceal her grin.

"But why?" Sebastian countered, his brow raising in amused puzzlement. "I am merely greeting my beautiful wife after a lengthy absence."

"It's been but a few hours, Ravenswood. Surely, you could not have missed me that much," Ivy laughed.

"Of course, he has! Nearly as much as I've missed my own wife," the Earl of Bentley declared as he too dismounted and wrapped Sara in an enthusiastic embrace. Alan swung her around in a complete circle as she squealed with delight in the most unladylike manner.

Yearning twisted Celia's heart as watched her friends' interactions with their husbands. The two women enjoyed something very rare in English society—genuine love matches with their soulmates. It was the type of relationship she could never hope for.

With a sigh, she averted her gaze and found herself caught by Gabriel's dark eyes. He watched her with a mysterious intensity from atop his horse. For a long moment, they simply stared at one other until Sebastian's attention turned to his friend.

"Mister Rose, have you ever seen a lovelier sight than this group of ladies on the road to Beaumont?"

"I have not, Lord Ravenswood," Gabriel drawled with a slight smile. "An enchanting collection of beauty rivaling that of any garden. And likely as sweet as any confection ever created." His tone was dulcet smoothness, its melodic nature sending a blush creeping up many of the ladies' cheeks.

Including Celia's. For she'd heard that voice in the dark stillness of a locked room. It was the same voice he'd used while calling her a sugarplum and demanding she find satisfaction in the use of his body.

Like an inferno, the unwelcome memory flashed through Celia. Flustered and suddenly desperate to escape Gabriel's mocking gaze, she twisted away. But instead of a hasty exit toward Beaumont, she abruptly landed on her bottom in the road. A moan of pain rose from her throat when she grabbed her ankle in reflex.

"Oh, my dear! Are you hurt?" Sara called out, already pulling free of her husband's playful embrace. "Here, Bentley. I must see to her."

There was a rush of movement, the sense of a much larger entity cleaving through the group. Before Celia could form an answer, Gabriel was at her side. Kneeling in the gravel of the dusty road, his hands reached under her skirts while Celia struggled to comprehend his speed in dismounting his horse and reaching her.

"Be still, now." His voice rumbled through her like a thunderstorm. "Is it your knee or ankle?"

"My ankle, I think," Celia whispered as Gabriel's fingers brushed over her stocking-covered upper leg before moving downward in a feather-soft caress of exploration.

"Then we must unravel these laces and relieve the pressure. Otherwise, you will suffer even more as time passes."

Celia stared at Gabriel's bowed head in dumbfounded amazement as he began untying the laces of her walking boots. His boldness was unheard of. His actions were completely inappropriate.

And utterly scandalous. Was he intentionally trying to ruin them both? No gentleman would dare thrust his hand beneath a lady's skirt in such a manner and certainly not within full view of others. Even if he only meant to ease her discomfort, it simply wasn't done.

But there was no ignoring the thrill of his gloved hand holding her foot steady against his thigh as he worked on the strings. A dangerous flash of pleasure overrode the pain, leaving her gasping in surprise. Gabriel glanced up at the slight sound, his jaw morphing into a block of steel as implications of this spontaneous rescue began sinking in.

And yet, he did not stop.

Gathering around, the other ladies pressed closer so they would have a better view of Gabriel's hand beneath Celia's skirts. Scandalized murmurs, like the darkening rain clouds overhead, swirled around them.

"Blast, why didn't I think of doing that?" With a huff of indignation, Lady Lydia popped open a blue sprigged parasol. She held it high so there would be no interference with the grandeur of the matching hat.

Raindrops plunked onto the graveled road. Fat, cold raindrops that would soon send everyone scattering in search of drier environs. Although they provided flimsy protection at most during a rainstorm, parasols sprung open like garden blooms.

Gabriel's shirt was becoming splotched by the drops, the cambric clinging to his skin in various areas. Celia swallowed hard. A smattering of curling dark hair peeped from the open vee of the garment. He was so close she could see the pulse of his heart beating in the vein running alongside his neck.

Good Lord.

"Come away now, butterfly, before you receive a soaking," Sebastian instructed his wife while sharing a nod with Gabriel.

That tore Celia's attention away from Gabriel's neck. A shiver of apprehension chased her nerves. Odd, but Sebastian's slight gesture toward his friend seemed as though it might be one of permission.

Throwing Sebastian an exasperated glare, Ivy ignored the directive and knelt beside her friend. "I shall send carriages back immediately for—"

Gabriel gave a low, nearly imperceptible growl that had Celia and Ivy's eyes widening. With graceful quickness, he scooped Celia up into his arms and rose to his feet. "No need. See to your guests, my lady. It will be quicker if I return Lady Celia to Beaumont myself."

CHAPTER 8

$\mathcal{A}$lthough the threat of a rain storm loomed overhead, Celia thought Gabriel moved with a suspicious lack of speed. And the way he held her could only be considered indecent. Positioned sidesaddle, she sat wedged between the man's legs. Her hip dug into his groin, and every time she wiggled in an attempt to create some distance between their bodies, Gabriel merely tightened his grip, which made her slide even closer due to the slick surface of the saddle.

He wouldn't even allow her to don her bonnet, saying the wide brim impeded his line of sight. She held it by the ribbons with one knee jammed into the crown. Her boots were tied together by their strings and now lay draped over the horse's neck. Cushioned by the fullness of her skirts, they did not needlessly bounce about.

"What is your horse's name?" Celia asked, hoping conversation would dispel the uncomfortable silence. Perhaps it would make their time together pass more quickly.

Gabriel did not respond for a long moment, then with an exasperated sigh, he said, "Arion."

The buckskin's ears flicked backward at the sound of his name and his master's voice.

Celia twisted to look at Gabriel. "But Arion was the swiftest of mythological horses. Yours, I'm afraid, moves incredibly slow. Were he responsible for carrying you away from battle and certain death, you would not survive as King Adrastus did."

"I would not discount his abilities, my lady. Arion is very sensitive to insults."

The horse tossed his head as if he understood everything being said, his silky black mane ruffled by the breeze.

Craning her neck to look past his body, Celia noted the distance between them and the other ladies increasing by the minute. Up ahead, Bentley and Ravenswood, with Sara and Ivy clinging to their backs, were already making the next bend in the road and would soon disappear from sight. She and Gabriel were essentially alone now. The realization was deeply concerting.

"I fear going any faster as it may increase your injury," Gabriel explained dryly. "Besides, I doubt it will actually rain on us." He adjusted Celia into a more favorable position, one which pressed her even tighter in the space between his legs.

"If you intend on manhandling me all the way back to Beaumont, I'd rather hobble the remaining distance on one foot," Celia bit out through clenched teeth. Why did he have to be so muscular? And why must he smell so divine? The heady scent of spicy cloves and leather was most annoying. "I'd probably make it there long before you."

"Oh, I couldn't allow that." Gabriel transferred the reins to one hand while steadying Celia with the other. "And why do you think I am manhandling you? I thought my actions to be most helpful."

"You consider this helpful? My reputation is being torn to shreds every second we are together."

Gabriel chuckled. "You have a very dark outlook on the

world, Lady Celia. Your reputation is in no more danger than it was two nights ago."

Celia's face heated in a rush of embarrassment. "Don't you dare bring that up. What you did to me was unconscionable."

He laughed again, bending forward until his mouth brushed her ear. "What *I* did, my lady?" Warm breath stirred the wisps of hair escaping her coiffure as the wind picked up. Celia stared stonily ahead as Gabriel continued in a voice smooth as melted honey. "I recall things a bit differently. If we are being honest, you used me for your own gain. Remember?"

Remember? How could she possibly forget? She'd thought of their encounter all through that night until dawn broke that next morning. She thought of it all during the following day while avoiding his presence. She'd thought of it during the visit to the village and the walk back to the manor. Blast it all, she couldn't get it out of her treacherous mind, and now, Gabriel had the audacity to inquire if she remembered it.

Worst of all, he placed all blame for the incident at her feet.

"I refuse to continue this ridiculous conversation. Do not talk to me any further, Mister Rose. Just return me to Beaumont. Hopefully, you will then disappear from my life."

Gabriel let out a heavy sigh threaded with amused exasperation. "Are you always this prickly, Lady Celia?"

"Only to scoundrels lacking good manners," she replied primly.

"Ah, I see," he said with a grin. "Am I to understand you've now included me on your extensive list of suitors?"

Celia truly could not help herself in that moment. Twisting around until her upper body was somewhat unencumbered, she drew back a hand and slapped Gabriel's smirking face as hard as she could manage.

The muted crack of her kid-gloved palm against his cheek sent Arion jittering sideways with an alarmed snort. Celia was forced to grab Gabriel's forearm to avoid being unseated until he reined the horse back under control.

The weight of his displeasure was evident in the restrained way one arm squeezed around her waist. There was a heart-pounding silence before he gripped her chin in the palm of his free hand and turned her face to his. Even the breeze seemed to steel itself for confrontation as he regarded her. Then his brow smoothed into an impassive façade, and not for the first time, Celia wondered how he came to have the thin, white scar slicing across his forehead.

"Try that again, my lady, and you shall find yourself over my knee for a bit of much-needed discipline. And unless I decide to show mercy, it will not be a pleasant experience for you."

Seeing the determined glint in his golden brown eyes, Celia swallowed hard and screwed up her courage. "You wouldn't dare."

A strange sort of fire lit Gabriel's gaze. His hand tightened on her chin, holding her immobile. The air surrounding them crackled with intense promise, and Celia hated that her entire body seemed attuned to his. His every breath was mirrored by her own, the heat of his chest burning her arm and the part of her upper body where it pressed against him. The discomfort of her injured ankle was forgotten as Gabriel's stare melted her defiance and turned her into a trembling puddle of confused desire.

Why did the thought of his hand striking her tender flesh in such a vulnerable area leave her eager to test his resolve? It was absolute madness taunting him like this, and she was a wanton harlot for entertaining the idea of being sprawled across his lap. The leather of his riding glove landing on her skin would no doubt leave a mark should he follow through with such brazen threats.

"Your first mistake is believing I won't do anything I damn well please with you, Celia Buchanan." His gaze narrowed and darkened, dropping to her lips. He looked as though he wanted nothing more than to devour her, body and soul. "Your second mistake is believing you won't enjoy every second of it."

"Always with the threats, Mister Rose." Celia's words rushed out in a shaky exhale of sarcasm. "Do you spend all your days dreaming up new ones? Or do you find yourself recycling those that failed the first time around?"

"Threats? I've found no need for them. I follow through with action." Gabriel released her chin, but his arm remained a secure pressure around her waist. He nudged Arion off the roadway and into the tall grass.

With a worrying twinge of awareness, Celia realized the gelding was being steered toward a strand of trees on the other side of the small meadow.

Clutching his arm even tighter, her fingernails dug little half moons into the fabric of his riding coat. Did he mean to abduct her? Ravish her? There was little hope of escaping her fate with an injured ankle. A familiar sense of premonition stole over her, leaving her light-headed. She'd been blessed since childhood with an uncanny knack for predicting when things happened. With this man, that ability was diminished and Celia did not understand why.

"What are you doing, sir?" She could not conceal the panic in her voice. Oh, blast her impulsiveness, anyhow.

"Dispensing with words and moving straight away to your next lesson."

Dread froze her limbs. She considered leaping from the horse's back.

Gabriel dropped the reins so they lay crisscrossed over Arion's neck. His arms wrapped completely around her waist, and a grim smile played across his firm mouth.

"Don't even think about it," he murmured.

"What?" Celia clenched her teeth.

"You know what I'm referring to. Jumping off this horse.

You'll only do yourself additional harm and make me angry." With a cluck of his tongue and pressure from his knees, Gabriel directed the horse's movements.

As they wove through the towering elms, Celia's apprehension increased. With the cloudy sky overhead, the copse of trees grew increasingly darker as they continued forward. Her apprehension increased as the dimness of the forest closed around them.

Still, they did not stop. It was almost as though Gabriel searched for something.

"How will you explain this detour to the others? You are thoroughly compromising me, Mister Rose, and I'll not stand for it. I won't."

"There will be nothing to explain. We are merely taking a necessary shortcut due to the overwhelming pain you are experiencing."

"Overwhelming," Celia echoed the word in disbelief then scowled fiercely. "I admit to feeling discomfort, but it most certainly is not a pain I consider *overwhelming.*"

Gabriel stopped the horse in the midst of a small clearing, and before Celia knew what he was about, he slid to the ground. Large hands encircled her waist, and she was swung down from Arion's back in a flurry of petticoats and skirts. He maneuvered her so her weight was borne against his wide form, her ankle protected from further injury. He practically held her aloft with just one arm, and she gripped his wide shoulders for greater stability before realizing it was unnecessary.

"Not yet, that is true." He smiled at her, plucking the bonnet from her fingers and tossing it aside. "But you may wish to hold off on that opinion until after I've finished with you."

"What are you talking about, sir?" Celia demanded, her words trailing off as it became crystal clear what the man intended.

Along the edge of the clearing, a large tree lay toppled. Bare of limbs and leaves, the trunk was the perfect spot for someone to sit. Swooping her up into his arms for the second time that afternoon, Gabriel stalked toward it and sat down.

Celia was trapped, nestled in the heat of his lap and the iron bands of his arms encompassing her. For the longest moment, Gabriel merely stared intently into her eyes as though searching for some mysterious sign. The color of his irises darkened to the color of molasses. Rich and warm. And although they were aflame with something Celia thought might be desire, there was a shimmer of gentleness in their depths as well.

She wasn't quite sure how she knew it, but Celia was suddenly quite positive this man would never intentionally harm her.

"You know exactly what will happen here," he finally said in a low, gravelly voice.

Celia's pulse leapt to life with the tenor of his voice. She may have foolishly put her fear aside. He sounded… dangerous. A shiver of apprehension trickled down her spine

And arousal.

"You've gone mad," Celia stuttered.

"Perhaps," Gabriel agreed calmly. Then, with scarcely any effort on his part, he spun her.

Around, up, and over, Celia went in a dizzying series of movements.

She was now indecently sprawled across that hard, muscled lap, attempting to catch her breath and surprised by his swift action. Her toes barely touched the ground while her head hung in such a way she could only see the forest floor and Gabriel's calves encased in tall riding boots. The black leather was shiny even in the gloomy light. She grabbed the closest one, her fingers barely making a dent in the leather although her nails dug into the material.

To her shameful horror, her skirts and petticoats were flipped up and bunched in the middle of her back.

"Hands," Gabriel commanded darkly.

Celia faltered, her heart lodging in her throat. Her skin felt alive, a mix of apprehension and perhaps excitement prickling her like thousands of hot needles.

"What?" she mumbled around a mouth gone dry with confusion.

Gabriel sighed. "Your hands, sugarplum. Give them to me."

This is insane. Why would I do that? Place myself completely under his control? And again, he calls me by that silly name.

"I demand you stop calling me that," Celia snapped in the most imperious manner she could muster whilst hanging upside down across this gentle monster's lap.

"I hope I am not forced to repeat my request," he murmured in a voice laced with silky threats and simmering desire. "But then again, maybe I do."

"Why do you want—"

The lazy slap to her bottom shocked Celia into silence. It didn't really hurt, but it certainly galvanized her to take him seriously.

"Stop asking questions, my lady, and do as I say."

Letting go of his boot, Celia quickly reached both hands behind her. An involuntary gasp choked her when he captured both in the palm of one large, gloved hand. He anchored them in the low dip of her back atop the heap of her skirts.

She was trapped. Like a lion capturing a mouse beneath one heavy paw, Gabriel now easily held her in place. And she'd willingly allowed it.

Trembling, Celia waited for whatever might come next, cursing herself for being so weak and stupid. The cool breeze of the wooded glen whispered around her thighs, curling little tendrils of air that reached the open gap of her fine linen drawers, and rushed over the heated flesh there. The sting was already fading away, but for some reason, the area was beginning to throb. And not in an unpleasant way.

Oh, God. She'd not considered the consequences of this. Had not realized what being over his lap would actually *mean*.

Exposure. Heat. Pleasure.

Excitement.

A sound escaped Gabriel that might have been either a groan or a curse. His hand tightened around her wrists, the leather of his glove soft and smooth on the exposed skin. Beneath her stomach and breasts and through the layers of her clothes, Celia felt him. She thought his lap and the muscles of his thighs somehow became even harder. Rigid. A vast expanse of edges and swelling flesh carved from warm stone.

"Are you ready?"

Celia startled. Ready? Of course not. But what else could she do when she was the one allowing this madness to continue? Surely, he wouldn't strike her again.

Unsure of her ability to speak, Celia curled her fingers around his and squeezed tight.

"Tsk-tsk, my lady. Situations such as this require words. Indeed, they are an absolute necessity." Gabriel's voice cascaded over her like summer honey. "Tell me you are ready for your lesson."

Perhaps it was a side effect of hanging practically upside down, but an odd, tingling sense of floating took over Celia.

He asked permission to punish her.

She would grant it.

What the hell was wrong with her? And how could she explain it when she didn't understand it?

"I—yes." Her quiet response echoed as if shouted from a mountain top.

"What a puzzle you are, Lady Celia," Gabriel murmured in surprised appreciation. "I shall enjoy piecing you together."

His hand carefully smoothed over her fabric-covered rump. Was he testing her resolve in allowing him to do as he wished? Celia bit back a moan but did not move. His touch traced the lines of the twin mounds, committing her to memory. His fingers trailed and roamed while flames ignited deep in Celia's body.

Dear Lord, this was something she never saw happening. How could his hands, so large and threatening, stroke her with such tender care?

"I'm imagining the rosy hue you'll turn under the weight of my palm, Celia." His murmur was soft and low. "How the imprint of my hand on your ivory white flesh will be shockingly pink before fading away. I'm imagining how you will squirm and gasp, both dreading and anticipating the next strike. And I know right now, you are wondering if I will even dare."

Smack!

The heaviness of his palm cracking over her bottom was unexpected. Gabriel's hand was so enormous it nearly covered both cheeks. Celia jolted forward in shock, biting back a cry before freezing still with awareness.

"That was only a preview, sweetness, of what I wish to do." Gabriel's breath was ragged, and yet control simmered in the way he handled her. "There's more. So much more than you could ever comprehend."

Celia shuddered but did not dare attempt an escape. She remained draped over his lap in a state of willing although dazed curiosity.

He wasn't done with her just yet as evidenced by his barely audible sigh.

"Damnit, Celia. I can feel your heat, smell your arousal. It is unraveling me."

Gabriel's hand slipped low. It ventured beyond the slit in her underdrawers. Then he was exploring her with just one finger. A devilish, sinful finger that dipped and swirled against the opening of her body for what could have been an eternity but was likely only a few seconds.

Celia let out a muffled cry, sensations flooding her. She

shuddered. Aching. Wanting. Needing. Because Gabriel still wore riding gloves and the leather burned like a firebrand on her sensitive flesh, igniting every nerve ending until her body screamed for more.

Her legs fell further apart, greedily inviting him to take everything.

But as quickly as her punishment had begun, it was over.

CHAPTER 9

Gabriel stood, hauling Celia up along with him. He had no intention of being so rough in his handling, but he gripped her upper arms so tightly he probably left behind imprints of his hands.

Celia could not hide her emotions. Wide, expressive chocolate brown eyes shouted everything at him. Things he had no right knowing. Her excitement. Her confusion. Her shocked arousal. It swirled around him, a heady mix of innocent discovery, and Gabriel fought the urge to place his index finger in his mouth. Fought against the rampant desire to know how sweet her intimate flavor would taste on his tongue. He wanted to lick his finger clean. Allow her body's essence to eddy and collect on his tastebuds. He wanted to savor and appreciate the taste of her and store the memory away for later when she was no longer under his control.

A surge of lust careened through him at the salacious idea. And Gabriel fought that, too. What occurred in the library was bad, but this, *this* was insanity. It would mean certain ruination if they were caught like this, and he was in enough trouble as it was with this girl. He could not continue inventing reasons and excuses to touch her. It was utter madness.

Because she was not meant for someone like him. That fact would never change.

No matter the circumstances. Or who his father was.

Once more supporting Celia's weight, Gabriel practically dragged her back to where Arion nibbled on the few blades of grass sprouting up amongst the carpet of leaves.

"We must return before they come looking for us." His gruff explanation came while tossing Celia onto the horse's back.

She instinctively grabbed the reins and a handful of Arion's jet-black mane. Her features tight, she stared down into his face. "I've said the same thing, but you ignored me." She sounded sullen, frustration leaching into every word.

"Well, we shouldn't dawdle any further." Gabriel turned, looking for her hat. The breeze had caught it up and carried it a few feet away.

"Is that what men call this? Dawdling?" Celia said peevishly to his back as he strode toward the bonnet with the intention of retrieving it.

The moment he bent over to pick up the pretty hat, Gabriel knew his mistake. He'd vastly underestimated the girl.

Celia twisted in the saddle, maneuvering so that one leg awkwardly swung over Arion's neck. Now, she sat astride, full skirts hiked up past her knees and an expanse of white silk stockings readily visible. While Gabriel stood awestruck at the magnificent sight she presented, Celia clucked her tongue to the horse. Setting her heels to his flanks, she held on tight as Arion, the traitor, obliged her command by bolting forward.

Celia's little yelp of surprised alarm almost made Gabriel smile. But then, concern for her safety erased any sense of amusement. There were many trees along the pathway leading out of the forest. She might fall off and seriously injure herself.

And if he let out the whistle sure to stop Arion in mid-stride, she could still end up taking a tumble.

Best that he allowed the stallion his head and trust in his sure-footedness. No doubt, the horse would quickly find his way back to the stables where a bucket of oats awaited him.

Raking a hand through his hair, Gabriel sighed.

It was a long walk back to the manor.

GABRIEL WAS MET by Alan when he entered Beaumont's foyer.

"Ah, there you are. We were preparing to send out a search party."

Gabriel scowled at his friend. "Is Lady Celia well?"

Alan grinned. "As well as can be expected. Her injury seems to be a minor one. Ivy insists she remains abed at least until tomorrow. I suppose I should inquire as to your own health?"

Gabriel's gaze narrowed. "What do you mean by that?"

Cocking his head, Alan considered him for a long moment. "Yes. I see precisely what Ravenswood is talking about," he remarked almost as to himself. Then he brightened, his next comment delivered most cheerfully. "Do not despair, my friend. These things do get a bit easier."

"What things?" Gabriel demanded impatiently. "Speak plainly as I find the mysterious nature of this conversation most annoying." He forced his hands to relax, suddenly realizing he was crushing Celia's hat in his irritation.

Alan shrugged. "Let us have this discussion in a more private setting than the foyer." With a hand on Gabriel's shoulder, Alan steered him into the drawing room. He then poured two drams of whiskey from a decanter on the sidebar.

Gabriel watched silently then, with a raised eyebrow, reminded his friend to continue the conversation. "As you were saying, Bentley?"

Alan chuckled and waved a hand. "The chase. The hunt. The pursuit. Oh, however you wish to name it, we men both enjoy and despise it. I must say, the two of you make quite the striking couple."

Gabriel tossed the bonnet into a chair and jerked off his gloves. He then snatched up the glass of whiskey Alan held out.

"Let me understand this. You and Ravenswood believe some manner of alliance exists between myself and Lady Celia?" Gabriel could not conceal his astonishment. Had he been that transparent in coming to Celia's aid after her tumble on the roadside? Had his attraction for the woman become so glaringly obvious that his friends now considered themselves to be matchmakers? Was it possible others could see this ill-advised weakness?

A faint sense of panic beat in Gabriel's chest. He had made the most dreadful of mistakes.

"Doesn't it?" Alan shrugged. "She's certainly a worthy prospect for a bride. And her family is well thought of. The Earl of Darby is a fine man. One who certainly would appreciate someone like yourself marrying his only daughter."

"Someone like me..." Gabriel's words trailed off in disbelief. "Have you forgotten exactly *what* I am? I've no family name. No estate. No real place in society other than the connection Sebastian graciously provides. Even if I owe him my life, his generosity is not without bounds." Sighing with frustration, he scrubbed his face with his hand. "While I am grateful for my friends' lack of discrimination in regards to my station, I know others hardly feel the same. I won't even begin to entertain the preposterous notion that I've become involved with Lady Celia, but rest assured her family would not welcome a bastard as a son-in-law."

Alan calmly sipped his whiskey. So calmly that Gabriel was reminded just how tightly he gripped his own glass.

"Granted, I do not know her very well, but Lady Celia hardly seems the sort to put stock in such things," Alan said. "Perhaps she wishes to marry for love instead of title? I mean, why hasn't she wed already? Any number of eligible men are constantly flitting in and out of her orbit. She could have her choice of husband many times over."

"Not every woman wishes to marry," Gabriel said tightly, fighting back an unfamiliar surge of jealousy. The thought of Celia marrying some stuffy, self-important lord was disturbing.

Besides the very real problem of his inappropriateness as a husband, there was the issue of his predilection when it came to sex. He preferred a darker manner of lovemaking—acts of wickedness no well-brought-up, innocent young lady would ever understand or welcome between her bedsheets. Regardless of whom he married, or more precisely, *if* he ever married, his bride must understand and accept that side of him. She must be a willing participant because he would never seek his pleasures outside of their vows. It was that sort of faithfulness which required a certain type of woman.

Lady Celia Buchanan was not that type of woman.

"Perhaps you are right." Alan grinned and downed his whiskey. "Being a happily married gent myself, I've an irrational need to see my friends attain the same sort of marital bliss. And if you require further proof of how perfect life can be with the right wife, you need look no further than Ravenswood and Richeforte. Hell, even Longleigh finally found his treasure and she was sitting right beneath his nose."

"I appreciate the advice. However, I'm not in the market for a wife." Gabriel set his half-empty glass down and retrieved Celia's bonnet and his gloves from the chair where he'd tossed them. "If you will excuse me, Bentley, I shall return this to its owner."

Alan waved a hand in dismissal, then, remembering some-thing of vital importance, his eyebrow rose in question. "Before you go, tell me how Lady Celia came to return to the manor alone and on your horse, no less. What actually happened?"

"I reached the conclusion it was inappropriate for the two of us to ride alone. My intent was to avoid any hint of scandal, so I dismounted and instructed Lady Celia to ride on alone. I would follow on foot." The lie stuck in Gabriel's throat but he choked past it. He would not sully the girl's reputation, and this seemed the most logical explanation for an illogical situation.

Alan threw back his bright blond head and laughed with such hearty enthusiasm that Gabriel knew a pang of unease.

"Ah, Rose, you are in the thick of things now. Indeed, you are in far deeper than you realize."

Gabriel's gaze remained stony as he regarded his friend. "Why is that? What did Lady Celia say was the reason?"

"That you lost your seat and she could not control your horse as it raced back to the stables without you. Knowing the lady's skill when it comes to horseflesh, I knew her explanation could not possibly be true. But it's best you repeat the tale as she relates it."

At least she did not say you accosted her in the forest, and she fled for fear of her safety and reputation.

Gabriel grit his teeth. He should have gone directly to her so they might correlate their stories.

"I'll thank you to disregard what I just said. Celia's version is the correct one," Gabriel muttered.

Alan was still grinning, pleased with the developments. Damn the man.

"You'll find her in the Rose Parlor with Ivy and Sara. They are keeping her company."

CHAPTER 10

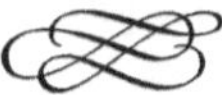

"The way he looked at you." Sara sighed, placing a hand over her heart. "I declare, I almost saw flames coming off the man. It was so terribly romantic."

"Romantic?" Celia snorted in amazement. She shifted on the divan, hiding a grimace when her foot slipped off the plush pillow it was currently propped upon.

"Oh, yes! Romantic. In the way his eyes lit up the moment he saw you. And how gentle he was while tending to your ankle. And, my goodness, when he scooped you into his arms and rode off with you, I thought I might actually swoon," Sara swore earnestly.

"Did you know there is an art to swooning?" Celia asked, determined to change the subject.

Sara cocked her head, looking exactly like a perfect, blonde porcelain doll. "Is there? And how does that work precisely?"

Ivy adjusted the pillow lodged beneath Celia's foot and frowned at Sara. "She's merely attempting to change the subject, my dear. Isn't that right, Celia?"

Celia averted her gaze from Ivy's penetrative turquoise eyes.

"It's far better than discussing Mister Rose's display of misplaced chivalry."

Ivy tsked as she returned to her seat opposite the dark rose-hued divan. Picking up the teapot, she refreshed their beverages. "One thing I will always say of Gabriel: he is absolutely genuine. And there is kindness there you might not see at first glance. The man has his demons, but many gentlemen claim such. Ravenswood trusts him implicitly, as do I."

"Does any of that matter?" Celia grumbled. "It's not as though I have leave to consider the man as a suitor. Why the two of you are so eager for that impossibility is quite puzzling."

The quick recrimination on her friends' features was enough that Celia flushed with regret. "I do not mean to imply Mister Rose is beneath me. You know a man's social standing matters little in my eyes. But it is true he is on the outskirts of our circle. Even if I wished it, which I don't, I'm positive my parents would never approve." She scowled with impatience. "Why does everyone insist on pairing the two of us, anyway? We've said no more than ten words to one another over the past year."

Ivy smiled. "Much can be said in just a few words. And while you may believe it goes unnoticed, I've seen the way you look at each other. Oh, I'll admit Mister Rose is a bit, shall we say, untamed. But there is no denying you share a mutual attraction, Celia. What harm can there be in exploring it?"

Before Celia could answer that dangerously probing question, there was a slight knock on the door. It swung open to reveal Gabriel, a grim expression on his features and her walking bonnet dangling from his broad fingers. She sucked in a breath at the sight of him, her cheeks suffused with heated embarrassment for what she'd done.

She'd stolen the man's horse, leaving him to walk nearly two miles. Under threat of a thunderstorm.

With nervous fingers, Celia gripped the handle of her teacup.

There was no concealing the tiny clatter when it shook against the matching saucer. The dark glint in Gabriel's eyes when they slid over her prone form was a mixture of pure fury and concern.

"Ladies, may I join you for a moment?"

"Of course, Gabriel! Shall I pour you some tea?" Ivy smiled, patting the seat of an unoccupied chair at the end of the divan where Celia's foot lay propped like a bizarre prize upon a fluffy pillow. Gabriel took the offered seat while Celia gulped in a desperate bid to contain her panic. He turned her poor bonnet over and over in his hands. She was sure, by the time it was returned to her possession, it would be hopelessly ruined.

"Yes, thank you, Lady Ravenswood," he murmured while staring at Celia with eyes hot and dark.

His gaze roamed with breathtaking insolence across her body as she lay stretched out on the divan. From her stockinged toes, over her legs, her hips, her bosom, and on up until, finally, their eyes clashed.

Burnished whiskey bored with dangerous intensity into sweet chocolate.

Sara cleared her throat and hid a smile by taking a sip of her tea. Celia clenched her teeth, perturbed by her friends' lack of alarm when it came to Gabriel Rose and his intentions. Could they not see how dangerous he was?

This was insanity. To lay thus, vulnerable and exposed. Although completely clothed with her feet only lacking shoes, Celia had never felt so... bare. And foolish.

Why am I frightened of him? After all, I am the one he accosted. The one he violated! He should consider himself fortunate that I only stole his horse. Oh, I hope his feet are blistered from walking! I hope he has stone bruises. I hope he is suffering from thirst and exposure. I hope...

Celia stirred with the intention of sitting upright, determined this man would not intimidate her a minute more.

"Stay where you are."

Gabriel's eyes pinned her in place, his command soft and resolute. Celia threw caution to the wind and defiantly pulled herself to a sitting position anyway.

There was only a small wince betraying the twinge of pain felt when her feet touched the floor. She set her teacup and saucer down on the low table in front of her. Then with a fierce glare, she leaned toward the man, snatched her bonnet from his hands, and impatiently tossed it onto the settee beside her.

A muscle ticked in Gabriel's chiseled jaw. A flicker of emotion revealed by tiny flutters just beneath his skin and the shadow of a faint beard.

"I shall require a moment alone with Lady Celia," Gabriel said, his gaze never leaving Celia. She noticed his hands had clenched into fists. That wasn't encouraging at all.

"We'll just step out into the hall and give you two a little privacy," Ivy replied, standing and shaking out her skirts. "But just a little, you understand. We must maintain appearances, after all." She winked at Celia and then linked an arm with Sara. "Just call out if you need us."

Celia wanted more than anything to beg Ivy and Sara to remain in the room, but her stubborn nature forbade it. Her chin tilted and she steeled herself for confrontation.

Once alone, silence fell as they stared at one other with mutual wariness.

"You've left me quite adrift, Lady Celia," Gabriel finally admitted with a sigh. "Indeed, I'm at a loss when it comes to you. If I possessed a single thread of self-preservation, I would stay far away from such temptation. But I'm finding it an impossible task. You both fascinate and sadden me, if you must know."

Celia reached for her teacup, taking a sip as a way of hiding her surprise. She wasn't sure of the correct response after such a brutally honest declaration.

"Have you considered courting me, Mister Rose? What I

mean to say is that I would not be averse to it," she impulsively blurted out. *Oh, blast it all. Why would I say such a thing?* "Your irrational behavior could then be explained away to others."

Gabriel's eyes darkened. "That is impossible."

Setting her cup back down, Celia took a deep breath and turned fully toward the man. "Why? Why is it impossible? And what have I done that saddens you? I'm afraid I don't understand."

Gabriel stood so suddenly that Celia fell back against the divan with a startled *"Oh!"*

He raked a hand through his hair, leaving the deep chestnut waves in a ruffled mess. "I'm saddened because someday you will belong to a man who has the right to claim you. We cannot be anything to one another because of who I am. Or rather, who I am not."

"That's ridiculous. Courting does not necessarily end with marriage, Mister Rose. Perhaps this might allow us to explore the fascination we seem to share and forever put it to rest. You are not without connections and wealth. Nor are you a pariah because of your birth. It will not impede your prospect of obtaining a wife of social standing at some point. Indeed, it may even help."

Gabriel leaned toward her with a growl. "I've no wish for a wife, regardless of her social status, and need your aid in gaining one even less. Do I make myself clear?"

Celia assessed him and the ferocity of his response. "Perfect- ly," she murmured. "Then there is nothing for it. You must abstain from contact with me until I leave Beaumont."

He appeared startled by her statement and then scowled. "Leave? Where the Devil do you think you will go with that injured ankle?"

"Mother and I will be off for Cornwall soon. We intend to visit Richeforte and Her Grace before their babe is borne."

"When?" Gabriel barked.

"I don't know precisely when. Babies have their own schedule, or so I'm told."

A hand raked through his hair while he muttered beneath his breath. "Seven hells." He pinned her with a steely glare. "I do not mean *that*. When do *you* intend on leaving?"

"Oh." Celia frowned at her mistake in misunderstanding him. "Mother only sent the letters yesterday."

His gaze turned even sharper as he loomed over her. "Because of my actions in the library?"

Celia broke eye contact first. She picked up the bonnet, fiddling with the ribbons. "No, it wasn't that," she finally admitted in a low voice.

Before Gabriel could respond, the parlor door flew open, and Lady Darby breezily floated into the room. Ivy and Sara were directly on her heels, unable to hide their curiosity when they saw Gabriel looming over Celia. He quickly stepped away but not before his position was noted. Lady Darby smiled broadly.

"Celia, my darling, I've finalized all the arrangements for moving into a separate room while you recover from your injury," she said cheerfully.

"Mother, that really is not necessary. I'm positive I will be back to my normal self by tomorrow."

"Nonsense. It's for the best and Lady Beatrix's departure this afternoon meant the extra room is available. I know you've not been sleeping very well the past few nights, my dear." Lady Darby kissed her daughter on the forehead and sat beside her on the divan. She then turned a sunny smile on Gabriel.

"Thank you so much, Mister Rose, for your assistance to my daughter today. I do regret you were forced to walk back to the manor. Celia is an accomplished horsewoman, so I can only reason that in her pain she was unable to control your horse. Thank goodness she suffered no additional harm during her ride back."

Gabriel bowed at the waist, his own smile benign. "Yes. Thank goodness."

"You simply must be Celia's escort at the next evening meal. After her ankle has healed, of course," Lady Darby said before turning to Ivy. "Lady Ravenswood, would that be possible? I would hate upsetting the seating arrangements, but I'm sure Celia would enjoy the opportunity to become better acquainted with her rescuer."

Celia choked on her astonishment. What in the world had gotten into her mother?

Celia's eyes narrowed. Of course. Matchmaking. But why was her mother focusing her efforts on the inappropriate, unattainable Gabriel Rose? There was hardly a good explanation other than she apparently saw something redeeming in the man and was suddenly willing to overlook his lack of title.

"Mother, I'm sure Mister Rose has no interest—"

"Of course, he does!" Lady Darby interrupted with a trill of laughter. She patted Gabriel on the forearm. "You *do* have an interest, don't you, Mister Rose?"

Gabriel simply nodded, but it was as effective as an impassioned speech on the floor of Parliament.

"I can certainly arrange it," Ivy said with a bright smile. "Tomorrow night, if Celia is on the mend."

Gabriel's crooked smirk was meant for Celia alone. "I would be delighted."

CELIA ROAMED the confines of her room later that evening. Mother insisted she remain abed but she refused. The forced inactivity chafed her nerves more than she could have anticipated.

She'd tried reading one of the several books Sara dropped off earlier, but none held her interest. For a while, she'd sat by the window as the clouds thickened, and the rainstorm that never materialized from earlier that day rebuilt itself and gathered strength. She watched the sun sink below the horizon, the swallows flying home to their nests for the night. When it became too dark to see anything other than the vague outline of distant trees illuminated by the lightning growing increasingly closer, Celia drew the drapes closed.

"I don't know why I must be confined to my room," she grumbled, trying to come up with some way of amusing herself. There was a twinge in the affected limb if she turned too quickly, but otherwise, her ankle was perfectly fine. There was no reason she could not walk on it.

"I could venture downstairs," she reasoned, but quickly dismissed that idea. Mother was obviously concerned about the injury, and Celia had not the heart to go against her wishes.

Perhaps she should spend this forced solitude preparing for the next time she saw Gabriel.

"Oh, Mother. What on earth are you thinking?" Celia asked the empty room. There was no understanding her mother's eagerness in pairing her with the man. It simply made no sense, especially when neither of her parents had ever indicated any preference for a single suitor over the last two seasons.

It seemed Mother *wanted* her and Gabriel pushed into close proximity.

Frustrated, Celia flung herself into a plump chair before the fireplace. Crossing her arms over her chest, she pondered what it all meant. Was this her mother's way of indicating approval without actually forcing the matter?

Her mind wandered to Gabriel and their conversation just before Lady Darby entered the parlor. Celia still felt the sting of his rejection when it came to the matter of courting her. She knew it wasn't a lack of interest driving the dismissal of her suggestion. Gabriel wanted her. Every action and glance directed her way indicated his desire. But he would not pursue her as a gentleman should.

And that fact left Celia aching even more. What untamed wildness existed beneath the thin veneer of civility Gabriel wore while moving through society? What would it feel like if the darkness she glimpsed behind his kindness was unleashed upon her?

There'd been a hint of recrimination in his tone when he'd asked why she would flee Beaumont. If the man believed she would leave because of what occurred between them, he was sorely mistaken.

He wasn't chasing her away. Far from it. Within this short timeframe, Celia found herself becoming hopelessly fascinated with the man. And that was dangerous.

Celia closed her eyes, remembering the way her heart began racing the moment Gabriel pulled her over his knee. The excitement had been both exhilarating and terrifying.

The thrill of Gabriel's fingers trailing so slowly over her flesh had left its mark. She might live the rest of her life feeling the slightly rough material of those black leather gloves.

Restlessness rushed through Celia. She needed to move. She needed a distraction. She needed something or someone occupying her mind other than Gabriel Rose. Twisted ankle or not, she would escape the deafening silence of this room and her own reckless thoughts. No one would know if she went now while everyone was at dinner.

Quickly, she selected a pair of slippers from the armoire. When she lifted her skirts and donned the footwear, she absently noted the faint, purplish bruising. It was visible even through her stockings.

A light shawl was selected as well, thrown over her shoulders for the moment, but useful in case she must conceal herself.

Celia was not sure exactly where she would escape to, only

that she must. Perhaps the conservatory. Or the music room. Even the Ravenswood portrait gallery.

Just somewhere other than this empty, quiet room where her own thoughts tormented her.

She opened the door slowly, peeking her head out to determine if the corridor was empty. Then bit back the tiny scream that rose in her throat.

Gabriel stood there in the shadows. Leaning with a casual, dangerous elegance against the paneled wall directly across from her bedroom door. He was dressed formally for supper in a somber-colored suit coat that fit him to perfection. It highlighted the muscles beneath the fabric, the dark iron grey complementing his features and the scruff darkening his jawline.

Does the man not own a single razor?

Gabriel's scarred eyebrow lifted in question.

"Going somewhere, my lady?"

"I-I thought I would visit the conservatory." It was difficult forming a falsehood quickly enough when she was so shocked by his presence.

"No. You will not."

The terse shutdown of her activities banged like a steel door in her face.

"I'm going crazy in this room. And you have no right—" Celia's protest broke off as Gabriel strode toward her.

"Who are you meeting this time, my lady? Lord Harvey? Or another unworthy gentleman?"

"How dare you accuse me! Besides, my intentions are none of your business," Celia shot back, horrified he would think she would intentionally conduct a clandestine rendezvous. "What are you doing here, anyway? Why are you lurking outside my bedroom door?"

His mouth stretched in a grim smile. "You may thank your mother for this. She requested that I check on you."

Celia shook her head, fighting down the panic choking her. "You are lying. She did no such thing. Why would she?"

Gabriel reached her, his hand cupping her elbow like a bear trap ready to snap shut. "I never lie, my lady. Lady Darby surely has her reasons. At the top of the list is gaining a son-in-law for a stubborn, wayward daughter who has rejected every suitor in her orbit."

"But not you, Mister Rose. She cannot possibly want you," Celia cried out in frustration.

Gabriel stared down at her, his arm sliding around her waist until she was firmly anchored against his body. The danger of the moment swirled around them both until Celia was dizzy with awareness of his hard form. His intoxicating cologne. The huskiness of his voice.

"You cut me to the quick, my lady. And yet, no one knows more than I just how unsuitable I would be as a son-in-law. However, Lady Darby insisted and I obliged. Despite my better judgment and suspicion of her intent," he muttered, the words laced with anger and accusation. "You should be in bed."

"And you should go to hell," Celia promptly replied, then clapped a hand over her own mouth, wishing the words back.

The corners of his lips quirked upward with amusement. "My prickly little sugarplum. Deliciously sweet but somehow covered in thorns." His eyes bored into hers while forcing Celia's retreat back into the bedchamber. The door slammed shut behind them with a swift kick of his booted foot.

Then Gabriel's mouth was upon hers. Hot and demanding. Insistent and possessive. Hard and yet so achingly soft. One hand cradled her face, his fingers sliding further until they wrapped around the thick braid of her hair. Gripping it as though it were a tether useful in controlling a wild animal, he held her in place.

He kissed her until she was faint, and even if her ankle had not been injured, Celia would have collapsed without his arms holding her aloft.

Alarm bells clanged inside Celia's head. Desire burst deep within her soul, clawing its way out of her body. It was so wrong for him to be in her room. Wrong that he was kissing her. Wrong that she welcomed the soft warmth of his hard mouth molding hers.

Thunder echoed, big and booming and so loud it seemed it was just outside the windows. Or was that her heart? She did not know, but one thing was certain. This man would ruin her, and she did not care.

Celia wrapped her arms around his neck. She nestled into his embrace. Reveled in the tight hold he had around her waist and the one of her hair. Sank into the treacherous depths of his mouth and lips as he took what he wanted with lazy insistence. She should push him away. She should call for help. She should do anything that would stop the inevitability of this man claiming her heart.

But she did not. She could only do one thing. The one thing that felt right. That felt true.

That felt like fate.

Destiny.

Her future. And his, too.

She kissed him back.

CHAPTER 11

Gabriel told himself he should stop.

But it was impossible. He couldn't stop when the girl in his arms tasted so sweet. Not when she was so warm and smelled so damned good it made him want to weep. She felt… right. It was the only way he could describe it.

Right in his world of everything wrong.

It'd been a long time since he had experienced anything so perfect. It was impossible to stop the continued onslaught of her innocent mouth. He plundered her sweetness, becoming drunk on everything that made Celia Buchanan who she was.

She was so tiny in his arms, although some considered her tall for a woman. As if God above specifically constructed her to fit his measurements, she molded against his frame like wet silk.

Bending slightly, Gabriel scooped Celia up, inwardly amused when she gave a muffled cry of surprise. She never stopped kissing him, however, not even when he stalked to a chair by the window and gently deposited her in it.

Only when he straightened did their lips finally part. Harsh pants for breaths hung suspended between them as Gabriel stared down at her. He must commit to memory this moment.

The moment when this lovely creature gazed at him as if he'd hung the moon and presented her with all the stars in the sky as gifts. He would, too, if it were possible to accomplish such a fanciful notion.

"Gabriel," Celia's whisper was one of longing.

It was the first time she'd used his given name. By God, Gabriel decided he would happily give the Devil his soul if it meant hearing her say it again while he was deep inside her.

"Shhh," he murmured. Looking around, he found the matching footstool and dragged it closer with the toe of his boot. "Let me see the extent of your injury."

Celia peered up at him, then, with a deep sigh, nodded her consent. She watched as he pulled the low, upholstered stool in front of her and sank upon it. Very carefully, he lifted her leg and placed her foot in his lap. He slipped off her shoe, then after a moment of hesitation, dispensed with the other as well.

His hands traveled over her ankle beneath the mound of her skirts, gently skimming the network of bones and tendons under her silk stockings. When he glanced up at her, she was watching him with an expression of dazed sensuality.

"May I remove your stockings, Celia?"

He promised himself he would stop if she asked, but she simply nodded her head and said, "Yes."

His hands trembled as they slid up until he reached her knee. A banding of ribbon held the stockings in place, and he expertly dispensed with the flimsy garments before she could change her mind. Pulling her injured ankle up so that her foot rested in his lap, he examined it. The bruises were turning an awful color, but there was relatively little swelling.

Gabriel's eyes met hers. "You did this trying to get away from me today, isn't that so?"

There was a flash of rebellion in her dark gaze, but her head moved in a quick jerk of agreement.

For several minutes, he stroked the softness of her skin,

marveling over the fineness of it until Celia drifted into a state of drowsy acceptance.

"I'm sorry I stole your horse," she mumbled, eyes half closed.

"Arion lived up to his name, I think." Gabriel's lips tugged upward with amusement at her slight frown of confusion. "He carried you swiftly away from danger, did he not?"

She was silent then said, "That depends on whether or not *you* are the danger."

"You know the answer to that, Celia."

A slow smile curved her lips. "Then I shall adjust my opinion of Arion's abilities."

"You like the danger, my prickly sugarplum." Gabriel kept her gaze captive as his head bent, and her eyes widened slightly. "Don't you? Answer me."

"Yes." The reluctant murmur seemed torn from her. She bit down on her lip with the admission.

"And this is dangerous for us both, isn't it?" he asked.

Celia nodded, eyes closing as though that simple act would make it easier to avoid the truth. The scent of her fear, and her arousal, tickled his nose. He was more than likely doomed to hell, but he thought it was the most intoxicating aroma he'd ever encountered. He forced himself not to breathe too deeply of it, certain it would make him do drastic, stupid things.

Gabriel's lips pressed against the worst of the bruising, soothing any lingering hurt she might have felt. When his mouth gently explored her ankle bone, she moaned. A slow lick of his tongue across the fine bones of the top of her foot pulled a strangled curse from her lips.

"Will you let me show you more, Celia?" His mouth moved over the paper-thin skin stretching across the arch of her foot. He bit down just hard enough, his teeth scoring the sensitive skin until she gasped in mortified pleasure.

"Y-yes," she surrendered with a low cry.

He hummed his approval against her flesh, his mouth

moving higher. From the arch of her foot. To the demarcation of her ankle. Along the smoothness of her calf. His lips were at her knee now, her skirts crushed and shoved upward as his mouth traveled a leisurely path of sin. "There's my good girl. I'll show you everything, if you allow me."

Celia's palm cupped Gabriel's cheek, momentarily stealing his attention away from the mysteriously sweet flesh of her inner knees. From his lower position on the footstool, he glanced up at the interruption.

"Who are you, Gabriel Rose? How have you captured me under your spell so easily?"

Celia's gaze bored into Gabriel's. Her beautiful dark eyes were shadowed with passion and that twinge of fear he'd sensed before. Indeed, they were nearly black, her lashes casting ebony smudges on her upper cheeks as she watched him. He never wanted her afraid of him, but he could admit her apprehension left him ravenous

"Who am I? I am a man possessed, Celia. A man determined to taste you."

Celia sighed, her fingers flexing along the hard line of his jaw. It was both a caress and a subtle restraint of his intentions. "But I know nothing about you. And you know nothing about me."

Gabriel caught an underlying note of insecurity in her tone. Celia believed his only interest lay in matters of lust. She had no idea how well he actually did know her.

Turning his head, he scorched her palm with a kiss before capturing her hand within his loose grip.

"I know you take cream and no sugar in your morning tea." He pressed a tender kiss to the inside of her knee. "I know your favorite color is emerald green." Another kiss burned the opposite knee. "You love to read but rarely sit still long enough to finish a book. You will dance every dance, rushing from ball to ball, but are left restless and aching for something you've yet to find. And you are fiercely loyal to friends and family."

His tongue slid along the contours of her kneecap. "I know you are frightened of all manners of insects but will save a beetle carried in with the morning's floral arrangements."

A whimper escaped Celia's throat as Gabriel revealed an incident which occurred during a house party at the beginning of the season.

"You are frightened of the dark, but you do not avoid the shadows. You've kissed other men but not in the same manner in which you kiss me." Releasing her wrist, Gabriel now used both hands to further spread her legs. His fingers stroked the texture of the skin he found there on her inner thighs.

Bloody hell. She's as soft as gossamer.

"Oh, Celia. I *do* know you. Perhaps better than you know yourself." His whisper tickled her skin, and she moaned at the sensation of his teeth nipping her with soft brutality. "But still, you have secrets I've yet to discover. Rest assured, I will seek them out. And I *will* uncover them all if you open to me just a tiny bit." "

Raising his eyes, their gazes clashed over the battlefield of her stomach and a mound of satin skirts. Then he watched her as his fingers coasted higher. And higher. Until finally they rested on the thin fabric of her undergarments. His thumbs framed the small slit in the material.

The look of reluctant lust on Celia's features was a siren's call Gabriel could not ignore. She was afraid but also helpless in her desire for him. The combination was heady. It turned him inside out. Turned him into a beast. A lion determined to claim a mate. To protect her from all harm except what he would do to her.

"I want to see you, Celia. Spread your pretty thighs for me so I can taste you. I want your sweetness coating my tongue. Filling my mouth. Because you are the most exquisite creature

I've ever had within my grasp, and I know with certainty you will eventually be my downfall. My utter ruin. Give me this gift, Celia, so I'm not forced to steal it from you. Let me see you and show you Heaven."

As he spoke, Gabriel shifted off the footstool. On his knees, he moved until his shoulders filled the space between Celia's legs. She was prevented from easing her thighs shut. It was impossible with his wide, muscular form wedged there.

Like a man coming to worship, he knelt before her.

A strangled moan leaked from Celia's throat when his thumbs spread the undergarment fabric apart, exposing pale, pink flesh to his avid gaze. Gabriel's jaw clenched with an aching hunger. It took everything within him not to fall upon her like a ravaging beast.

Damn, she was beautiful. All wet silk and cream and heat. Every crevice and fold begging for his mouth.

A wash of light scarlet colored her neck and cheeks. Her hands fluttered in a bird-like motion as if she considered stopping him.

Which was very foolish now that her sweet, feminine scent was in his nostrils and the flavor of her skin permeated his lips. He would not stop now. This was fate. His. Hers. Their unavoidable destiny.

"Grip the arms of the chair, Celia. Do not let go until I give you permission."

Celia hesitated, then did as Gabriel requested. Her head fell back against the cushioned seat in surrender. She trembled, the tiny flutters tickling his fingertips as he held her open. Their eyes remained locked as he gave her a crooked grin.

"You may wish to scream, but I advise against it."

Celia nodded, clutching the chair with such ferocity her knuckles whitened.

"If you should find it difficult remaining silent, I shall help you," he continued. "My hand over your mouth, perhaps?"

He recognized the confusion and a glint of fear in the depths of her velvety brown eyes. She was working out such a scenario in her head and how he might accomplish such a feat.

What it would mean to be under his control and so helpless. So vulnerable. He was hard as stone imagining the depraved things he would do with her if given the opportunity.

"A single stocking would serve well as a gag." Gabriel's tone turned contemplative, a wicked smile tilting his lips upward. "Or maybe I should utilize something more intimate." His fingers stroked the fabric of her underdrawers.

Celia's eyes widened all the more. "I-I shall be quiet. I swear it."

Gabriel hummed his approval.

His head lowered.

His mouth covered her sex.

He drank her in as though she were the finest of spirits.

And he became a man undone.

Could Gabriel feel her shaking? Could he feel the imperceptible tremors quaking just below the surface of her skin?

His breath was so warm. Celia tensed, her exposed flesh reacting in the most elemental way to Gabriel's nearness. Leaning her head back against the chair, she stared at the coffered ceiling above her and waited in a state of horrible anticipation for *something* to happen.

Then his mouth was on her. Determined and hungry. Unavoidable. And so gently possessive, Celia's world tilted.

"Oh, God." The whimper escaped her, and Gabriel responded with a dark chuckle of pleasure.

"Focus on me, Celia, and save those prayers until I'm done with you."

His tongue traced her, learning the shape of her flesh. He licked and nibbled, absorbing every tiny sound Celia made. And his hands remained locked on her, keeping her spread wide as his firm lips and hot mouth drove her to the brink of utter madness.

Celia gripped the chair, her fingernails digging into the

ornately carved wood. Shifting her gaze from the ceiling, she stared at the man kneeling before her. With her skirts bunched up around her stomach, she could only see the thick, russet-hued wealth of his hair and the vast width of his shoulders as he bent to her. But it was enough. Enough that she understood what he was doing to her and experienced a strange sense of willing helplessness. Enough that she comprehended just how deeply their lives were becoming hopelessly entwined. She should be afraid of him. Of his strength and how he controlled her so effortlessly. Her heart thumped painfully as she tried pushing away *those* memories from the past. She must focus on the pleasure Gabriel was giving her.

There was pleasure before, remember, you silly girl? Pleasure, then dark moments of terror.

Celia squeezed her eyes shut. *Don't think about that. Think about this. Here. Now.*

Now. This moment in time when Gabriel was staking his claim with teeth and lips and tongue. There was no going back from this. This was something she would not be able to pretend never happened. This was something she could not shove into the deepest recesses of her mind.

Gabriel explored her with exacting thoroughness. The swipes of his tongue danced between full and lush and razor-like intensity. She relaxed in his hold, melting into the grip he maintained on her. It was as though he waited patiently for that moment of surrender. That moment when her mind accepted everything he demanded she accept.

When she began floating in a hazy dreamlike sea of pleasure, his methods abruptly changed.

She was wet from his ministrations. Fevered from the heightened state he'd driven her to. Swollen with lust. And too enthralled to protest when the intensity of his attentions rose to a crescendo.

Gabriel growled with satisfaction, the rumble tickling her

most intimate place. The rough stubble shadowing his jaw and upper lip abraded her skin but Celia did not mind it. It only heightened every sensation, leaving her incredibly sensitive to every pass of his mouth.

"Your sweet quim tastes like fucking ambrosia," he whispered. He lavished her folds with the flat of his tongue before spearing it into the warmth of her body.

Celia choked back a gasp at the coarseness of his muttered words, then moaned in appreciation when his tongue pressed harder on her clitoris. His thumbs spread her even wider, parting soft, dark curls and exposing her center.

There was no escaping what would follow. Celia knew it was useless to even attempt squirming away. She wanted everything he was doing in this moment and anything he planned on doing next.

Gabriel sucked the tiny knot of nerves gently between his teeth, holding it steady. His tongue began an unrelenting lashing of the sensitive tissue. Over and over. The speed, the tempo, none of it changed, not even when her hips rocked with greedy insistence up into his mouth, wanting more. It remained a constant assault. A persistent motion that carried her into the heart of a raging storm and refused to let her go.

Celia could not help herself, even with the threat of being gagged. She let out a strangled cry of delight, her body no longer her own. Every heartbeat, every drop of blood, every nerve and vein belonged to Gabriel. The climax washed over her without warning. Ecstasy wrung quivering moans from her throat, and Gabriel's response was instant and instinctive.

His hands slipped to her bottom. Cupping the cheeks of her buttocks within his large palms, his fingers dug into the plumpness thorough the fabric. Her hips were slightly elevated until the core of her body was more easily devoured.

Then he sucked all of her wet, swollen flesh into his mouth, drinking in her release. Demanding everything. Taking all without mercy.

Celia trembled. She hovered in a state of suspended pleasure. Orgasmic tendrils curled and invaded every inch of her body and soul. She was flung to the stars beyond the moon while plummeting to land in a cloud of feathers at the same time.

Gabriel's moan of possession echoed in the room. He continued feasting as he appeased his hunger.

His mouth softened as the peak receded, but he continued tenderly licking all her aching, yet satisfied parts. Lassitude crept over Celia until she could barely open her eyes. She sagged against the cushion of the chair, breathing deep, trying to still her racing heart. As she slowly floated back to earth, she became aware of Gabriel murmuring words against the skin of her thighs and the quivering flesh between them.

"*Ma douce fille. Ma dragee piquante.*"

The love words spoken in French made Celia's heart clench with something dangerous. Something wild and unknown. Something she'd never felt before and had no idea how to manage.

My sweet girl. My prickly sugarplum.

Gabriel lowered her until she was once again completely seated in the chair, his hands sliding away from her bottom. Then he moved up her body by incremental degrees, straightening her undergarments and pulling her skirts back into place so her legs were once again properly covered.

With a smile, Gabriel pried her hands off the chair, lifting them until they looped around his neck as he bent over her. He braced himself, his hands mimicking her grip on the chair arms. There was a glint of satisfaction in his molten gaze as Celia stared at him in wonderment.

He pressed a lingering kiss on her mouth, his firm, warm lips brushing over hers and breathing in her tiny pants of air.

Celia tasted herself on his mouth. It was both strange and exotic. Intimate and inappropriate. Her arms tightened around his neck as longing overcame her.

Oh, how she wanted to taste him in the same manner he'd tasted her. She began to tell him so, but he brushed another kiss across her mouth and she remained silent.

Gabriel did not straighten his form, nor did he remove Celia's arms from around his neck. He maintained his stance with a certain degree of arrogance and said, "Shall I pleasure you once more before your mother arrives and attempts trapping us into marriage?"

"My mother?" Celia frowned, still a bit woozy from the entire experience. "Whatever are you talking about? No one is being trapped."

"Nothing changes the fact that your mother sent me here, Celia, nor what her intentions may be to that end. I've made it quite clear I have no desire to marry."

Celia sat straighter in the chair, the motion bringing her nearly nose-to-nose with Gabriel. "I don't expect you to marry me. And I don't want to marry you, either. I believe I've made *that* perfectly clear."

His hand raised and Celia steeled herself. However, to her surprise, he merely touched the center of her bottom lip using his thumb. Staring deep into her eyes, he softly rubbed the plump flesh in a repetitive motion that was hypnotic. He pressed even further, gently forcing her mouth to part. His thumb raked over the barrier of her teeth then stopped as if he were daring her to actually bite him.

Celia's breath stilled. Panicked and wanting. And he watched her with such intensity she wondered what he might be thinking of doing. An overwhelming urge swelled deep inside her. A desire to suck his thumb into her mouth and swirl her tongue around it.

Where on earth did that come from?

With a crooked smile of satisfaction, Gabriel slowly removed his hand. The moment was over and Celia blinked at how quickly the atmosphere changed.

"Good. Then we are in accordance and can present a unified front should your mother persist in throwing us together," Gabriel replied calmly. He straightened, moving away from her while pushing the stool back into place. With great care, he lifted Celia's injured ankle and settled it on the plush piece of furniture.

"There. All set. I shall take my leave now that I've seen to your welfare."

Celia's cheeks turned bright pink. *My welfare. Is that what it's called? That entire episode where his face was nestled between my thighs? My welfare?*

A sense of self-preservation overcame Celia. Lifting her chin high, she favored him with her haughtiest stare. "Thank you for your concern, Mister Rose. Even if it is unwarranted."

Gabriel leaned back in, his lips brushing over her temple. "Mister Rose? Tsk, tsk, Celia. After tasting your climax in my mouth, I'd say we're on a first-name basis. What occurred just now was most definitely necessary. And let's not forget how well you followed my instructions."

Celia's face flamed hot. Damn this man. How did he manage the impossible feat of making her moan his name one moment and then curse him the next? It made no sense why she was so vulnerable to his charms. It was infuriating. She grit her teeth seeing his smug expression. How dare he toy with her, pursue her so recklessly, all while proclaiming he had no desire for a respectable relationship. How dare he use her for his own twisted amusement.

"I did not seek out your attention, Mister Rose."

"But that was you kissing me as though you need my breath to survive, wasn't it? And that was you spreading your legs wider for me. Moaning with every lick. Every nibble."

Celia sucked in a breath. "Please go away. And stay away."

"Impossible." He laughed, nuzzling into her hair. "I think I should kneel before you once more. Do you know why? Because you are most amendable just after you come. As are most women."

His arrogance was astounding, but deep in Celia's belly, there was a nervous, excited flutter. Somehow, she needed to regain control of herself and this dangerous situation.

She pushed at Gabriel's broad chest with balled fists. He did not budge from his position. He loomed over her. A lion guarding his kill. Watching her with those sharp, golden-brown eyes as though he found her efforts greatly amusing.

"Next time, I'll have you on your knees, my little sugarplum. And it will be you pleasuring me."

Celia could not help herself. Her gaze drifted, landing on the prominent bulge marring the flat front of his trousers.

Dear Lord, the man had no shame. No restraint. And for some bloody reason, Celia apparently liked it.

She liked it too much. It sickened her how much she hung on his every word despite her outrage.

"Your words are as coarse as your manners." Her exasperated huff hung between them.

Gabriel's eyes narrowed, then his head bowed slightly. "I apologize, my lady. One should not expect too much from a bastard. I shall see you tomorrow. Rest well."

His lips pressed against her forehead in a brief caress, and then he was gone. The door clicked behind him before Celia could even muster up an admonishment at the derogatory term used in describing himself.

Later, much later, restlessly tossing and turning in her bed, Celia wondered why the faint self-recrimination in Gabriel's voice bothered her so terribly.

CHAPTER 13

Once again, Gabriel spent a night cursing his damnable weakness when it came to the delectable Celia Buchanan.

The failure to distance himself was becoming an infuriating exercise in delusional behavior. He had nothing to offer her, despite his wealth. Nothing of value remotely capable of overcoming his lack of title. And nothing would ever excuse the fact he was the bastard son of an opera singer who had, unfortunately, fallen in love with a man of higher social standing.

The Earl of Darby should marry off his headstrong daughter as quickly as possible. Lady Darby's strangely complacent attitude in throwing her daughter to a wolf like himself should be discouraged as well. In the interim, Gabriel decided he must physically place the girl at arm's length before they found themselves in a tangle of consequences and scandal.

But even as Gabriel made those hard decisions, he could not help but remember the soft, warm taste of her in his mouth. The sweetness of her climax and those intoxicating gasps for air that escaped her lungs as he pleasured her. She was an addiction now. One he should forget.

Or, at the very least, learn to live without.

~

GABRIEL INTENTIONALLY AVOIDED any interaction with Celia until it was time to gather for the evening meal. As promised, Ivy arranged it so that he and Celia sat beside each other. Because he was so readily accepted by the Earl and Countess, his presence at the table was not out of the ordinary. Oh, some thought it quite scandalous a bastard was seated among the ton, but Ravenswood was not deterred. Gabriel was accustomed to the murmurs, but he wondered if Celia truly objected.

Offering his arm as he escorted her into the dining room, Gabriel took note of Celia's barely noticeable limp.

Bending close, he murmured, "Are you well enough to walk?"

Celia gave a tight nod. "I am fine, Mister Rose."

She said nothing more while Gabriel held her chair so she could slide into it. When he took his own seat, he leaned in again. "Would you tell me if you are still in pain, I wonder?"

"It is not your concern if I am or not, Mister Rose," she primly replied. Without looking at him, she methodically unfolded her napkin and laid it across her lap. Still keeping her gaze averted, she nodded permission for the servant to fill her wine goblet. "Indeed, *I* am not your concern at all."

Gabriel nodded with grim acceptance. "I agree, Lady Celia, but for the sake of Lady Ravenswood, let us make the best of this situation. After tonight, we shall endeavor to stay far away from one another."

Celia cast him a glance from beneath long dark lashes and scoffed. "The promise of such action has not come to fruition thus far. You are to blame for that, Mister Rose."

Gabriel leaned back in his chair, idly toying with the stem of his wine goblet. "I take full responsibility for my behavior, my lady."

Celia huffed. "How refreshing, Mister Rose. And unbelievable."

They spoke in low murmurs, but Gabriel knew attention was directed their way. From across the table, Lady Darby gave him an encouraging smile. There was no concealing the small glimmer of hope it contained.

The muscle in Gabriel's jaw clenched. "Should I leave, my lady? Tell me to go and I shall this very instant."

"And give others even more fodder for their tongue-wagging?" Celia sighed in resignation. "No, Mister Rose. You shall stay and suffer with me."

Suffer. It was an appropriate word for the remainder of the meal. Because it was pure torture. Sitting in such close proximity to the woman he wanted so desperately while she did her best ignoring his presence.

He allowed her insolence, of course. What else could he do when she only responded when he asked pointedly direct questions? It was not as though he could throw her across his lap and spank her as he had in the forest.

From the opposite ends of the table, Sebastian and Ivy wore duplicate frowns aimed in his direction. They recognized the increasingly cold hostility yawning between Gabriel and Celia but could not make sense of it. Indeed, the crackle of that ice was affecting the other guests. To the point those seated in close proximity lost all interest in any semblance of conversation.

A yawning chasm of silence grew outward from the middle of the dining hall where Gabriel and Celia sat. Lady Darby appeared somewhat distressed, her gaze darting between her daughter's icy countenance and Gabriel's.

"I hope your injury is fully healed, Lady Celia," Robert remarked from across the table. His chin still bore evidence of the wound Celia inflicted upon him, but it had not diminished his interest in her. "I join others in expressing my concern for your well-being."

Gabriel glared at the man. A need to leap across the wide, mahogany expanse, through the elaborate candle and lily centerpieces, and over the delicate chinaware and crystal goblets burned his stomach with unrelenting intensity. His hands itched to wrap themselves around the young lord's throat and squeeze until no further bleating issued from his mouth.

He sipped his wine instead as Lord Harvey continued.

"Do you plan on joining the festivities planned this evening?" Robert tipped his glass in Celia's direction. "I humbly offer my escort, if that is the case."

"Thank you, Lord Harvey," Celia coolly replied. "I've not yet made my decision."

"I will sit with you, Lady Celia, should you decide not to take part in the dancing," Sara offered, leaning past Robert with a wide smile. "We shall keep one another company."

"There is no need for you to be sidelined." Celia nodded at her friend. "I may dance after all."

Gabriel's brow knitted into a frown. If Celia intended on making him jealous, he would quickly ruin those plans.

"I do not mind keeping Lady Celia company." His hand moved from his own lap to her silk-covered thigh, his head tilting as he favored her with a sidelong glance. "You should not risk further injury, my lady. We shall be bored together." When she stiffened beside him, Gabriel allowed himself a tiny smile. Concealed by the tablecloth and the table itself, he squeezed gently, his fingers warning her to stay and accept his touch.

Celia's own smile was grim. "But Mister Rose, that would be torture beyond comprehension. Surely, you have other matters that better occupy your time." Her tone left no doubt she would be the one suffering from his presence. Her own hand disappeared beneath the tablecloth. It was accomplished with such grace and subtlety no one, not even Gabriel, noticed. Then to his utter surprise, he felt a prickling of pain.

It was almost too preposterous to be true. Celia, armed with her dinner fork, stabbed the silver tines into the top of his hand. It did not hurt, for she pressed with restraint, and Gabriel was hard pressed not to crow out loud with laughter.

"Torture is a relative term, my lady," Gabriel said solemnly.

Celia shot him a heated glare, then pushed the weapon into his skin with greater purpose.

With relative ease, Gabriel shifted his hand, grabbing the handle of the fork. His fingers covered hers in a crushing grip.

"Time in my company might not be as horrible as you think." He squeezed Celia's hand until her grip on the fork loosened. It fell soundlessly to the carpeted floor.

"That is so true," Lady Caroline chimed in. "Mister Rose is always entertaining. And so knowledgeable of a great many subjects. I imagine this is a result of your education in France, isn't that correct, Mister Rose? The French are so very advanced in all things."

Gabriel smiled at the widow simpering from the opposite side of the table. "Most assuredly. Excuse me for a brief moment, please."

Ducking beneath the table allowed him an excuse at avoiding further conversation with the widow. But wickedness was second nature to him. While retrieving the fork, he would give Celia Buchanan something to think about.

Gripping her injured ankle, his fingers tightened as he leaned toward her with deliberate intent. She could not move away when he lightly bit the outside of her thigh, his teeth breaching skirts, petticoats, and stockings.

Celia gave a strangled squeak of alarm, batting frantically at his head as though he were a cantankerous poodle. Gabriel ignored her and calmly emerged from under the table, fork in hand.

The paleness of Celia's cheeks, the shock at his brazen actions before she schooled her features into a mien of serenity, spread a grin across Gabriel's face.

"A new fork for the lady, please. She dropped this one," he instructed a servant while handing over the utensil.

Robert watched them with a suspicious glare, although his tone was artificially light. "I do hope you have games planned for us, Lady Celia. They are the highlight of every house party. I know I enjoy them immensely."

The stare Gabriel leveled at the young lord was nothing short of glacial. "There shall be no games tonight."

Celia smiled brightly at Gabriel. Her cheeks were much rosier now than they'd been just seconds ago when he'd nipped her thigh like a lion toying with its food. "Thank goodness you have no control over these matters, Mister Rose." Her attention turned to Robert. "If others wish it, I am happy to oblige. But those who persist in bending the rules will not be invited to join." It was a subtle warning. Robert Harvey and his tendency to take more than he should would not be tolerated.

"You already play a dangerous game, my lady," Gabriel murmured under his breath for her ears alone. "My advice is that you do not begin another."

"I will remind you, sir, your advice holds no weight with me," Celia immediately shot back. The fierce statement lay cloaked by an easy smile for anyone watching their interaction.

"You are infuriating, you do know that, right?" Gabriel's voice strummed with frustration, but Celia was correct. He had no say on her actions. Why he continued this madness of inserting himself into her life was beyond comprehension.

Momentarily defeated, he sunk back in his chair.

Realizing he would say nothing more on the subject, Celia flashed the other guests a stunning smile.

Gabriel's hands tightened into fists as she cheerfully quoted Shakespeare, "You can't lose a game if you don't play the game. So, let us all play, shall we?"

CHAPTER 14

*C*elia was achingly aware of Gabriel's displeasure. It rippled off him in little waves of discontent and lapped at her feet.

He was furious. Enough that it kept him from lurking in the shadows as he usually did in such situations. During the hour she remained in the ballroom, Gabriel stood like a sentinel.

Disturbingly close and stonily silent.

Despite her deep-seated inclinations toward rebellion, Celia remained seated, fuming even as she did so. She should accept one of the many offers to dance. She should stroll the terrace while on a gentleman's arm. Enjoy the balmy night air and the fragrance of roses and jasmine. Maybe even grant a stolen kiss or two.

But thinking about those things made her stomach clench with distaste. How had Gabriel ruined those things for her? How had she given him the means of destroying any chance she possessed of finding a suitable husband? One perfect for her unfortunate situation?

Celia rubbed her leg in an unconscious gesture. Glancing in Gabriel's direction, she found him staring directly at her. She froze in realization. She was assuaging the very spot his teeth had nipped.

Gabriel smirked, his golden-brown eyes gravitating to her thigh. And when he looked back up, their eyes connecting, Celia shivered with awareness. Gabriel appeared ravenous. As if he might pounce upon her and finish devouring her for dessert. Only the thinnest veneer of civility kept him from following through, and Celia wondered how long it would be before that shell cracked into a million pieces.

So attuned was she to him, Celia did not hear Miss Paula Heaton. The young lady asked her question a second time while sliding into an unoccupied chair.

"Will you still conduct the games, Lady Celia?"

Celia tore her gaze from Gabriel's narrowed one, focusing instead on the pretty girl sitting beside her. "Yes, of course, Miss Heaton," she replied with a smile. "Are there others still interested in such pastimes?"

"Please, call me Paula, if you like. And yes, so far, there are nine of us, including yourself. We are ready to begin if you are."

Gabriel's glare burned Celia. She could feel the heat of it, the intensity of his disapproval, but she refused to acknowledge him. He would not dare try and stop her. He would not dare.

His deep, rumbling voice surprised both Celia and Paula Heaton. Together, they stared up at Gabriel as he bent at the waist and executed a respectful bow.

"Gather them, Miss Heaton, and meet myself and Lady Celia in the library."

Gabriel grasped Celia's arm as they exited the ballroom. With his jaw set in a tight line, he was obviously furious. Marching her along, his anger made him forget the tenderness of her ankle.

Only when she stumbled with a small gasp of pain did the man come to his senses. With a muttered curse, he halted in the middle of the wide corridor. Celia found herself hauled up alongside him, his gaze impenetrable as it searched hers.

"Does it pain you?"

"It does not," Celia replied stubbornly, tossing her head back. "Just a twinge from being manhandled by a monster."

"If you are lying to me, I shall throw you up over my shoulder and personally deposit you in your bed," he grunted. "Where you shall remain until I know for certain you are completely healed."

"An impossible scenario," Celia ground out. "Your concern is deceiving when you drag me along like a hangman leading me to the gallows."

Gabriel's gaze flared, an instant spark promising retribution for her insolence. But then his eyes softened. His grip loosened so his hand now cupped her elbow. "I forget myself with you, Lady Celia. Indeed, I forget my place. Forget I have no right to touch you or even speak to you. But you have a way of inciting all manners of emotions inside me. And I am just a man, after all."

Celia sighed, her lips tight with annoyance. "Gabriel, don't ever believe you haven't the right. You've more than most men of my acquaintance."

He appeared startled by her words, but Lady Caroline Robertson's approach interrupted whatever Gabriel might have said in response.

"Ah, there you are! Come, come, let us get these games started," she trilled, clapping her hands with delight.

"You are joining us?" Celia asked curiously.

"In a chaperone capacity only, my dear. And I thought I'd keep Mister Rose company. Surely, he attends for the sole purpose of keeping these young bucks in line." The widow's appreciative glance swept over Gabriel's form.

Celia's fists tightened. She recognized the lascivious glint in the other woman's eyes.

"How kind of you, Lady Robertson," Celia said, stepping away from Gabriel, although he seemed faintly disturbed by the distance she placed between them.

The others joined them in the corridor. There were more men than women but that wasn't unusual. Lord Harvey hung at the back of the group, his dark eyes bouncing between Celia and Gabriel.

"Well, it seemed a necessary endeavor. However, do not worry I shall watch the participants too closely." Caroline sidled closer alongside Gabriel until their arms were a hair's breadth from touching. "I won't ruin everyone's fun."

The lady's true intent and interest were so blatantly obvious, Celia was hard pressed not to roll her eyes. Playing these games was not so appealing anymore. In fact, she'd lost all interest in the entire affair. Seeing the politely indulgent smile Gabriel bestowed upon Caroline sent a sharp ache through Celia's heart.

And that was upsetting because the emotion stemmed from a tiny fissure of jealousy. It was something she could not examine too closely.

They continued into the library as a group, the doors shutting with a faint click of finality.

"What shall we do first, Lady Celia?" a young lady inquired. She blushed when one of the five men in attendance grinned at her boldness.

Celia sank onto one of the burgundy-hued divans. Her cheeks grew pink upon recalling the last time she was within the confines of this room. Upon this very piece of furniture.

And how she'd used Gabriel Rose's body in a quest for glorious pleasure in that magical hour after midnight.

Peeking at Gabriel through the sweep of her lashes, she knew he was remembering those moments as well. His full, plush lips curved upward, and the scoundrel actually winked at her.

Celia's lips tightened with irritation. What was he doing here, anyway? In the months since she'd become aware of his existence, Gabriel never took part in such silly activities. He never danced. Never showed any interest whatsoever in any woman. His demeanor remained the same whether he was ignored completely or shamelessly flirted with. He may play cards or join the gentlemen for cigars and brandies, but he carefully maintained a distance between himself and members of the ton.

His presence in this library was surely some new method devised simply as a means of torturing her.

"I suggest Kiss The Candlestick," Robert interjected.

Celia let out a sharp laugh. "Oh, not again."

"Yes, it is a game played far too often," Sir Jasper said. "You are always so clever, Lady Celia. I'm sure you can think of something rarely done."

Celia watched as Lady Caroline inclined her head toward Gabriel. He responded by bending slightly so she could whisper in his ear. Whatever she said sent a smile spreading across his face.

Jealousy, pure and simple, hit Celia's body like a lightning bolt. Without considering the ramifications, she blurted out, "We shall play Hot Cockles."

There was a moment of stunned silence before Gabriel rumbled, "You most certainly will not." He glared at her, his eyes burning coals of dark golden fire. Beside him, Caroline bit her lip in amusement.

"I-I would not feel comfortable playing that game, Lady Celia. It's entirely too scandalous," Paula said, uneasily.

"I'm all for it," Robert chimed in.

A chorus of agreeing voices echoed him, although three of the others still had yet to voice an opinion.

"It is the majority wishing to play," Celia pointed out. "And it's no more scandalous than Guessing The Kiss."

Robert maneuvered his way toward Celia, his eyes alight with an odd glow. "Once again, you devise the perfect entertainment for the evening, Lady Celia."

She spared the persistent Lord Robert Harvey a glance while squaring her shoulders. "I shall go first and choose the lap to lay my head. Paula, if you do not object, we shall use your pretty scarf as my blindfold."

Again, there was a rumble of dissent from Gabriel, his eyes burning with fury over Celia's willingness to play the game. A game in which she would lay her head in someone's lap while allowing another to strike her hand, palm up, in the middle of her back. Correctly guessing the striker was how one claimed victory.

Despite Lady Caroline's tugging of his arm, Gabriel stalked toward Celia. He stood close enough to touch her knees where she sat on the divan. Celia's head tilted back so she could match him stare for stare.

"You will not play such a game, my lady." His growl was a warning for her and the gentlemen silently vying for the opportunity to be either the one whose lap Celia's head rested or the one striking her.

"You do not have to take part, Mister Rose. I imagine that striking a woman, even in jest, does not interest you." The jab she inflicted referred directly to the incident in the forest.

Gabriel's eyes flared with a blaze of heat over the reminder. His fists clenched at his side, and for a moment, Celia feared he might do the unthinkable. He might plop down, haul her across his sturdy knee, and spank her until she cried for mercy.

Just the idea of such a thing sent a flush of embarrassed arousal through her entire body. Despite that, she managed to retain her defiance.

"You are free to leave, Mister Rose," Robert drawled. "As you are not a member of the *ton*, I imagine our ideas of amusement are quite foreign to you." He reached past Gabriel and took Celia's hand, drawing her up to her feet. "Choose me as the lap, Lady Celia."

"If you wish to keep that hand, Lord Harvey, I suggest you remove it from Lady Celia's person." Gabriel's possessiveness radiated from that simple statement. He was publicly laying claim, and Celia gaped at him in shock.

"You do not dictate who may touch me, Mister Rose. You forget yourself."

"Celia..." His growl was another warning as was the dropping of her title.

She was in grave danger. But instead of frightening her, the knowledge sent a wave of terrified desire coursing through Celia's veins.

"Mister Rose," she answered as calmly as possible.

In a flash, he had her arm, tugging her free of Robert's loose grip.

"A word in private, my lady."

"What do you think you are doing, Rose?" Robert objected angrily. "You cannot just drag her away."

"Will any one of you stop me?" Gabriel shot back, his eyes hard and his jaw clenched. He ignored the stares of the other guests and dragged Celia closer alongside his body.

Celia allowed it, although she wasn't quite sure why. She should not go anywhere with this man, not when he practically vibrated with frustration over the deliberate attempt at making him jealous. She'd hoped for some reaction but perhaps she'd pushed a bit too far.

"Leave us. Now." Gabriel's command was as quiet and as deadly as that of any king. Rather than question the authority in his voice, the others obeyed. Even Robert, grumbling beneath his breath over this commoner's audacity, did as Gabriel demanded.

In a matter of seconds, Celia was alone with Gabriel. A *very* precarious place to be when she melted like ice thrown into a fire the moment he dared touch her.

He hauled her against him until her toes barely touched the ground. Held against his chest like some sort of coveted prize as he glared down at her.

"Are you that desperate for a spanking, Celia?" His voice was a silky thread wrapping around her and pulling tighter until Celia could hardly breathe without moaning. "Answer me. And truthfully."

Celia swayed in his grip. "No. I don't know."

His laugh was dark. "Oh, you know exactly what you want, sugarplum. And I know exactly what you need. But tell me this. Whose lap would you have chosen to lay your head? Which man would have been granted the honor of your warm breath curling around his cock? Felt your trembles when your backside was struck? Heard your little gasp of pain and delight?"

Celia's eyes closed on a pang of desire so intense it left her dizzy. "The strike would be to the palm of my own hand in the center of my back," she managed the explanation in a choked whisper. His brutal words should have her gasping in shock instead of sending lust spiking through her veins.

Gabriel's mouth brushed over her lips. "Do you think any man would be able to resist striking that sweet, plump arse when it's practically begging for his hand? Do you think he won't dream of thrusting his cock into you while turning your pale flesh a bright red? Marking you with his palm prints? Impossible." His free hand came up and cupped her throat, his palm resting so firmly against it that he surely felt it every time she swallowed. His eyes dropped to that point, narrowed with frustrated lust while his fingers flexed slightly.

"Whose lap would you have chosen, Celia?" He repeated the question.

Celia knew a momentary panic. Her heart beat so fiercely she wondered if Gabriel could hear it.

"Yours." The admission was borne of desire, one heightened when his fingers tightened.

"My punishment, correct?" Like feathers brushing lace, he stroked the sides of her throat in tiny movements. "Because I dared stop your reckless behavior."

Celia hesitated. She'd not thought of it that way. She'd only thought of the pleasure found in being that close to Gabriel. Her opportunity to revel in the hard-hewn strength of his thighs beneath her cheek, the weight of his hand holding her head in position. Only now, in this moment, did she realize the highly sexual position she would have willingly placed herself for the sake of the game. Her head in one man's lap while another struck her from behind.

The images conjured in her brain were staggering.

Her breath escaped in a rush of regret. "I'm sorry."

"I know you are. Now, let us call the others in and we shall continue the course you set us upon."

Celia froze. "What? No. I no longer wish to play." She struggled against the grip he had on her upper arm and the warm fingers wrapped around her neck. Gabriel held her easily, however. She could not twist free of his grasp and his lips twisted as he watched her try.

"Shhh. Do not fret, sweetness. Do you honestly think I would allow another man to strike you? He would die a quick death if he dared. No. It is my lap you will find yourself draped over and the only hand you taste the bite of shall be mine."

Oh! He cannot do this. He cannot possibly be serious. A public display of discipline? I'll never survive it. Nor the scandal.

"Gabriel. You cannot."

His fingers tightened even more. His lips brushed hers again, and just before his brutal mouth claimed hers, he murmured, "Your punishment, Celia. And mine as well."

CHAPTER 15

Gabriel released Celia. His bottom lip stung where she'd nipped him in desperation.

He grinned. "Do you think that will dissuade me from what must happen?"

Celia's eyes were wide. She was shocked by her own actions, but then the chocolate depths of her gaze darkened with a hint of steel.

It only made Gabriel more determined to see her bend to his will.

"I won't allow you to do this in front of others," she snapped.

Gabriel's eyebrow cocked. "In private then?"

Celia stomped her foot. "Deuce it, but you are maddening."

"We'll call it a courting ritual, if you like. Start an interesting trend. Prospective beaus turn prospective wives over their knees to test compatibility." Gabriel considered her, rubbing a thumb over his wounded lower lip thoughtfully as though such a scenario were a true possibility. "As for our own situation, it's evident we are a match. You enjoy such activities. And I most certainly relish them."

A noise that sounded like outraged frustration issued from Celia's throat. That defiant chin of hers tilted higher.

"We are not courting, Mister Rose. And you've made your stance on marriage perfectly clear."

Sebastian's words rose in Gabriel's mind at that moment. His friend's annoying, unwanted advice that he find a wife and settle into his own home.

It pricked at Gabriel. The impossible idea that he might possess his own family. His own happiness. His own contentment.

His own life.

It was becoming more tempting by the second to heed Sebastian's words. And to consider fulfilling it with this woman despite the obstacles between them.

"Perhaps I've reconsidered," he stated nonchalantly.

Celia's eyes flared. "Have you now? I wish you luck in your search for a wife."

She struggled in freeing herself from his grasp, but Gabriel would not let her go so easily. His arm slid around her waist, his mouth dipping closer to hers. "Did you not suggest we undergo an engagement of sorts to better explore this attraction between us?"

Her back stiffened. "I did. And you refused. It's too late to avail yourself of the offer now. I've rescinded it."

"Have you now?" Gabriel mocked, eyes narrowed while drawing her firmly against him. Her hands balled into fists, two ineffective weapons resting lightly on the wide plane of his chest.

God's blood. Her stubbornness made him ache all the more. How he wished to tame this woman. Make her beg for him. Hear her screams of pleasure and moans of satisfaction.

Before he could say more, the library door swung open. Lady Caroline's head appeared in the opening, her eyes wide at seeing the close embrace between Gabriel and Celia.

Celia tried jerking free again, her cheeks blushing pink. Gabriel merely arched an eyebrow at the intrusion and held her even tighter.

"What is it?" Gabriel barked. Their bodies were no closer than if they shared a waltz, but the fact Celia was alone with him for more than a few minutes was scandalous on its own.

"Ahh, a necessary interruption, Mister Rose. You are needed in Lord Ravenswood's study. The footman said something about an unexpected visitor?" Caroline's gaze swept over them, boldly curious and perceptive. The library door opened even more, giving the small group still standing in the corridor an unobstructed view. Lord Harvey's features were pinched with fury. Indeed, the man looked as though he might suffer an apoplectic episode.

"The Earl requires your presence, Mister Rose," Celia said tightly. She'd gone completely still, no longer fighting Gabriel's hold.

"If it were anyone other than Ravenswood, I would tell them to go to the Devil." Gabriel's mouth brushed her ear, making note of her imperceptible shiver. "You've been granted a reprieve." His arms finally loosened enough so she could back away. "But this conversation is not over, Celia. Nor shall I forget your punishment."

Gabriel rapped on the door of Sebastian's study, his knuckles striking the wood forcefully.

Annoyance was evident in his actions. Annoyance at being interrupted. Annoyance at leaving Celia behind in Harvey's company. The summons to Sebastian's study effectively broke apart the group intent on playing parlor games, but Gabriel did not trust Harvey when it came to Celia. The man wanted her badly enough that he might do something extreme if it meant she would be his.

"Come in," Sebastian called out, and Gabriel wasted no time pushing through the door. His impatience was hard to conceal. For whatever purpose Sebastian had summoned him, he wished it over quickly.

Sebastian stood up from behind a huge burlwood oak desk. With a tumbler of whiskey in his hand, he gestured toward Gabriel. His smile was both pleased and mysterious. "Ah, here is the man himself, Lord Banbury."

Gabriel swung toward the person Sebastian addressed. The other man stood near the fireplace, his body half turned so he could watch Gabriel stride forward.

A curious sort of premonition flooded Gabriel. A feeling that something momentous and life-altering was imminent. He recognized Lord Heath Banbury. And the young earl's sudden appearance at Beaumont could only mean one thing.

"Lord Banbury," Gabriel almost growled the two words, his nostrils flaring with distrust.

"Our father has died," his half-brother stated without preamble. He took a gulp of whiskey from the cut crystal glass held tight in one hand.

The atmosphere swirled with tension. Silence hung heavy and it seemed no one was interested in breaking it.

Gabriel's heart twisted with hate. Hate for the man who'd abandoned him as a child. Hate for the man who'd cast aside Gabriel's mother as though she were something dirty. Something to be ashamed of. It was difficult keeping all his emotions in check as he stared at Heath.

When Sebastian pressed a tumbler into his hand, Gabriel took it automatically. The contents were downed in one gulp before he managed a cold response.

"I don't care."

His half-brother shared many physical characteristics with

Gabriel. The same build, although Heath was not quite as large or muscular. The men did possess the same stubborn jawline and hawklike nose. Their eyes were different hues, however, with Heath's the piercing blue of his own deceased mother's.

The two men had never actually engaged in conversation before, but through his contacts, Gabriel knew Heath's reputation. The man was decent. Honest. Despite having a reprobate as a father, Lord Banbury was an exemplary gentleman although he was quite popular with the ladies.

The younger man cast a glance at Sebastian who shrugged his shoulders as if to say, "I told you so."

"You don't understand what he has done—" Heath began.

Gabriel cut him off with a low snarl.

"You are right. I don't understand. And I don't give a tinker's damn what he has done. I wanted nothing but answers the last time I saw him. Instead, he used his cane and gave me this scar." Gabriel swept a hand through the heavy tumble of his hair while glaring at Heath. The fury seeping from him was like poison spreading through the room. "A useful reminder I was better off without him in my life. I want nothing from that man. Then or now."

"Gabriel, you should hear Banbury out," Sebastian murmured. "He's traveled two days without rest to deliver this news in person."

Gabriel rounded on his friend. "And you should keep your opinions to yourself. My lord."

Sebastian's hands rose in surrender, a smile tilting his lips at Gabriel's grudging use of respect. "Understood."

Heath cleared his throat, his dark blue eyes troubled as he continued despite Gabriel's increasing anger.

"I know Father failed you, Gabriel. I know your hatred for him. He told me often enough how you ignored his commands and then his pleas for reconciliation. And he related how you fought the one time you saw each other. How angry he became and how he struck you." Heath advanced toward Gabriel; his jaw squared with determination. Darkened circles rimmed his eyes, and the rumpled condition of his clothing spoke of his exhausted state. "I can't say I blame you for despising him. Our father was wrong in his treatment of you. And even more so in the treatment of your mother."

"Did you not understand what I said, Banbury? I don't care. Now excuse me, I have other more important things requiring my attention." Gabriel dismissed Heath and gave a deferential nod to Sebastian. "I trust the two of you will keep the knowledge of my father's identity in confidence."

"I'm afraid I cannot do that." Heath took a deep breath. The look he gave Gabriel was a strange mixture of sympathy and regret. "Soon, everyone will know precisely whose son you truly are."

"Those who matter already know who I am. And they know my reputation. The company I keep. The dangerous men I call associates. Do not force me into a position where I must personally ensure this never becomes fodder for the rumor mills." Gabriel's tone remained calm, but his hands clenched into fists, his eyes darkening with the violence coursing through his veins. He burned with the desire to shut his half-brother's mouth permanently.

"A useless threat, I'm afraid," Heath said.

"And why is that?" Gabriel snarled.

"Because our father named you as his heir. Like it or not, four days ago at dawn, you became the new Marquess of Rosenthorne."

CHAPTER 16

Gabriel slammed a fist into the surface of Sebastian's desk.

"I don't want it."

There was a moment of silence before Sebastian gave a low chuckle. "It seems you haven't a choice, my friend."

Gabriel glared at him. They were alone now. Now that Heath had been shown to a guest room. Now that Gabriel's life was essentially ruined. Now that everything he knew of himself was questionable.

"I learned the marquess was my father the year I turned sixteen. He did not acknowledge me then and it doesn't need to happen now."

Sebastian turned his tumbler over in his hands. "It's not so simple, ignoring a matter of such magnitude."

"Banbury may have it."

"According to Banbury, he cannot claim it as long as you are alive. Your parents' marriage before your birth made you the legal heir. No matter that Rosenthorne wed another soon after your mother's death and later fathered another son. You are firstborn. You, my friend, are the new marquess regardless of your reluctance to claim it. And I know you have your own wealth, but you just came into a windfall."

"I've no need of his damned money. He threw my mother aside, Seb. Abandoned her in the cruelest manner and left me in the care of strangers. Then he promptly procured himself a new wife. Along with a new son." Gabriel paced before the fireplace in restless agitation. "If I were legally his and my mother his wife, why did he abandon us both? I don't believe he married her. After all, he only confessed this to Banbury while on his deathbed. Perhaps he suffered a state of delirium."

"There is proof. A marriage license and the minister who performed the ceremony. The marquess swore to it in that statement crafted along with his barrister's assistance and witnessed by his physician." Sebastian refilled their glasses with whiskey. "It seems Rosenthorne intended on atoning for his misdeeds."

Gabriel slanted Sebastian a look full of suspicion. "Are you not surprised by this momentous revelation that Rosenthorne is my father?"

Sebastian sighed. "I learned that secret shortly after we arrived in England. But like you, I had no idea you were his legitimate son. It wasn't that difficult to guess if one took the time to look. You bear an uncanny likeness to the old marquess. And to Banbury."

Gabriel scrubbed his jaw. "Over the last two years, you've said nothing."

"It's not my story to tell. Gabriel, think hard on this before you walk away. It is an opportunity to gain everything you ever wanted. An opportunity to claim the woman you want."

Gabriel's jaw tightened. A muscle ticked along its clenched length. He knew precisely what Sebastian meant by that. His status as a bastard had just been shattered. Now, as a bachelor with a lofty title, he would find himself besieged by women eagerly hoping they might become a marchioness.

"Damned if I want a woman whose only interest lies in the titles a man holds," he growled.

God's blood. He was a bloody marquess. The title was thrown into his lap simply because a man died and decreed it so. The same heartless man who'd married Eleanor Rose in secret before hiding her away in shame until she bore him a son. It was all too fantastical to believe.

Now, there were no obstacles standing in his way when it came to Celia Buchanan. If he wanted her, he could claim her. Indeed, her parents would likely present her on a silver platter for the taking.

And Celia would hate him forever if the choice of a husband was not her own.

"I know your life has suddenly been turned upside down," Sebastian murmured. "And your future is now something you must plot out. I will assist in any way I can, Gabriel, and your friends will be at your side as well."

"I have no idea how I am to operate in such a world, Seb. I've spent my life in the shadows. I'm the man others do not acknowledge unless necessary. The thought of losing my anonymity, being recognized as a marquess. It may be too heavy a burden for a man like myself."

"You will know what to do. I will help you every step of the way. Along with Richeforte and Bentley."

Gabriel's throat clenched when he thought of the surprising path he'd been tossed upon. He was having trouble accepting the idea. How would Celia take this shocking news? Would she distance herself from him? Or become one of the vapid, empty-headed, marriage-minded ladies crowding London's ballrooms?

"I must speak with Lady Celia." Gabriel downed the remaining whiskey and set the glass down on Sebastian's desk.

He could not discount the sense of urgency he suddenly experienced. Suddenly, it was all he could think about. Seeing her and her reaction to this incredible news.

"You will seek her out sooner rather than later?"

Gabriel allowed himself a small smile. "I shall do so this very instant. And hope she'll listen as I try explaining things. The lady was rather perturbed when I left her in the library, so my chances with her are far from ideal."

Sebastian's head cocked. "Does this mean you will accept the marquessate?"

"I will consider it. But I can make no promises on a final decision. Yet."

GABRIEL SEARCHED for Celia for over an hour. Whispers hung in the air behind him as he moved through Beaumont's various rooms in his hunt. No one knew Celia's whereabouts, but rumors were rife concerning Heath Banbury's unexpected appearance and what it meant.

He ignored all questions until he came across Ivy.

The young countess already knew the surprising turn of events. Taking Gabriel's arm, she guided him outside the Blue Drawing room where several games of whist were taking place. A small measure of privacy existed in the corridor, even with guests coming and going and servants bustling about.

She squeezed his arm, beaming up at him. "This is wonderful news, Gabriel. It truly is."

"Tamp down your excitement for the moment, my lady. I've yet to accept the marquessate. It's too much of an unknown. Too much responsibility." Gabriel shook his head. "And God's blood. When I think of the duties required by Parliament of any lord, I become nauseous."

Ivy's beautiful features glowed with encouragement for her friend. "Nonsense. If Ravenswood can manage it, you can as well. Perhaps even better for you do not possess the same hot temper as my husband. Besides, my understanding of Parliament is that it is simply a gathering of men who harumph, argue, and pat each other on the back for their accomplishments. While we must keep your secret for the moment, I have every confidence you will take on this responsibility. And excel at it."

"I've never wanted anything from my father. Now, everything is suddenly mine. I'm trying to process all of it."

Ivy sobered. "I imagine it is difficult reconciling your feelings for the old marquess and this opportunity. It will help having people surround you who care for you." She was quiet for a long moment, then carefully asked, "You still intend on informing Celia?"

"I'm searching for her now but have had no luck." Gabriel sighed, raking a hand through his hair. "Perhaps she has already retired?"

"Oh no, she's not gone to bed just yet! She's down on the terrace lawns with a few other guests. They're engaged in a bit of competition."

"I'm afraid to even ask for an explanation." Gabriel groaned.

"Nothing too scandalous." Ivy grinned. "They are catching fireflies. When the game ends, whoever has the most in their jar receives a forfeit from the person of their choice. The fireflies are released unharmed."

Gabriel felt a twinge of annoyance. "I'll hazard a guess this game is yet another one of Lady Celia's ideas?"

Ivy laughed. "It is. And it's quite beautiful. If you hurry, you may still take part in collecting the little creatures. Perhaps win a forfeit of your own. My lord." That last was added in the most teasing of manners and Gabriel's jaw clenched as he stomped away.

He heard laughter and giggles as he approached the terrace overlooking the mansion's rear lawns. A mix of men and women raced back and forth under the light of the Chinese lantern. They carried nets and scarves, swinging them wildly through the air.

If Celia was one of the ones dashing about the wide expanse of lawn with a damned injured ankle, Gabriel decided he most certainly would haul the lady over his knees and give her ass more than a few swats.

He spied her almost at once.

She was seated in a well-lit portion of the lower garden terrace. From a low bench near the central fountain, she watched the others as they captured the illuminating insects. She did not look at him when he sat beside her.

"You dislike bugs. Why have you organized such a game when this is the case?" Gabriel asked, genuinely puzzled by this girl.

"Did you know it's believed fireflies light up as a way of attracting other fireflies? It's some sort of ritual." Celia ignored his question. "Attracting a mate is the ultimate goal."

"How fascinating," he said dryly. But the curve of her neck was far more intriguing. The shell of her ear infinitely enthralling. He could not help himself. He reached out and trailed a forefinger along the sweet line of her jaw and fantasized about tracing the contour with his tongue.

Celia's eyes briefly closed. Then she sat up straighter, smoothing her skirts in a brisk, businesslike manner. "Was your summons to Lord Ravenswood's study a matter of great importance?"

The question reminded Gabriel of the momentous change in his life. "Potentially."

Celia turned further toward him. "That's a very cryptic statement. What does it mean?"

"May we speak in private?" Gabriel countered.

The lights from the torches placed around the boundaries of the lawns lit her face, highlighting the smooth planes and deepening the color of her eyes to nearly ebony black. A curl escaped her coiffure to brush her jaw, and she pushed it back into place with an impatient movement.

"Is this not private enough?" she asked.

"No."

His one-word answer creased her brow.

"We are alone, Mister Rose. No one can overhear whatever it is you feel you must say."

"I do not want to chance being interrupted," he shot back.

"Hmmm," Was her reply.

She stood, surprising him as she addressed the lords and ladies still running about like crazed rabbits across the green lawn. "Let us take the count, everyone!"

Those participating in the game came forward carrying small jars filled with the glowing green-yellow lights of the fireflies. Gabriel was not happy to see Lord Harvey among the participants. The man's expression hardened, obviously perturbed to see Gabriel as well.

For the next few moments, there was some back and forth over who had the most fireflies in their jar. Eventually, the conclusion was reached that both Lord Harvey and Lady Jane Bostick were tied for the honor.

"I claim a forfeit from Lady Celia," Lord Harvey crowed.

Gabriel almost growled.

"I am not playing the game, Lord Harvey. You may only claim a forfeit from those participating," Celia said.

Lady Jane piped in, "I claim my forfeit from Lord Harvey. Perhaps he will do the same and the game has a satisfactory conclusion."

Lord Harvey scowled before realizing it was a very ungracious gesture on his part. "That would be agreeable, Lady Jane.

When the fireflies are released, we will fulfill the forfeit, if you wish."

"I'd like that, I think," Lady Jane said shyly.

"Gather down in the center of the lower lawn," Celia declared. "Lady Jane, you may be in charge of the release."

The players of the game all began talking amongst each other, and Lord Harvey took Lady Jane by the elbow to lead her down onto the lawn. Within a few moments, Celia and Gabriel were alone once more.

"There, Mister Rose. Privacy." Her tone was almost mocking.

"I require more than this," he replied sternly. "Much more."

Celia shrugged as though it mattered little what he wanted, but she bent to his wishes. "We may enter the rose garden maze, if that will suffice."

Gabriel nodded silently. He allowed her to lead the way as they approached the maze. The sweet scent of roses surrounded them as they stepped just inside the entrance. The bushes at the beginning of the path were thick but not terribly high. Gabriel and Celia could easily be seen in this section, but no one would be able to hear their conversation.

"What has happened?" Celia asked once they were out of earshot and mostly beyond the eyesight of other guests.

"Much," Gabriel murmured.

Celia's eyebrow rose. "Again, with the cryptic statements."

Gabriel hesitated. The rest of his life depended on this moment. Leap or retreat. Seize or forfeit.

All of it or none of it.

Those were his choices as he stood on a rocky precipice.

He wanted all of it.

Because suddenly, here in the quietness of this maze, with the aroma of roses and rich green grass surrounding them, with the distant hum of others laughing and the light of the torches illuminating this girl's face, he wanted everything. And above all else, he wanted Celia Buchanan.

"Certain events have occurred that change the nature of our relationship." Gabriel paused at the confusion evident in Celia's features. She did not quite understand what he meant. Clenching his jaw, he gathered his courage.

"I want you to be my wife."

CHAPTER 17

"What?" Celia blinked.

Surely, she must look like a fool as she gaped in dazed shock at the man. Funny how it sounded as though he had just requested her hand in marriage.

No. Not *requested.* The arrogant cad demanded.

"I want you to become the next Marchioness of Rosenthorne." Gabriel's features were as pale as newly woven silk. The scar slashing his eyebrow in half glowed a faint white in the flickering light cast by the torches at the beginning of the maze.

This was most confusing. "I've no desire to marry the Marquess of Rosenthorne."

Gabriel scrubbed his chin and let out a sharp laugh.

The faintest hint of insecurity glimmered in his demeanor and Celia was puzzled by it. This man was always supremely confident. So assured of his position. His power. He may be Ravenswood's enforcer, the earl's man in all things, but only because it was Gabriel's choice. He held the reins of his own fate and lived as he wanted.

"I want you to marry me," he clarified.

"You are not making a great deal of sense, Gabriel." Celia

shook her head in an attempt at clearing the cobwebs. She was obviously missing a great deal of information during this odd conversation. "How precisely would marrying you make me a marchioness?"

Gabriel took her by the arm.

"Come, sit down so that I might explain better. That bench there, it will provide the privacy required for this tale."

Celia eyed the stone bench Gabriel waved at. It was further into the rose hedge maze, shrouded from any lantern light. It was just a shadowy heap in the darkness.

Her heartbeat answered with a thud of fear. "I see no need of going any farther."

Gabriel's head tilted as if he suddenly understood a great many things about her. Celia swallowed and met his penetrating stare.

"Come with me, Celia." His hand took hers, his long fingers clasping lightly around her own. The tone of his voice, both gentle and unyielding, persuasive yet darkly commanding, touched something deep inside her. And her fate was sealed when he uttered one additional word.

"Please."

Celia hesitated, her heart thumping as she considered Gabriel's request. She understood she was safe with him, even in the dark. What she could not comprehend was *how* her obedience was so easily compelled. She let out a breath and gave a barely perceptible nod.

He led her to the bench, tugging her down beside him. His fingers remained tangled with hers, his bicep pressing against her shoulder. His arm was huge. Hard as the stone bench they sat upon but much, much warmer. Hot. Unyielding.

It was dark in this corner of the garden. Darker than she'd anticipated.

A bubble of panic rose in Celia's throat but Gabriel must have sensed her unease.

"Settle, Celia. Take a deep breath and release it slowly."

His voice rumbled through her in a soothing, melodic river of sound. Celia did as instructed, leaning into him as though absorbing his calmness was possible. She focused on her breathing and the steady cadence of his as the dizzy wave of fear subsided with surprising quickness.

A few seconds passed before Celia felt steady enough to speak.

"I'm better now."

Gabriel's dark eyes watched her like a lion sizing up prey. "How long have you been frightened of the dark?"

Celia startled at her secret fear voiced aloud. "I'm not. I just…"

Gabriel's fingers tightened upon hers, his mouth quirking with a sympathetic smile. A smile that was also laced with steely determination. "You will not lie to me, Celia. As my wife, I will expect your honesty. Even when you are uncertain or afraid."

Her stare turned sharper. "I still do not understand what you are talking about."

"My father has died."

Another wave of dizziness swept her. "Your father?"

"Yes, my father. And on his deathbed, he claimed me as his heir. I am to be the new Marquess of Rosenthorne. Once the queen approves my father's wishes, that is. And if I accept."

"Marquess?" Celia's mouth fell open at the unexpected declaration. Her heart plummeted as if she'd suddenly leapt from a cliff. If Gabriel was unattainable as a husband before, he was truly out of reach now. The Rosenthorne title was too lofty to be risked with someone like herself. Someone less than worthy.

"I am as shocked as you at this turn of events, but this title means nothing to me if you will not become my marchioness."

Celia's chin tilted higher with distress. "It matters not if you are a marquess. We cannot marry."

There would be no shortage of women vying for Gabriel's

attention now. He would soon forget her, and she prayed that happened quickly. For both their sakes.

"And why not? I've no interest in marrying anyone else. And you must marry eventually."

Celia grit her teeth at his persistence.

"I-We do not suit one another, Mister Rose. It's obvious if you look beyond the superficial veneer of attraction we share."

"You wanted a faux courtship. Well, there is no need pretending now." Gabriel sighed when Celia remained silent. "I see I've a bit of work convincing you otherwise."

"You possess more ups and downs than a rowboat tossed about in a hurricane, Mister Rose," Celia grit from between clenched teeth. "I fear it is impossible keeping pace with your moods."

Taking her by the shoulders, Gabriel turned her until she was fully facing him. One hand cupped her chin, holding her still while he studied her face. His eyes turned darker, a glint of wicked promise shimmering in the sun-sparked depths. "Marry me, Celia. I will keep you safe and care for you the rest of our lives. Your burdens will become my burdens. Your joys will be my joys. Your pleasure, my goal. And your happiness shall be my lifelong pursuit."

"I don't understand why you've suddenly decided this."

"You needn't understand why I want you." Gabriel stood suddenly, pulling her up along with him. "You need only say yes."

"I-I cannot." Celia's words escaped in an agonized whisper. "I *cannot.* You are too possessive. Too intense. Too much of every-thing that makes you unsuitable as a husband. *My* husband. You care too much, Gabriel Rose. It's as plain as if you wore a banner proclaiming it to the world. I am not the wife for you. And you are not the husband for me."

"Possessive? Yes. That is one thing we do agree upon." Gabriel chuckled. His firm lips brushed over hers and she shuddered in reluctant compliance. "Intense? Yes, that too. Because every touch we share feels like flames licking at my soul. You're goddamn right I care too much. The problem is that I care about you. Celia, give me your fears. I will conquer them and shatter any doubt that you and I belong together. Give yourself to me and I shall do the same."

In the distance, Celia heard a collective cheer from the crowd gathered on the lawns. Seconds ticked by as she and Gabriel stared at one another, and for some strange reason, the darkness began receding. A warm, lovely glow spread from the darkest corners of the garden, tendrils curling and weaving through the roses' thorny branches until Celia was convinced something magical was occurring.

It was the fireflies. The tiny insects were fleeing their brief captivity in glass jars, escaping the brightly lit lawns for the safety of the dark. They were nearly frantic in their attempts at reaching the edges of the shadows. Searching out all the secret, hidden places while lighting the way at the same time. It was both beautiful and heartbreaking.

Celia's own destiny seemed carried along on the wave of sparkling lights. This moment would decide her fate. The premonition swamped her, leaving her shaking with excitement and dread.

"You wanted me when I was nobody. And now that I am to be titled, you reject my offer. I wonder why that is." There was obvious puzzlement in his voice.

Celia knew he would stop at nothing in solving this mystery.

She did not protest when Gabriel's arm slid around her waist. She did not attempt freeing herself as the fireflies lit up the darkness and Gabriel's hand cradled her jaw. When his lips crashed down on hers in a searing claim of her soul, she had no defense.

"Be mine, Celia." The command was growled against her mouth.

She could not tell him the truth. That as an untitled commoner, she'd thought he might be perfect husband material. He probably would not have expected much from her as a wife. Would not have any recourse when her dark secret cast a shadow over their relationship. Gabriel's eventual disappointment would have been countered by his elevated status as the husband of an earl's daughter. He would have accepted her as she was, and he would have been left with no recourse.

But Gabriel's potential elevation as a marquess was disastrous. The title would never allow consideration of anyone less than perfect as his bride.

Gabriel's hand anchored her chin until Celia met his heated gaze.

"Do not force me to make this decision for you, Celia. Because I will and I won't regret it. Not for a single goddamn second. And neither will you, I promise you that."

As the light of the fireflies receded and the darkness encroached once more, Celia shook her head in denial.

"You don't want me as a bride, Gabriel. Not now."

The rejection lit something wild and desperate inside Gabriel. Before she could react, he drew her tighter against his body, caging her with heat and desire. His mouth covered hers, swallowing anything she might have said. He devoured her, his tongue thrusting against hers in a silent demand that she return his kiss.

There could be no retreat, not with the rose bushes and the darkness surrounding her. Celia could not help herself anyway when he kissed her like this.

She was always drowning in him. Always fighting to reach the surface when he took her in his arms. It was inescapable when she truly had no desire to escape. The haven his arms created felt right. Like paradise. Like home and safety. It was all an illusion, but she craved it just the same.

Her arms came up, not to push Gabriel away but to clutch at

his broad shoulders. It was like embracing a huge oak tree. His body was solid and warm and so much larger than hers. Celia was cocooned by warmth. Safe. Wanted. Desired.

When the kiss deepened, she gasped and met him full measure. And why she surrendered was a mystery she did not think could ever be unraveled.

Gabriel's hand cupped her breast. Even through the gown's fabric, his palm scorched the flesh. Celia sighed, pressing closer into his touch. Gabriel was always warm, an inferno of heat and muscles and temptation.

His mouth traveled from hers and made a searing path down the column of her neck. Open mouth kisses were interspersed with sharp nips of his teeth to the delicate skin. Celia gasped at the overwhelming sensation of being consumed and worshipped. She was held in such thrall she couldn't muster the concern that his hands were involved in sinful things.

"Be mine, Celia." His demand was repeated while nipping her ear.

One palm openly stroked and caressed her breasts, his fingers pinching the nipples with deliberate intent until the sting penetrated the layers of cloth. When that same hand dipped into the bodice of her gown, forcing the material to gape and allow him better access, Celia did not stop him. She arched her back, offering herself up like a sacrifice to a lion.

Gabriel's growl of pleasure reverberated through Celia. Somehow, between the wicked fingers plucking at her breast and the scorching fire of his mouth on her throat, she had not noticed his free hand gathering fistfuls of her skirts. His palm now skated dangerously close to her aching, needy center.

A yearning that he touch her there as he had in the forest swamped Celia. She trembled in his embrace, hips tilting toward his hand. All conscious thought left her mind, leaving it a blank canvas that only Gabriel could paint with color.

God help her if she actually accepted his proposal.

"Ma dragee picquante."

My prickly sugarplum.

He muttered the words against her neck, fingers ripping the delicate fabric of her drawers with careful brutality. One thick digit slid inside her wet heat while his other hand twisted the hardened peak of her nipple.

Celia moaned in distressed pleasure, writhing with need and want and the terrible knowledge she could never fully be his.

"Yes, Celia. Come on my hand now," Gabriel crooned in her ear. "Show me how this sweet, little quim will squeeze my cock when I take you the first time. Moan for me as I fuck you with my fingers. Show me that you belong to me. You're so goddamn tight and sweet."

A wave of desire crashed through Celia at the filthy words Gabriel uttered. Her knees buckled until only his massive strength held her aloft. Clutching his shoulders tighter, her fingernails dug into the dark fabric of his coat. The pressure created by his finger built until it was an unmanageable force.

A thunderstorm roiled through Celia, sweeping her up into the heavens and shattering her with flashes of lightning.

"Fuck," Gabriel groaned as her climax began shaking its way through her body. "So beautiful. So perfect. So fucking mine."

There was a murmur of voices. Others. People nearby. Caught in a whirlwind of ecstasy, Celia became semi-conscious of the chance of discovery. But she couldn't stop riding the waves of pleasure. She may have even tried crying out, but Gabriel anticipated it before the sound broke free of her throat.

He quickly spun her around, his large body blocking anyone from witnessing his actions. Now, she sagged against him, her back to his front, and he held her so tight she could not wiggle away.

Withdrawing his hand from the gown's bodice, he clamped it over her mouth while the other remained wedged into the heat between her thighs. His broad, blunt finger stubbornly coaxed more of her response until she was limp with satisfaction and moaning with delight. The coolness of the night air danced across her thighs as Gabriel's forearm held her skirts aloft.

"Do not come any closer," he snarled.

Celia jerked at the feral quality of his tone, but the finger still inside her continued stroking with persistent tenderness. There was a fierce possessiveness in his voice and she shivered.

Celia felt the motion as Gabriel turned his head and glanced over his shoulder.

"If you value your lives, you will leave this garden immediately. Now."

His words were directed at others. Not her. Celia stiffened in Gabriel's embrace when she realized that the group hunting fireflies had discovered them. They gathered at the beginning of the rose garden maze, no doubt puzzled and maybe even horrified by the suggestion of Gabriel holding her captive.

No matter that she was safe from their prying eyes. And relished being held in such a commanding way by this man.

She should be fighting to get away, but that would turn matters even more dire. The situation was painfully clear as it was. There would be no doubt as to what had occurred between them. How Celia had been compromised. How she hadn't fought it and had gone willingly to her ruin.

This was scandalous on a monumental scale. Gossip would spread quickly. It would be demanded that Gabriel marry her, taking the decision ultimately from her hands.

She would be his after all. Despite her fears. Despite the rejection of his proposal. Despite the fact he would be one of the most powerful men in England and she the most unworthy bride imaginable.

She would be his.

She *wanted* to be his.

And she wasn't sure she was all right with that.

"Let her go, Rose. Damn you, if you think I'll stand idly by while you attack her, think again," Robert demanded in outrage, his voice quivering with emotion. "Lady Celia, come away with me now. Away from this blackguard."

"Take one more step and I'll dispatch you first, Lord Harvey," Gabriel replied coldly. His palm, however, was hot as fire as he cupped Celia's sex. His finger moved slowly out of her inner channel and slid through the moisture there. Finding the tiny bud of nerves, he stroked her with increasing intensity.

Celia sucked in a strangled breath behind the barrier of his hand. Lust was stirring again, and Gabriel knew it. She sensed his wicked grin before he thrust even deeper, his finger hooking in a manner that sent stars dancing before her eyes.

Thank God, no one saw the full effect of this man destroying her. How easily he accomplished destruction with just a crook of his finger. As far as the others were concerned, they'd simply caught Celia and Gabriel locked in a passionate embrace with only kisses passing between them. Scandalous and certainly ruinous but hardly the full truth of what was truly happening

Lifting his hand the tiniest bit from Celia's mouth, Gabriel whispered in her ear, "Tell them you are unharmed, Celia. Better yet, tell them all how much you love my hands on your body, my finger inside you. You do like my finger inside you, don't you? If not, tell me to stop and I shall."

She almost swooned from the fiery rush of his breath and the sharpness of his teeth nipping her ear lobe. Her head shook in protest that he might cease doing these wicked, wonderful things.

"I'm in no danger." She addressed the crowd at Gabriel's back. Her tone rose higher when his finger twisted in the most devilish of ways. "Please, please go away."

He grinned against her neck as his free hand clamped once again over her mouth. What should have infuriated her only left her boneless and compliant to Gabriel's will.

"Good girl," he murmured. "And it's true. You are in no danger with me, and you never will be."

The pleasure in his voice caused by her surrender lit a strange flame inside Celia. This man was the key and he would unlock her in ways she could never imagine.

Rumbles of confusion met Celia's statement. No one seemed inclined to follow her shaky plea. It took Gabriel's drawled command to get the desired effect.

"You heard the lady. Run along now. All of you."

The people Celia could not see began retreating, their outraged murmurs drifting over the garden.

He may have been a bastard with no social standing, but no one dared challenge Gabriel. Celia could only imagine the power he would yield as a marquess. It would be terrifying.

"By God, you will pay for this outrage, Rose," Robert declared, his voice quivering with anger. He stood somewhere behind them, reluctant to abandon Celia to someone he deemed unfit. "This is not the end of this."

"I should hope it's not," Gabriel replied to the other man, even as his finger glided in and out of Celia's body with lazy, secretive intent. Robert let out a frustrated curse before he finally stomped away.

Now they were alone once more in the darkened silence. There would be no further challenges to Gabriel's claim upon her.

"No, this is definitely not the end of things, is it, Celia? And do you know why? Because there's still more to come," he whispered, his full attention centering on her. "And I'll be damned if anyone steals your pleasure while I'm in the process of giving it to you."

Removing the hand over her mouth, he tilted her head back and used his lips to ensure her silence. He devoured her, bringing her once again to the edge of insanity before pushing her into its silky, darkened depths.

Celia plummeted and flew into the stars with his fingers guiding her journey.

Moments later, when his hold finally eased, Celia turned in his arms. His erection pressed against her belly. It was heavy. Hard. She shivered with awareness of his own unsatisfied need. The fact he'd done nothing to ease his own torture twisted her heart with shocking affection.

She was safe with him. He'd not harm her, but should Gabriel decide he'd take her right there on that stone bench, Celia knew she would not stop him.

In a haze of morbid curiosity, she watched as he deliberately licked his finger clean of her essence. Why did she feel this sudden compulsion to take his finger into her own mouth? To lick and suck any part of his body he'd allow her to devour? She wanted to taste him as he'd tasted her.

Gabriel's whiskey-hued eyes glittered as though every dirty thought in her head was being screamed aloud. "Soon, sugarplum. Soon."

The husky promise sent another stab of lust curling through Celia's body. If he asked it, she knew she would fall to her knees and take him into her mouth. He could teach her the many ways of pleasing him, and she would gladly accept the tutelage.

She should be mortified. Scandalized. Humiliated by this public display of Gabriel's hold on her. But Celia could not muster up even a smidgen of outrage. Even as he proved his ownership, she wanted more.

And that would be her ultimate downfall.

Falling for a man who would eventually despise her.

CHAPTER 18

*L*ady Darby did not appear very upset over the fact her daughter was recently ruined and would be expected to marry as quickly as possible. The fact her daughter would become a marchioness no doubt eased the sting of scandal.

"These matters must be taken care of with the utmost haste," Lady Darby commented with a serene smile.

"Of course, my lady," Gabriel murmured. "My intentions are to leave at first light to meet with my father's barristers. He has already petitioned the queen to recognize the marquess's will, but I shall see to it personally as well."

"I have every confidence you will see to every detail." Lady Darby nodded in approval for Gabriel's haste. "I must say, however, you are a most unexpected marquess, Lord Rosenthorne."

Gabriel frowned when he realized his future mother-in-law was calling him by his father's title. "I am not Rosenthorne yet, Lady Darby."

"A small matter of details." Celia's mother laughed with a wave of her hand. "And you've always been Rosenthorne. It has merely taken a bit longer for that fact to be acknowledged. Will you accompany him, Lord Banbury?"

Gabriel's half-brother was in the process of yawning behind his hand and quickly recovered his composure. "I hope to avoid it, if that's possible. Having just arrived a few hours ago, I thought I would stay a few days and enjoy Lord and Lady Ravenswood's gracious hospitality."

"You are welcome to stay as long as you wish, Banbury," Sebastian agreed. "And we do apologize for disturbing your rest this late in the evening for these unexpected circumstances."

"Thank you, Ravenswood. I hope my time here will afford me the opportunity of becoming better acquainted with my new sister-in-law. And soon enough, my brother as well." Heath smiled at Gabriel. "We've much to catch up on after your return from London."

Gabriel's hard stare did not waver from Heath. The comment regarding Celia fired up Gabriel's possessive nature, but when Heath looked his way, it was to give him a benign smile.

"There are many favors owed me, and I anticipate this entire matter will be quickly facilitated," Gabriel said with a grim smile.

"Excellent." Lady Darby gave Celia a quick embrace. "Celia? You should stay here while I travel home and retrieve your father for the ceremony."

Celia had remained silent during this impromptu meeting in Sebastian's study, and she gave her mother a wan smile now.

"I could go to Tristan's instead," she replied almost tonelessly.

Gabriel did not like Celia's strangely compliant state. It was as though she'd been operating in a daze since the two of them exited the rose garden. Even now her gaze remained averted, unwilling it seemed to meet his own.

No, he didn't like it. And he liked the idea of her overprotective brother's involvement even less. Tristan was a friend but sometimes those things did not matter when it came to younger sisters and their ruination.

"Not a wise choice, my darling." Lady Darby laughed softly. "I'm afraid your brother may react rather badly. Best that we break the happy news once the ceremony is over. I shall have a difficult enough time restraining your father from violence."

"Do you think they won't soon learn of this?" Celia asked with a flash of fire in her gaze. "It is the topic of everyone's conversation at this very moment and will spread like wildfire over the next two weeks."

"Lady Celia is correct." Heath took a sip of brandy, waving the glass at the occupants in the room. "You won't be able to keep this a secret. Just as Gabriel cannot keep his identity a secret."

"Ivy and I can help manage some of the rumors," Sara offered. "We shall say this is the result of an ongoing romance. That Celia and Gabriel share a common affection and planned on announcing an engagement soon."

Gabriel scoffed, drawing everyone's attention. "No one will ever believe that."

"Nevertheless, we shall put it out there," Alan chimed in with a nod toward Celia's mother. "With your permission, Lady Darby."

Celia sat up straighter in her chair, chin tilting higher, and Gabriel almost groaned aloud. His new fiancée was almost certainly preparing to blurt out a protest.

"What about *my* permission?" she bit out angrily. "All this discussion over what my future shall consist of and not one of you has expressed an interest in my opinion of the matter. What if I have no wish to marry Gabriel? What if I should have no wish to marry at all?"

Emotion made her voice crack on the last three words. Lady Darby tsked with sympathy and reached for Celia's hand.

"There, there, my love. I realize this is not an ideal situation, but it does seem to be the best solution. Besides, I have detected some manner of affection between you and the marquess."

"He's not a marquess yet," Celia muttered beneath her breath. "And I won't bow before him like the rest of you are apparently content to do."

Heath sipped his brandy, hiding a smile. Lady Darby pressed a hand to her heart in dismay, and Sebastian shuffled some papers upon his desk as if he'd not overheard Celia's statement.

Gabriel's jaw clenched.

Ivy and Sara both appeared distressed by Celia's words, but it was Ivy who broke the tension first.

"My sweet friend, listen to me." She took Celia by the hands, drawing her up to her feet. "What you believe to be the end of your life is truly the beginning of an adventure. You and Gabriel feel something for one another, and that is something to be grateful for."

"Would you accept this if it were you?" Celia demanded with a touch of hysteria in her tone. "Would you blindly go along with this farce? This sham of a marriage?"

A frown creased Gabriel's brow. He'd not considered how trapped she'd feel when he coerced her into accepting his proposal.

Ivy had the grace to blush with Celia's heated question.

"No," she admitted, her mouth curving with a rueful smile. "And I did fight when my marriage was forced upon me."

"Like a wildcat," Sebastian interjected. "Even after I threatened her."

Ivy waved her hand at her husband to hush before her attention returned to Celia. "Of course, I could have refused more strenuously, and Ravenswood knew it. I could have run away. Hid away in the country. Married another man."

"Over my dead body," Sebastian growled.

Ivy ignored that and continued. "There were few options

open to me, but I was not helpless. I chose to marry the earl. Because in my heart, I knew the truth. Regardless of everything else, we were meant to be together. I ask that you do the same as I did, Celia. Look into your heart. You will see the answer clearly if you do that one thing."

"It was the most intelligent decision she's ever made," Sebastian interjected, laughing softly when Ivy shot him an exasperated glare.

Silence hung in the room for a long moment before Gabriel said in a low voice, "I will speak with Celia alone. Now."

"Already behaving like a true marquess," Alan said with a smirk. His comment earned a dark glare from Gabriel.

"If my presence is no longer required, I shall return to bed," Heath remarked, setting his glass down on a nearby table. Taking Celia's hand, he pressed a kiss to the back of it as she returned his smile. "Goodnight, dear sister. We shall speak more tomorrow as I'm certain you have questions and Gabriel will not be here to provide answers."

"She's not your sister. Yet," Gabriel grumbled. He did not like the easy friendship he sensed forming between Celia and Heath. It left him feeling like an outsider. An imposter with no business claiming his father's title. A nobody who should stay in the shadows. "And I shall explain things without your assistance, Banbury."

Heath tilted his head before nodding. "As you wish, brother."

"Seven hells. Stop calling me that, Banbury." Gabriel hated that his tone was decidedly peevish. "We hardly know one another well enough for such familiarity."

An expression of saddened regret flashed across Heath's features as he joined the others in their departure. "I hope to remedy that, Gabriel."

Gabriel did not respond. Instead, he reached for Celia's hand, tugging her to him with a restrained show of strength. She collided against his chest with a soft, exhaled "Oh!"

"Gently, Rose," Sebastian said with a frown as he paused in the study's doorway.

"It goes against my nature, but for her, I will be," was Gabriel's reply. He inclined his head in deference to Lady Darby. "I shall escort your daughter to her bedchamber once we are done here."

"I suppose no further harm can come in allowing you some privacy. The wedding will happen regardless." Lady Darby accepted Lord Banbury's arm as they stepped into the corridor and gave her daughter a bright smile. "Good night, my dear. I will see you in the morning before I leave for home."

The door clicked shut and then Gabriel and Celia were alone.

Gabriel did not let go of her wrist, although she tried jerking free.

"Not so fast, sugarplum," he crooned. "As Banbury said, we have a few issues to settle between us. This whole situation has taken on a life of its own, but we will resolve everything before this wedding takes place."

CHAPTER 19

"What is there to resolve, Gabriel?" Celia demanded. "We will be married. As you wished."

Gabriel's eyes bored into hers. A muscle worked in his jaw, and again, Celia thought she saw a flicker of uncertainty in his gaze.

How odd that he seems apprehensive. Does he regret the course our lives are now on? Does he wish we'd never acted on the attraction we share?

Celia's hands grew clammy with anxiety. Whatever Gabriel was thinking in that moment was quickly shuttered until she could no longer see it in his features. After the explanation of how he'd come to be named Marquess, she still did not understand why he wanted her for a wife.

He sighed as if greatly disturbed by her show of reluctance.

"I need you to want this marriage as badly as I do, Celia. I cannot do this without you at my side. Frankly, I do not want to even try. You know as well as I that should we not go through with this, the consequences will not be pleasant. You shall be ruined, and I will end up banished or perhaps find myself facing your brother on the opposite end of a pistol."

That statement sent a bolt of icy fear streaking through Celia's body. If she did not do what was expected of her, the very real possibility existed that someone could die.

Tristan. Or maybe Gabriel.

Emotion swelled in Celia's throat, choking her with the reality of her situation.

Gabriel's hand cupped Celia's jaw with firm tenderness. "We are attracted to one another. I care for you. The title ensures it is a good match. And there is no denying we were caught in a comprising situation."

"One of your making, Gabriel."

A tiny smile lifted the corners of his lips. "Yes. You are right, and I'll be damned if I am sorry for that moment we shared in the garden. I know there is more to your objections. Some other reason for fighting this that I've yet to uncover. You remember me saying once that I would discover all your secrets? This one is the most important. So, tell me, Celia. Tell me the truth. Why would marriage to me be distasteful?"

Celia's lips clamped shut. Reveal her secret? She could not. But she also did not know what to do. Perhaps she could blame her reluctance on something many young ladies in her position likely experienced. She wanted freedom. A right to choose her own husband. The right to follow her own path.

Gabriel's eyes sharpened, his hand gripping her wrist just a little tighter. "I will know if you lie to me, Celia. And I punish liars." His head dipped toward hers, his nose gently brushing her temple in a frightening juxtaposition to the harsh words. "I enjoy administering punishments, if you want the truth of the matter."

Celia's breath escaped in a shaky puff of air. "You won't hurt me. I know you won't."

Amusement briefly lit the whiskey-colored depths of his

gaze. "No, but I will make sure you are extremely uncomfortable. Now, no more stalling. Tell me, Celia."

Celia trembled. Her pulse pounded so fiercely, forcing its way through her veins, that she felt faint. And before she knew what was happening, the words bubbled up, escaping her throat in a helpless admittance of guilt.

"I am not pure. I am not the one you deserve as a bride." She choked on a sob. "Don't you understand? I am not a virgin, Gabriel. I cannot possibly become your marchioness."

He froze in place, his features turning to stone but not before she saw the hurt he could not conceal. His fingers closed with almost painful intensity on her wrist before he caught himself. For a heart-stopping moment, Celia thought he might cast her aside in disgust. Instead, his grip loosened.

"Do you think that matters, Celia? To me, of all people? I was nothing more than a bastard until earlier this evening. If you are worried you might sully the title I now carry, do not fret. My father's actions were a defilement on their own." His laughter was a bitter sound, his eyes pinning her with the promise of sinful fantasies and punishments. "Besides, do you honestly believe I don't already know everything about you? Especially something of such magnitude? I'm well aware of the fact you are not a virgin. You might be surprised to know that the how and why of it matter very little to me."

The dark intensity of his demeanor should frighten her, but Celia only felt a macabre fascination. An unlikely calmness settled over her now that she'd voiced her dark secret aloud. This revelation could ruin her. Any other gentleman would reject her upon learning she did not come untouched to the marriage bed. But Gabriel apparently did not care. He wanted her beyond all reason.

Maybe, if she was brave enough to let him in, he might possess the power to destroy all her carefully constructed walls.

How Celia longed for the opportunity to be wiped clean. To

have the nightmares and fears purged at the hands of this man. Could he build her broken body back up until she was stronger than ever before?

"So, you are not pure, Celia Buchanan. Well, neither am I. We're the perfect pair, don't you think, to become the new Marquess and Marchioness of Rosenthorne?"

Gabriel's palm cupped her chin, his fingers digging slightly into her cheeks. The pressure reminded Celia of her promise to be his. She'd agreed to this when they were alone in the garden. And she abruptly realized there was no backing out at this juncture.

How could she even consider it after revealing her terrible secret? No one else would want her now. Thinking of the dishonor and scandal this could potentially cause her family caused a small moan of distress to rise in her throat.

Gabriel heard it. His hand drifted up and buried itself in her hair. His fingers were soothing and yet inexorably firm against her scalp.

"Whatever happened in the past shall remain there, Celia. Our future is all that matters. The *only* thing that matters." A smile of something resembling pain twisted his lips. "Trust me to do what is best for you. Trust me to do whatever is necessary to keep you safe. But understand this, sugarplum. You are mine now. Mine. And I am not a man who shares his possessions. Should you ever seek the attention of another man, even if that man is my own brother, I will not hesitate to erase him from this world and have you witness his demise."

His words made her shiver. Gabriel Rose was a dangerous man who had likely killed before. God above, he'd just warned her he would not hesitate to take a life if he believed it was warranted. Giving herself over freely to a man who considered her one of his most prized acquisitions was probably the most rash decision she'd ever made. And the only one that felt completely right.

Gabriel took a deep breath and seemed to gather himself. The uncertainty and pain she witnessed earlier disappeared. Left in its place was the confident, arrogant man she knew so well.

He smiled in that charming manner of his. The one Celia could not resist. The one that somehow twisted her into a wanton creature prone to surrender.

She was his. And Gabriel wanted her just as she was.

With all her flaws and mistakes.

He placed a finger beneath her chin. The heat in his gaze incinerated the fog surrounding her. Everything became crystal clear when he asked her a question for which he already knew the answer.

"Do we understand one another, Celia?"

Celia mutely nodded, staring at him. Of course, she understood even if she wasn't quite sure just what he expected from her as a wife.

Anticipation curled in her stomach as she waited to see what he would do next. It sent her heart racing. Made her mouth dry. Chased goosebumps across her skin.

"Excellent. Now, get on your knees for me." Gabriel's voice was smooth as poisoned syrup and just as deadly. "I wish to see how well my future wife follows commands. And just how much she trusts me."

Celia swallowed hard. "Now?"

"Yes. Now. And Celia? No more questions unless absolutely necessary."

Celia's lips tightened with the light admonishment, but she sank to the floor with shaky gracefulness. The thick Turkish rug carpeting the Earl of Ravenswood's private study cushioned her knees. She eased back into a questionable position of comfort and waited for what would come next. The pop and crackle of the fire in the grate accentuated the shallow breaths she desperately inhaled in an attempt at calming herself.

"Mon douce fille," he murmured. His hand curled under her chin, tilting her head back so he could stare down into her wide eyes. When she trembled, his thumb passed over her bottom lip in a fleeting caress.

Celia gasped softly, surprised by the spark of arousal she experienced. Gabriel's lips twitched with amusement as he did it again. Heat flared in his gaze as he tracked his thumb's movement across the plump flesh. His touch was firmer this time, gradually pressing between her upper and bottom lip as if seeking entry into her mouth.

Celia's hands fluttered. Where should she place them? On his thighs? On her own?

"Behind your back, Celia," Gabriel said as if reading her mind. Celia did as he instructed, and Gabriel swore softly under his breath when the position arched her back. Her breasts thrust out in an almost obscene manner and his gaze swept over her in a heated rush. "Now, open your mouth."

Celia did that, too. Her reward was Gabriel's thumb sliding between her lips and beyond the barrier of her teeth.

"Suck."

The command was a dark, husky rasp of lust, and Celia hesitated only a second before closing her lips around his thumb. She applied a gentle, hesitant suction, her cheeks hollowing out a small bit. This was so strange but oddly arousing at the same time. Instinctively, her head bobbed until the digit was drawn further into her mouth before withdrawing and allowing it to slide almost free. It was an unconsciously sultry motion that was beginning to excite her and definitely affected Gabriel.

He groaned, thrusting his thumb deeper into the recesses of her mouth. Celia swirled her tongue around him in an experimental gesture, and in the next instant, she was no longer on her knees.

Gabriel's hands gripped her upper arms with almost painful strength, holding her aloft. The sudden motion of being jerked to her feet was startling. Mostly because for some bizarre reason, she'd enjoyed kneeling before him. Relished the idea she'd given him pleasure instead of receiving it. She'd liked being under his control.

But why had he stopped her? Had she done it wrong? Disappointed him with her inexperience? Did he think simply because she was no longer a virgin that she was proficient when it came to lovemaking?

A frisson of unease swept through Celia at the reminder of her lost innocence.

No matter her reputation and what Gabriel might conclude after watching her over the past year, she was hardly an expert. Her encounters with the men in her social circle were limited to kisses and nothing more. At least until Gabriel Rose entered her world and gave her glimpses of what the shadows truly held.

Even after what she'd been through, Celia could not explain why she sought the danger of this man's attention. There was always the potential for tragedy. To be hurt as she'd been hurt in that darkened horse stall so many years before. That night she turned sixteen and learned that what felt amazing could not always be trusted.

"Lesson over," Gabriel said gruffly, staring at her with an expression blended from disbelief and unadulterated lust. His erection pressed into her as evidence of his arousal. His shallow breaths matched her own. "And lesson learned. You, my darling, are the perfect wife for me. I cannot wait to show you what it means to be completely mine."

CHAPTER 20

The mission was completed with relative ease.

Within a week of his father's death, Gabriel's petition was granted. He was officially recognized as the new Marquess of Rosenthorne.

And that came with all the perks and problems entailed by a title. With the stroke of a pen and royal signature, Gabriel was now responsible for nearly two hundred souls in his employ and the production of several crops cultivated at Rosenthorne Park.

Gabriel also procured a special license from the Archbishop of Canterbury. Once a minister was procured, he could marry Celia immediately.

"You did not hesitate in securing one of the most eligible women in all of England, did you, Lord Rosenthorne?" the queen remarked with detached curiosity when he was ushered before her. "It is well that we would have approved the match had you bothered following the required steps."

"An enviable union," Carraway, his father's barrister, declared jovially upon learning the news. "Quite fortunate to have captured a lady from such a well-connected family."

"An excellent match, I'm sure of it," an assistant to the archbishop said when handing over the special license. "Congratulations, Your Lordship. I wish you years of happiness."

Yes. Apparently, everyone considered it an exceptional match with the exception of the bride.

Gabriel still found himself disturbed by Celia's revelation of her secret. Not because of her previous relationships, but because he suspected there was much more to her past than she was admitting. Was this why she'd never entertained the many marriage proposals over the years? Could she be under the mistaken idea that her worth was diminished simply because she was no longer a virgin?

Gabriel despised the archaic rules of society that measured a woman's worth based on purity and the size of her dowry. He'd made it clear to Lady Darby that the sizable amount received from marrying her daughter would be placed in a special account. Only Celia would have access to the funds and she could spend the money as she saw fit. Gabriel had no need of her dowry. Not with his own personal fortune and the new influx of riches from his father's estates.

He scrubbed a hand over his face as the coach rattled along a rutted portion of the road leading to Wiltshire. This portion of his journey was necessary, although he faced it with much dread. The main residence for the marquessate was Rosenthorne Park, and he wondered how much of his father's presence would exist within its halls.

Gabriel's jaw tightened. By God, he would make the manor *his* home. His and Celia's. Together they would fill it with laughter and light. Children. Happiness.

And he would take his rightful place in society. A place denied him for almost twenty-eight years.

He'd discovered the idea of marriage, once an abhorrent undertaking, had quickly become his greatest desire. He was eager to wed Celia. To claim her as his own. She would serve as a valuable asset while he navigated this new phase of his life. Her grasp of society's rules would guide his path among the *ton*.

Indeed, his acceptance would be molded by her delicate hands.

It would not matter that his father wed his mother in secret before casting her aside for fear of social stigma. Noblemen just did not marry actresses or opera singers. It was acceptable to install one as a mistress, but marriage? It was an abomination in the *ton's* narrow view. Gabriel supposed it was to his father's credit he never annulled the marriage before his birth. Perhaps his parents might have even worked through the difficulties caused by their different stations had his mother not died. Surely, they must have loved one another at some point.

But if love was the reason a marquess could marry an actress, what explained Rosenthorne's treatment of his newborn son? Gabriel was shuttered away like a dirty secret just as his mother had been. He was ignored and isolated for years, and on his sixteenth birthday, his father unwisely attempted reconciliation.

Gabriel would not accept nor listen to any explanations put forth by the marquess for his heartless actions. They'd argued to the point of violence. That surly insolence of Gabriel's earned him the distinctive scar bisecting his eyebrow. The bloody wound caused by Rosenthorne's walking cane brought the brief altercation to an abrupt end.

Gabriel fled the boarding school where his father paid a dear tuition every year. He was quickly absorbed into France's underground world. A place where survival depended on the development of instincts never tapped into. And somehow, he survived on the fringes until the fateful day Sebastian Cain saved his life in a whorehouse alleyway.

Until his arrival in England, Gabriel had been unaware he had a half-brother born three years after his own birth. Tragically, or perhaps prophetically, the marquess's second wife had also died in childbirth. Gabriel felt pity for the woman. By all accounts, the second marchioness was a very sweet, young lady when she wed the much older Lord Rosenthorne. It was hardly a love match, and it appeared the marriage was one of convenience only. But the lady did bear the marquess a son. It was naturally assumed Heath was the heir until the secret emerged regarding Gabriel's legitimacy.

Gabriel had not yet formed a bond with Heath, but he appreciated the similarities in their lives. Both grew up without their mothers. And both learned their father's secrets only upon his death.

Upon arrival at Rosenthorne Park, Gabriel immediately met with the estate's steward. Mister Kinsey was reportedly one of the more trustworthy servants his father employed. While Gabriel had no intention of making changes when it came to the staff, he would be watching matters very closely.

"You'll find things in order, Your Lordship," Mister Kinsey said as they sat together in the study. The ledger books sat in a pile between them. "Your father's estates turned a handsome profit last year and are on pace to do the same this one as well. Of course, there were unfortunate incidents regarding some employees who were not the best fit here at the estate, but in general, matters have run very smoothly, indeed."

Gabriel regarded the thin, elderly man who so earnestly addressed him. His instincts told him the steward was being truthful. There was no deception in his tone or mannerisms. "You've dismissed some of the staff?"

"Thirty-six, milord, which also includes some stable workers. I've already begun the hiring of new individuals to take their places. I've also instructed the steward at Rosenthorne Hall in Mayfair to see the staff is adequate for your lordship."

Gabriel nodded. "I would like to stay apprised of the progress on that front."

Mister Kinsey bobbed his head. "Of course. If I may be so

bold as to inquire if My Lordship and the Marchioness will be residing here? Or one of the other estates?"

Gabriel had thought long and hard about this particular subject. Truly, he had no desire to walk the same halls on a daily basis. Did not want to sleep in the same, overly large bed that had belonged to his father. But as the new lord and master of all his father had owned, Gabriel knew it was necessary if he was to establish himself. He could not hide away at one of the lesser estates. No, he must stake his claim. Here. Boldly. Quickly. No hesitation.

He *was* the new Marquess of Rosenthorne. There must be no doubt in the minds and opinions of others.

"We shall make our home here. There will be a complete overhaul of the manor, beginning immediately with the master bedchamber, followed by this study. The rest I shall leave up to the discretion of my future wife. When we return, I expect the bedchambers completed and a team waiting and ready to do the marchioness's bidding."

To his surprise, Mister Kinsey was not rattled by the request. "Of course, my lord. We most certainly shall begin at once. Indeed, I suspected this would be a requirement upon your assuming the title. Therefore, I've taken the liberty of securing the necessary workers required for the task. I need only your direction and preferences when it comes to materials and general aesthetics of the space."

Gabriel leaned back in his chair, impressed by the man's initiative. "I believe we shall do well together, Mister Kinsey."

"I hope to meet your expectations, my lord. And that of the marchioness."

That was something the estate steward and new marquess had in common. Gabriel wanted nothing more than to exceed Celia's expectations and desires. He would begin by giving her full rein to redecorate the manor in any manner she pleased.

IT WAS another four days before Gabriel's carriage pulled into Beaumont's circular drive.

He was tired. Hungry. Travel weary. But as he trudged up the mansion's steps and entered the grand double doors, only one thing mattered. The need to see Celia. To touch her silky skin and inhale her soft, delicate rose scent. He'd been dreaming of her for days, which had not improved his mood in the least. Was there ever a time he'd been so fixated on a woman? And could he help the fact his obsession now bordered on the obscene? Drawing his gloves and hat off, he tossed them to Alfred, Beaumont's butler.

"Welcome back, my lord," Alfred bowed. "Anna has your rooms prepared and at the ready."

"Thank you."

Gabriel had entered the foyer, expecting Celia would greet him there. She would rush into his arms. Plant a kiss upon his lips with that breathy, little sigh he was coming to crave. Instead, Sara Bentley peeked out of one of the many doorways surrounding the central foyer and then hurried forth.

"The marquess returns," Sara exclaimed. "How wonderful to see you, Rosenthorne!"

He was still adjusting to the title and found it irksome that the surname his mother had given him should be shunted aside. It was even more bothersome that he was now expected to answer to the name of a man he despised.

"You may still call me 'Rose', Lady Bentley. In fact, I rather prefer it."

Sara's head tilted at the faint bitterness of his tone. "Of course. It is fortunate the names are so similar. Much easier to remember."

"Yes, it is." After a brief pause, Gabriel pointedly asked, "Where is Celia?" He did not care or even know if it were proper to inquire of one's future wife with such overriding impatience.

Obviously, it was not acceptable because Sara let out an exasperated sound and frowned discouragingly. "She's gone riding with Lord Banbury and a few others. The Earl and Countess are among them. Lord Bentley and I stayed behind as I was feeling unwell earlier but that has passed."

Gabriel could not contain the thread of possessiveness curling throughout his body. "When will she return?"

"I don't know, but you have time to refresh yourself after your long journey before they come back to the manor." Sara turned and smiled as her husband approached. "Bentley, look. Lord Rosenthorne has arrived."

Alan grinned, shaking Gabriel's hand as he drew near. "Back to claim your bride, I see."

"Only to discover she is traipsing about the countryside with others," Gabriel growled.

"And on your own horse, no less," Alan remarked cheerfully. "Oh, do not fret, Rose. We all know Lady Celia's skill when it comes to horseflesh. Arion is in excellent hands."

Gabriel did not mind at all that Celia had taken Arion for her own use. Everything he had was hers anyway. A peculiar jolt of pleasure assailed him knowing she rode his horse by choice.

"And not to worry over Celia's ankle injury," Sara interjected helpfully. "It has healed completely. Indeed, she danced several times last night without a single twinge of discomfort."

Again, Gabriel experienced the same disturbing twinge of possessiveness, only this time the string pulled taut around his heart like a cruel noose. Seven hells, if this was what marriage consisted of, this constant tug of worry and stomach-rolling uncertainty regarding his wife and her actions, he might not survive.

"Did she now?" he bit out.

"It was all great fun. I'm sorry you missed it, Rose. I'm sure we shall have more of the same tonight, and you shall have your opportunity to dance with her as well." Sara glanced past Gabriel as a servant carried in the travel valises and stood expectantly. "Oh, here are your things. You do want them taken to your chambers so you can settle in, yes? The housekeeper has had everything ready for days, just waiting for you to come back." Sara's smile was graciously pointed. "We shall inform Celia of your arrival the minute she returns from her ride."

CHAPTER 21

Celia knocked on Gabriel's door, tentatively at first, then with greater conviction.

She'd come straightaway upon learning he'd returned only an hour before. Ivy pointed out the way to his suite of rooms with a small grin while Celia clenched her teeth.

Her apparent eagerness to reunite with her recent fiancé was a source of amusement for both Ivy and Sara. Before Celie could escape their collective delight, Ivy leaned in close.

"No one shall disturb you. In fact, no one ever goes in Gabriel's wing of the mansion with the exception of the maids."

When horrified disgust crossed over Celia's features, Ivy quickly shook her head. "Silly girl. Not for *that*. They go only to accomplish the tasks for which they are employed. Sebastian would never stand for that sort of nonsense. Nor would I. And Gabriel, well, he would never do that in this house."

And now, Celia stood in that corridor outside Gabriel's door. Her leather-clad knuckles stung from rapping the thick English oak with increasing force. Her pulse raced with anticipation at seeing him again after so many weeks apart.

It was surprising, really. How much she'd come to enjoy his company, even when she'd tried so hard to avoid him.

She knocked again, her chin lifting. *Why isn't he answering?*

Perhaps he was asleep. Or in the bath. Or maybe he wasn't in his room at all. Or maybe a maid was in there after all and…

The door swung open with such abruptness that Celia was forced back a step in retreat.

Gabriel wore only a large white cloth wrapped about his body. The edges were tucked in on one corner, the material slung low on his hips.

Celia swallowed hard. She saw nothing else other than muscles. His chest, God, his chest was a vast expanse of smooth planes. Hard ridges. Bulges. A smattering of dark hair in the center called for her fingers to entwine and explore.

She felt a bit faint. Especially when her gaze dropped lower. The cloth draped so far she could see matching demarcations marking the outer portion of his pelvis. A trail of dark hair began just below Gabriel's navel and disappeared into the white fabric. On his stomach, droplets of water glistened in the light of the corridor sconces. The liquid slid lazily along that trail of hair, holding Celia's gaze hostage until the cloth finally absorbed it.

"Ahhh, my future wife graces me with her presence. And it appears you came straight from the stables, did you not?"

Startled by the simmering anger in his tone, Celia met his gaze. Her knees actually shook when she saw the flare of desire evident in the darkened depths.

"I came at once when they told me you were here." She cleared her throat, hoping to sound a bit stronger than she felt. "So, it is done then? You are the new marquess and a special license has been granted for our marriage?"

Gabriel leaned onto the door jamb, one shoulder propped against the wooden frame. His hair was damp. Swept off his forehead, it curled a bit at the nape of his neck. It made him seem much younger, like an innocent, mischievous youth. A direct contradiction to the wicked scoundrel Celia knew him to be.

"So eager to become my wife," he drawled.

"I'm anxious to avoid scandal," she shot back in an elevated voice.

When a lock of hair flopped over his forehead, his scarred eyebrow lifting in disbelief, Celia nearly reached up with the intent of sweeping it back for him.

Her lips tightened and her hand clenched into a fist instead. She must remain immune to the rakish image he currently presented. Difficult though the task would be. "Did the queen give— "

"Yes, yes, my prickly sugarplum. And I would wed you tonight if your parents were here to witness the ceremony. The queen's blessing means there will be no backing out of our engagement. Not that I would allow that."

"I've no intention of jilting you at the altar, Lord Rosenthorne." Celia took another step back into the safety of the corridor, but Gabriel caught her by the wrist.

His eyes deepened in color until they were a deep, rich hue. Almost as black as his thick eyelashes. His jaw tightened and he tugged her so close she could smell the sandalwood scent of his soap. The towel around his waist dipped even further.

Celia's heart pounded with awareness. Beneath the fabric of her riding habit, her nipples hardened into tight buds. She could not forget the way he'd caressed her before. How he'd worshipped her with his tongue and teeth.

"You will call me by my given name, Celia. I am not a title where you are concerned."

"The cloth," Celia stuttered in her panic. "It is in danger of falling."

"And if it does, you will see everything there is of me." His tone was almost teasing, but in stark contrast, his face remained hard and unforgiving.

Celia could not determine if he was upset with her for being just outside his door, or perturbed she wasn't already in his bed.

The bulge hidden by the fabric was growing larger by the second. What would it feel like to hold him in her hands? To caress him and drive him past the point of madness as he so effortlessly did to her? She licked her lips which were suddenly dry. What would he look like completely bared to her? His body was massive. His cock surely matched in proportion. Would she find it repulsing or exciting? Would it hurt when he pushed into her body?

More importantly, would he stop if she cried out?

"Christ, don't look at me like that, Celia."

His low murmur startled her. Realizing her gaze was practically assessing the area between his legs, she shook herself in an effort to regain her senses and peered up at him. "Like what?"

"Like you are as hungry for me as I am for you."

"I-I don't know what you mean." She was rattled by his ravenous gaze and her body's heated response. How could it be this man seemed the only one capable of inspiring such roiling emotions simply by looking at her?

"Yes. You know precisely what I mean." Gabriel released her wrist with an exasperated sigh, taking a step back into his rooms. His hands gripped the edge of the door, his knuckles whitening. "But now is not the opportune time to address the matter. I cannot take you in hand in the manner you so desperately need and as I so fervently crave. I must wait until we are properly wed."

Celia frowned. "Take me in hand?"

"Yes, my pet." His eyes raked her form until a shiver of forewarning trickled down her spine.

She still wore her emerald green riding habit, complete with kid leather gloves dyed to match and a jaunty hat accentuated with a peacock plume. A short quirt used for guiding her horse while riding sidesaddle dangled from her wrist.

His gaze touched on it and a tiny smirk flickered across his firm lips.

There was that tingle in the pit of her stomach again. The one that recognized the darkness in Gabriel and in herself.

Whatever he was thinking was a complete mystery, but the man possessed the capability of looking through her and straight into her thoughts. Celia suspected Gabriel saw everything about her.

Without thinking of the consequences, she goaded him. "Will you be able to restrain yourself until we are married? I don't believe it is possible."

Gabriel's nostrils flared in acknowledgment of her rash challenge.

"Is that so?" His melodic voice curled around Celia like a ribbon of sin. "I think you have no idea just what you are attempting to provoke. Do you want restraint, sugarplum, or do you wish to experience everything?"

"Everything." She tossed back, trembling with her own boldness. And she did. No matter how frightening it might all be. She trusted him not to harm her, even if that belief was a reckless one.

Gabriel's eyes flared with understanding, the irises turning so dark and fiery, Celia wondered if she might burn to a cinder from the heat of his stare.

When his lips curled the slightest bit, she was irrationally struck with an urge to press her mouth to the corners of his and taste his amusement.

"And so you shall." The door was already swinging closed when Gabriel added in a voice laced with conviction. "But not until we are truly husband and wife, and there is no possibility of escape for either of us."

AFTER GABRIEL so unceremoniously shut the door in her face, Celia had no choice but to slink back to her room.

There, she considered her future husband's cryptic statement. There were so many things of which she remained naïve when it came to matters between a man and a woman. Gabriel would most certainly teach her, but it was an unavoidable truth that her previous experience with intimacy was a disastrous event.

Memories of the awful night five years before often flooded Celia's mind. During the dark of night, the bedside lamp would often burn low and she would awaken in a state of panic. Heart pounding, drenched in a cold sweat, and gasping for air. Imagining the hand was still clamped so tight over her mouth that she could not draw a proper breath.

During those terrifying moments between consciousness and sleep, Celia would remember Bryan Flannigan's hot breath brushing across her cheek. His calloused fingers pushing into secret places in ways she'd thought both exciting and shocking at first.

And she always remembered how the pleasure disintegrated into the foreign sensation of flesh tearing when he pushed her skirts higher and shoved himself into her body.

How would she ever forget digging her nails into his lightly muscled forearms, trying without words to make him stop? Despite her struggles, Bryan's sinewy body, lean and hard from years of working menial tasks, had surged forward. Taking her innocence and shattering the trust she'd placed in his hands.

It was difficult understanding how she once found Bryan's attention exhilarating. His teasing kisses always suffused her with warmth and filled her head with wicked thoughts of allowing him to do even more. She indulged in silly, impossible daydreams. Fantasies in which she and the handsome groomsman were married. They would live in the country, far from society's censorship and her parents' disappointment. Bryan would find work in another nobleman's stable to make a living. He would come home to the little cottage they shared. He'd call her 'lass' and give her sweet kisses on the cheek.

How stupid she'd been. Bryan was ten years older than her tender age of nearly sixteen that summer. Celia recognized now the whole affair was borne of immature infatuation on her part. She allowed him to take advantage, and Bryan relished the opportunity to take her innocence. She'd been a silly, headstrong girl caught up in her first romantic crush and she'd paid a dear price for her naivety.

She'd been so caught up in Bryan's affections. Eagerly agreeing when he said they must keep their relationship a secret or else he'd lose his employment. She accepted everything he'd said she must do. Believed the bounder's promise that they would be together forever. Believed him when he whispered if she would let him kiss her, touch her, it would prove how much she loved him.

She allowed him liberties, even when her inner voice screamed she should rethink matters. She let him talk her into meeting him in the stables that night. Eager to see the surprise he said was special and only for her. She'd gone willingly. Gave in without a peep, until it all went too far. When she attempted pushing him away, he simply laughed and captured her hands in one of his. He continued as he pleased until she cried out in muffled pain from behind the hand clasped over her mouth.

Only then did Bryan stop.

Withdrawing abruptly from Celia, he reached down between his legs. He began working himself with his own hand until a groan echoed in the secluded, darkened stall.

When Bryan collapsed against her with a huff of satisfaction, his hand still clamped over her mouth, a splash of hot liquid landed on Celia's thigh.

When he finally leaned away from her, the face Celia once thought so handsome, with his blue eyes and shock of reddish blonde hair, was now that of a stranger.

"You better keep your bloody mouth shut about this if you know what's good for you," he'd sneered at her, his Irish heritage evident in the dismissive lilt of his voice. "I'll not go swinging from the hangman's noose just because a toff's whore daughter couldn't keep her legs from spreading. So, you keep that maw shut, or I'll do it for ya."

And with that, he hopped up to his feet. While Celia lay sprawled in the musty straw lost in a state of dazed, pained confusion, Bryan shoved his cock back into the confines of his trousers. "Clean yourself up and get back to your room before someone comes looking for you."

She never saw Bryan again after that night. Descending into a state of melancholy, Celia discovered hiding the bruises on her upper arms from her mother difficult but not impossible. But there was no concealing the nightmares she suffered for months afterward. She began insisting on a lamp being lit during the night, even when her older brother, Tristan, teased her about being afraid of the dark and how she was too old for such childishness.

Celia brushed aside Lady Darby's attempts at discussing her daughter's odd behavior. Eventually, her mother stopped her worried prodding, attributing Celia's condition to the impending introduction to society. That rationalization apparently suited everyone. Even Celia, herself.

After screwing up the courage to enter the stables a month following the incident, Celia learned Bryan left weeks before. He'd collected his wages and abruptly left for other employment. Celia did not know where or for whom. She only cared that the man was far from the Darby estate.

Celia overcame the fears plaguing her with great determination. She made herself dance with the various men seeking her out. She even allowed their kisses. It was strange, but somehow, the fear morphed into something entirely different over the years.

Soon, she *was* different. Drawn to men who snatched inappropriate liberties. That reckless feeling of adrenaline, the fear of getting caught, was enthralling. Addictive. She did dangerous, scandalous things in the shadows. And she realized it was imperative she must find a husband who did not give a pauper's halfpenny for anything that transpired in her past. It left her searching for the perfect mate, with little hope of ever finding him.

That is, until she met Gabriel.

Gabriel Lawrence Rosenthorne. Now, the new Marquess of Rosenthorne and Lord of several lesser estates.

He was the perfect blend of dangerously imperfect and socially acceptable. A man battling his own secrets and demons and yet possessing admirable strengths and qualities. She was marrying a man who might have been crafted specifically for her.

But was it possible he truly did not care about her past? Nor learning the identity of the man who took her virginity?

Gabriel's cold indifference on that particular subject seemed too good to be true, but it was part of the reason she agreed to wed him.

He said he didn't care.

She hoped he meant it.

*M*any of the guests who traveled to Beaumont for the Ravenswood house party had already departed for festivities at other country estates. It was routine for the *ton* to attend endless rounds of soirees, hunting parties, and balls during the summer. One did not sit at home simply because the Season was on hiatus.

Were it not for her impending wedding at the Earl of Ravenswood's estate, Celia and her mother would have left as well. They would have either traveled back home or followed through with Lady Darby's plan of visiting Grace and Nicholas in Cornwall.

As it was, Celia found herself waiting for her mother and father to arrive at Beaumont. She did so with anxious nervousness, eager to have the wedding done and over with. She did not deal well with the anticipation. A knot had formed in the pit of her stomach on the night Gabriel announced he was marrying her. It had resided there since that evening.

Sara and Alan were among those invited to stay and witness the wedding. Of course, Heath, Celia's future brother-in-law, remained at Beaumont. He served as her constant companion during Gabriel's absence. Celia found the man quite entertaining. He possessed a dry sense of humor that often left her wondering if he was jesting or not. Although they moved in the same circles, she'd never spent time in his company prior to all of this. Now, she was coming to regard him as an unlikely ally and friend.

Lord Robert Harvey departed a few days after Gabriel left for London. Her former beau was certainly displeased with the situation.

"I shall not extend my congratulations on this marriage, Celia," he said with grim finality. "The man you are taking as a husband will never be of our social standing. No matter how many marquessates he may inherit. Are you so willing to tie yourself to such a man? A complete nobody?"

"It is too late to do anything about it at this point," Celia had said with a sigh. Although she strongly objected to his characterization of Gabriel being a nobody, she let that argument go. "My mother has agreed. My father certainly will. And Rose will not release me from my own consent to marry him. It is useless fighting it. He will obtain the queen's consent for this hasty marriage, and then I am certainly left with no choice."

That evening as Celia finished dressing for the evening meal, there was a knock on her bedroom door.

"I will get it, miss," the maid said with a smile. Since her own maid, Katie, traveled with her mother, Celia was using the services of Mrs. Frazer. The elderly woman served as a lady's maid when needed, although her usual duties were as an assistant to Annie, Beaumont's housekeeper. She was a bit flighty but terribly sweet, and quite talented when it came to arranging intricate hairstyles.

"Good evening, milord."

"Good evening, Mrs. Frazer," Gabriel said, looking past the woman to where Celia sat at the dressing table. "If Lady Celia is ready, I've come to escort her to supper."

"How nice. Yes, I just finished her coiffure, and all milady requires now are her slippers." Mrs. Frazer opened the door further. "I'm sure Lady Celia will not mind if you would like to wait inside while I fetch them for her."

Celia blushed, remembering the last time Gabriel was inside this room. How he'd gently removed her shoes and then kissed the place between her legs with ravenous hunger.

"Thank you, Mrs. Frazer. I would love to. And perhaps I may offer my assistance. I know you suffer with the limitations of a painful back." His voice was a low rumble. It conjured up even more memories for Celia. Memories where he told her what to do while describing his plans for her.

His smile touched Celia from the other side of the room. She still sat at the dressing table, frozen in place by a surge of desire so strong she thought her knees would buckle if she tried standing. It was ridiculous that he affected her this way. It was ridiculous that she hungered for the slightest bit of attention this man showed her.

"Oh, that would be lovely," Mrs. Frazer replied happily. "Here you are, milord." She handed over a pair of gold-heeled slippers with dainty bows of a darker hue accentuating the toe. A slender strap would wrap around the ankle, securing the shoe in place. Gabriel dangled the shoes from his index finger by way of that same strap.

He watched Celia's reaction as he approached and knelt before her.

"Shall I?" he murmured, studying her through the sweep of his dark lashes. Celia bit her lip and gingerly placed her foot on his bended knee. Even through the fabric of his trousers and the silk of her stockings, she felt the muscles in his leg. They were hard beneath the arch of her foot, and Celia nearly curled her toes with pleasure when his hand encircled her ankle while sliding the shoe into place.

It was so erotic and yet so simple a thing. The way he silently slid the strap into place around her ankle and fastened the dainty buckle, his large, blunt fingers surprisingly dexterous when it came to the delicately wrought mechanism. The corners of his mouth lifted as he adjusted the bow, apparently amused by the whimsical detail, and then reached for her other foot to repeat the process.

"I hope to see these same shoes at some point in a far more intimate setting," he said in a low voice, his hand lingering on the angular lines of her ankle. He caressed the fragile bones for a heartbeat of a moment. "In fact, I would like to see you wearing these and nothing else. Would you like that, too, sugarplum?"

Celia's eyes fluttered shut at the scandalous image his words conjured in her mind. *Yes.* Yes, she would like that very much.

"All done, then. Thank you, Lord Rosenthorne." Mrs. Frazer's cheery voice interrupted the quiet, heated magic of the moment.

Celia blinked, realizing Gabriel had already risen to his feet and now waited for her to accept his hand. His smile was a crooked grin, his eyes raking her from head to toe as she stood and slipped her hand into his. The warmth of his grip soaked into her senses. She relaxed, the tension seeping away as he tugged her closer. The delicious scent of his cologne drifted over her in a subtle cloud of evergreen and spice.

"Come along, Lady Celia. It is our very first appearance as an officially engaged couple, and everyone is eager to see how we handle this new phase of our relationship."

Word spread quickly of Celia and Gabriel's hastily announced engagement and their impending marriage. And news of Gabriel's inheritance traveled even faster. It was the main topic of conversation at supper. Ivy gleefully said the reveal of a secret romance was being swooned over, and many society hostesses were planning their guest lists to include the *ton's* newest couple.

Celia suspected it was just a matter of time before the news reached her brother. Knowing Tristan, he would surely intercede on her behalf. And while she thought he had a healthy respect for Gabriel in the limited capacity of their acquaintance, it would hardly stop him from attempting a rescue of his dearest baby sister.

But was that truly what she wanted now? Rescue? Was that scenario even possible after she'd revealed her terrible secret to Gabriel? It wasn't. And she knew for a certainty she would become Gabriel's wife. Momentum had grown to the point where there was no backing out of it now.

She anticipated her parents' arrival any day, and the wedding would then take place. Celia was unsure of Gabriel's plans after that, nor did she know what to expect. Most bridal couples went away on extended honeymoons, but in their case, Gabriel had serious, pressing duties now. His presence would undoubtedly be required for various estate business.

Heath cheerily suggested the new couple begin with a visit at Greenbriar Fields, his home in Oxfordshire. Gabriel's reply was noncommittal.

"Later, perhaps. I wish to acclimate myself to my new station and marital status at Rosenthorne. And there is work being done there requiring Lady Celia's approval and input."

"Already ripping out the old wallpaper and tossing the furniture, I suppose?" Heath mused with a nod of approval. "Can't say that I blame you there, brother. The entire estate needs a good overhaul."

Celia sensed Gabriel was perplexed by this somewhat affable newfound brother of his. He seemed unable to decide if Heath was truly an ally or a threat in disguise.

She admitted having the same thoughts initially, but Heath

never exhibited the slightest indication he could be a villain in the making. In fact, Viscount Banbury was very much like Gabriel. Straightforward. A little arrogant. A great deal charming. His reputation would bolster Gabriel's own as he entered the dragon's lair otherwise known as the *ton*. For although many would accept a previous bastard's rise to prominence, there would be others refusing to acknowledge Gabriel's claim to the marquessate. It might not even matter to some that the queen herself sanctioned the old marquee's will. Gabriel would be shunned. And Celia along with him.

When the other ladies decided they would migrate to the drawing room following supper, Celia stood up from the table. A helpful footman quickly eased her chair back out of the way.

"If you will excuse me, I believe I shall retire for the evening."

"I do hope you are not unwell, Lady Celia," Sara said, with a concerned frown.

"Oh, just a slight headache. Caused by an afternoon in the sun on horseback, no doubt. I'll be perfectly fine by morning." Celia shot a glance at Gabriel.

He'd still not uttered a word about her riding Arion. She hoped he did not mind that she borrowed his mount. In fact, she'd considered the act one of helpfulness as the stallion required the exercise.

The men began discussing their own plans. They would remain in the dining room where they could smoke their cigars and indulge in a glass of port while discussing various business dealings.

Gabriel, after a second of hesitation, followed her to the dining room doors.

"Rest well, Celia," he said, briefly touching her elbow, his hand a firebrand of heat on her skin. "Knowing this is likely your last night of going to bed alone."

Celia stared up at Gabriel's ruggedly handsome face. His statement should not leave her feeling as though she were melting. It was greatly irritating. She could not go through a lifetime with this man feeling constantly aroused by the simplest of words.

"Goodnight, Lord Rosenthorne." She deliberately used his title and saw his eyes darken with her insolence. Quickly stepping away from the dining room's entrance, she glanced back to see him resting a shoulder against one of the double door jambs.

The thunderous expression on Gabriel's face was oddly assessing, but Celia dismissed it with a shrug. There were surely times over the course of their marriage when he would look at her as though his new wife vexed him a great deal.

She hoped Ivy understood her reticence to join the other ladies. The women who remained at Beaumont were eager to discuss every detail of the ceremony, small and intimate though it would be. Over the last two weeks, Celia managed a distant smile whenever the subject came up. She could not shake an impending sense that catastrophe was inevitable.

How surreal it was that she would be married soon. And to a man who was essentially a stranger. A handsome one, but a stranger, nonetheless. She wondered what type of husband Gabriel would be. Indulgent? Strict? Would he overlook her little quirks? Laugh at her need for a lamp burning by her bed so the room was not completely dark? Or would he hold her close and whisper in her ear until the shadows receded?

Celia was lost in thought as she walked down the softly lit corridor headed toward the room she was staying in. Worrying over such matters truly was giving her an awful headache. Rubbing her temples, she did not notice when one of the many guest room doors cracked open.

Before she had an opportunity to struggle, Celia was grabbed and pulled into a room. Hard hands held her fast, arms wrapping around her waist from behind and a hand quickly clamped over her mouth, muffling her surprised scream.

"Shhhh!" Lord Robert Harvey admonished in a low, aggravated voice. "It's only me. Shhh, you don't want anyone to hear us, do you?"

Dragging her further into the room, Robert reached behind him and pulled the door shut. The lock clicked into place.

They were alone now in an empty guest room with only a single lamp burning for illumination. Celia wiggled in the man's tight grip and tried to breathe.

A quick rush of panic flooded her. It was crippling. A deafening roar filled her ears. For a second, she thought she might be incapable of moving a single muscle to free herself.

Her captor never noticed her distress, blithely explaining his actions as if Celia was a co-conspirator in his plans.

"Listen, I'm taking you away from here. It's our only chance before that bastard drags you to the altar and shackles you to his side forever." Robert breathed heavily, both from exertion and apparent adrenaline.

Celia's head shook back and forth, her words muffled behind Robert's hand.

"I know, sweetheart. I know. But do not thank me just yet. Wait until we are clear of the house and safely away from here. I've planned everything. In fact, my valet waits for us in the woods with horses for our journey."

A laugh bubbled up in Celia's throat, incredulity chasing away her panic. *His valet?* The man Robert referred to was at least seventy years of age. Far past the prime age to assist in a kidnapping.

When Celia choked on her giggle, her fear subsiding quickly in light of such absurdity, Robert harrumphed in her ear.

"This is most certainly no laughing matter, Celia."

She bit his hand in response when it slipped from across her mouth.

"Owww!" Robert snatched his hand away, glaring at her in recrimination. "Whatever did you do that for?"

Celia took a huge gulp of air. Taking advantage of his shock, she jerked free of his hold. Bolting forward, she placed an over-stuffed brocade upholstered chair between them as a barrier.

"You were suffocating me, you dolt." She glared at him in the dimly lit room. "Just what the Devil do you think you are doing? Grabbing me like that in the corridor?" The demand was accompanied by the gesture of her hands settling on her hips.

"Rescuing you, of course. I've come to carry you away from the dangers of marrying beneath your station," Robert replied with arrogant conviction. "To save you from being ostracized. Or worse, being made a laughingstock."

"Do I appear in need of rescue?" Celia bit out. "And my future husband is a marquess. So, it's you who should worry of being ostracized by *him.* Rosenthorne will soon be capable of destroying a man with just a few simple words." Her head tilted. "Rather than just by using his fists."

Robert waved a hand in her direction. "He would never lift a hand against a nobleman. He wouldn't dare. The bastard would swing from a noose if he tried."

Celia's head tilted, remembering the rumors she'd heard in the past of Gabriel's aid to the Earl of Ravenswood. And then there were his own words of warning just days ago, threatening the life of any man she happened to show an interest in. Robert Harvey had no idea the danger he was currently in.

"You foolish man. Don't you realize what will happen if he should discover us? He will most certainly kill you if he discovers us like this. And I can't say I would blame him for it. You have no idea what he is capable of, although surely you've heard the same rumors as I." Celia crossed her arms over her chest, giving Robert her sternest look. "Now, you will step aside from that door and allow me to go on my way. While I haven't any idea how you managed sneaking into the earl's home, you'd best pray neither he nor Gabriel catches you here."

"I won't have my plans of rescuing you disrupted, Celia. And I'll not leave you behind to marry a monster," Robert replied with exaggerated patience. "You will thank me for this one day, I promise you. When we are husband and wife, this will be nothing but a horrible memory."

Celia stomped her foot. "You thickheaded imbecile. I don't require rescue and I most certainly will *not* marry you! Now, open that door before I take matters into my own hands."

"That's precisely what I like about you, Celia." Robert grinned. "That feistiness is one of your better qualities."

"Open the door, Robert," she demanded again, fists clenching into little balls. To think she enjoyed kissing this man before Gabriel laid claim to her. He seemed silly and inconsequential compared to the man she would soon marry. And his inability to appreciate the danger of this situation confirmed her suspicion that he was quite possibly simple-minded as well.

"You have no idea what is best for you, Celia. Your infatuation with that man has clouded your judgment and I—"

A thunderous roar sounded from the other side of the locked door. Celia winced, her heart pounding with recognition and a shiver of fear.

"Celia. Unlock this door at once."

It was Gabriel. The unmistakable fury in his voice made her somewhat nauseous.

"I cannot, Lord Rosenthorne. The way is blocked," she shakily replied. To Robert, she hissed, "Now, see what you've done? Move away from the door before you are struck with—"

Before she could complete the warning, the door splintered apart, flying open and sending shards of wood sailing through the air. Celia wasn't sure if Gabriel kicked it open with his booted foot or simply pounded one of his massive shoulders into it, but the door now hung crooked on its hinges, the wood shredded and in pieces.

A chunk of the wood had struck Robert's arm, ripping a hole in his coat and leaving a bloody gash above his elbow. He stared stupidly at the wound and turned to see Gabriel coming through the mangled door.

"Look what you've done, you beastly bastard," the younger lord accused while picking a shard of wood out of his hair. "You've ruined a perfectly fine suit coat and…"

The words trailed off as Gabriel strode quickly toward him. A huge hand clasped around Robert's throat, strangling anything else he might have said.

Celia stared at her fiancé. A roiling thunderstorm of anger, possessiveness, and blood lust surrounded him as he held Robert aloft until the man's toes barely grazed the floor.

"You fucking dared touch what is mine, Harvey?" Gabriel's melodic voice came out in a low, guttural snarl. Then, as if she were an afterthought, he directed his next question at Celia. "Are you harmed, Celia? Did he hurt you in any way? Because if he did, I will kill him right here. This very second. And I will enjoy making him suffer."

Gabriel obviously tightened his grip on Robert's throat because the man began wheezing in the most horrible way. Celia shook herself from her stupor. If she didn't do something, it was possible Lord Robert Harvey might die right before her eyes.

Rushing forward, she clutched Gabriel's bicep. It was like grabbing a hunk of solid iron.

"I am unharmed. Please, Gabriel. Please let him go. You are choking him."

Gabriel's gaze swung to her, fixing on Celia's concerned features with blazing intensity. "I warned you this would happen."

"Yes. You did," Celia replied calmly, her voice somehow remaining steady, although she trembled with dread. "However, this incident is simply a misunderstanding. I've not the slightest bit of interest in Lord Harvey. If I did, I would have accepted his marriage proposal instead of yours. I would have accepted his offer to run away with him. But I did not. And I was in the middle of explaining matters to him when you broke down the door. Please release him as I asked you."

"Run away with him?" Gabriel's eyes flared with renewed fury. "Over my dead body. And his."

Robert sputtered; his face was turning a peculiar shade of red now.

"Let him go, Gabriel. Now." Celia put every bit of strength she possessed into that command, and surprisingly, Gabriel obeyed.

The stranglehold he had on Robert was finally released, but still, he shoved the man away in a brutal show of disdain.

Robert stumbled, hitting the wall with a thud that left him both coughing and groaning.

"Thank you," Celia said in a soft voice, willing Gabriel to look at her. Her hand remained on his arm, and she felt the muscles bunching beneath the fabric of his coat. Heat rolled off him, his anger slow to dissipate. But the depths of his gilded whiskey-colored eyes revealed something entirely different. And her own reaction frightened Celia the most.

There was a spark of fear there. Of desperation. Celia knew instinctively that Gabriel believed she could reject him. As a man and as a husband. She might abandon him. She may even declare him unworthy of being married to someone like herself.

And there was the glimmer of vulnerability in a man who'd gone through life alone and unwanted. A little boy who'd lost everything and who now grasped hold of the first person who was truly his, refusing to let go.

Celia's heart softened. She could not ignore the tenderness that seeped into her own gaze as she stared up at him. For swirling along with the fear he could not conceal was concern for Celia herself. That protective glint reminded Celia of her own promise. She'd given her word to this man, promised herself to him. He'd vowed to protect her, and in his gaze, she saw that he believed he'd already failed in the undertaking of that duty.

"I'm perfectly fine, Gabriel. I'm unharmed, truly," Celia whispered, moving closer so he understood she sought and welcomed his protection. Emotions careened and crashed through her. The aching need to hold and assure him was almost overwhelming.

"What the Devil is going on here?" Sebastian's voice, quivering with outrage, echoed from the shattered doorway. "And, Lord Harvey, why is that you are in one of my guest rooms when you are no longer a guest here at Beaumont?"

Gabriel never broke eye contact with Celia while jerking his chin in Robert's direction. "He came with the intention of abducting Celia."

"And why did you take your anger out on the helpless door?" Sebastian barked. "Damnit, Rose. That hellish temper of yours will be your undoing."

"He had her locked in here and would not let her pass," he murmured, and Celia wondered if he might pull her even closer and kiss her in that moment. A public display of possession and his intention to keep her. Something was happening to her. It transcended physical attraction and desire. It made her palms damp and her mind go to mush whenever she thought of Gabriel Rose. She'd never expected that she'd feel this way.

Love. That's what it was. Love for this rogue turned Marquess. For this man who would kill another for her. How could she fall in love with such darkness?

From the corridor where they stood peeking into the room, Ivy and Sara gasped in collective outrage.

Sebastian leveled a glare at Robert. "That was rather stupid of you, wasn't it?"

Robert scowled. "Perhaps. But that does not excuse the attack on my person. Call for the constable, Lord Ravenswood. This matter must be dealt with at once."

Heath's laughter was terse. "Dear God. You cannot possibly be that naïve."

Gabriel's jaw tightened as he dragged his gaze from Celia's and stared at Robert. "Yes. It will be dealt with immediately. I intend on seeing you arrested for attempted kidnapping. Sebastian, while summoning the constable, you may also call for the minister." Pulling Celia closer, he protectively tucked her under his arm. "Go near her again and I *will* kill you, Harvey."

She somehow controlled her trembling body, still reeling from the realization she'd fallen in love with this man.

The firmness of Gabriel's tone left no doubt. He would not be swayed from his decision.

"Lady Celia and I will marry tonight."

CHAPTER 23

Not long after the constable dragged Robert Harvey away from the manor house, the minister of the village chapel appeared on Beaumont's doorstep. The bedraggled man was more than a bit perturbed that he'd been roused from bed in order to perform a wedding.

"An ungodly hour," the man proclaimed, although, in reality, the clock had just recently struck the hour of ten.

After perusing the special license, huffing beneath his breath over the highly irregular circumstances, and finally accepting a rather large donation to his parish, the minister finally conceded. He would perform the ceremony but only within the confines of a holy place.

As a group, they all traipsed across the green lawns and gravel paths to the small chapel on Beaumont's grounds.

"Must we do this tonight?" Celia asked as Gabriel entwined his fingers with hers during the walk to the building.

He slanted her a quelling look. "I'll not take the chance of another former suitor bursting through the doors, intent on carrying you off to Gretna Green before I make you a marchioness."

"I don't know if that was Lord Harvey's intent or not," Celia replied tiredly. "Oh, did someone inform his valet that the plan was foiled? The poor man has been standing in the nearby woods for hours now, waiting for his master to return with a hostage."

"It's been taken care of," Ivy piped up from behind them. "I've also had essential items moved from your room into Gabriel's suite for the night."

Celia stiffened and Gabriel's hand tightened.

I have forgotten what comes after the ceremony. When Gabriel has every right to take anything he desires.

"Courage, sugarplum," Gabriel said in a low voice meant only for her ears. "This part will be over soon enough. Then the only thing left is the begging for your parents' forgiveness for my impatience. And hoping your brother does not shoot me on sight."

"Tristan would not. He likes you."

Gabriel's smile was almost sad. "Perhaps. But then again, this is the first time I compromised his sister. He's bound to be angry with me."

He said not another word until they were repeating their vows. And when he pressed a hard, possessive kiss upon her lips to seal her fate, Celia wondered how it had all occurred so rapidly. The entire ceremony was a complete blur.

"A toast to the new groom and his bride!" Alan cheered as they stood outside the chapel. Heath leaned in, placing a chaste kiss on Celia's cheek, and Alan and Sebastian quickly did the same. Ivy and Sara embraced her much more somberly than she expected, sensing how disquieted she was by the evening's events.

Celia pondered how the night was the same after the wedding as it was when she first entered the chapel. The moon still shone high above them, and the fireflies continued their mystical dance in the darkness. Crickets chirped in a reassuring cadence in the distance. Everything was the same and yet everything was different now.

Her life had changed in a matter of fifteen minutes. Clad in the same dark lavender gown she'd worn to supper and holding a hastily constructed bouquet of hothouse roses and lemon branches, she'd been married. The sharp aroma of lemon oil contrasting with the delicate scent of the yellow blooms told her it wasn't all just a dream.

Almost in a daze, Celia glanced down at her hand. A pear-shaped topaz of bright blue glittered in the moonlight. The ring had belonged to his mother. It was one of the few things he had that belonged to her and now it was hers.

"Take care with it, Celia," Gabriel had warned while placing it on her finger during the ceremony. "It is one of my most precious of possessions, and I have so few things that belonged to her. I treasure it, and now you, above all things."

Celia had managed a nod, painfully aware of how heavy the ring sat on her finger. It held the weight of his lost childhood. The pain of abandonment. The sorrow of desertion and an absent father.

"Come with us, Celia," Sara prodded gently, giving Celia an encouraging squeeze and breaking her out of her reverie. "We shall help you ready for bed while the gentlemen share a glass of brandy to celebrate this happy occasion. Lord Rosenthorne will be up shortly, don't worry."

"As if we could keep him away," Ivy scoffed, her expression softening when Celia's expression showed her distress. "Do not be afraid, Celia. Your new husband, as rough as he may seem, will take care of you."

"I should like some brandy as well." Celia's voice was shaky. She did not miss the look which passed between Ivy and Gabriel and his subsequent nod of agreement. And that made her almost angry. That her actions would now be scrutinized and either approved or denied. Under English law, Gabriel now had complete control of her life. Her fate. Her happiness and her despair.

When her chin took on a mulish tilt, Gabriel smiled while excusing himself from the other men.

Placing a finger beneath her chin, he lifted until her gaze met his. "One glass, Lady Rosenthorne. And mark my words, I will know if you exceed that."

Both Sara and Ivy averted their eyes during this exchange, but they certainly heard Gabriel's low murmur. Ivy bit back a grin of comprehension and whispered something in Sara's ear which made her giggle.

Celia considered a moment of defiance. She would, and could, drink as much brandy as she liked. And he couldn't stop her. But for some reason, she simply nodded her head, disappointed by the sense of belonging she felt when he leaned forward and kissed her forehead.

How could he be so damned charming and tyrannical at the same time?

How odd was it to hear herself referred to as 'Lady Rosenthorne'?

It would take some getting used to, but she truly was his marchioness now.

THE CLOCK WAS STRIKING midnight when Gabriel turned the door handle to his suite of rooms. Passing through the sitting area, he entered the bedroom and paused. A lamp on the bedside table and the low fire cracking in the fireplace lent a rosy glow to the masculine space. When he inhaled deep, he caught both the faint smell of woodsmoke and the far more feminine scent of roses and lemons.

A wave of tenderness overtook him as his gaze drifted over the mound of blankets on his bed and the body they conformed around. His bride. His wife. His Celia.

She was finally his and she waited for him in his bed. Anticipation swelled to almost unbearable portions, even as he reminded himself he would not press her tonight. It had been a long, trying day for them both. And he was certain Celia would not welcome his advances after enduring the stress of a near abduction and subsequent marriage.

On a table near the fireplace, he noted a decanter of brandy and a glass. The decanter verged on empty.

Gabriel frowned. Had she imbibed more than the single drought he'd allowed her?

With a sigh, he sat on a bench positioned at the end of the bed and began removing his clothes. He'd slept in the nude for years and had no intention of changing his habits now, regardless of the risk he might offend his new wife.

But perhaps this was not the night he should insist on such matters. *Select your battles carefully now. And plunder the rewards later.*

After pulling on a thin pair of muslin sleeping pants, he padded back over to the bed, and for a moment, stood looking at Celia. She faced away from him, her hair streaming over the pillows in a gorgeous, ebony-hued banner of silky waves. He could just make out the linear curve of her body beneath the coverlet, and her position was such that he could see the shell-like crescent of her ear and the softness of her rounded shoulder. Her hand was curled upon the pillow, her palm open, her breathing measured and relaxed.

Moving as quietly as possible, he pulled the covers back and then reached to turn the lamp down.

"Please don't extinguish the lamp."

A thread of concern laced through Celia's softly spoken request. She remained lying as she was, the words directed from over her shoulder. Gabriel was puzzled by the directive, but he did as she asked.

"All right." He hesitated for a moment, then slid into the bed, settling himself beneath the sheets and propping his pillows just so behind his head. Lying there beside her, he breathed deep of her unique perfume and waited to see what she might say next. In all honesty, he wasn't quite sure what to do with a woman in his bed with whom he had no intention of making love.

"Thank you," Celia breathed. The words came out only slightly slurred, but Gabriel caught the subtleness of how the brandy affected her.

"Celia," he murmured, placing a hand on her shoulder and pulling her until she lay on her back, staring up at him. The flickering light cast by the lamp illuminated her features, and he was shocked to see fear dancing in the dark depths of her eyes. "How much did you drink?"

Her giggle ended in a half-sob. "Enough? Maybe more?" She flinched when his hand cradled her jaw and slid into her hair.

"You were only to have one glass, sugarplum," he admonished. Why was she suddenly behaving as if she were frightened of him? Did she think his demeanor toward her would change simply because they were wed now? Yes, it was true he would spank her on occasion, and punishments would certainly be a part of her life due to her naturally defiant nature, but never would he intentionally harm her.

Indeed, he had a gut feeling Celia would enjoy the punishments he crafted with her in mind. She'd already exhibited a shy willingness when it came to exploring the darker aspect of sexual relationships. But he certainly had no desire of terrorizing his beautiful little wife.

"You cannot tell me how much I shall drink or not drink, Gabriel," she mumbled with false bravado. "You don't *own* me, you know. And besides, I needed it to get through this night."

"Silly girl. Of course, I will tell you what you can and cannot do. You are my responsibility now and one I do not take lightly. My instructions, my rules, are always intended to keep you safe. Even if you believe they are capricious and unfair."

"This whole ordeal is unfair!" she cried out, attempting unsuccessfully to jerk away from his caressing hand.

He simply tightened his hand in her hair, and while she groaned at the pressure, it did not stop the flow of her confused words. "It is unfair you have married me when I do not know your feelings for me. It is unfair that I don't even understand my feelings for you. It is unfair I melt each time you touch me. And it is unfair that I am so frightened of what you might do to me that I cannot bear it."

"Shhhh," Gabriel soothed her, the hand previously tangled in her hair now sliding to cup the nape of her neck. He could better control her in this manner, and he held her fast with that hand while the other slid across the flat plane of her stomach and curled around her waist. She was caught now, unable to move away unless he allowed it. "Calm yourself, Celia. There is nothing to be afraid of. I've no intention of making love to you, if that's what has you in such a state. I realize more than you can know now is not the time to exert my power to do as I wish. You are exhausted and overwrought with emotions. And soused as well. Tonight, we share only a bed and the comfort of one another's arms."

Celia stilled in her efforts of escaping his embrace. "You... you will only hold me?" The last word was accompanied by a hiccup of relief. Her breath, sweet with brandy, brushed across his lips, and Gabriel steeled himself against the reaction of his own body. He would not make love to her, but damned if his body was receiving the message on that front.

The soft, creamy hue of her nightclothes was a perfect foil to her dark hair and dark eyes. She was the Devil's own temptress.

Gabriel wanted to unwrap her from the confines of that silken gown, expose her bit by bit to his hungry gaze, and feast upon her sweet skin until he was drunk with lust. Damn Ivy and Sara for dressing her in such provocative clothing.

"Yes. That is all," he answered with some difficulty. Desire made his voice husky and low. "But I know you disobeyed me. You drank more of that brandy than you should have. And there are consequences for instances of disobedience. But not tonight, pet. Tonight, we sleep. And later, we'll discuss your punishment."

Celia slowly relaxed as he spoke, believing him when he said nothing intimate would occur. Rather sleepily, she sank back into the pillows with a hum, her eyes closing from the warmth of his body surrounding her like a welcomed blanket.

"You can't punish me," she said, snuggling closer with a confused frown at her own compliance. "I'm a marchioness now, and husbands do not punish marchionesses."

Gabriel smoothed Celia's hair back away from her brow, watching as she slipped into sleep. He could not ignore how her hand crept up until it now rested on his bare chest. It seared his skin like a firebrand.

Reclining against the pillows, he folded his hand over hers, holding it there with gentle force. A smile tipped the corners of his mouth up as he considered the drowsy, inebriated assertions she made.

His new wife had much to learn about what her husband would do to her, marchioness or not.

And how much she would come to enjoy it.

AT SOME POINT during the night, Gabriel lowered the light of the lamp until it was almost extinguished. Then he lay awake for a long time, one arm propped behind his head, the other pinned to the mattress by the weight of his new wife.

She used his body as if she were a spoiled empress and he the most comfortable of pillows, her arms and legs in a tangled sprawl. Despite her standoffish behavior during the ceremony and even earlier when he entered the suite, Celia possessed no qualms when pressing closer to him. She practically straddled him, one leg thrown up near his hip, the other entwined with one of his legs. Her arm lay haphazardly across his stomach, her fingers touching bare skin and setting him ablaze with awareness.

Gabriel shifted, growing more uncomfortable by the second. He hadn't been with a woman in weeks. And that abstinence was making this even more difficult than he thought it would be. His cock was a hardened staff of iron beneath the bedclothes, and Celia's knee rested dangerously close alongside it.

Damn, how he wanted to roll his new wife over onto her back. Press his lips to the perfumed softness of her breasts. Discover all the places on her body that reacted to his touch. He would make her cry out loud with satisfaction and revel in the fact he'd been the one to do that to her.

But he'd already made his promise. He would not touch her this first night they shared. He would let her sleep in peace and keep his hands to himself.

When Gabriel's muffled sigh of discontent ruffled her hair, Celia snuggled even closer. Her breath passed from between softly parted lips and feathered his shoulder. She slept like the dead, unphased by his agitated shifting. The deepness of her slumber was both a blessing and a curse.

God's teeth. How can I lay with her like this and not touch her? Fuck, why should I? She's mine. My wife. I've every right to do as I please.

I should *do as I please.*

Hoping he could relieve the pressure building in his groin, Gabriel moved his arm from behind his head. Remaining on his back with Celia cradled on his opposite side, he carefully reached between his legs.

Giving his aching cock a squeeze, he nearly groaned aloud at the sensation, even as he breathed deeply of the rose and lemon scent emanating from Celia. He really shouldn't be frigging himself while she lay right beside him. He was a bloody degenerate for even entertaining the thought. But still, his hand found its way beneath the blankets and into his sleeping pants until his hand closed around his bare flesh.

If the deep inhales and exhales coming from Celia were any indication of her unconscious state, Gabriel thought it possible he could ease the ache pounding within him while also keeping his vow.

He gave himself a quick stroke, his hand forming a circle around the base of his cock and moving upward. It wouldn't take him long to come to a finish. He felt as though he might burst at any moment, especially when he thought of the woman lying beside him in the quiet darkness of the night. He could imagine her hands drifting over him. Learning his shape. His strength. Her whispers that she wanted him just as badly as he wanted her.

Lust surged through Gabriel like a hot tidal wave. Eyes closing with the fantasy, his hand loosened then tightened, moving again and again. Up and down. Gripping harder. A bit faster. Almost violently. But oh, so necessary. Because if he held any hope of stemming the maddening desire that he sink himself inside Celia's softness, this must be done.

Bliss shimmered just beyond his reach. He hovered on the verge of exploding. Seconds from plummeting over the precipice.

Almost there. *Almost...*

"Gabriel?"

Celia's soft voice broke through the haze of pleasure of his impending climax. Gabriel clutched himself, trying desperately to stave off the inevitable. She raised herself up on her forearms. Now, she would discover just how depraved he really was. How hungry he truly was for her.

CHAPTER 24

"Celia, turn away from me this instant."

Gabriel's voice was a guttural growl. And while the darkness she'd woken to frightened Celia, his response only intrigued her.

"But the lamp has gone out. And, and I cannot sleep without it."

"It did not go out, I turned it down. Now, please. Do as I say. Turn over." His tone reeked of anguished hope that she would do as he commanded.

Celia could just barely make him out in the dark. Her new husband was a mountainous form beside her in the bed, but oddly enough, it was comforting to have him so close. Heat emanated from his body, and although she wasn't quite sure what awoke her from such a deep slumber, she was warm and cozy because of his nearness.

Peering at him, she leaned closer, her hand sliding up from his stomach to his chest. It was heaving beneath her hand, distracting her from the realization she'd woken with that same hand on his stomach and her legs thrown over his. "Are you ill? Or perhaps injured in some way?"

He let out a bark of a laugh that sounded pained. "Jesus Christ. I'm two seconds from exploding in my own hand with your name on my lips, Celia. For the love of God, please roll over. I cannot stop this from happening."

Celia wasn't quite sure if he meant what she thought. Having overheard conversations she had no business hearing in the past, she was aware that men sometimes pleasured themselves. Especially if a woman was unavailable.

However, she was right beside Gabriel. Why would he feel this was necessary if she was his wife? Did he not think she was worthy of such attention? Well, she was. Even if she didn't quite understand it all and the thought of any man pushing his way into her body left her drenched in a cold sweat, this was Gabriel. Her husband. And he would not harm her. She was certain of that.

In a swift movement, she leaned fully across Gabriel so she could increase the lamp light. Her breasts swung in front of his face as she reached for the lamp's lever, and he let out a groan of helpless lust.

"Celia, I swear on all that is holy, if you don't distance yourself immediately…"

She sat back on her haunches. The low light illuminated Gabriel's face. Celia found herself entranced by the raw emotion that darkened his eyes. Beneath the coverlet, it appeared his hand was between his legs, and a flush of heat pinkened her cheeks. He *was* pleasuring himself.

"It's either this or I take you, sugarplum," he said in an almost forlorn voice. "And I promised you would not have need to fear my attentions tonight."

In response, Celia pulled lightly on the coverlet until it finally fell away past his hips, exposing him from head to knee. In the lamplight, his chest gleamed like bronzed slabs of granite, the muscles lining his abdomen rippling with every breath. For some strange reason, Celia was possessed by a desire to explore those intriguing ridges with her mouth. But what arrested her attention more than anything was the shape of his body beneath the fabric of his sleeping pants, and the outline of his hand where he gripped himself so tight, Celia wondered if it was painful.

It certainly appeared painful.

"Does it hurt?" she asked hesitantly.

"*Fuck,*" Gabriel muttered beneath his breath. Then, in a somewhat normal, but strangled voice, he said, "Yes, but not for reasons you think." His gaze searched hers, the depths nearly black and so mysterious Celia wondered if falling into an abyss would have the same effect. "This has become all too common for me since I've met you.

"Can I... help somehow?" She did not wait for permission. As if her hand belonged to someone else, Celia watched herself tug his pants down, exposing him fully to her gaze.

Gabriel growled when her fingers brushed across his knuckles, but he didn't stop her actions.

The sight was fascinating. Beautiful. And lord above, more erotic than anything she could have ever imagined. She stared as Gabriel held himself tightly, fingers wrapped just below the thick, mushroom-like head of his cock.

Celia swallowed past a lump in her throat, her fingers aching to stroke the velvety-looking skin to discover if it was as soft as it looked. Even in the soft glow of the lamp, she saw the vein running down its length. It throbbed with the strength of his heartbeat, keeping time in perfect cadence.

Gabriel's sex was in perfect proportion to the rest of his body. There was only one word that accurately described him.

Massive. The man in his entirety was simply overwhelming to the senses.

"Damnit, you shouldn't even be awake. Why the hell are you awake, Celia?" As if he couldn't help himself, Gabriel indulged in a quick stroke as Celia watched in utter fascination. His eyes fluttered shut before pinning her with blazing intensity. "You're not going to look away, are you?"

Celia met his eyes, a sense of inevitability overcoming her. This was where she was supposed to be. With this man.

At his mercy.

Waiting to come alive.

Slowly, she shook her head, unable to even form words.

"Fine," he snarled softly. "Watch me, Celia. Watch me as I fuck my own hand and dream it's you that I'm making love to. Don't you dare look away until I'm done. Do you understand me? Don't you fucking look away."

Celia nodded obediently, strangely excited by the fierceness Gabriel exhibited. His eyes burned in the dim light as if they were lit coals. They scorched Celia, flaring with twin flames of lust when she bit her bottom lip.

"Every time you do that, every time you bite that luscious bottom lip, I want to sink my teeth into it and suck it into my mouth, Celia. Every goddamn time. You're driving me utterly mad," he muttered.

Her breasts felt heavy. Her nipples ached with such acuteness, she unthinkingly rubbed them with the palm of her hand through the silkiness of her nightgown. But that only increased the inferno of heat that had been growing between her own legs. With an agitated noise, she shifted her thighs in an effort at alleviating the tingling sensation.

The corners of Gabriel's lips tipped up in recognition of her distress.

"Tsk, tsk, pet." Using his free hand, he caught her chin, holding her steady. "You've had your pleasure over the last few weeks at my hand. Now, you will watch as I have mine. And maybe, I'll reward you for your patience, although that's not a guarantee."

He then grabbed a handful of her hair, tugging her until she had no choice but to come closer, her face hovering inches above the corded muscles of his belly. His fingers tightened, holding her there. He began stroking himself, the urgency from before tempered by the knowledge there was surely no need to rush matters now. Celia knew he could take his time and she still would not turn away.

His fingers tightened, both in her hair and around his cock. "I should have you open that pretty mouth for me so I can slide into it." The strokes were leisurely but with purpose. He was in control now, something Celia suspected had been lost for at least a few moments when this all began. Yes, he was in control, and he would not relinquish it so easily.

"Would you like that, sugarplum?" His scarred eyebrow lifted as he questioned her. "Would you fight me if I tried? Or would you drink me in as though I were the finest brandy, and you were dying of thirst? I think you would. I think you would like me holding you still, shoving myself down your throat until you had no choice but to swallow me."

His breaths were harsh, increasing in pace with the motion of his hand. Celia watched as he commanded, fascinated when a bead of clear liquid seeped from the head of his cock. He rubbed a thumb over it, spreading it into his flesh, and groaned at the sensation. The fact Celia could not tear her eyes away seemed to exhilarate him.

"*Regarde-moi pendant que je reve de te baiser, ma chere femme.*"

The demand was a singsong litany of lust and sin. In her own agitated state, Celia did not completely grasp much of what he was saying until seconds later. The husky order set her ablaze.

Watch me while I dream of fucking you, my sweet wife.

Whatever Gabriel wanted, she would surrender without question. He'd mentioned many times making use of her mouth, but this was the first time she found herself wishing he'd make good on the threat.

Abruptly, she realized she could take matters into her own hands.

Or mouth.

She bent closer, and before there was a chance she might change her mind, or Gabriel stopping her, Celia took the flared head of his cock into her mouth. It was all she dared, but it was enough.

"Fuck, *yes,*" Gabriel hissed in surprise, his hips bucking upward in desperate search of the warm recesses of her mouth. His hand remained locked around his flesh, and although her hair was still within the tight grip of his other hand, he did not push or insist she take more of him. He simply retained his hold and let her determine the extent of her actions.

"Don't you dare stop. Stay, Celia. Stay. Stay. *Sweet Jesus.*" The words ran together as he stroked himself harder and faster, and Celia, for some unknown reason, was compelled to swirl her tongue over the thickness in her mouth. Instinctively, she hollowed out her cheeks as if she were sucking on something particularly delicious.

Gabriel grunted, and in the next instant, he yanked her backward. A noise like a small pop echoed in the room when he lost the suction of her mouth.

Then he groaned, rumbling a low noise of agonized satisfaction. For an endless moment, Celia's breath matched his as the climax sent shudders through his body and fluid pumped from his sex in arching ribbons. It smeared across his naked groin.

Celia absently wondered what it tasted like.

His fingers loosened by degrees. First on her hair, then on his cock. A deep breath escaped him. All the tension she'd sensed from the moment she came to his room earlier that afternoon seemed as if it had drained away.

He was silent, then said, "Once again, you surprise me, Celia. Thank you."

Celia felt a pang of sympathy. He sounded exhausted. He probably was. After all, he'd traipsed back and forth over England the past few days and topped it all off by getting married.

With quick movements, Gabriel removed the sleeping pants, using them to wipe away the remnants of his seed. The garment was tossed onto the floor before he fell back against the pillows, pulling Celia alongside his hard form.

"You're welcome," she whispered, wondering if he would now use his hands and mouth to give her the same blissful attention as he had done before.

She trembled with need, the junction of her thighs wet and aching. The taste of him, clean with a hint of soap and salt, left her even more ravenous. It was as if her new husband had fed her some manner of addictive opiate. She could not comprehend how this had happened. How she went from nervous and agitated, to unsatisfied and agitated.

Gabriel laughed softly. The self-assured air he usually exhibited returned with amazing speed. He was back in control once more. "I do know what you need, sugarplum. And usually, I would delight in giving you everything you crave. But not only will I honor my vow of not touching you tonight, but you've also earned a punishment for drinking more brandy than you should have. Did you think I would forget about that?"

Celia frowned. "That is not fair. You touched me and I touched you. And I truly needed that brandy. You can't say that I didn't. It's been an exceedingly tiresome day."

Positioning herself in the bed so that she could lean onto his chest, she folded her hands beneath her chin and willed him to touch her in the manner she needed.

Her efforts were in vain; however, Gabriel's expression softened. The tenderness in which he regarded her eased Celia's frustration a tiny portion.

"I know it's not fair, pet," he breathed. His hand passed over her head in a caress that made her eyes flutter shut with both sleepiness and a sense of belonging. Her head dropped. His heartbeat sounded like a thousand drums in her ear when she pressed it to his chest. Steady. True. Right. This felt right.

"But I always keep my promises," he continued in a low voice, stroking her hair and smoothing the tangles. "Good or bad, I keep them. And this one pains me more than you can possibly imagine."

CHAPTER 25

A loud banging on the outer chamber door startled Celia awake.

It was barely morning, the room still grey with the receding of the night. The lamp by the bed was no longer lit. Celia frowned. It'd been burning when she'd fallen asleep the night before, cradled in Gabriel's arms. How was it that she slept without that comforting light?

Before she could inquire what was happening, Gabriel rolled from the bed in a singular motion.

Celia had forgotten he had removed his sleeping pants after their passionate encounter. Now, she found herself staring at her husband in fascination.

Dear God. He is completely nude.

Gloriously, wildly nude, and on full display for her admiration.

His entire backside could have been inspiration for one of Michelangelo's statues. Gabriel's muscular physique was a true work of art. Celia's mouth went dry as her eyes traversed the width of his back, watching the muscles of his large shoulders clench and unclench. She'd never noticed how long his hair was.

It lay in wavy darkness just beyond the nape of his neck, leaving her with the desire to twine her fingers into the curls.

Past the expansive breadth of those shoulders, his body tapered down to a narrowed waist and trim hips. But it was the unexpected sight of his buttocks that drew a quick breath of appreciation from somewhere deep in the center of Celia's chest.

They were so exquisitely sculptured they might have been constructed of fine marble. Round and firm. And smooth. So damned smooth Celia imagined running her hands over the pair of them so she could determine for herself if there was any roughness to them.

She must have let out a noise more alarming than the intermittent pounding on the suite's door. There was no mistaking the fury of the person making all the racket.

Gabriel glanced over a shoulder, confusion etched across his features. Upon realizing Celia was staring unabashedly at his naked body, he grinned.

"Sorry, sugarplum, but you will become used to seeing me thus. I usually sleep in the nude."

Since his sleeping pants were unusable, Gabriel half turned and tugged the gold-colored coverlet from the bed. He quickly wrapped the length of damask around his waist but not before Celia glimpsed just a small portion of his impressive front. She blushed a fierce red, remembering how she'd boldly taken his flesh into her mouth. Remembering how much she liked it and how she'd felt like a beloved goddess suddenly subservient to a more powerful ruler.

Gabriel tsk-tsked. His eyes sparkled with mischievous intent. "Keep looking at me like that, pet, and I'll send whoever's pounding on that door straight to the Devil. Then, I'll make good on the invitation your eyes are extending."

Celia should have looked away with that ominous warning, but instead, her gaze locked with Gabriel's. As they measured one another for a long moment, a new sense of connectivity linked the two of them. Whatever happened from this day forward, they were in it together.

"Stay in here, Celia," Gabriel said in a more somber tone than before. "You aren't exactly dressed for company this early in the morning. And if trouble has come looking for us, I'd rather you not prove so accessible."

Wide-eyed, Celia nodded and watched as Gabriel padded from the bedroom and into the sitting room portion of the suite. As an afterthought, he drew the door behind him, leaving it cracked open so Celia was not left isolated.

The moment he was out of sight, Celia slid from the bed, pulling on the matching wrapper to her nightgown. She quickly hurried to the door and peered through the opening.

Gabriel strode across the room as best he could with a coverlet draped around his hips. He flung open the door with a low snarl.

"What the Devil do you want?"

The answer came in a swift punch to his jaw. Gabriel stumbled back, barely managing to maintain his grip on the coverlet.

"Where is she, you reprobate?" Tristan demanded in a low voice filled with rage. "Where is my sister?"

Gabriel rubbed his jaw and faced his new brother-in-law with a rueful shake of his head. "In my bed. Where she should be."

Tristan glared at Gabriel. "You just gave me the reason I need to kill you."

Gabriel's eyebrows rose high. "Why would you do that?"

"Why? It is enough that you have ruined her! Now, you are brazenly going about the business of shaming her. I'll have your head for this, Gabriel. Friend or no."

"Your sister has not suffered at my hand," Gabriel said calmly, brushing away a tiny drop of blood from his lower lip.

"What are you doing here anyway? Did you arrive with your parents?"

"The entire countryside is abuzz with news of your potential rise in station. Along with the rumor you have thoroughly compromised my sister," Tristan growled. "I came the moment I received word. And it doesn't matter, but I passed my parents on the road an hour ago. They told me of your plans to wed Celia, but I don't intend on allowing that to happen. Now, Rose, do you prefer pistols? Or rapiers?" The use of the old surname was done intentionally by Tristan. He did not know the title of Marquess was already bestowed upon Gabriel.

Celia pushed through the door, surprising both men with her sudden appearance. "You shall choose neither! Will you make me a widow before I've a chance to be a wife, brother?"

Tristan exhaled a sigh of relief upon seeing his sister, furious though she may be.

"Celia, sweetheart, are you all right?" Tristan exclaimed, stepping around Gabriel. He gave her a quick embrace, looking her over as if she suffered numerous injuries, although truly, he was the one who looked the worse for wear. His hair was wet and tangled from the wind and morning dew. His coat was askew, and his boots flecked with mud left imprints on the floor rug. Eyes wild and dark with worry, he examined her more closely. His jaw tightened when he realized she wore only her nightclothes. "What are you doing here in his chambers?"

Gabriel waved a hand in Celia's direction with an air of exasperation. "Explain it to him, pet. I doubt he will listen to me."

Tristan shot Gabriel a deadly stare before turning back to his sister.

"Come away with me, Celia," he urged in a heated plea. "I can scarcely believe Ravenswood approves of Gabriel's actions, but the moment our parents arrive we will leave Beaumont at once and—"

"I'm not leaving, Tristan, at least not until Gabriel decides we should. I am where I am meant to be. After all, we were married last night. A rather hasty ceremony, but one deemed necessary." Celia pulled her robe tighter around her body at Tristan's expression of confusion. "You see, Lord Harvey took it upon himself to try and abduct me to save me from marriage to Gabriel. It was decided I'd be safer as a marchioness, rather than just as the future fiancée of a marquess. This is why we did not wait for Mother and Father's arrival."

"Married," Tristan repeated the word as though in shock.

"That's right. Married." Gabriel raked a hand through his hair, settling the dark strands into some semblance of order. He tightened his grip on the coverlet. "Do you think I would dishonor Celia and the lord and lady of this house in such a manner were she not my wife?"

Before he could answer, Celia leveled a stern look upon Tristan. "Did you leave Violet behind? She let you come without her?"

"I came by horseback as it was the quickest way of reaching Beaumont. You know she's not an accomplished rider. Yet." Tristan had the good grace to look somewhat ashamed of his hasty rush to judgment. "She did beg me not to do anything foolish."

"And yet, here you are," Gabriel mumbled.

Celia quickly took Tristan's hands. "You have always been the impulsive one. But I adore you for caring about my welfare."

"Which is now mine to worry about," Gabriel reminded them both.

Tristan opened his mouth to respond, but a voice interrupted.

"A family reunion, is it?" Sebastian yawned, leaning against the doorjamb. He was dressed haphazardly in dark trousers and a white shirt that billowed open and revealed his wide chest. He was also barefoot, apparently forgoing shoes in the rush to Gabriel's suite.

"Ravenswood," Tristan acknowledged the earl with a nod of his head. "You must forgive my intrusion of your household this morning."

"My butler nearly broke a leg in his rush to inform me we'd been invaded by Viscount Longleigh on a mission to save his sister." Sebastian grinned. "And although my wife begged that I stay abed and not insert myself into the fray, I had to make sure there was no threat of bloodshed."

"As you can see, it is a family matter. One easily resolved," Gabriel replied calmly. "Longleigh has been assured of Celia's safety. As her husband, I appreciate his concern, even if it is now unnecessary."

"Quite so, Rosenthorne," Sebastian said. He motioned at the tight-jawed Tristan. "I'm positive the marquess understands the depths of your affection for your dear sister. But, my good man, you have interrupted their first morning as man and wife."

CELIA'S PARENTS arrived only hours later. Lord Darby, Gabriel, and Tristan immediately ensconced themselves in one of the drawing rooms to go over the details of the dowery, although Gabriel still insisted that the archaic practice was unnecessary.

Lady Darby retired to her previous guest room to rest following the long journey from Darby Woods.

Celia was completely prepared to pace outside the drawing room had Sara and Ivy not pulled her away for their own whispered conference.

"Was he gentle?" Sara asked with a frown.

"More importantly, did you enjoy it?" Ivy asked, her brow arching high.

Celia stopped herself from squirming under their very direct questions. She could not tell her two friends that nothing happened between her and Gabriel on their wedding night.

Well, almost nothing.

"Yes." She decided her answers would at least be honest, if not the complete truth of the situation. "Gabriel was surprisingly considerate, and it was not as painful as it could have been."

There.

That should satisfy the two women. God, is this what all married women did when given the chance? Discussed the merits of marital relationships and what occurred between man and wife as though it were part of everyday conversations?

Her cheeks pinkened at the thought of her friends learning exactly what she'd done last night.

"Oh, thank goodness," Ivy breathed in relief. "If you are blushing, then I'm convinced you found it pleasurable and my worry for your welfare is all for naught. We are very lucky women, Celia. We have husbands who care for our pleasure and will do anything to ensure it. Not many wives have this luxury. Treasure it."

Sara squeezed Celia's hand. "The best part is that it gets even better after the first time. I imagine the marquess will be hard pressed keeping his hands off you now. Lucky girl."

Celia could only nod as though in complete agreement, then with a silent sigh of gratitude, turned toward the drawing room as the door opened and the men filed out, Gabriel at the forefront. Seeing her father emerge with a pleased smile, Celia hurried to him and accepted his embrace.

Lord Darby pressed a kiss to Celia's temple. "It appears your mother's worries these past few years were unfounded, daughter. You've caught yourself a marquess. And a fine man at that." He nodded at Gabriel where he waited for them to join him for breakfast. "I know you will be very happy." Then Lord Darby winked at Celia and said under his breath, "And I've informed your husband that marquess or no, should I receive word of your unhappiness, it will be dealt with swiftly. But I doubt it will ever come to that. Your mother informed me, and I see it for myself. Rosenthorne is already enamored of you."

The following day, Celia and Gabriel prepared to climb into the carriage which would carry them to Rosenthorne Park.

Gabriel's personal items in his suite of rooms were being packed up and prepared for transfer to their new home while Lady Darby assured Celia the same was already done for her own belongings.

"I shall make sure all of your favorite things are sent to Rosenthorne Park, my darling," her mother said, dabbing at tears in the corners of her eyes. "I believe the marquess will take very good care of you, even if the circumstances of your wedding are a bit out of the ordinary. How I do wish I'd been here to see you walk down the aisle."

Celia patted her mother's arm, wishing her mother had been present as well. "I do regret the haste, Mother. And I do wish I could still travel with you to see Grace and Richeforte before the season begins. Perhaps, Rosenthorne and I may visit them after we are settled."

Lady Darby sniffed back more tears and enveloped Celia in a warm embrace. "I know this is all part of you having your own life, but it is still quite difficult to think you will no longer be at Darby Woods. I shall miss you dreadfully."

"You are always welcomed for a visit, my lady," Gabriel said to his mother-in-law while snaking an arm around Celia's waist. "In fact, everyone is welcome. Even you, Longleigh."

Tristan shot Gabriel a hard look. "If I suspect my sister is unhappy, you can bet that I will pay you a visit. Perhaps sooner than you might think.

Gabriel's shoulders lifted in a shrug. "Please do. And bring your lovely wife as well. I know Celia will enjoy seeing someone familiar."

Heath grinned at the back and forth between the two men. "We're all one big family now. I, for one, cannot wait for Christmas."

Lady Darby smiled at the man's good-natured teasing. "I'm sure it will be a grand time."

"We should be on our way, Celia. If we make good time, we should reach Rosenthorne Park by tomorrow afternoon." Gabriel squeezed her waist and Celia nodded in agreement. Then she found herself swallowing her tears as Tristan pulled her from Gabriel. He enfolded her in a warm embrace.

"Violet and I shall come as soon as it is agreeable to you both. And for all my blustering, I know Gabriel to be a good man. He will take care of you. I know he will." Tristan released her and clapped a hand on Gabriel's shoulder. "Watch over my sister, Rosenthorne."

"With my life," Gabriel replied. He stepped back then, allowing everyone else to say their goodbyes. And he remained stoic as his half-brother wrapped Celia in an enthusiastic hug.

"I shall see you soon, sweet sister," Heath said jovially. "If not at Banbury Lake, then most certainly at Rosenthorne."

His embrace was followed by several from both Ivy and Sara, and affectionate ones from Sebastian and Allan. Her father kissed Celia's cheek and shook Gabriel's hand.

"Be mindful of my daughter's wellbeing, Rosenthorne," he said.

Gabriel nodded. As if in afterthought, he pulled both Heath and Sebastian to the side of the circular drive, speaking in a low voice. Whatever he said apparently puzzled the two men for Sebastian's eyebrow lifted high and Heath frowned. But Celia had no opportunity to discover what their discussion could possibly be about because, with sudden finality, it was time to leave.

Gabriel handed Celia up into the coach on loan from the Ravenswood stables. Arion would be fetched at a later date as Gabriel did not trust anyone other than himself to ride the stallion.

Celia took the seat facing forward and waved out the glass window to her mother. Gabriel did not take the opposite seat. Instead, he settled in beside her, his wide shoulders turning so that he did not take up so much of the space.

How odd it felt to be leaving in such a manner. Unsupervised and alone with a man in the close quarters of a coach. Shooting a glance at Gabriel, she wondered if he felt the strangeness of the situation even more keenly than she did. After all, he'd arrived at Beaumont as a normal man. He left it as a highly connected marquess with an enormous estate and his own personal wealth.

"I hope you don't mind that I am sitting beside you," he murmured, watching as she blew a kiss to Sara and Ivy.

"I don't mind," she said quietly, turning back to him.

"I realize it is far more crowded this way, but I have difficulty when it comes to riding in reverse." He was almost sheepish while making this confession.

Celia's head tilted, waiting for further explanation as the coach lurched forward.

Gabriel grunted, bending his head so he could stare out the window beside him. "I become nauseous when occupying the jumpseat." The admission seemed pulled from him.

"I shall sit opposite of you, Gabriel. It does not bother me to ride in reverse."

It seemed impossible that this muscularly fit man possessed such a commonplace weakness. And that he was obviously embarrassed by its existence. The unexpected insight into her husband sent a tiny pang of tenderness straight through her heart.

Gathering her skirts, Celia went to move but Gabriel captured her wrist. He twined his fingers with her gloved ones.

"Stay beside me, Celia." His lips quirked with a rueful grin. "It's a long journey, but you and I shall alleviate the monotony together."

When they were younger, she and Tristan would play games while traveling. Usually, this dissolved into a rather serious competition over who counted the highest number of black sheep in passing fields.

She couldn't imagine Gabriel playing such games, even in jest.

Gabriel urged her closer until Celia was nestled under his arm. He smelled amazing and her cheeks flushed pink remembering how he'd bathed in the corner of the suite that very morning.

He'd not hid his nakedness. Celia found herself looking anywhere but his direction when he rose from the tub like a dripping wet Adonis. During her own bath the night before, he'd fled the suite and did not return until late in the night. She'd been asleep by then, but when he crawled beneath the coverlet, she naturally gravitated to his warmth.

It was puzzling that he'd not yet insisted on asserting his husbandly rights. She could not reason why he seemed determined not to touch her. She was his now. He was entitled to do whatever he wished and Celia almost wished he would. It would end this strange state of limbo between them.

"How will we do that?" she inquired, referring back to his statement of banishing boredom during their journey.

Gabriel simply grinned, his arms tightening around Celia's shoulders. "I shall come up with something, I'm sure."

CHAPTER 26

The first leg of the trip passed rather uneventfully. Celia was content watching the scenery pass by her window while Gabriel sat lost in his thoughts.

He'd never spent so much time alone with a woman before, at least not one who was truly a lady. Of course, there'd been many hours in the company of women whom he'd slept with, and a few of those ladies had been of the gentry. But those incidents were pale, colorless events when compared to the moments he enjoyed with Celia.

Everything about her was fascinating. From the curve of her jaw to the straight line of her nose. And her eyes. God help him, but staring into them was as if he were drowning in huge vats of melted chocolate. The sooty thickness of her lashes intrigued him with every downward sweep. He wondered what she was thinking as she stared out the window. Did she regret marrying a man who was essentially a stranger?

There were little things about his new wife that Gabriel wanted to peel away, layer by layer. Things like the unmistakable air of innocence that clung to her like a sweet perfume. Why was that, when she'd admitted she was no longer a virgin?

Who had she been with? Someone from her social circle? Someone she interacted with even now?

Despite his statement that he did not care what she'd done in the past, Gabriel was discovering that held no truth. He was not curious because of any censorship of her behavior, but rather he was ravenous to know what made his little wife who she truly was beneath that glittering social veneer. He wanted to know what made her laugh. Made her cry. What she liked most about him. Whether she liked her hands bound during sex or if she preferred to initiate exploration.

Yes, there were many things he'd yet to learn about Lady Celia Buchanan Rosenthorne. Many of those would be answered the first time they made love, and while he was dying to uncover every secret she possessed, he could not explain why he'd not taken her yet.

It had not felt right taking her under Ravenswood's roof. True, he'd already crossed so many boundaries when it came to establishing intimacy, but their first time together as man and wife should be done in his domain. In his home. In his bed. Where he was lord and master.

That type of chauvinistic attitude was commonplace among the *ton*. Gabriel attributed his own tendencies to the fact he was naturally dominant. Regardless of his upbringing and new elevation to Marquess, he'd always dictated his own path in life. He'd done as he pleased, when he pleased, with whomever he pleased. From the age of sixteen, he'd charted his own course and people followed him because of it.

Life as a marquess would probably exacerbate this forceful trait he carried. He already recognized the change in his demeanor. He demanded and others obeyed, or at the very least, deferred to his wishes.

It was partly the reason he'd instructed Sebastian and Heath to see to Lord Harvey's release from the constable's custody. Now that Gabriel was wed to Celia, the man wouldn't dare infringe on his claim. He no longer posed a threat and had hopefully learned a valuable lesson.

Staring at the slender fingers of his wife's hand as she absently removed her traveling gloves, Gabriel wondered how well Celia would accept being commanded. She would probably resist at first, but he sensed a submissive spirit hiding behind all of her feistiness. He would delight in uncovering it for their mutual pleasure and bringing it to the surface.

Only one more night to endure, this one spent in a sleepy inn on the road to Rosenthorne Park, and then he would find out for himself if his wife would do anything he asked of her.

CELIA NAPPED CUDDLED against Gabriel as the coach moved in almost a measured cadence. The drivers called out to the horses occasionally, and the popping of a whip interspersed their shouted commands. The vehicle's rocking motion was often jolted by a wheel landing in a hole and rolling through it, but it was a much smoother ride than it might have been.

How Celia slept at all was a mystery. This journey was an excellent reminder of why Gabriel preferred riding as a means of travel. While traveling by coach was intended as a comfortable way of reaching one's destination, the brawniness of his size made that impossible. His shoulders took up most of the seat's cushioned back, and his legs, when stretched, reached the opposite bench with no room to spare.

He shifted in an attempt at becoming more comfortable, and in doing so, disturbed Celia's slumber. Her brow creased in a tiny frown as she tried readjusting her cramped position.

I should move to the opposite bench. She'll have more room and I can watch over her.

But even the thought of riding in reverse made Gabriel's mouth water with sour nausea. This particular weakness was a curse. It was not just carriages which had this effect on him. Traveling by boat did as well. He'd thought he would actually perish when crossing from France to England alongside Sebastian two years ago.

"So, it's seasickness bringing the mighty Gabriel Rose down to his knees?" Sebastian had laughingly asked while Gabriel hung his head over the side of the ship that first hour on board. He'd not had the strength or willpower to dispute the earl's assumption then.

The memory brought a wry grin to Gabriel's features. That was the last time he'd been on the water for any reason. Even now, he was loathe to even try paddling a rowboat around a small pond.

Celia sighed, making a little sound of frustration as she moved her shoulders until she sat upright rather than snuggled under Gabriel's arm. There *was* a simple solution. He could move, giving her the entire bench.

Gritting his teeth, Gabriel slowly slid Celia away from his body. He lowered her to the bench while at the same time, he moved to the opposite side.

For a long moment, he quietly sat as the coach rocked along. It was a beautiful day, the sun shining bright overhead as the noon hour approached. Soon, they would stop to water the horses and dine on the meal Ivy had Cook prepare for them and the coach drivers. Packed in an enclosed wicker basket, it barely fit in the baggage compartment when the luggage was also added.

Gabriel leaned against the seat cushion. Perhaps this wasn't as bad as he remembered, this riding backward. If he concentrated hard, he could almost forget he was not facing forward.

Glancing at Celia, now stretched on the opposite bench like a cat lounging in the sun, made matters much easier to bear. She mumbled in utter contentment, her body curved into a fetal position and head pillowed by an outstretched arm. Her opposite hand curled under her chin, and the traveling gloves she'd held in her lap for the last hour drifted to the floor in a small heap of blush pink kid leather.

Gabriel decided he would retrieve them in a few minutes. Right now, he found enjoyment in watching Celia sleep. Her expressions, from pensive to relaxed, proved endlessly fascinating. Enough that he could almost ignore his increasing nausea.

The coach hit a rather nasty rut in the road, and Gabriel bit back a groan while at the same time reaching out to steady Celia on her solitary bench. He did not wish to see her go flying off the cushion. Using his hand, he braced it upon her hip and held her in place.

Another hole and Gabriel felt sweat bead up along the edge of his hairline. A grunt slipped from his throat as the coach lurched sideways.

Damn it to hell.

With a deep breath, he leaned forward, placing his elbows on his knees. Concentrating on Celia's features might help steady his constitution. He took another deep breath, dropping his head in an effort to quell the sickness.

When his head lifted, it was to find Celia's eyes wide open, watching him.

"Why are you over there, Gabriel?"

Her question was softly asked. Concern glinted in the chocolate depths of her gaze.

"Watching you." His reply was just as soft.

"But your aversion—"

"Doesn't matter."

He reached out, brushing back an ebony curl that had fallen over her brow. Celia moved as if to sit up but Gabriel stopped her. His hand lightly gripped her shoulder, keeping her in a prone position.

"Stay as you are," he murmured, swallowing hard when the coach lurched in the opposite direction.

"No," Celia said. "This is silly. And I'll not have it." She brushed away his hand and pushed herself up. "Come here."

Grasping a handful of Gabriel's coat lapel, Celia tugged him back onto the bench beside her. Then, in a surprising move, she hitched up her skirts and straddled him as though he were a new pony.

"There," she breathed through a smile. "That's much better, don't you think?"

"Just what do you think you are doing, Celia?" Gabriel gritted through his teeth.

"Making you forget about being sick," she whispered, running a hand through the thickness of his hair. Her fingers lightly traced the pale white scar tracking diagonally through his eyebrow. "How did you get this, Gabriel? I've always wondered and now… now, I've the courage to ask."

"It doesn't matter."

She frowned but her fingers remained gentle, ghosting over the old wound until Gabriel wanted to close his eyes and muzzle into the palm of her hand. "To me it does."

A bump in the road sent Celia's lower body colliding with his in the best way possible. It was like a lightning bolt striking between his legs. He tensed, trying to stave off the urge to grind his growing erection against her softness.

"May I kiss you, Gabriel?" Her voice was low and husky, her eyes dancing with mysterious lights. "And for every kiss, will you tell me one of your secrets?"

"You never need permission to kiss me, sugarplum. All of those belong to you now. But if we are to trade secrets, I will demand the same of you. All those you carry deep inside you are mine now. And I will have them. One by one or all at once."

Her features immediately tightened, the teasing mood evaporating like the morning mist. "I've no more secrets to tell."

Gabriel's hand wrapped lightly around her throat, his thumb teasing the pulse beating there in the delicate hollow. "But I think you do. And as I said, those belong to me now. Everything about you is mine." His free hand slipped around her body and cupped one of her buttocks in a firm grip. Even through the fabric of her gown and her underclothes, his fingers were hard reminders of his overwhelming strength. He was so much larger than she. So much stronger.

Her breath came in short gasps of air as he simply held her in place, poised like a beautiful statue on his thighs.

"Gabriel…"

His name fluttered on her lips in a plea for more.

"Yes, pet," he rasped. "A secret for a kiss. Starting this very moment." His fingers tightened slowly, both around her neck and on her buttocks. "You go first."

Her eyes flared with heat. "That is unfair. I asked you first. And I was distracting you from being ill."

Gabriel chuckled. He found it amusing how she believed she had the upper hand. While her ploy did work—his nausea had passed—she'd soon learn he controlled their interactions. Yes, she held the power to determine their duration, but he held the reins to the outcome.

"And I've said before that you will find many things to be unfair as my wife. As my marchioness." He tilted her head back by exerting pressure at the nape of her neck. "Now, do you want that kiss or not? A secret first."

She trembled at the sternness of his voice, and just when Gabriel thought their game was at its end, she licked her lips.

The motion made his cock twitch, remembering how she used those lips on him just two nights ago.

"I've never felt this way with anyone but you, Gabriel. You —" She swallowed hard. "You make me feel wild. Uncontrolled. Like something that must be tamed."

Her confession hung in the air between them, flushing her cheeks with the prettiest blush of honesty.

"Well done, Celia. You've earned that kiss. Good girl."

Her pupils dilated with something Gabriel recognized quite well. Lust. Pleasure. Surrender.

With a low growl, he crashed his mouth to hers, kissing her with all the pent-up frustrations swarming through his brain and body. It was not a gentle, sweet kiss, but one harsh and insistent, demanding she give him the rest of her secrets.

He was becoming addicted to the thought of taking them.

Celia kissed him back with a moan of sweet surrender, falling into him and letting him arrange her as he desired. Her sex pressed against his own. Heat built like an inferno as their tongues clashed and mated and sought the hidden pieces of each other's souls.

The absence of the coach's rocking motion alerted Gabriel that they'd stopped. With a growl of frustration, he swung Celia off his lap. She landed in a flurry of skirts beside him with flushed cheeks and reddened lips. She also had the pink imprint of his fingers against the creamy skin of her throat.

She stared at him in a daze. "Why did you stop?"

Gabriel straightened his coat and then twitched her skirts into place. "We've stopped to water the horses and to eat the noon meal if you like. The drivers require rest as well."

"Oh," Celia said, her cheeks blushing even redder than before. "I didn't realize…"

Gabriel captured her hand, lacing his fingers with hers and bringing them to his mouth to press a soft kiss upon her bare knuckles. "It is understandable, pet. It's easy getting lost in our kisses. I look forward to the moment I do not have to stop."

CHAPTER 27

After pulling into a small copse of trees and eating their lunch, Gabriel aided Celia back into the coach and they continued on their way. The sun had already sunk below the horizon when the vehicle rattled into the courtyard of the inn where they would stay the night.

"Stay close to me, Celia," Gabriel instructed as he helped her step down from the coach. "While reputable and the proprietor is an honest man, ruffians are always a possibility at places such as these."

As inns went, The Gilded Rooster was better than most. The sheets were clean, the food plain but wholesome, and the innkeeper and his employees were attentive to their guests. Gabriel considered this establishment to be one the safer places he'd stayed, but that assessment came before the acquisition of a beautiful, wealthy wife who needed protection from vagabonds and thieves.

With a possessive hand on her elbow, he escorted Celia to the crowded main dining room and selected a table near the fireplace. His size and warning glare discouraged many a man's interest in their arrival.

A pretty, dark-haired barmaid placed a mug of ale in front of Gabriel, her face wide with a smile. "I thought it would be a few months before you came back this way. It's good to see I was wrong."

Celia's head tilted in question, her gaze darting from the girl to Gabriel.

"Hello, Tessa," Gabriel replied quietly, nodding toward Celia. "A glass of sherry for the lady, if you please."

Tessa glanced toward Celia as if noticing her for the first time. "We do not have sherry. Water, perhaps?"

"Wine, then," Gabriel answered for Celia. He watched her during the entire exchange with Tessa. He had a fair idea of what his wife was thinking when it came to his involvement with the barmaid. And while he had slept with the girl many months ago, he had no intention of doing it again. Marriage for him meant fidelity. He would not break his vows for any reason.

Tessa shot him an exasperated look but scurried off as Celia glanced around the large, noisy room with great interest.

"Obviously, you've been here before. Tessa is a good friend, it seems." Celia's gaze returned to clash with his. The chocolate depths of her eyes glittered with an emotion that might have been jealousy. "Should I be concerned about other barmaids?"

Gabriel's mouth twitched in a smile. "She's not a friend. But I did share a few nights with her, if that is your concern."

He did not miss seeing the hurt he'd caused his wife. Her eyes watered and her chin trembled the slightest bit before she tossed it higher.

"I'm not an imbecile, Gabriel," she flung at him. "I'm quite aware you slept with the girl. She just devoured you with her eyes as if you were a meal."

"A long time ago," he finished quietly for her. "Celia, it was a very long time ago."

Her lips tightened. "It must have been quite memorable."

Gabriel took a sip of the ale. "For Tessa, perhaps. Not for me."

Tessa returned just then with the glass of wine. Setting it down without so much as a glance spared for Celia, she focused her attention on Gabriel.

"Will you be needing two rooms then?" The girl's tone was seductive while reeking of familiarity. And she moved so close that her upper waist brushed against Gabriel's shoulder. She then made a great show of bending over to check his mug of ale, her breasts on display in the low-cut gown.

"Just one," Gabriel replied. "It's already arranged."

Celia's temper was rising. The look she gave the barmaid was nothing short of murderous. Gabriel could not help the thrill of pleasure coursing through him at the thought of Celia's possible jealousy.

"Oh. A room for the lady, of course. We're terribly busy, as you can see." Tessa's tone was smug. "But you've no need to sleep in the stables, Gabriel. I'm sure accommodations may be found, same as last time." Her giggle left no doubt as to her invitation. "You were quite satisfied with them, as I recall."

"Why should my husband be required to spend the night in the stables?" Celia asked, ice dripping from her voice. "Or anywhere other than with myself?"

Gabriel bit back another grin. He would not allow this to go too far, but he was wildly curious about this side of his new wife.

Tessa's attention turned to Celia, her jaw slackened with confusion. "Husband? Gabriel married you, did he?"

Celia stood slowly, staring the other woman down as though she might leap across the table and begin a brawl. The interaction between the two women was drawing attention. Other patrons nudged each other, nodding in Celia's direction with hungry, curious stares.

"Tessa!" The innkeeper shouted from the other side of the

room. "You've other tables, girl. Get these ales and leave Lord and Lady Rosenthorne be."

Tessa's eyes widened. Her gaze bounced between Gabriel and Celia. "Lord Rosenthorne?"

"The new Marquess, if you must know," Celia nearly growled at the dumbstruck woman. "And my new husband."

"Sit down, Celia," Gabriel said in a low voice. "The men in this room are enjoying your display of temper entirely too much for my liking."

Celia's eyes flashed with rebellion, but she sank back into her chair as he commanded. Her eyebrow arched high as she stared at Gabriel. "Dearest husband, Tessa did not realize you are the new Marquess of Rosenthorne?"

Gabriel shrugged his massive shoulders. "Word has gotten around, but obviously she did not."

"Tessa!" Mister Jonsey yelled again over the joviality of the room. "The ales, for damnation's sake!"

Tessa seemed shellshocked. An expression of disappointment crossed her features. Grimacing, she dropped a quick curtsey directed at both Gabriel and Celia. "Beg your pardon, milady. Milord. I must see to the other tables now."

While she hurried away, Celia leveled a glare at Gabriel. "How long would you have allowed that to go on?"

"I'm not sure. I'm still unaccustomed to being Lord Rosenthorne. It's easy to forget sometimes I have a new identity," he replied casually. "What I was then and what I am now will surely clash on occasion."

Celia's eyes flared with helpless anger. "I meant that woman's shameless flirtation. You were doing nothing to stop it."

"Are you jealous, sugarplum?" Reaching for Celia's hand, Gabriel rubbed a thumb over the blue stone of her wedding ring.

"Don't be ridiculous," she snapped. "I merely despise being made to look foolish."

She was angry, but she did not pull her hand away. Gabriel realized she was searching for a means of steadying herself. He was her balance in this world now, and their connection was paramount to this marriage being a successful one.

"It is perfectly all right to be jealous, Celia. I know I am. For example, should any man in this room think twice about taking you from me, I'd have his head on a platter. Perhaps I would even serve it to his friends. Just so everyone would know how deadly serious I am when it comes to protecting what is mine." Another sip of his ale, and he said, "Your reaction to a rather forward barmaid is an encouraging development. I think I rather like that fierce side of you."

Celia's stiffened. "I would like to retire to our room now."

Gabriel frowned. "Without your dinner? I won't allow that. You must eat. There's another long day ahead of us tomorrow, and I'll not have you weakened from lack of sustenance."

"I'm not hungry."

Her stubbornness was going to get her in trouble if she wasn't careful.

Gabriel smiled with a little tsk of disappointment. "I did not ask if you are hungry, Celia. I said you must eat. And you will." His manner remained calm as he spoke, but a thread of determination wove through his words.

Celia's rebellious side flared.

"I shall go to our room on my own if you are going to be so beastly. I do not require your escort."

She went to stand, but Gabriel halted her immediately. His hand snaked out, snagging her wrist in a tight grip. He squeezed until she sucked in a breath. "You've no idea how beastly I can truly be, *mon douce fille*. I would suggest you cease this attempt at making me angry, lest you find out."

"I'm making *you* angry?" Her eyebrows shot upward, twin

arches of indignation. "I'm retiring, Gabriel. Whether you like it or not. You are my husband, not my master."

Gabriel gave her a considering look as a tiny smile lifted the corners of his mouth. Still keeping hold of her wrist, he raised his free hand and summoned the innkeeper. As the man hurried over, his expression harried from dealing with the many patrons crowded into the dining area, Gabriel downed the remainder of his ale.

"Mister Jonsey, will you please see that two meals are delivered up to our room? My wife is feeling unwell and requires my immediate attention."

CELIA FLOUNCED AHEAD of Gabriel as they traipsed the inn's corridors to reach their assigned room even as her husband held fast to her arm. His fingers were a tight vise wrapping just above her elbow, and while a relaxed smile played about his lips, she felt the tension coursing through him.

Truly, she did not understand just why she was in fact so very angry with him. He could not be held accountable for situations in his past, just as she could not be held responsible for her own. Perhaps Gabriel was correct in his assessment, however. Maybe she was jealous.

Jealous of a pretty barmaid with intimate knowledge of her husband.

I should not care how many women he's been with. I shouldn't. And I'm not. I just prefer not having them so blatantly paraded in front of me. And I won't be commanded as though I am some hapless pet he's recently acquired. I will do just as I please. As I've always done.

"Your thoughts are so very loud, Celia. I hear every single one of them." Using a key, Gabriel turned the lock on the door to their room and pushed her inside. "In a few moments, you will lack the ability to think at all. You will only be able to feel."

Giving him a mutinous glare, Celia stood by the window. A few of their bags had previously been placed there by the two Ravenswood coach drivers. Those same men were down in the dining room, enjoying a pint of ale. They'd watched closely when Celia confronted the barmaid. She knew they were also there for her protection. To assist Gabriel if any trouble should emerge during the trip to Rosenthorne.

The corner room was probably the largest The Gilded Rooster offered their guests. It was brightly lit with the warm glow of lamps and a small fire burning in the grate. A bed which appeared surprisingly comfortable was positioned in front of a second window while a sturdy dressing table occupied the other corner. Its mirror reflected Celia where she stood. There was even a small table flanked by two oak chairs where one could sit and dine.

Gabriel closed the room's door and, with deliberate movements, removed his suit coat. It was thrown over the edge of the bed.

"Take off your gloves, Celia."

For a brief second, she considered disobeying him. Perhaps he ordered other women around, women like that silly Tessa, but she would not be bullied. Her chin tilted higher.

Gabriel's scarred eyebrow rose slightly, daring her to attempt defiance.

With a shrug, Celia abruptly stripped the gloves away. She threw them so they landed on top of his coat.

Without a word, Gabriel caught one of the two chairs with the toe of his boot and dragged it away from the table. Sitting down, he watched her silently for a long moment, then said, "Remove your travel jacket."

Celia grit her teeth. Would he have her disrobe completely

before him? While he sat like a king on a wooden throne and commanded her?

"You've no need for it here, pet."

That was true. Beneath the emerald green, short-waisted jacket was a lovely gown of a paler shade of green, its trim matching the jacket.

Gabriel leaned forward, resting his forearms on the top of his thighs. Peering at her from beneath a sweep of dark eyelashes, he said, "You will do as I say, Celia. Even if you are angry with me."

She nearly stomped her foot in her fury. "No, I will not."

"You are racking up quite a list of infractions." His smile was dangerous, sending a responding heat trickling through Celia's veins. She shivered although she was becoming quite warm from his gaze. "Not including those incurred before our marriage."

He might have been the Devil himself in that moment. Staring at him from across the room, Celia made note of the silky darkness of his hair. The fiery light in his eyes. The way his lips curved upward in a smirk constructed of both sinful pleasures and punishments.

"I will find great enjoyment in collecting your penance." His voice was a low husky promise.

Before Celia could respond, a knock came at the door.

"Who is it?" Gabriel called out, keeping Celia pinned to the spot with the fierceness of his gaze.

"Tessa, milord. With your supper."

Celia snorted in disgust, whirling away so she now faced the window. Pulling the curtain back slightly, she could see out into the dark night and the courtyard below illuminated by lamplight.

But what held her attention was the wavy reflection in the glass of the room behind her. She watched as Gabriel rose from the chair and unlocked the door. Tessa entered with a small cart holding two covered platters, a bottle of wine, and two goblets.

Tessa looked from Celia to Gabriel, head cocked as though aware of the tension between the couple. In the window's reflection, Celia saw the young woman lean against Gabriel and whisper in his ear.

Celia's lips tightened. *Brazen tart.*

Gabriel took a step back with a barely imperceptible shake of his head. "This is all we require tonight, Tessa. You may come back in the morning and retrieve the cart."

Tessa frowned at the dismissal, but she obeyed Gabriel. Celia huffed again. No doubt, that woman had been on the receiving end of many an order from Gabriel Rose. Her single-minded pursuit betrayed the depths of her interest in the man.

Once the door closed again, Gabriel resumed his seat in the oak chair. The suppers waiting on the cart were ignored as he rolled up his shirtsleeves to expose leanly muscled forearms.

"Come to me, Celia."

His voice was a low rumble that did such strange things to Celia's insides. She dared not look at him for fear she would launch herself into his arms. Why she felt so tightly wound, like a string ready to snap, she wasn't sure. There was electricity in the room now, its sudden appearance turning things dark and murky. Whatever this man meant to do, she suspected she would allow.

Willingly, or perhaps not.

"No," Celia said in a voice that trembled with exquisite anticipation and only a small amount of dread.

"No?" He echoed her refusal as though surprised to hear it. "That was not a request, wife. Come here so we may address this matter properly."

"Will you snap your fingers next?" Celia whirled around; her eyes blazing with uncertainty and irrational anger. "Summon me like a stray foxhound to your side?"

"If need be," Gabriel replied calmly. "Although I doubt that will work with you. Bringing you to heel will require different measures."

"Bring me to heel?" Celia stared at him in disbelief while repeating his words.

The next moment she was striding across the room. Upon reaching him, her hand flew with the intent of delivering a resounding slap across his handsome face.

Gabriel caught her wrist before the blow could land. A split second later, his boot swung out, taking her feet out from under her so that she tumbled awkwardly across his lap. With quick, precise movements, he arranged her body. She was thrown over one knee, his other leg trapping both of hers while effectively pinning her in place. His heavy arm and huge hand splayed across her lower back.

Celia was so stunned that she was speechless. Then fury erupted like a wild summer storm.

Squealing with alarm, she twisted and turned in a futile attempt at escape.

Gabriel chuckled at her efforts which only infuriated her even more.

"Be still, my little thorny sugarplum. And refrain from crying out as well. That is, unless you enjoy having an audience."

That ominous threat succeeded in arresting Celia's movements. Horrified that he might actually follow through on his statement, she immediately stopped struggling.

"See? You *can* obey my commands without creating greater problems for yourself." Gabriel was the embodiment of serenity. His hand continued pressing down on her back, his fingers splayed wide. "Being a brat is never acceptable, but I know how to handle you when you act like this. And I imagine, given your nature, this will be a common occurrence."

Celia choked on an enraged sob, but even so, she did not move. Instead, she hung over his knee in a state of suspended trepidation. She was becoming lightheaded. Whether that was from her current position or the impossible situation, she did not know.

"Now, let us sort this out in a manner which will bring us both resolution. It is acceptable that you have strong feelings when it comes to our marriage. I have them as well. I understand this lashing out is simply your way of dealing with your emotions. Emotions you've probably never experienced before. You are frightened of what is to come in our marriage. Worried about being a wife in a new home and with new responsibilities. This is all new to you, but you must remember it is new to me as well." Gabriel sighed, and with his free hand began pulling the pins from her hair and tossing them aside. Eventually, her coiffure unraveled enough that the tresses tumbled down her back in a cascade of ebony-hued waves. "What I am about to do will accomplish two goals."

"And those are?" Celia bit out in a strangled voice. He sounded so caring and protective when he spoke like this. All while threatening to punish her. She did not understand why the two sentiments meshed so well when he addressed her. Nor why she liked it so much.

"It is my duty to ease your anxiety and prove my complete and utter devotion to you." Gabriel's head bent closer, his breath warm in her ear. "So, I will allow you to stand, Celia, but you must do exactly as I say. Do you understand?"

Celia wished for the strength to tell him to go to the Devil, but her body was clamoring for something. Something that was turning her into a needy, desperate mess. Unable to form a rational thought. Unable to think of a reason why she shouldn't do as Gabriel demanded.

"Celia, I am waiting for an answer."

Her head jerked in a nod. "Yes. I understand."

"Good girl. Now, up you go."

The firm, praising quality of his words had the surprising effect of melting Celia's worry away. How odd that she experienced a wave of calm. She felt it in her bones as she slid from his lap and stood, aided by Gabriel's hands guiding her.

"Remove your traveling garments."

The command gave her pause, but an arch of his eyebrow reminded her she'd just agreed to do as he instructed.

Although disrobing would be easier if she had a maid, she managed well enough. In a matter of minutes, she'd removed the gown and now stood dressed only in a light corset, an ivory-hued chemise with matching stockings, and her undergarments. She also retained the shoes because when she bent to remove them, Gabriel made a noise in his throat and shook his head.

His eyes raked over her form, turning darker by the minute, the pupils eating up the irises until they were shimmering pools of deep brown.

"Celia," his voice cracked a little. "You are truly the most beautiful thing I've ever seen. I can scarcely believe you are mine."

Celia ducked her head, blushing from the compliment. Her hands came up to cover her breasts, which seemed so very exposed, but he stopped her once again.

"Do not hide from me, Celia." His breath was harsher now, and a darkened intensity permeated the room, matching his demeanor.

Her hands dropped to her sides, waiting for his next instruction and hating herself for wanting to do whatever would please him.

"Do you see the dressing table there? I want you leaning over it, facing the mirror with your backside to me."

Celia paused. It was a position which would display her body in the most brazen way.

"But before you do…" Gabriel's voice was a silky caress of all things wicked and sinful. "You will remove everything with the exception of your stockings."

He wanted her completely naked? Celia's heart stuttered. She wasn't sure she could do that. Everything inside her rebelled at the thought of being so exposed. She must have appeared somewhat dazed because Gabriel cupped her chin in the cage of his large, warm hand.

"Remember what I've told you about breathing, pet," Gabriel said, his eyes blazing as he stared down at her. "This will help you work through all the emotions you are feeling right now. I promise you."

"I'm not angry anymore," she whispered desperately.

He only smiled as though he knew she was attempting to avoid whatever he had planned.

"Remove your clothes, Celia."

There seemed to be nothing else she could do but submit. Closing her eyes, Celia spun around.

"You must undo the laces." She was surely blushing bright pink from head to toe with embarrassment.

"Of course, sugarplum."

She stood quivering, waiting for the feel of his fingers tugging at the corset's ribbons. But he seemed content to let her wait for it was several seconds before she heard him rise from the chair and approach her.

"Do you remember I once told you I would happily take the job of dressing and undressing you, Celia?" His voice was a husky murmur as he reached for the ribbons. A few sharp tugs and the boned corset sagged forward, slack enough that Gabriel could draw it over her head, and then it was tossed aside. The warmth of his body seared her backside as he came closer. "My desire for that has not lessened. Indeed, seeing you like this only increases my need for every part of you."

His fingers trailed the outline of her bare shoulder blade with the delicate violence of a firebrand. Celia shivered when she heard the raw desire in his tone.

Then cool air brushed her skin as he stepped away.

"Continue," he ordered softly.

She could not turn and face him as she stepped out of her underdrawers and pulled the chemise over her head. But she felt the heat of his gaze looking his fill of her naked back and bare buttocks. The blush staining her skin deepened.

"So lovely," Gabriel murmured in appreciation. Then in a sharper tone, he said, "Over the dressing table, Celia. Reach your arms out to the sides and grasp the edges."

For the first time in five years, Celia found herself wishing for complete darkness. Biting her bottom lip, she mustered her courage and padded over to the piece of furniture. With a deep breath, she bent over and then sucked in a gasp when the cool wood came into contact with her tightly budded nipples.

"How gorgeous you are when you obey me, Celia. You are in the perfect position for both punishment and pleasure. Press your cheek to the table's surface. Stay just like that, and I swear there will be more rapture than pain."

She knew when Gabriel came closer because the air in the room changed. It swirled with his lust and her fear of the unknown. A bead of sweat formed between her breasts and rolled down until it was absorbed by the oak.

Gabriel gathered her hair, pulling it so it draped over her shoulder in a silky cascade of ebony waves

The sudden slap to one buttock took her by surprise. Jolting forward from the contact, she choked on a cry.

"Stay where you are, Celia," he warned. In quick succession, he delivered two more swats that had her biting her bottom lip even harder to contain a sob.

"That, sweetheart, was owed for the night we became engaged. The night I warned you there were consequences for playing your damnable games despite my warnings. Do you understand?"

"Y-yes," she managed.

"And this is for this evening. It is not so much of a punishment as it is a way of helping you understand how things will be between us. Sometimes, there will be discomfort before there is satisfaction. For both of us."

Before Celia could even fathom what he meant by that, the palm of his hand landed another six, no, eight more times on her bottom. But with the sharp, stinging sensation came an unexpected sense of relief. Maybe even a bit of pride because, although Gabriel struck her soundly and without mercy, Celia remained in the position he wanted.

Flat across the dressing room table, fingers digging into the oak wood.

She did not realize tears were rolling down her cheeks until Gabriel's palm smoothed over both her buttocks, his touch easing away some of the pain. She relaxed into his touch as though it were a healing balm.

"There now, pet. It's over." He leaned over her, his bare chest grazing her back.

When did he remove his shirt?

With a gentle finger, he swiped one of her tears up and sucked it into his mouth. "Now comes your reward. Spread your legs for me, Celia."

Celia did not even question the why of it. She reacted simply out of instinct, her legs moving apart as though they were independent of her willpower.

Gabriel's mouth touched the place between her shoulder blades. Softly. Reverently. He traced the line of her backbone, his lips hot and warm on her skin. Moving even further down, his hands palmed her buttocks in worship of her shape.

Fingers massaged her flesh, feathering away all of the aches until Celia could think of nothing but the building pleasure. When his mouth suddenly moved over the curve of one full cheek, his tongue swiping the satiny expanse in a lavish caress, Celia gasped in shock.

A tiny whimper escaped her throat when Gabriel gripped her hips. He kept her in place, the brutal tenderness of his fingers biting into her skin. "Stay, Celia." His whisper skated across her flesh, chasing the goosebumps that popped up.

Then she sensed him crouching down lower and lower still, until his mouth was suddenly between her legs. Hot and invasive, his tongue traced the outer folds of her sex as he nuzzled deeper into her.

"Gabriel!" Celia cried out, her fingers digging into the edges of the table. Everything inside her, every emotion and the pulsating of her veins pooled where his wicked mouth was centered. "Oh, God. Please… please… *more*."

"You will not beg God for your pleasure. You will beg me."

A thousand needles of pleasure encroached all at once. Gabriel growled, his tongue sweeping through the moisture seeping from her body. He sucked at it with a greedy hunger, his teeth grazing her button of nerves until Celia nearly screamed from the intensity of it. Before she knew what he was about, Gabriel's tongue sharpened into a point. He speared it at that little button over and over until Celia was shattering into a million pieces. Flung through the universe and all the stars as if she were a flaming arrow.

Gabriel feasted fully on her, never letting up as she rode the waves and trembled with the aftershocks. Only when she whimpered did he show mercy. The caress gentled into a slow, intense worship.

The climax left her shaken. Weak. Delirious. Never had she gone through such an experience before. She did not know how she remained upright. Her legs were as wobbly as a newborn filly.

One of his hands left her hip, and a second later there was the sound of fabric rustling as he stood to his full height. Celia knew what it meant, but she could not bring herself to move away. She could not even muster the strength to close her legs. Instead, she remained draped across the table in languid contentment.

"I cannot wait any longer to claim you, my sweet Celia. Thorns or no, I'm taking you now." Gabriel's arm inserted itself between the tabletop and her abdomen. He lifted her from the desk, and Celia instinctively braced herself with palms flat on the wood.

Their eyes met and clashed in the mirror's reflection. Celia could not look away from the half-crazed desire she saw in Gabriel's features. He looked wild. Savage. Feral.

And she looked the same.

There was no other sound in the room than their harsh breathing until Gabriel spoke.

"Will you be mine at last, Celia Rosenthorne?"

The question was unexpected.

Celia's heart twisted with that surprising pang of tenderness. Once again, Gabriel was on the verge of madness, and yet he asked permission before claiming what was his.

How could she deny him what they both wanted? Even if she was terrified by the thought of how it would surely hurt, there was no question of surrender.

When she slowly nodded, an expression of savage gratitude flashed across her husband's face. Her head dropped, waiting for him to begin.

With one arm still wrapped around her waist, he used his free hand to gather her hair. The unruly mass of ebony waves was quickly wrapped twice around his fist. A rope he would use as a means of control.

He tugged until Celia had no choice but to meet his gaze in the mirror.

"You will watch me as I fuck you, sweet wife. You will not look away as I make you mine. And do not bow your head to me. I may occasionally place you on your knees, but you are a goddamn marchioness and you bow to no one. Including me."

CHAPTER 29

Celia's eyes blazed as she returned his stare. Gabriel was positive he'd never seen a more glorious sight than the mirror's reflection. His wife was surely what God intended as perfection when he created women. Her breasts, high and firm, were just the right size for his hands to cup, her nipples a shade reminiscent of dusky pink roses. Their coloring was an entrancing contrast to the startling warm ivory hue of her skin. His arm, where it wrapped about her waist, was so much darker than her tender flesh. To the point he could pose as a pirate, marauding and taking what he willed from a captive maiden.

Keeping Celia's head tilted back, Gabriel moved his arm from her waist. The sweet flare of her hip called for his hand; he gripped the flesh there in a subtle warning that she maintain her position. Ass out toward him, hands bracing her upper body on the dressing table, and her back arched until her breasts jutted out as if she wanted her nipples to kiss the cold surface of the mirror.

"Yes, Celia. Just like that. Stay. Stay like that as I slide inside of you. This time, I want to see your face when you come. I want to see you explode for me." As he spoke, Gabriel maneuvered into position, sliding up behind her until his cock hungrily thrust in the direction of her core. Celia let out a soft moan when she felt him there, so huge, so hot and hard. So ready. He was going crazy with anticipation, but something kept him from surging forward in a greedy rush.

His cock nudged her opening, and he nearly combusted when he felt the soft, silky wetness of her earlier orgasm. Easing his way until only the flared head of his sex was inside her, he kept a tight grip on her hair, keeping her head tilted back so he could watch her face.

He wanted to see her eyes as he claimed her. See everything she was experiencing. See just what he did to her and what she did to him in return. He wanted to go slow.

But she was making that incredibly hard. She was so goddamn tight. So lush and wet. An inferno of lust and desire. She was everything goddesses were made of, and he was merely a man. A man unable to contain his need for her.

With a groan, Gabriel thrust further inside her, watching as Celia's eyes widened with shock and pleasure. He wasn't even in halfway, and already her inner walls were clenching around his girth as if in protest of his size. Yes, he was large, but it wasn't as though she were a virgin and incapable of taking all of him.

Do not think of the men she's been with.

"Fuck, you are so tight, pet. I feel you squeezing my cock with every breath you take. I feel your heat burning me. Your deliciously wet quim sucking me in deeper," he whispered, leaning forward and nipping at her neck. "And I already know just how splendid you taste. I'm still licking you off my lips. Savoring you and making plans to take even more."

Her shocked gasp spurred Gabriel on. Especially because he detected both a tiny hint of fear and helpless need in the sounds she made.

"Open up and let me in all the way, Celia. Open for me.

Open, for God's sake, before I go insane… before I hurt you." Gabriel's hips snapped forward, burying himself a bit farther.

Celia cried out in a low, desperate plea.

"Does that mean you want more, sugarplum?" His gaze bored into hers in the mirror's reflection. "Or do you want me to stop? If it's mercy you want, then say so now while I have the willpower to stop."

Celia was so damned gorgeous. She might have been an untamed lioness, her pupils so dark they swallowed up the irises of her eyes. An expression suspiciously similar to pain flashed in those shadowy depths and Gabriel hesitated.

Perhaps he was hurting her. Perhaps he'd hurt her before during that spanking, and stubborn girl that she was, she kept it from him.

Fuck. This was a horrible idea. Why did I think she was ready for this? For me? And how could I have ever thought she wanted me as badly as I want her? I'm still a bastard when it comes straight down to it. A bastard with no right to touch her.

But before he could withdraw, Celia reached up with one hand, burying her fingers in the shaggy waves of his hair. Curving her arm around the back of his neck, she kept him from moving away.

"Don't stop, Gabriel. I want this. I want *you.* No matter what came before us, I want you." Her whisper was fierce, daring him to take her. "You can wipe away everything, can't you? I want you to. I want you to erase all that came before…"

Gabriel sucked in a breath. The thought of fucking the memory of the men before him out of her memories had his cock swelling to impossible proportions.

Thank God. She won't stop me from doing anything I want with her.

"Yes, pet. I will," he crooned, pulling her hand from his hair and moving it so it was braced once more on the dressing table. "And you will keep your pretty back arched for me." When she did not move fast enough to suit him, he slapped one cheek of her bottom with a cupped palm. She became even wetter around the tip of his cock, and it made him smile. "I expect immediate obedience, Marchioness, and once I receive it, you will be rewarded again."

Celia arched her back even more. A whimper escaped from her mouth, although she frantically bit her lower lip to keep it contained.

Gabriel's chuckle was dark with appreciation. "That's it. You learn quickly, don't you?"

He surged inside her then, all the way to the hilt, and nearly wept with the flood of sensations. Keeping their gazes locked, he began moving in and out of her body, dragging his cock almost to the point of exit before gliding back in. Reaching forward, his fingers pinched the hardened bud of one of her breasts until she began squirming against him in a rocking motion.

Gabriel ground his teeth together from the sheer pleasure. Celia was like nothing he'd ever experienced before. His addiction, his *obsession* for her expanded until it reached every corner of his soul. Coursing through his veins until there was no choice but to accept she was part of him now.

"Just like that, *ma chère femme*. Yes. Keep moving just like that. You feel so good wrapped around me. So goddamn good that I find myself losing control, and I'm trying so hard not to hurt you."

Celia hissed in a combination of pain and desire as he pinched the tips of her breasts just a little harder, and in the next instant, the same hand administering that almost cruel caress, curved around her throat. He held her like that, tugging her hair with one hand, controlling her while squeezing her with his other hand until she cried out from another sudden climax, her body releasing every band of tension and accepting him in the most primal way.

It was too much, that surrender of her body and the softening of her flesh. The way her sweetness invaded the darkness of his soul and illuminated him from the inside out. Before Gabriel could stop it, his climax barreled through him. It felt like a thousand volcanos erupting at once, drowning him in fiery lava. With a helpless groan, he thrust harder into her silken depths as though the violence of his possession could erase both of their pasts and all of his pain.

"Mine." The word came out in a guttural grunt as he released his hold of her throat so she could fully catch her breath. "*Mine. Do you understand, pet?* And as surely as you are mine, I am now yours. Always."

She gulped in huge breaths of air, letting out a moan-laced sob of surrender as she collapsed forward onto the table, her body trembling with the force of their combined orgasm.

Gabriel bent over her, brushing the thick mass of her hair to the side so he could press a soft kiss upon the nape of her neck. He kissed her over and over, languid, warm kisses where the salty-sweet flavor of her skin permeated his mouth.

Regardless of his future as a reluctant marquess, this woman would face it beside him. Gabriel's heart soared with relief all while aching with uncertainty. He'd never had anyone he could call his own until this moment. And although he was a man most unworthy, Celia was his now. He would never let her go.

Gabriel dragged his trousers back into place. He'd not had the patience to remove neither them nor his boots earlier. Which meant he'd taken his new wife like a whore in a back alley.

Grimacing with regret for his callous treatment, he scooped Celia up and carried her to the bed. Laying her down on the sheets, he pulled the coverlet around her and then set about ensuring her care.

After wetting a bit of cloth with water from the pitcher and basin, he returned to the bed. She let out a drowsy moan of protest when he urged her onto her back. The coverlet was flicked back so her body was again exposed and he could tend her properly.

"What are you doing?" she asked with dark eyes half-lidded. Reaching up, she traced the scar slicing across his eyebrow.

Because he had not yet dimmed the lamps, Gabriel could see the confused glint in the chocolate-hued depths of her gaze. As if dazed, she belatedly realized she was bare. Her hands slowly came up in an effort to conceal her breasts.

With a soft *tsk* of disapproval, Gabriel trapped her hands in one of his own and stretched them above her head.

Her eyes widened.

"Be still, Celia, so I can take care of you."

"You don't have to. Please." She struggled in what could only be considered a flash of panic. "Wait."

Gabriel frowned, his grip tightening just enough that she stopped writhing and stared up at him. "I *want* to, Celia. And I will. Has no man done this for you in the past?" The very question set his teeth on edge with jealousy, but it affected Celia much differently.

She froze in place, her eyes as wild as a trapped animal. Indeed, it seemed she barely breathed as Gabriel passed the cloth between her legs in a softly, soothing motion.

It came away tinged with splotches of red mingled with his own seed.

Gabriel did not move. He stared at the obvious signs of blood as though they could not possibly be real. Then his gaze lifted to Celia's.

"You were a virgin." The statement came out in a growl. "You *lied* to me?"

Celia's face darkened with confusion. "I did not lie."

Gabriel moved the cloth back between her legs, eliciting a soft cry from Celia. "Explain this to me then, wife?" He folded the cloth carefully so that a clean side was presented, but inside he shook with dread. Seven hells. Had *he* injured her himself? Had he been that goddamn rough with his surprisingly delicate little bride?

"I cannot as I don't understand." Embarrassment sent a shocking wave of pink to infuse her skin. She was so damned lovely spread out like this, but Gabriel ignored the temptation. He moved the cloth between her legs once more, taking note when she winced and gentling his actions.

"It's very simple, my lady. Either you've slept with others in the past or you have not." Gabriel's tone became coolly impersonal. He effortlessly slipped into a role he knew quite well. That as an interrogator. Someone who knew ways of enticing even the most seasoned and hardened of criminals to spill all their secrets.

"Gabriel, please." She was pleading with him, but for what, he did not know. Mercy? Understanding? Absolution?

Guilt rose to choke Gabriel, along with the dread of suspicion. Either he'd hurt her enough that she bled or she had lied in a desperate attempt to avoid marriage.

Marriage to him.

"I'm waiting for an explanation."

Celia let out a sob of such anguish it nearly ripped Gabriel's heart into pieces. But while she squirmed against his grip in a series of useless movements, he held her in place, his face an emotionless mask.

"I do not know. I don't, I swear it!" she cried out in a soft wail. "It only happened once, but the pain was so unbearable. I begged him to stop, to let me go. But he did not. He held me down and kept going... and going... until he..."

Gabriel could not believe what he was hearing. Someone had attacked her? Someone forced themselves upon his sweet, fiery Celia? Someone stole from her the singular prized possession a young woman of society could offer a man?

Rage began slowly building inside him. A lust to maim and kill the man responsible for this atrocity against his wife beat like war drums inside his veins.

But the blood he'd cleaned from between her thighs reminded Gabriel he was certainly not innocent by any means. Thinking she was experienced meant he'd taken Celia as roughly as he would have fucked a courtesan in a brothel. He'd spanked her, toyed with her, and plunged inside her tight depths with a single-minded determination to feed his own obsession. Yes, she found her pleasure, but at what cost?

Releasing Celia's hands, Gabriel slowly rose from the bed. Immediately, she yanked the coverlet over her body and up to her chin. She watched as he silently washed the cloth out in the basin and then discarded the water in a separate bucket behind a small bathing screen.

Picking up his discarded shirt, Gabriel thrust his arms through the sleeves, buttoning it with cold efficiency. He could not stem the anger bleeding through his actions, nor did he consider how it might appear to Celia.

His glare was truly not meant for her, but it was directed in her direction, regardless. She was a convenient vessel for his frustration.

"Who was it, Celia? And why did he not face the consequences for his actions? Many a man has been forced to the alter based on such behavior."

The question startled Celia. She stared up at him, her lush bottom lip clenched between her teeth. "Perhaps my parents did not care to see me married to a cruel beast."

"Who. Was. It?" Gabriel bit out in a voice that made men tremble in their boots upon hearing it. He was the most feared man in all of London's underground, and yet the look in this girl's eyes shifted from fear to stubbornness in a matter of seconds.

"You do not get to ask me that, my lord. Before I agreed to marry you, you said the past did not matter. It still does not matter. I will not tell you the name of the man because it will change nothing. You knew my secret. You knew I was not pure before you dragged me into Ravenswood's chapel."

"Celia, what I have discovered just now changes matters. I want the man's name. Otherwise, I shall conduct my own search, and I won't care who I hurt or kill in discovering his identity."

Celia scooted up in the bed, unsuccessfully hiding a wince of pain. "You will *not*, my lord. You will abide by the terms of our agreement, or I shall petition the queen for an annulment."

"Don't be foolish," Gabriel scowled.

"No. You are the one being foolish," Celia snapped back, moving until she leaned against the bed's headboard. "You are the new Marquess of Rosenthorne. You have a mountain to conquer in proving yourself worthy of the title. Will you jeopardize everything over a matter which cannot be altered or erased? Will you have others know I did not come to this marriage a virgin? More importantly, will you shame my family? My parents have no knowledge of what occurred to me, nor does my brother or anyone else for that matter. You are the only one to whom I've revealed my secret, and I only did so because... because..." Her fierce statement broke off in a choked sob.

"For what reason did you tell me, Celia?" Gabriel demanded. "Did you hope I would reject you? Did you tell me for the sole purpose of avoiding marriage to a bastard only to have your efforts fail?"

Celia's eyes narrowed, even as a tear slipped down her cheek. "You are not a bastard, Gabriel. And I told you because I could not bear to witness your disappointment upon discovering your bride had already served another man's pleasure."

Gabriel's jaw clenched. Heaven help him, but she was right. He had insisted it did not matter who she'd been with before him. It still did not matter, but the entire situation had become rather murky now. He wanted the name of the man who'd harmed her, and he wanted Celia to willingly provide it.

More than anything, he wanted her trust.

Celia's jaw tilted as they stared at one another, and Gabriel growled with frustration. With quick, jerky motions, he tucked in his shirt. Forgoing the cravat, he shrugged into his dark burgundy-hued coat.

"Keep this door locked and do not wait up for me. I won't return until long after you've fallen asleep." He turned the doorknob and hesitated as if reminded of something. "I will have one of the coachmen stand watch for your safety until I come back. Enjoy your dinner."

Celia bit her lip, obviously concerned about being left alone, but her chin rose even higher. "I wish you a pleasant evening, dear husband."

Gabriel did not respond to the faint mockery in her tone as he exited the room, locking the door behind him as he went.

CHAPTER 30

Gabriel sent Jeremiah to guard the door to their room, and then he found a table and ordered an ale.

He ordered another when that one was done, then sat and stared at the fire for a long time.

"Begging your pardon, milord."

Gabriel glanced up to see a man standing at his table. He might have been the same age as Gabriel himself, but it was difficult saying if that was truly the case. His face was haggard, although there were faint indications he'd been a rather handsome man at some point in his life.

The dark air of desperation and imminent poverty stamped across the man's features were evidence of a rough, hardscrabble existence. He was Irish as well, which was yet another strike against a man choosing to live in England.

"Yes?"

"You're the new Marquess of Rosenthorne?"

Gabriel glanced around the man for Tessa. Seven hells, but he needed another ale. "I am," he said in reply to the man's question. Tamping down his impatience, Gabriel turned his attention to the man who'd disrupted his reflection on the episode shared with Celia.

"Heard you were looking for workers at Rosenthorne Park. If ya are needing stable hands or carpentry, I've got years of experience. Good with horses and fixin' anything that needs fixin'." The man ducked his head, twisting his cap in his hands. "I've worked at some of the largest estates in England. Name's Flannigan."

Gabriel did not care where this man had worked, nor what his name was. He simply wanted another ale before retreating to his room where his wife, no doubt, was crying herself to sleep in a room lit by a single lamp.

"We are in recent need, that's true. If what you say is true, then you may seek out my estate manager there," Gabriel said, distracted by the sight of Tessa coming toward him with a fresh tankard of brew. "He will know of the positions available."

The man smiled, sweeping his thinning reddish blonde hair back under a threadbare cap. "I'll do that, milord. It's said you and the marchioness are newlyweds. She's a right beauty, she is, milord, if you don't mind my saying so. You're certainly a man what has the luck. A man rising above his common status is something most of us can only dream of."

A man born to the aristocracy might have berated Flannigan for his inappropriate compliment, but Gabriel distractedly waved the man's words away. He was bound to hear such sentiments from others with his first steps into the venerable House of Parliament. Taking his seat among gentlemen who'd been there for years would certainly result in hearing statements far less flattering than Flannigan's.

Tessa set down the tankard of ale before Gabriel with a loud thump, but she did not linger. Which was good, considering he'd once again made it clear he had no interest in her flagrant offers. She flounced away with a flip of her hair, and Gabriel smiled to himself. The pretty tart could not hold a candle to the gorgeous wife waiting for him upstairs.

"That will do, Flannigan. Now, if you will excuse me, my preference is to not conduct my business affairs in a public tavern. I wish to finish my ale in solitude before retiring for the evening."

"Of course, milord." Flannigan's lips tightened with the dismissal, but his tone remained even as he continued. "I'll be sure your man of affairs knows ya gave me your blessing."

Flannigan retreated with a bow, but Gabriel barely took note of the man's leaving. With a relieved sigh, he applied himself to drinking his ale.

It gave him something to do rather than brood over the argument with Celia.

DURING THE NIGHT, Gabriel found himself lying on his back with Celia sprawled across him. He stared up at the wood-beamed ceiling, watching the low shadows cast by the lamp dance across the plaster surface as his wife slumbered.

It was surprising how she gravitated to him even after an argument. It was as if she instinctively knew his dedication to protecting what was his. Regardless of the harsh words they traded with one another, she was now his responsibility. He would scorch the world until it melted away like cinders for her.

Gabriel sighed, embracing her a bit tighter. The scent from her hair tickled his nose. Roses and lemons. Fresh. Clean. Sweet.

Celia's hand laid curled over his chest and he gently picked it up, admiring the sight of his mother's ring on her finger. He may now be a marquess with untold riches at his disposal, but this ring and the woman now wearing it were the two most precious things in his world.

Pressing a soft kiss to her fingertips, Gabriel considered how much he was coming to care for Celia. He would do whatever was necessary to keep from losing her. And if that meant honoring her wishes and forgoing his search for the man who had assaulted her, he would do that, too.

Even if the decision burned a hole in the pit of his stomach and left behind the taste of ash in his mouth.

He would do it for Celia.

THEIR ARRIVAL at Rosenthorne Park the following afternoon threw the entire estate into a full-scale panic. It seemed the marchioness's suite of rooms was hardly fit for occupation, mostly because of the need for Celia's desires when it came to décor. The designer hired to update the stale, old-fashioned rooms of the mansion had done what he could up to the point of gaining Celia's choices.

After enduring an hour of introductions to the staff, Gabriel took Celia by the arm.

"I know you should have your own suite as Marchioness. I will pay whatever is required to expedite the process now that you can select décor and finishes. I instructed them to wait for you, but it is an inconvenience for you."

Celia stared at him with a calmness she did not feel. Was he that eager to rid himself of her company? Had their explosive night of passion the previous evening proven too intense for her new husband?

It'd certainly been intense for her. Indeed, she was still sore from his attentions. Still wincing every time she sat down too forcibly. But even though she'd wept until she fell into a deep slumber during the long night, she'd woken in the morning nestled under Gabriel's arm as though she was meant to be there. She'd lain perfectly still, accepting the heaviness of his forearm thrown across her midriff. Accepted the warmth of his breath stirring her hair as it feathered across her cheek and down the side of her neck.

Although she'd witnessed him frowning over the silliness of her request, Gabriel had not extinguished the lamp in their rooms during the two nights they'd already shared. Indeed, he'd given her the strangest look the following morning while turning the wick down. As bright sunlight streamed past the drapes and lit the space, Celia wondered if he were trying to solve the puzzle of why she needed the lamp at all. And she wondered if he might someday make the connection between her fear of the dark and the incident when she'd lost her virginity.

And *that* was something she did not understand. She'd bled after Bryan's attack in the stables. Suffered for hours, the space between her thighs sore and painful. She had not emerged from that night as a virgin and accepted it as fact over the past five years.

Last night with Gabriel had not been as painful. There'd been unimaginable pleasure, but it was obvious she'd bled afterward as if she were an untried virgin. How that could be was most puzzling. Could it be attributed to Gabriel's considerable size? His hefty circumference? He was much, much larger than Bryan. Perhaps it was a simple matter of her flesh adjusting to such things until she was accustomed to lovemaking with her husband.

"Celia? Did you hear me? Your suite of rooms will not be ready for another two weeks. Perhaps longer. I can make arrangements for your things to be placed in one of the guest rooms which have yet to be renovated or..." Gabriel hesitated, his jaw clenching as he watched her reaction. "Or I can have you moved into my rooms. They were just finished today, so the odor of paint and varnish may be offensive. If you would rather not subject yourself to—"

"I do not mind so much. Really. If I will not be a bother, I prefer to stay in your apartments," Celia quickly interrupted.

"Of course, it is of no bother. I will have my items moved into one of the guest rooms so that you are undisturbed." Gabriel looked stoic enough to break in half, his body rigid as an oak.

Celia's head tilted. "Why would you move to a guest room, Gabriel? I do not mind sharing the suite with you. And if you do not mind my presence, I'd much rather you be there with me. Unless, of course, it is not the thing for husbands and wives to share a room." Celia bit the tip of her fingernail in thought. "I know the Earl and Lady Ivy share his chambers. As do Lord Bentley and Lady Sara."

Gabriel's eyes glowed as he stared down at her. "I don't give a tinker's damn what everyone else does, Celia. If you wish to share my rooms, I would be more than pleased to see you in my bed every morning when I wake. Even more so if you are naked and ready for me."

Celia blushed, glancing around to determine if anyone else had overheard that scandalous statement. Really, Gabriel had the most disconcerting habit of stating his thoughts aloud for anyone to overhear.

"Does that shock you, *ma petite dragee?*" Gabriel asked, pulling her closer until she felt the heat of his body. It came off him in waves. The man was always so warm. "I will serenade you with love songs every morning and press a thousand kisses to your lips and your pretty breasts. Would you like that?"

Celia could think of nothing she wanted more. She melted with his words, wondering how the argument from the night before could be forgotten so easily. Not that she would dare complain, but such swings from hot to cold were enough to make her head swim. It definitely made her wonder if she would ever resist this strange attraction.

Gabriel watched her closely, his eyes flaring with molten

appreciation when she swayed against him in a show of submission.

"I would like that very much, my lord."

"Then it is settled. You have free rein when it comes to renovating our new home. Except for my study and the master suite, you may do as wish. In fact, I heartily hope you do so. I've no patience for such things."

Celia smiled. Gabriel was a man of action. Of course, he would not enjoy involving himself in the minute details of fabric choices and wall colors. And while she enjoyed time spent outdoors and quiet times reading her books, she found the prospect of redecorating Rosenthorne Park to be an unexpected surprise. Gabriel's trust in placing such a daunting task in her hands made her stomach flip with excitement and a desire to make him proud of her efforts.

"I shall do my very best, Gabriel," she said, then added teasingly, "Although I will not hear of your complaints when I've wallpapered every parlor with images of books and the formal dining room has horses of Greek mythology galloping across its walls."

"If you love it, then I shall, too." Gabriel lifted her hand and pressed a warm kiss to her gloved knuckles. He ignored the giggling of the downstairs maids watching them. Miss Ellenston, the housekeeper, shooed them to return to their duties.

"Do whatever pleases you, pet," he breathed, finally releasing her with a silky promise. "I know I shall reap the rewards of my tolerance one way or another."

CHAPTER 31

Their first dinner as husband and wife in Celia's new home was a daunting one.

The dining hall was cavernous and dark, decorated in shades of Rosenthorne's heraldic colors of deep burgundy and gold. Heavy drapes covered the windows, a remnant of the old marquess's command that they stayed undrawn as a way of protecting the equally dark wood furniture.

The six ornate crystal chandeliers running down the center of the room and positioned strategically over the dining table were in terrible need of dusting. Celia overheard Mrs. Ellenston explain to Gabriel that the room was next on her list. With the hiring of new, eager-to-please servants, it would receive a thorough cleaning over the next few days.

For a formal meal, Celia should have taken her chair at the opposite end of the table, and if there'd been guests dining with them, she would have. But it seemed quite silly to sit so far from Gabriel when they were the only two in attendance excluding the footmen positioned on either side of the room's double doors.

Gabriel's eyebrow lifted when Celia slid into the chair on his left.

"Breaking the rules already, Lady Rosenthorne?" A teasing note flitted through the question, and Celia gave him a saucy grin.

"You'll soon discover it is my natural inclination, Lord Rosenthorne."

"You forget, sugarplum, that I know more about you than you realize."

Celia ducked her head as she opened the linen napkin and laid it in precise folds across her lap. He may have just become a marquess, but he occupied the seat at the head of the enormous table as though he'd been there his whole life. A steady, unwavering confidence exuded from the man, a confidence only those born to nobility could emit.

"So you have said before. It places me at a distinct disadvantage since I know practically nothing about you, Gabriel Rose."

"We began this game in the coach on our way here." Celia's use of his previous name resulted in a fleeting smile across Gabriel's features. Leaning forward, he braced his elbows on the table and steepled his fingertips. His gaze caressed her mouth, a fiery hunger in the whiskey dark depths he did not bother to hide. "What is it that you wish to know, sugarplum? I hold no secrets when it comes to you."

It was a subtle reminder that Celia could not make the same claim. She held her breath, hoping he would not once again insist on the name of the man who had abused her in the past. But he simply watched her, patiently waiting for her question.

Swallowing hard, Celia blurted out the first thing that popped into her mind.

"How did you come to have your scar?"

Gabriel's smile widened. "You begin with the most obvious of my mysteries."

Celia blushed. "I do not mean to offend. It's just I've always wondered and there are rumors."

"I'm far from offended. Tell me some of these rumors." His melodic voice put Celia at ease. "They may prove more interesting than the truth."

Celia took a sip from her water goblet. "A jealous husband gave it to you after discovering you with his wife."

"I would never sleep with another man's wife," Gabriel murmured, revealing more of his character than he probably realized. "What else?"

"You got it whilst fighting pirates off the coast of Malta." Celia grinned. "That's my favorite. I can imagine how it occurred. You were swinging across the deck, brandishing a sword, when a dastardly pirate cut the rope as you flew past."

"Very imaginative but never happened."

"All right. It's been said you were completely soused and fell from your own bed, hitting your forehead on a chamber pot."

Gabriel grimaced, leaning back from the table as the first course was served. "Hardly a flattering image."

"It's not nearly as bad as the one where you and Lord Ravenswood came to blows over a woman while you were both in France."

Gabriel shook his head. "Only once has that come close to a reality. And it occurred after I arrived in England and after the Earl married. Lord Bentley was also involved in the defense of Lady Ivy, so I did not act alone. Fortunately, no blows were exchanged that night." He sipped his wine, head tilted as he considered her. "And I was given this scar many years before that."

"Those are all I can recall at the moment. There are so many, you see. For all your tendencies to remain in the shadows, you have long been a source of gossip." Celia dipped her spoon into the bowl of chestnut soup. "I regret that won't change with your new title. In fact, there will probably be many more outlandish tales spread about you."

"My concern is that you will suffer because of these cruel rumors. I won't have you sullied simply because the irregular circumstance of my inheritance places you in the same crosshairs as myself," Gabriel said, his tone vibrating with such fierce protectiveness that Celia blinked in surprise.

"It won't be as bad as all that," Celia murmured. "We shall make a game of it. Anytime either of us hears a rumor, we shall invent one even more outlandish simply for our own amusement."

Leaning back in his chair, Gabriel gave her a considering look. "I believe that is an excellent idea." He was silent for a long moment, then said, "The scar came from my father. He appeared at the boarding school in France when I was a lad. Tried convincing me he'd done what he thought best in the situation." Gabriel sighed, remembering the altercation that day. "But he'd done what was best for *himself*. Not me. And it was certainly not in my mother's best interest. He abandoned her when he was needed the most. I wanted nothing of his explanations or excuses. We argued and eventually came to blows. He struck me across the face with his cane, and as I stood bleeding, he blamed me for causing the injury."

A distressed sound escaped Celia's throat.

"I did not wait to see what else he would say or do. I stormed out of the room, gathered my things, and slipped out into the streets of Paris. And I learned during those years on my own that the only person I could rely on was myself."

"So, you did not know he'd married your mother? That you were his son in every sense of the word?"

Gabriel shook his head as the footmen removed the bowls of soup and servants brought in the next course of roasted pheasant and creamed peas. He waited until they could once again speak in private. "No. And even had I known, I doubt it would have made much of a difference. Being legally recognized as his son would not have changed his actions when it came to sending my mother away so her existence would not embarrass him."

There could be no mistaking the angry resentment Gabriel's words contained, but Celia recognized an even deeper emotion her husband carried inside. Pain and betrayal seeped from him as though they were being squeezed out.

"I'm sorry, Gabriel. I hope your father experienced remorse for his actions and for hurting you."

Gabriel stabbed at the piece of fowl on his plate. "Perhaps he did. I cannot explain why he decided to make me his heir. No one knew he was my legitimate father. He could have gone to his grave keeping my mother and myself a secret."

"But he did claim you." Celia was determined that Gabriel not keep this hurt bottled up inside him. "And that must count for something. Perhaps one day he would have sought you out again so you could reconcile your differences. He might have played a role in your life and atoned for his mistakes."

Gabriel scrubbed a hand over his face and gulped down the contents of his wine glass, motioning for the footman to refill it. "Perhaps." His features hardened, a muscle ticking along his jaw. "No more questions, sugarplum."

Celia nodded in agreement. She was silent for a long moment, using her fork to toy with the pheasant on her plate, then said, "When may we send word that Lord Banbury come for a visit? It will be pleasant becoming better acquainted with my new brother-in-law. He is quite charming."

Her husband made a non-committal sound. His eyes darkened as he tilted his wine glass until the ruby-red liquid swirled around the glass bowl.

"I think you will enjoy the opportunity of becoming closer to your brother, too," Celia pressed. "He is family, of course."

Gabriel gave her an unfathomable look. "*You* are my family now, Celia. And the only one I will ever need or want."

The possessive note in his voice made Celia's heart swell. And the way he was looking at her now, with eyes dark and sinful, his lips curving just enough to have her wondering what he found so amusing, made her pulse race. He'd looked at her in the same manner just the night before. When he had taken her with such violent deliciousness and later argued over the reluctance to spill her secrets. Did all men look at their wives in such a way? As though they could not wait to devour them?

"Dessert, milord," one of the servants murmured while clearing their used dishes away. "Sugarplum brandy cakes."

The dessert was set before them, and Celia admired the pretty picture it made. The cake, a sponge-like creation soaked in sweetened brandy, was decorated with beautifully sugared plums and a dollop of fresh cream. It was too gorgeous to even eat.

"Oh, it's so lovely!" Celia exclaimed with a clap of her hands. "I don't believe I've ever seen a prettier dessert. Your chef is very talented, indeed."

Gabriel's gaze flickered between the lavish dessert and Celia herself.

"Don't you want dessert?" Celia asked, scooping up a bit of the cream and licking it from the spoon. It was as delightful as she expected.

"Yes. I'm ravenous for it."

"Then why are you not eating it? It's very good."

"That is my intention. To feast until I can take no more."

Celia's head tilted at the husky quality of his voice. It vibrated through her, and she suddenly realized he was not speaking of the desserts on the plates before them.

"Leave us." Gabriel waved a hand at the servants, and without so much as a single word, the two men quickly abandoned their post. Now, she was alone with her new husband, and he looked as though he seesawed between spanking her for some unknown transgression or rewarding her for tempting him.

"Will you do something for me, pet?" Gabriel asked in a voice brimming with sexual connotations.

Celia's hand tightened on the spoon, her mind racing with thoughts of what he might do. "Yes, my lord."

I'll do anything you ask of me. Why that is, I cannot even begin to understand. But I will. Because being with you erases the darkness that chases me. It makes me feel whole. Safe. Needed.

She could not say such things aloud, even if her face most likely conveyed every thought as though it were shouted from the rooftops.

Gabriel's fingertips drummed against the tablecloth in a soft staccato. His eyes burned into hers while Celia shivered with awareness.

"Come stand before me."

"Why?" Celia boldly asked. The air in the room shifted, and the heat of his gaze flared, the dark whiskey-hued depths of his eyes glimmering with promise and retribution.

"Because I told you to do so, pet. And because I want my dessert spread before me. Gasping my name and clenching my fingers."

There was no denying what he wanted.

"But here, Gabriel?" Celia stuttered. "The servants…"

"In case you haven't noticed, they are practically terrified of me. Not one soul will pass through those doors," he drawled. "Now, come here."

Celia laid her spoon beside the plate, and after a moment of consideration, she plucked a plum from the dessert and popped it into her mouth as she stood from her chair. Her little moan of satisfaction as the sugared fruit burst in her mouth drew a low chuckle from Gabriel.

"Is it good?" When Celia nodded in response and pushed

away from the table, Gabriel's lips curved in a sultry smile. "There is no comparison to what I'm about to taste, Celia."

He shoved his own plate and wine glass aside as Celia sidled between his legs. Her back was to the table, and because she was standing and he remained seated, her breasts were at the perfect height for his mouth. He could kiss her there if he wanted, and suddenly that was all Celia could think of. Gabriel's wet, warm mouth worshipping her breasts. The scrape of his stubbled chin against her aching nipples. The sting of his teeth when he nipped her flesh before soothing it with laps of his tongue.

"I cannot seem to get enough of you, Celia. You've invaded my shadows, and now I want to keep you there with me forever." Gabriel did not touch her as he spoke, his hands resting casually on the arms of his chair, but Celia vibrated with his words, regardless. "Pull your skirts up for me."

Her hands shook, but she did as commanded and then stood waiting, great drifts of fabric clutched in her fists.

"Such a good, obedient girl when it suits you." His low laughter made her blush. "Up onto the table, pet."

"Gabriel…"

Her hesitation had his scarred eyebrow rising high. With a hard swallow of trepidation, Celia obeyed. Still clutching her skirts, her undergarments exposed to his fiery gaze, she moved onto the table and then sat with her legs dangling. The way Gabriel stared made Celia feel like she was indeed a confection for devouring.

"How pretty you are. My own little sugarplum waiting to be consumed." Moving his chair closer, Gabriel's hands roamed up the inside of her legs and spread her wider. His long, broad fingers found the opening in her flimsy undergarments, and with a sudden movement, they were ripped apart.

Celia gasped in shock, her legs automatically closing, but Gabriel prevented that. One hand gripped her thigh, holding her open, while the other swept against her sex. Celia trembled.

She clutched her skirts with such violence the silk might never recover.

"Already so wet for me," he murmured, trailing a finger down her seam in a teasing manner. "And so fucking sweet."

Celia watched as he plucked a plum from his dessert and dipped it in the cream. She thought he would plop it into his mouth, but instead, he ran the piece of fruit over the lips of her vagina and nestled it into the folds.

She gasped for air, and when his eyes met hers, the darkness she saw made her a little afraid for her own sanity.

"You asked if I would eat my dessert, Celia. And I will. I'm going to devour the sweetness of your hot little quim now, and you will refrain from reaching your climax."

"I don't... I don't understand," Celia muttered, distracted because her body was so heated. Her inner channel was already clenching with need. Her thighs were slick with a wave of moisture just from his words.

Why did he not seem to experience the same wild desperation she did? How did he maintain this cool composure when she was already on the edge of exploding? It wasn't fair.

"Oh, you understand me, pet." Gabriel chuckled, leaning closer and pressing a soft kiss on the sensitive skin of her inner thigh. "You understand every word I've said. And you will do as I ask because you want to please me, isn't that right?"

Oh, she did want to please him. To the point she would willingly forfeit her soul to the Devil.

Her head bobbed with desperate jerks.

"Tsk. Tsk. Words, Celia. Use them." He slicked a finger through her wetness and pushed the piece of fruit more firmly into her folds until it nudged against the button of nerves there.

Celia swore she saw stars. She moaned, caught on the edge of insanity and ecstatic to be there. This man held the unique ability to turn her into a greedy, trembling mess. "Yes. *Yes.* I want to please you, Gabriel. I shall do as you say. Oh, please."

"There's my good girl."

Gabriel's breath was so hot on her exposed flesh that Celia wondered if it might melt the sugar from the plum now wedged into her sex.

Their eyes met over the mound of skirts and her quivering stomach, and his command was a rough growl. "Remember, this dessert is mine. You will not come unless I grant permission. And, sugarplum? There are consequences for disobedience."

Celia did not dare breathe as his head lowered and his hands slid around to cup the sides of her buttocks. In this position, he held her firm and slowly licked from her opening to the piece of fruit and back again, his tongue spearing inside her.

She almost exploded that very moment. Her legs shook as she staved off a multitude of sensations.

Gabriel licked and nibbled and lavished every bit of her flesh with his mouth. Every now and then, his nose would bump against the fruit, pushing it harder against her clitoris, and Celia would brace herself against the impending combustion. It happened often enough that she suspected this action was absolutely on purpose.

"Gabriel… Gabriel…" she moaned in supplication, her body on fire for him.

She could no longer take watching him feast on her. It was too much for the senses. Leaning back onto her elbows, her head tilted until all she could see was the sparkle of a crystal chandelier above her and the swirling design of the plaster ceiling.

"Do not come yet, *ma chere femme.* Not yet." He began eating the fruit, his teeth occasionally grazing sensitive flesh and distracting her from the orgasm building inside her. And Celia thought she could obey him. She focused on the sting from his teeth as he feasted and was able to sway her body from its natural inclinations.

Realizing her strategy, Gabriel doubled his efforts, his mouth lush and sinful and so, so hot. The plum was certainly gone now, and there was nothing left but his mouth and tongue and the trembling of her body.

Then Gabriel slid two fingers inside her sheath, curving them upward and stroking a hidden spot inside her. Celia bucked wildly as he sucked her clitoris into his mouth with greedy intensity.

How could she withstand such an erotic onslaught? She could not. It was not possible. With a low cry, Celia gave in. She flew apart and came back together against his mouth while he ate her with even more ferocity, feasting as though he would never have enough of her. His fingers plunged and curled inside her, filling her and forcing her to stay on the crest of the wave before tumbling into another abyss. And as he devoured her, Gabriel muttered one word against her flesh, imprinting his claim on her body and her heart for all eternity.

"Mine."

Gabriel scooped his nearly insensate wife up from the dining room table and settled into his chair with her in his lap. He cuddled her close, staying in that position for the longest time as he allowed both of them time to recover.

He'd just experienced the singular most erotic moment in his life; more than a few seconds were needed to calm his own heartbeat. To quell the racing of his blood and allow his massive erection to subside before he could even think of carrying Celia up to his room.

"I'm sorry," she whispered against the curve of his neck where her face was currently buried.

"Why is that, pet?"

"For disobeying you. I tried so hard not to." Her voice was small and worried.

Gabriel smiled against her hair, nuzzling his nose into the fragrant strands. He had intentionally pushed her over the edge, making it impossible for her to obey his order. "I know you tried. It is part of the fun when we play games such as these. Even when you fail, there is still reward to be found in the punishments I give you. Now, do not fret. You are still my good girl."

Celia snuggled closer, looping her arms around his neck as she kissed a spot just below his ear. "You always know just what to say and do, Gabriel. It is just as Ivy and Sara said. I am indeed a fortunate woman to have such a husband as you."

Gabriel embraced her tighter, his heart swelling. "Rest now, Celia. In a moment or two, I shall carry you up to our room and begin anew."

Celia stirred against him. "Again?" Her voice was soft and she sounded so tired. It'd been a long day for them both, but Gabriel found his obsession with his wife did not subside simply because he married her. No, if anything, his desire had multiplied. He could not get enough of her.

"Yes, again. And again and again, until I've had my fill and I'm satisfied that you won't walk or sit for the next few days without being reminded how deep I was inside you. So, yes, again until I am ready to stop."

Celia shuddered the tiniest bit. "That sounds unpleasant. Perhaps even uncomfortable."

"I will take great care with you, Celia," Gabriel swore with a smile. "You will be as invested as I am in our mutual pleasure."

She said nothing else, although he sensed her frowning in protest. With a tiny sigh, she settled against him, dozing off with her head cradled in the crook of his neck.

Gabriel relaxed into the chair, letting himself enjoy this moment. This moment when he held his wife in his lap in the middle of a vast, ornate, dusty dining room, her skirts over-flowing the chair's confines as she slept in his arms. The taste of her, sugared plums, and cream still lingered in his mouth.

It was perfect.

~

Mister Kinsey met Gabriel outside his study the next morning and followed him into the room holding a stack of letters.

"Your correspondence, Lord Rosenthorne," the man said, setting the bundle down on the wide desk.

Gabriel eyed the daunting pile with a sense of dread. "Christ. Is all that for me?"

Mister Kinsey smiled in understanding. "Mostly half is official correspondence regarding responsibilities of the estate. The other will be invitations and social engagements Lady Rosenthorne will likely address. Your father employed a secretary for such things. If you like, I will facilitate the hiring of someone for both you and milady. As well as a valet for milord."

Gabriel scrubbed a hand down his face. "I've managed thus far over the last twenty-eight years to dress myself. I don't believe I require a valet."

"Of course, milord." Mister Kinsey's head tilted. "Milady's maid will arrive soon, yes? Mrs. Ellenston has selected a young lady as a temporary substitute."

"There's no need." Gabriel waved away the offer. "I will see to my wife's demands until her maid arrives."

Mister Kinsey ducked his head, a flush of embarrassment coloring his face at the thought of a marquess acting as lady's maid. "Very good, milord."

"See to the hiring of secretaries, Mister Kinsey," Gabriel stated as he sifted through the post. It rarely occurred, but at this moment, he was feeling extremely inadequate. This task of being a marquess was proving more difficult than he imagined. The only bright spot so far was that the position delivered the delectable Celia into his grasp. "I've no idea what I should do with most of this."

"I'm happy to assist," Mister Kinsey offered. "The most important piece of correspondence I spied in this stack is an official post from the secretary of the Prime Minister. I imagine he requires your appearance in his office before taking your seat in the House of Lords. You will need to set up your own offices there."

Gabriel winced. He'd been dreading this summons, having been warned of its arrival by Sebastian.

What he knew of Parliament was that a small group of wealthy lords held the position of deciding the fate of the common Englishman. Unfair, true, but a reality, nonetheless. And now, he would straddle the two sides of his heritage in a different way. Commoner and nobility attempting to reconcile with each other.

A trip to London was apparently necessary, but the thought of leaving his bride so soon was not a pleasant one. Of course, he could take Celia along with him. Perhaps she would enjoy shopping and seeing to their house in Mayfair before the season began. In the meantime, work could continue here at the country manor without Celia being unduly inconvenienced.

The more he thought about it, the better the idea sounded.

He'd left her in bed this morning, having exhausted them both the previous evening. After leaving the dining room, he'd carried Celia up to his room and plied her with kisses and caresses that lit them both on fire. Then, contrary to his earlier words regarding punishments, he slowly made love to her until she was desperate for release and begging him.

Afterward, she'd curled up beside him, her fingers twirling through his hair and brushing the heavy locks from his brow. She'd kissed him sweetly, so soft and compliant in his embrace that Gabriel found himself becoming more entranced by the second.

His body was now stirring with incessant hunger as he thought of waking her, his fingers searching between her legs, his mouth at her breast, and a hand gripped tight in her hair. If he must journey to London, she would go as well.

He could not abide being parted from her for longer than a day. That much was clear.

THEY DEPARTED A WEEK LATER, once Celia's maid arrived at Rosenthorne Park along with most of her personal belongings. Gabriel's items had arrived the day before, including Arion who nickered with pleasure at seeing his master.

Celia felt as though she were caught in a whirlwind, one which began the moment she'd agreed to become Gabriel's wife. From Beaumont to Rosenthorne Park, and now to Rosenthorne Hall located within the fashionable district of Mayfair. She traveled in the marquess's grand coach along with her maid while Gabriel followed behind on horseback.

That development in itself was disappointing. Celia greatly missed Gabriel's presence inside the coach. Sighing, she glanced out the window, grateful that this trip into London was quicker than the journey from Beaumont to Rosenthorne. It was only a day of travel to reach their destination, and she looked forward to spending more time with her husband.

She was still learning so many things about Gabriel, his wicked sense of humor being the most pleasant surprise. There was also his unfailing commitment when it came to her wellbeing. Including those times following their moments of intimacy. He was so tender. So masterful. So riveting. Celia found herself hanging upon his every word like a besotted schoolgirl. Eager for his attention and the burning ecstasy she felt when he touched and kissed her.

While he'd not punished her again following that night at the inn, Celia could not help but wonder the other things he might do should the occasion arise. The spanking he'd given her, while not terribly painful, certainly left an impression. Admittedly, she'd both enjoyed and hated that particular punishment.

But what else was there to experience with her husband? What would please him as well as herself?

She sighed again as the countryside slowly morphed from pastoral fields to bustling city streets. They were entering London, and soon, she would find herself in a new situation as the wife of a powerful marquess. A marquess with no real experience in dealing with the intricacies of the *ton* and all its cruelty and pettiness. Celia would be the one to ease his way into this life, and her stomach clenched with apprehension for the daunting task ahead. Any hint of scandal, either real or imagined, must be avoided during these first few weeks of their introduction to society.

After all, the two of them were already under scrutiny based on the circumstances of their hasty marriage.

Pulling into the circular driveway, Celia gazed up at the imposing grey stone façade with awe. While many of the residences in Mayfair were fashionable townhouses like the one her parents owned, Rosenthorne Hall was a separate building nestled within a sprawling plot of land. A high, black iron fence enclosed its entirety, the grounds kept very much in the style of nearby Hyde Park. It was lushly beautiful, the feeling of privacy unusual within the confines of the crowded city where people jostled elbows. She'd never had the pleasure of visiting the home. The old marquess was notoriously reclusive, and there'd been no events held there for many years. In fact, Gabriel's father had rarely been in residence, and the house sat in a suspended state as a result.

"How very grand it is, milady," Katie, her maid, breathed from the other side of the coach. "It is like a fairytale castle."

Upon entering the border of Mayfair, Gabriel trotted ahead of the coach so he could arrive at Rosenthorne Hall first. Now, as the vehicle rolled to a stop, Celia watched from the window as he dismounted from Arion's back. He handed the reins over to a young stable boy with a warm smile and words she could not hear.

Celia's breath caught in her throat at the sight of him. Her husband was so brutally handsome. Somehow, the cloak of power he'd inherited just a month ago had only intensified his appeal. The man exuded arrogant confidence, his demeanor both aloof and approachable. It was an odd juxtaposition, and Celia wondered if others would find the combination difficult to resist.

She, herself, could not, and the proof was evident in the shameless way she lusted for him.

He'd made love to her tenderly every night of the past week leading up to their departure for London. It was a sweet seduction of slow, gentle thrusts, the sweetest of loving words, and the most scandalous of instructions. She thought perhaps he was building her up, preparing her for something she might not agree to without this careful planning. What that might be, she did not know, but a tiny part of her was eager to experience more.

Even if it frightened her.

The coachman jumped down from his perch and snapped open the steps. When the coach door opened for her descent, Gabriel was already there and taking her hand in assistance, his lips lifted slightly in a self-conscious smirk.

"Welcome to Rosenthorne Hall, Marchioness."

He helped her down, leading her away as a groomsman stepped closer to take one of the coach horses by the bit. Celia did not pay much heed, but upon looking back to ensure Katie had descended the coach safely, she caught a glimpse of the man holding the horses.

Celia's heart stuttered with fear.

It cannot be. It simply cannot.

Bryan Flannigan winked, his cruel mouth lifting in a smirk in acknowledgment of her shock.

The sun dimmed as everything swirled about her in a kaleidoscope of sights and sounds. She heard Gabriel's cry of alarm as though it came from a great distance and felt his heavy muscled arms slide about her waist. He was holding her up even as she fainted.

Celia clutched his arm.

"Gabriel," came from her lips in a shallow, weak puff of air before the world went black and sucked her down.

CHAPTER 33

Celia awoke in a state of confusion.

She lay upon a huge bed, the curtains of the canopy pulled back in great swaths of gold brocade. Overhead, that same fabric gathered into elegant swoops, meeting in the middle and held in place by a beautifully carved medallion of roses and entwining thorny branches.

"Celia?" Gabriel's face appeared before her, his eyes wild with concern. "Seven hells, you just took twenty years off my life."

When she went to prop herself up, Gabriel's hand restrained her. "No. Do not move. I've called for a physician, and he will determine if you are well enough to rise from this bed."

Celia frowned. How had she ended up in this bed when the last thing she remembered was standing in the gravel driveway?

And then you saw him. Bryan Flannigan. The man who stole your innocence. Who so cruelly forced his way with you. And who laughed at you while you cried in pain.

A sob caught in Celia's throat. What was the man doing here? At Rosenthorne Hall? Five years had passed since that night, and still, she felt the terror. The darkness of the stall and his hand clamped over her mouth, suffocating her while he hurt her.

He must be one of the new hires. But why had he sought employment in the service of the marquess? Did he know she was the new marchioness?

Thinking on the moment in the courtyard, Celia recalled his smirk of satisfaction. He'd not been surprised to see her, and that made her heart thump faster with fear. He'd known she would be there and had relished her shock.

"The physician should be here shortly, but until then, you will remain just where you are," Gabriel repeated, his hand going to her shoulder and gently pressing her back against the pillows.

"Don't be silly, Gabriel." Her voice sounded so far away, even to her own ears. "I merely fainted. Women do it every day."

But not her, she admitted to herself. She'd never fainted before in her entire life, although she'd faked it on numerous occasions in the past to escape overeager males. The real thing, however, was an odd experience she certainly did not recommend.

A strange little laugh bubbled in her throat at the irony of the situation.

Gabriel frowned with intense concern. "I'm not married to those other women, Celia."

"I'm perfectly fine, I swear it." But was she really? Her fingers felt icy and her head was still swimming with enough terror to make her dizzy.

"That is to be determined," Gabriel replied, annoyance evident in his tone. "Fainting dead away in my arms is an alarming event."

"I'm sure I'm not the first woman to do so, my lord." Celia thought injecting a bit of humor into the situation would ease Gabriel's worry. She was mistaken.

Brow furrowed, his expression turned dark as a thunderstorm. "I've never cared for another woman the way I care about you, Celia." His hand cupped her chin. "You will allow the doctor to examine you. I must know that you are well. That the demands I've made upon you these past few weeks have not damaged you. If this is a result of something I've done…"

Something unknown glittered in the depths of his eyes with that abrupt confession. Possessiveness, yes, but it mingled with something undefinable. It was warm and beautifully entrancing and capable of melting Celia's willpower to resist his commands.

She became lightheaded, exhilaration and amazement swooping about her stomach with the uplifting force of a thousand fluttery butterflies. Her heart tightened painfully but not from fear. This was much bigger. More encompassing and empowering. It both weakened her and made her invincible. A paradox of emotions. Two sides of the same coin. Soft and yet unyielding. Giving and taking. The conqueror and the sacrifice. Light and dark. She was all that at once. A perfect match for a man like Gabriel because he was all those things and more.

The realization that she loved him hit Celia with the sudden clarity of a lightning bolt. It was stunning how it rolled over her, leaving her a pile of mush in his hands. Easily bent to his will and desires. Eager to do whatever he asked of her, no matter how infuriating or silly she thought it might be.

"Please," Gabriel added, and Celia melted even further, the terror over Bryan Flannigan's sudden reappearance in her life easing when his thumb rubbed gently over her bottom lip. "Do this for me, sugarplum. Let me take care of you."

"Most likely, it is simple exhaustion stemming from recent events in your life. I understand you only recently married, my lord?"

"Two weeks ago," Gabriel replied.

The physician smiled knowingly. "Ah, then that explains it. I see this many times with newly married wives. I would not worry over much, Lord Rosenthorne. Your wife appears to be in perfect health."

Gabriel eyed the doctor with a critical stare. "Are you positive? I'll not have her fainting again only to have you diagnose some malady."

"I'm quite sure," the doctor said in a jovial manner. "Your concern is unfounded, my lord. I've found women faint on a regular basis. Perhaps it is on account of their fragile constitutions, but the condition always resolves itself rather quickly. Lady Rosenthorne is no different than my other patients with the same complaints."

Celia refrained from a rather biting comment. She and her "fragile" constitution would like very much to kick the good doctor in the shin. The man was quite handsome and surprisingly young for his profession. No doubt, there were many women who "needed" his medical expertise. He was definitely a charmer, but for all his popularity in treating members of the *ton,* the man knew nothing about her, nor what she'd endured in the past. She was far from being a frail, brittle creature.

"So, may I get up from this bed now?" she asked in an exasperated tone, earning a sharp glance from Gabriel.

The peevish note in her voice was simply not complementary of a marchioness, and the flare in Gabriel's gaze was a stark reminder of her new status. Swallowing hard, she amended in what could only be considered a breathless, flirty explanation. "That is, I would very much like to see my new home. We only just arrived, Doctor Franklin, and right away, I was carried to this room and put to bed. Please say I don't have to remain in it for very long."

Gabriel's head tilted, an eyebrow raising in dark amusement at her obvious tactic.

"If you are feeling well, you most certainly should do as you please, Lady Rosenthorne," Dr. Franklin said with an encouraging smile.

"Thank you. How refreshing to discover your sage advice matches my feelings on the subject. Why, I might have just had the capacity of diagnosing myself all along!"

Celia found she could not move when Gabriel suddenly moved closer. Standing beside the bed, his hand clamped over her shoulder, keeping her pinned against the pillows. "It's best you stay where you are. Just relax and let me tend to you. Even when you are somewhat petulant, I enjoy seeing to your needs." His fingers drifted up and caressed the curve of her throat, his touch sure and possessive. "In fact, I insist upon it."

Celia flushed, catching the meaning behind his words and his actions. She was behaving rather brattish, and Gabriel would not hesitate in correcting her once they had a bit of privacy. He might even punish her for speaking so freely to the doctor. Why her blood began racing through her veins at the very thought was a puzzle she'd yet to work out.

"I will walk you out to your carriage, Doctor Franklin. The marchioness and I both appreciate you coming so quickly." Gabriel moved away, and Celia thought it was as if the sun had retreated. When he glanced back at her while escorting the doctor to the bedchamber door, Celia shivered at the promise in his dark gaze. "I'll return in a moment, darling. Do not think of moving from that bed. Not even one inch."

Celia should have thought twice, but her chin tilted high in a challenging manner. "I anxiously await your return, dear husband."

Gabriel's eyes burned at the unspoken challenge in Celia's voice, a smirk twisting his lips. "Not as much as I do."

❧

GABRIEL TOOK the stairs returning to the master bedchamber slowly. He could not erase from memory how Celia had appeared just before she fainted. How frightened she appeared. It was as though she'd seen a ghost, her features so white and pale that she might have been an apparition herself. He literally panicked when she slumped in his arms. His usual, calm demeanor was almost comically obliterated by fear and irrational terror for his wife's well-being.

He barely remembered bolting up the stairs, holding her body against his as if he could protect her from whatever caused her pain.

While the doctor's examination left him with the peace of mind Celia had not fainted from an unknown physical ailment, Gabriel could not ignore the fact *something* had happened.

The question was: what triggered it?

Gabriel dismissed the upstairs staff milling nervously about on the second-floor landing. Even Katie, Celia's maid, was dismissed before he reentered the master bedchamber.

It was gratifying to see Celia still abed. She wore her traveling dress, although the hat and gloves had been removed. Even her hair remained twisted into a modest bun. During his absence, she'd moved and now sat propped against the headboard, numerous fluffy pillows piled high behind her. Her dark chocolate brown eyes followed him as he shut the door and then leaned against it with arms crossed over his chest.

"I'm glad you are feeling better," he murmured.

Celia returned his stare. "I did not need the physician. I told you it is common for women to faint. Perhaps I overheated or did not eat enough lunch." She shrugged. "Even the coach ride could be to blame."

"Hmm," was Gabriel's reply. He considered that for a few moments then came closer, arms still crossed as he studied her. "Have you ever been to Rosenthorne Hall before?"

Celia shook her head. "It's well known that your father

rarely entertained. In the years since my coming out, no events have taken place here. Why do you ask?"

Gabriel knew he was missing something important when it came to this fainting business, but he could not reason it out. "I thought perhaps something about this place triggered a memory of something terrible. Or even sad."

Was he wrong in thinking perhaps her face paled just a little bit more? There was a secret here, but damned if he could uncover it.

She let out a shaky laugh. "I hope you will not call for a doctor every time I sneeze, for heaven's sake. I don't know if I would like becoming one of Doctor Franklin's regular patients, although I understand why some women would."

Gabriel's mouth tightened. "Did you enjoy your *examination* by the good doctor?"

Her eyes narrowed at the unmistakable note of jealousy in his tone. He couldn't hide it.

She shrugged. "You called for him, husband. Remember?"

"So I did. I trust you recall my warning regarding certain situations?"

Celia flinched, and while Gabriel felt a pang of regret for reminding her of his violent tendencies, he wasn't sorry that it was true.

"Even more egregious than your flirtation is your impudence. Certainly not very marchioness-like, wouldn't you agree?" His hand reached out, brushing aside a tendril of hair that fell across her smooth brow.

When Celia sighed, Gabriel sensed her gratitude that the subject had changed. He should investigate further into why that was, but the spark in her eye intrigued him more.

"I know I must work very hard at being a marchioness you will be proud of, Gabriel." Celia's chin tilted up in that familiar gesture he recognized so well.

"We both must, sugarplum. Together, of course." Gabriel

took her hand, pulling her up from the bed. Turning her around, he began slipping the buttons of her gown from the moorings.

"I have Katie to see to this, my lord." Her voice trembled, but she allowed him to silently continue. His fingers were deft, and soon, the gown fell away from her bosom.

"Your maid is of no use to you right now, Celia. Nor to me. This is just between us."

With her gown loosened, Gabriel began working on the laces of her corset.

Encouraged to step forward from the puddle of clothes left behind on the floor, Gabriel held her hand and helped her hop back up onto the edge of the mattress. Kneeling before her, he untied the laces to the delicate heeled boots she wore, slipped them from her feet, then slid her stockings down her legs as well.

Celia allowed him these liberties, but when she was left in nothing but her chemise and undergarments, she stopped him by placing her hands on his shoulders.

"I can remove the rest of my clothing, Gabriel." Her eyes were shiny with surrender. "I want to do what pleases you."

He stared up at her for a long moment, then shrugged out of his riding coat. "And so you shall, pet. But not tonight. Tonight, you will rest and we shall address these matters tomorrow."

She stuttered in disbelief. "You mean you aren't... I mean, we will not—"

"What kind of husband would I be if I took advantage of your weakness right now? But do not fret, sweet wife. I will administer your correction tomorrow, and you will certainly remember the lesson. Now, keep your chemise on until I can retrieve your nightrail from the lady's chamber adjoining this one. I believe Katie is already there putting away your belongings."

Celia watched silently as he padded to the door connecting

the two suites together and disappeared. He returned very quickly with a flimsy concoction of soft pink muslin.

"I will not complain if you were to visit Madam Maurer's shop in the near future," he murmured, slipping the garment over Celia's head.

"What do you know of Madam Maurer?" Celia asked, a hint of amusement in her voice as he began pulling the pins from her hair.

"What every other red-blooded male in London knows, of course. Her creations for women's lingerie are sinful and certainly more to my liking than these virginal gowns you possess. I give you full rein to purchase whatever strikes your fancy there. In fact, I insist upon it. I've already set aside pin money for your use, but whatever the cost, I will cover all of your expenses."

"Would you go with me?" Celia asked breathlessly, touching Gabriel's arm with the tips of her fingers. She gripped his muscles as he swung back the bedclothes, encouraging her to slide beneath them.

"Would you like me to?" When she nodded, Gabriel teased her, "How scandalous of you, Lady Rosenthorne. I think I would enjoy it as well. Perhaps after I've concluded my meetings in the House of Lords, we can arrange a day to spend together in the city."

The anxiety he'd sensed in her earlier was easing away. She smiled up at him as he kissed her forehead. "I'd like that very much, Gabriel. I truly would."

"Then we shall do as you wish."

CHAPTER 34

Gabriel did as he promised. He simply held her during that first night at Rosenthorne Hall. Celia did not know what well of strength the man drew from when it came to his self-imposed abstinence, but she could not manage the same restraint.

Her body practically buzzed with awareness of her husband. Every move Gabriel made had her skin tightening in response. When he nuzzled her hair, she could not help from wiggling back into him, her bottom nestled against the tops of his thighs. She ached for him, and not having him was frustration amplified a hundred times over.

As he dressed the following morning, Gabriel laughed at her interest in helping him. It was an excuse to touch him, and he knew it. Still without a valet and with no intention of employing one, he quickly dressed himself.

"You've more experience in the intricacies of women's fashions than I have in men's clothing, Gabriel," Celia grumbled, giving up and plopping into a high-backed chair near the fireplace. "I find it most vexing to discover I've no skill at all when it comes to something as simple as tying your cravat. A woman should know such things, don't you think?"

"I think it is far more important to know how to *remove* such items," Gabriel said with a sly grin. He shrugged into a russet brown coat and straightened its edges. "You will not overexert yourself today while I am gone. Explore as you will, but no lifting and no moving of furniture or anything of that nature. I do wish I could be here with you for this as I must learn the layout as well, but Mister Harold and the housekeeper, Mrs. Chason, will show you around. Then you can give me the tour, personally."

Celia drank him in. Her husband was so incredibly handsome. Even if his hair was a bit shaggier than the average lord and the brawny width of his shoulders might be considered beastly by some. He had shaved away the fine stubble on his chin, but by the next morning, he would be forced to do the same again. It was one of his concessions in looking the part as the new Marquess of Rosenthorne. Civilized brutality mingling with the potency of savage, male beauty.

Seeing his arms bulging even beneath the fine cloth of his coat, Celia remembered how they'd wrapped around her during the night when she woke from a frightening nightmare. It'd been years since she'd had one so intense, but Gabriel had taken immediate control, soothing her back to sleep.

She woke that morning with dark circles under her eyes and the understanding she must confront Bryan. Convince him that he could not possibly work for the marquess and be so close to her. It was for his own safety and her sanity. Should Gabriel become aware of just who was working in his stables, he would likely exterminate the man without a second thought. The thought of even talking to Bryan made her nauseous, but it must be done.

Swallowing down the sickness, Celia smiled at her husband

from the middle of the enormous bed. He pulled on a shirt, his fingers nimbly fastening the buttons.

"You look so very handsome, Gabriel."

For all his natural confidence, Celia knew he was nervous. The strangest emotion melted through her, swelling her heart until she recognized it for what it was. Pride. Pride that he was her husband. There was nothing she wouldn't do to ensure his success when it came to being part of her world. Even if she must hide certain things from him, things like the existence of Bryan Flannigan and what he'd done so many years ago. The scandal would ruin Gabriel before he even had a chance of establishing his dominance of the *ton*. And she could not let that night in her father's stables ruin everything her husband deserved to have in his life.

She *would* not let it happen.

"Thank you, pet. I don't know when I shall return today. I must meet with Carraway and discuss arrangements for dowry funds. Once they are transferred into your own account, only you will have access. I will not dictate how you spend it, nor will I have an accounting of its spending. It is yours."

"You are too good to me, Gabriel." Celia bit her bottom lip, realizing just how true that was. She'd married a man who surpassed all her expectations when it came to husbandly attributes. A man who would protect her from the world if necessary.

Gabriel leaned over onto the bed, his hands on her shoulders. He pulled her closer, landing a sweet but fiery kiss on her lips. "I'll do anything for you, Celia. Do you understand? Anything and everything. Even when you don't know what it is that you need, I will provide it. And should I need to burn the world down giving it to you, I shall."

∽

AFTER DRESSING with Katie's help, Celia made her way down to the foyer. Mister Harold, the butler, kindly showed her the various rooms on the main floor. Along the way, he introduced various maids and footmen, imparting tidbits of information about the enormous house. She was shown the kitchen, the ballroom, all five drawing rooms, and the library.

Mister Harold also took her by Gabriel's study. Peeking inside, Celia could see her husband had already put his own touch on the space. It was warm and superbly decorated in muted tones of gold and deep scarlet. The colors of the Rosenthorne marquessate.

"Which way should I go to reach the stables?" Celia asked Mister Harold.

The elderly man gave her directions, and with a sick feeling, Celia exited the house.

The sun was a fiery ball in the morning sky as she followed the gravel path leading to the large building at the back of the manor. The stables bustled with energy as groomsmen and stableboys mingled with skilled workers making repairs. It appeared some parts of the structure had fallen into disrepair over the years.

The head stablemaster offered to give her a tour, but Celia declined. She would rather not keep the man from his work, she explained with a tight smile. But the real reason was she was more comfortable exploring alone without any witnesses in case Bryan made contact.

There were several horses inside their stalls. Arion occupied a roomy box stall. He nickered at seeing Celia's approach, hanging his head over the stall door and tossing it to gain her attention.

"Hello, sweet boy," she crooned, rubbing his large head with the heel of her palm. "Are you settling in?"

She glanced around as she spoke, apprehensive that she would see Bryan, yet even more anxious when she did not. Was it possible the man had left on his own after seeing her? Had he realized the danger of staying?

Please let that be the way of it. It will solve so many problems.

"So, you found a man t'marry you. Even if you were damaged goods."

Bryan's voice was rough and coarse, and when Celia whirled around, she was taken aback by his physical appearance.

He was no longer the boyishly handsome man for whom she'd suffered her first crush. Having only had a fleeting glimpse of him the day before, she saw him quite clearly now. He was gaunt, his hair thinning and his features sallow and pinched.

He smiled cruelly in recognition of her shock. "Aye, I may look different, but you, milady, you look as fine a picture as you did that night in the stables." His watery blue gaze moved over Celia, taking in the obvious wealth of her clothes and the pearls adorning her ears before dropping to the ring on her finger. His eyes gleamed with avarice.

Celia drew back her shoulders, determined not to cower despite the overwhelming terror at seeing him again. "You did not damage me, Bryan. And yes, I am married now. To one of the most powerful men in all of England. While I shouldn't give a farthing for your wellbeing, I cannot help but warn you that is it very dangerous for you to remain here. You must leave. For your own safety."

Bryan's head tilted as he laughed. "For my safety, lass? I am in no danger."

"If my husband discovers who you are, what you *did*, he will kill you. I promise you that."

The man smirked, then with a quick glance around to see if anyone watched them, he sidled closer. He made a pretense of straightening Arion's halter where it hung on a hook beside the stall door and ignored the agitated shaking of the stallion's head. "Was your husband himself what gave me a job."

Icy cold dread permeated Celia's blood. She stared mutely at the man, unable to even voice words, struck silent just as she'd been that terrible night so many years before.

Bryan clucked his tongue. "You didn't know? I'll clear matters for you. You see, I saw you at that inn just after your marriage. You and him. I asked the marquess that very night if he had need of servants, and he directed me to Rosenthorne Park. But the estate manager said I would be of more use in town. Now, your husband probably doesn't remember me, but that's all right. I'm not here for him."

When he stepped toward her, Celia instinctively retreated.

"No, lass. I'm here for you. Do you remember back then I told you to keep your mouth shut or it would go badly for you? Now, it's you worrying that I can keep me own trap closed. After all, we don't want the marquess finding out who's been with his wife, do we? We don't want all those toffs knowing milord married a whore what spread her legs for the first man who told her she was pretty."

Celia trembled when Bryan reached out and ran a finger along the length of her arm. His gaze was contemplative as he stared her down. She smelled the faint odor of sour ale. It emanated from his body and breath.

Is that the cause of his physical decline? An abundance of drink?

"Such finery. I imagine you have lots of pretty things that can keep a man's mouth shut, don't you? Fine things that will keep a man in the things he enjoys. Drink. Women. A turn of the cards now and then." His eyes once again touched on Celia's wedding ring. She folded her hand over it as though that would protect it from avarice.

"You won't… you won't leave, will you?" Celia managed to say, her heart thumping so hard she felt faint again.

"Why would I?" Bryan's laugh was derisive. "I'll stay because you won't say a word about us, and you'll pay for my silence. Pay any price I name just so your new husband never learns the truth. You'll pay to save your own pretty hide."

Bryan was right. Celia would give him anything he demanded. Not to protect herself but to shield Gabriel. The thought of his being ostracized because of her past, of his possible ridicule by the society of which he was now a reluctant member, strengthened her resolve and made her sick at the same time.

Knowing she would give this vile man anything he wanted after he'd stolen so much from her was an abomination.

"Give me what I want. And I keep my mouth shut." Bryan's blue eyes blazed with smug satisfaction. He already knew the answer. He knew Celia would do anything he desired. "Deal?"

Celia nodded as she turned away from him. She stroked Arion's glossy forelock, fighting back tears of resignation and shame.

"I'll take those earbobs for the first payment. Hand them over."

Celia slowly removed the delicate jewelry and placed them in Bryan's grime-encrusted hand. She would not think of the day Tristan gave them to her. Her eighteenth birthday had been the occasion. Her brother said with an affectionate laugh that all women deserved pearls of some sort.

Despite her resolve, a tear rolled down Celia's cheek. It was quickly swiped away. She did not want the creature tormenting her knowing how deeply affected she was by the loss of her brother's gift.

But she was too late in hiding her sorrow.

Bryan grinned. "All fancy ladies like yourself get pin money from their husbands. Hand those coins over instead if you want to keep your pretty trinkets. Easier to spend and I won't have to spend time fencing these bits."

"I haven't received my pin money yet." Celia's voice was hollow. "I've only been here a day and… and the marquess has more important matters to attend."

"I don't care. Better get your hands on it quick, milady,"

Bryan sneered. Spying the stablemaster headed in their direction, he picked up Arion's halter as though inspecting its strapping. "Bring it to me in two days' time. And if you don't, I'll take something else in its place."

His tone left no doubt as to what he referred, and his ravenously greedy gaze confirmed Celia's fears. The man would take anything he could get. Whether of monetary value or pieces of Celia herself, it truly did not matter.

The thought of Bryan laying hands on her after she'd experienced the fiery sweetness of Gabriel's kisses made her stomach roil in revolt.

"I will bring what I can," she whispered, her features twisting in defeat. She could not stand his repulsive presence a moment longer. She fled the stables, hurrying back to the safety of the manor before she vomited.

CHAPTER 35

"There goes the Bastard Marquess now."

Gabriel sighed, ignoring the words spoken in such crisp, cool tones. He was already aware of the slur falling from the lips of certain gentlemen outraged by his rise in fortune and rank. Following the aide, he continued down the corridor, headed for his private office in the House of Lords. It was a temporary space since most of the building was still under construction after the devastating fire of 1834.

Gabriel could not resist glancing back to see who had spoken so derisively. He found the cold eyes of the Earl of Clayton, a man recently back from the edge of financial ruin. Gabriel himself had aided Sebastian Cain in that endeavor nearly two years before. A matter of revenge at the time for the man's intended seduction of Ivy.

"Lord Clayton," Gabriel called out as he continued striding down the hallway. "I do hope you aren't foolish enough to make the same mistakes as in the past. You may not recover so quickly the next time."

The aide guiding Gabriel through the maze of corridors and chambers nodded, saying under his breath, "The earl is certainly one you would do well to avoid, milord. He is a rather disagreeable sort when crossed."

Gabriel gave the younger man a tolerant smile. "The same could be said of me. Although some might argue I'm far worse."

The reception he'd received amongst the gentlemen trickling back for the next Parliament session was certainly an odd mix. Gabriel found himself ignored, discussed as though he were not within hearing, and surprisingly enough, jovially welcomed by more than a few. And as the day wore on, he found himself gradually gaining confidence in both his duties as marquess and his skills at fitting in with this new life. It really was no more difficult than handling issues for Sebastian. A sense of excitement trickled through him as he considered all the things he could do from this seat of power. The injustices he could help alleviate and the positive change he might have a part in, based on his own decisions and convictions.

He ended that first day with several personal offers to cover his sponsorship at White's, the premier gentlemen's club, as well as invitations to apply at Boodles. Sebastian had already secured Gabriel's membership at both clubs, so he declined the generous offers put forth by others.

There were also numerous invitations for social events that he and Celia should attend. The first would take place that same evening at Lord and Lady Buckholt's Grosvenor Square home.

"Just a small gathering. Perhaps twenty guests and an informal dinner. Should be grand fun. However, should I fail in securing you and Lady Rosenthorne, my wife might actually murder me," Ethan, Lord Buckholt, lightheartedly claimed. "She's dead set on having the honor of hosting this season's most in-demand couple before anyone has a chance to snatch you up."

"If Lady Rosenthorne agrees, we shall certainly attend. She is recuperating after the strenuous demands of this last month as well as the journey into London just yesterday."

Ethan waved his hand in understanding. "Of course. We do hope to see you there, but it is only the first of many parties this season."

Gabriel couldn't be sure he was prepared for this test of acceptance into the *ton* so quickly. He realized Ethan and his wife, Margaret, the countess of Buckholt, were just the sort of friends he required in his new role. What he knew of the couple was complimentary, and they held much in common with the friends Gabriel already counted as his. Young, very much in love, and highly connected as well as respected.

If Celia decided they must attend the Buckholts' gathering, Gabriel would happily do as she wished and accompany her.

Indeed, this could be the perfect event for easing his way into society with Celia at his side.

WHEN GABRIEL ARRIVED HOME, Celia met him in Rosenthorne Hall's cavernous, white marble foyer. Frowning, he thought she appeared even more fatigued than she had the night before. The nightmare she suffered must have been more distressing than he initially thought.

"Celia, did you go against my orders and take part in moving things and unpacking your belongings?"

Celia shook her head, her chin lifting as she came close enough that Gabriel could press a kiss to her lips. She blushed at the unexpected show of affection.

"I did as you asked, my lord, and did nothing more than watch others while they worked."

"I'm glad to hear it and yet disappointed to not have a reason to mete out a punishment." Gabriel slipped an arm around her waist as Celia flushed even brighter pink with his husky words. "The Earl of Buckholt and the countess have invited us to dinner at their home tonight. I told him I would not commit unless you gave your blessing."

Celia smiled. "Oh, I would love to. Margaret, the countess, is very sweet. How kind of them to think of us." She regarded Gabriel, her gaze expectant as she asked hesitantly, "Did your day go well then?"

Gabriel nodded. "It did. And yours, little wife?"

A strange expression passed over her face before she gave him a bright smile. "It was fine although confusing. This house is so huge that it's easy to get lost. I wandered through most of the rooms this afternoon, attempting to gain an understanding of its layout."

"I've thought the same. In fact, I've yet to explore all of it. Did you have a chance to visit the stables? I know your fondness for horseflesh, so if none of the mounts here appeal to you, I shall take you to Tattersalls. You may choose a horse to be kept here while we are in residence. Then we can both ride when I've the time and if you are available. I would enjoy spending those moments with you."

Celia grew a shade paler with the mention of the stables, and Gabriel thought it strange. But once again, she smiled radiantly at him.

"Oh, that would be lovely, Gabriel. And very thoughtful. However, I do not think I shall spend much time riding while we are in London."

Gabriel frowned, knowing how much she enjoyed the activity. Her reluctance to share that time with him was far more disturbing than anticipated, but he shrugged it off. No doubt, she just required time to adjust to both married life and life in society's crosshairs.

"We shall discuss it later, but right now, let us make a decision as to whether we go tonight or remain at home," he said, giving her yet another kiss because he could not seem to help himself. "I will do what you think is best. After all, you have all the expertise in such matters."

He sensed how she struggled with the decision, but in the end, she agreed the opportunity was too great to let pass. They would attend the dinner later that evening.

It was a strange thing, Gabriel decided. This preparing to go out into the world as an official married couple. Celia's maid went about getting all the necessities ready, and he watched as Celia was dressed for the evening knowing he would be the one undoing all those preparations at night's end. This first time making love to his wife within the walls of this house would be something they would both remember.

Once they were both ready for the evening, they descended the stairs and exited onto the stone terrace as the coach was brought round. Celia's unease was pronounced when one of the grooms appeared. Stepping forward to take one of the horses by the bit, the man held the matched black geldings in place.

Celia fumbled with her reticule, dropping it.

Gabriel retrieved the small bag, holding it out to her with a puzzled tilt of his head. She clutched it so tight her fingers were crushing the beaded fabric.

"I shall not embarrass you, *petite femme*, if that is what has you so nervous," Gabriel murmured, drawing her startled gaze away from the coach.

She stared at him in surprise. "What do you mean?"

Gabriel shrugged while adjusting the lightweight cloak Celia wore over a gown of deep sapphire blue. His fingers lingered on the curve of her collarbone, the expanse of skin exposed by the gown's scooped bodice. "It is our first true appearance in society as husband and wife. It's only natural that you might be concerned over my reception as marquess. However, I shall be on my best behavior so you have no cause for worry."

Celia's features softened. "I am not worried. You shall know precisely what to say and do. You always do."

Taking her gloved hand in his, Gabriel wished he could strip it away and press his lips to the warmth of her creamy skin. How he loved touching her. Inhaling her delicate scent. Hearing her musical laughter. "But never on so grand a stage, sugarplum. I am nervous, if you must know the truth. And I am not invincible to the distress it will cause me if I should prove to be an embarrassment to you."

Her mouth tightened. "You must not think that, Gabriel. Do not allow the *ton* to keep you from being who you are."

"Having you beside me is all that is keeping me sane right now, Celia." He handed her up into the coach, then settled on the seat beside her. "And I will *never* be as proud as the moment I enter the room with you on my arm."

Celia turned toward him, brushing away the lock of dark hair that was forever falling across his scarred brow. "I am the one honored, Gabriel. Never doubt that for an instant. You were born for this world, and it's time you claim your place in it."

The small, intimate party at Lord Buckholt's had swelled from twenty attendees to nearly double in size. Margaret, however, apparently anticipated this possibility. Her manner remained calm and steady, despite having just pulled off the upset of the Season.

Already on a friendly basis since the beginning of the Season two years prior, Celia embraced the petite blonde woman. Gabriel was encouraged by the lady's enthusiastic greeting and warm smile of welcome when Ethan introduced them.

Gabriel followed Celia's lead, taking the well-wishes and numerous invites all in stride, never revealing his inner conflict.

He was an imposter among these glittering, polite faces. He had killed before. Ruined those who'd deserved it. Gambled alongside the very worst reprobates and visited too many brothels to count. He'd seen a few of these gentlemen in some of those disreputable places. The men he recognized, all highly respected lords, ducked their heads at Gabriel's scrutiny. A few smiled sheepishly while clapping him on the back and welcoming him into the inner circle of society.

These people accepted and celebrated him. Apparently, they did not care Gabriel's father had abandoned him to be raised as a bastard. Did not care his mother was an opera house performer whose husband banished her after the wedding, ashamed of her lack of social status.

None of that mattered. Because what mattered now were the possibilities of everything Gabriel was capable of as a powerful marquess. The favors he could grant. The hopes he could crush. The lives he could change. And the dreams he could make come true.

As the evening wore on, Gabriel slowly learned a valuable lesson about his newfound influence and its impact on those around him. The *ton,* this new world into which he'd been thrust, was no different and no better than the murky underground he'd survived for years.

And he realized with sudden clarity, his experiences before becoming the Marquess of Rosenthorne would serve him well.

"With the Season beginning soon, you will find it difficult getting away from London for longer than a few days, but will you take a honeymoon, Lady Rosenthorne?" Margaret asked during dinner.

"Please, I'm still 'Celia' when amongst friends, regardless of the new title." Celia smiled at Margaret, her eyes straying to where her husband sat at the other end of the table. "And I am unsure of Lord Rosenthorne's thoughts on the subject. It's been a whirlwind since we've married."

Lady Amelia Palmerton arched an eyebrow. "Such a hasty engagement and la, the wedding details are simply fantastical." The woman's tone was almost snide, concealed by the genial smile she wore pasted on her features. "Is it true, my dear, that the marquess had Lord Harvey taken into custody by the local constable? It's being said the poor man spent a miserable night in a cell with the village drunk before Lord Ravenswood directed that he be released."

Celia slanted a glance in Gabriel's direction, obviously unsure how she should respond.

With a heavy sigh, Gabriel nodded in agreement that he would take on the old dragon. He cleared his throat, drawing Lady Palmerton's attention.

"It was absolutely necessary. The man could not be trusted around the marchioness, having attempted an abduction just prior to his detainment. He was released *two* days later, at *my* direction, and suffered no harm that I am aware of."

Lady Palmerton held a hand to her bosom in exaggerated shock. "But still, my dear Marquess. One does not go about such matters in such a barbaric way! There are certainly more genteel ways of handling things. You simply must learn that life as a peer of the realm is very different from the rough and tumble one you led before your father's death resulted in your new title." The lady's censorship was quite obvious, as was her general dislike for Gabriel.

He regarded her with a steely, imperious stare. "Should I have done the honorable thing and challenged him to a duel? I chose the most rational of options available. I'm sure Lord Harvey appreciates my restraint. The man lives because of my discretion. Hopefully, he will think twice before attempting such foolishness again."

Lady Palmerton's lips thinned. "Well, I believe it was simply savage behavior."

Seated beside Celia, Lord Palmerton frowned at his wife's insistence on continuing with the subject. Everyone else at the table had quickly fallen silent, curious to see how the new marquess navigated the disapproval by one of society's dragons of propriety.

Gabriel's smile was cruel patience. "I must disagree with you, Lady Palmerton. Savagery would have involved beating the man to a bloody pulp, which I fervently wished to do. I will not abide any man laying a hand on my property nor harming the people I care for."

"It is good that many gentlemen do not share your propensity for violence, Lord Rosenthorne," Lady Palmerton primly replied.

Gabriel took a sip from his wine glass and found Celia staring at him, an expression blended of both horror and pride stamped over her pale features. She'd not known it was he who ordered Lord Harvey released the day following their marriage.

With his gaze caressing and fiercely possessive, Gabriel raised his glass to her. It was an apologetic salute in light of his following words.

"And I find it appalling more men are unwilling, or perhaps unable, to protect what is theirs. Marquess or no, I will do whatever I deem necessary when it comes to my wife's safety. And the next man to test my resolve may not find himself so fortunate to escape with his life."

"I am the luckiest of women to have such a husband as Lord Rosenthorne," Celia said quietly. "And he is more the man because of the old marquess's absence in his life."

There was a moment of stunned silence among those gathered, then Lord Buckholt slapped the table with the palm of his hand.

"Hear, hear!" Ethan exclaimed, raising his own glass in agreement. "To the protection of our loved ones, regardless of the methods."

As everyone else raised their glasses, with the exception of Lady Palmerton, Gabriel met Celia's gaze across the vast expanse of table separating them and felt his chest swell with a curious emotion. It was near to bursting as awareness flooded his body until he almost couldn't breathe.

The protection of our loved ones...

Loved ones. Celia was *his* loved one.

His.

She was not just his wife. Not just a possession. She was not just his marchioness. Nor was she only an anchor in this new world. No. She was so much more. She was his beloved. His moon and stars and the sun around which he rotated like a moth encircling a flame.

Celia was his everything. And he would die or kill while protecting what was his. If that made him a beast in the eyes of London's society, then that's precisely what he would be.

CHAPTER 36

*I*t was closing in on midnight when they finally arrived at Rosenthorne Hall.

Gabriel helped Celia descend from the coach and then stepped aside so she could continue on without him.

"I shall join you in a moment, my sweet. There is a matter of new upholstery for the coach I must mention to the coachmen. In my opinion, it is rather threadbare." He smiled down at her, placing a finger beneath her chin and lifting it. "And I'll not have my beautiful marchioness riding about Mayfair or the thoroughfares of London in a threadbare, somewhat shabby coach."

"It is not that bad, considering it has most likely not seen any use in many years," Celia replied.

"It's bad enough that I immediately noticed its condition earlier tonight. Go on up onto the terrace. I shall only be a minute or two."

Celia nodded and ascended the terrace steps, intending on waiting for Gabriel there so they could enter the manor together. Gazing up at the night sky, she pondered the appearance of so many stars when the peaceful quiet was disrupted by a man's rough whisper.

"Have you something for me, milady?"

Celia stiffened in fear before half-turning toward Bryan. "Have you lost complete leave of your senses?" she hissed. "The marquess is only steps from us."

"He pays no attention to you and me. Although he should. You are a pretty sight, I'll say that much for ya." Bryan sidled closer. "Do you have what I want?"

"You only blackmailed me this morning. I've not had time to ask my husband for money," Celia snapped back in a low whisper. "And this popping up in an attempt to intimidate as you did earlier this evening will not get your funds any quicker. You will make my husband suspicious if you do not keep your distance."

"The way milord was eating you up with his eyes, I'd say he doesn't notice anything else when you are around. And I think you won't have a problem gettin' whatever you want from him." Bryan laughed and Celia closed her eyes at his crudeness. "Maybe after he tups ya tonight, you ask for it, right? I've a powerful thirst and no coin to quench it. Makes me tongue loose, if you get my meanin'."

"You said I had two days." Celia tried hiding the panic in her voice but failed. Her heart was beating so fast; she feared any second now Gabriel would turn and discover her speaking to this man. He would discover her secret. And he would hate and despise her for stooping so low as to be with someone so despicable and for the threat to his burgeoning social standing.

Even this limited contact with Bryan made Celia feel dirty. As though she should scrub her skin raw in an effort to erase any sign there'd ever been anything between them.

Bryan leaned forward, his sour breath wafting through the air. She nearly gagged, both from the toxicity of his breath and her terror at being caught with him.

"Aye, you are right. I did say two days. Shite, what was I thinking? To compensate for me time, bring some pretties in addition to the coin. I got a half pound for those earbobs. If you show up with nothing, I'll be taking something more personal from ya."

His lecherous laugh sent a wave of horror tumbling over Celia. That was the stuff of her nightmares. The thought of reliving everything this man had done to her left her frozen with fear until footsteps sounded on the terrace behind her.

Celia whirled around. Gabriel was stalking in their direction. His features were etched of stone, but his eyes were alight with fierce concern.

She nearly swayed with relief as he came closer and Bryan, obviously realizing the danger for himself, retreated a bit. A gruesome semblance of a harmless smile pulled his gaunt face even tighter. He bowed at the waist in a grudging show of respect.

"Is something amiss?" Gabriel asked, his hand sliding under Celia's elbow. He squeezed her there, probably not even aware he was practically holding her up.

"Um, no. He was merely curious as to whether or not I prefer to ride in the mornings," Celia managed to say calmly.

"And why does one of the grooms have a need for this information?" Gabriel's voice was calm, but a dangerous thread lurked there. He was suspicious and Celia scrambled for an explanation that would appease him.

"Apparently, at his last place of employment, the lady of the house enjoyed taking a morning ride every day. He wished to have a horse ready for me if that was the case."

For a long moment, Gabriel said nothing as Celia held her breath. Head tilted, he studied Bryan's face until recognition lit his gaze. "Ahh. Flannigan, right? I remember you approaching me at The Gilded Rooster recently. So, it appears Mister Kinsey had work for you, after all."

Bryan executed a bow. "That he did, milord. Pardon me boldness in speaking with Her Ladyship. I mean well enough, that I do."

Celia almost choked at his sinisterly innocent words but quickly recovered with a light cough. "I do believe the night air is turning disagreeable, Lord Rosenthorne. I'd like to go inside now."

Gabriel's inscrutable gaze remained on Bryan for a few moments longer before he said to Celia, "Yes, of course. Come along, then."

Celia allowed her husband to lead her away, and she did not dare turn back to see Bryan's reaction. She imagined his once handsome face was twisted with rage that his torment of her was interrupted.

Soaking in Gabriel's strength, she took a deep breath. She needed guidance for the right words when reminding her husband of his promise of pin money. As for the bit of jewelry Bryan demanded, she would paw through her jewel case and find something of little value both monetarily and emotionally.

Without thinking, she twisted the wedding ring on her finger, conflicted about how she could obtain any meaningful funds in such a short timeframe. It was doubtful Bryan would be content with anything she gave him.

"What has you so worried now, *petite femme?*" Gabriel asked as they entered their suite of rooms.

"Nothing. I think tonight went exceedingly well, don't you think?" Celia replied, tossing her reticule onto an occasional table.

Gabriel regarded her with an unblinking stare, his jaw setting itself in a stony line. "It did. But that is not what I asked you, is it?"

Celia forced herself to act surprised by his seriousness. "Whatever is the matter, my lord?"

"You, sugarplum. You are not yourself and you cannot hide that from me. I will have an answer. What has you reacting like a scalded cat? Jumpy and looking over your shoulder."

"I've no idea what you are talking about, Gabriel," Celia

replied. She was saved from saying anything further when Katie entered the room to help undress her for the evening. The girl yawned behind her hand and drowsily stood by the connecting door to the lady's chambers.

"I will help Her Ladyship tonight. You may go back to bed, Katie," Gabriel said, his tone curt with frustration.

Katie nodded, and with another yawn, she departed for her room in the servant quarters. Once they were again alone, Celia stripped away her formal gloves and then sat at the dressing table. She began removing the pins holding her intricate coiffure in place, working in silence with her eyes downcast. When that was done, she finally met Gabriel's stare in the reflection of the glass.

He was frowning, a muscle ticking in his jaw as he watched her.

"I know you are not telling me something, Celia. And for the life of me, I cannot reason out why you've been acting so strangely since we arrived here yesterday."

Celia let out a little laugh of dismissal. "It is nothing, Gabriel. Just a bit of tiredness is all. Nothing more. Please do not worry so."

Taking her hand, Gabriel pulled her up until she stood before him. His eyes darkened into melting pools of nearly black ink, his mouth quirking at one corner. Slowly, he spun her so she faced away from him and began unfastening the buttons running down the back of her gown.

"I don't believe you, pet. At least, not entirely. And I will do as you ask for now and cease my questioning of your odd behavior. But tell me this at the very least. Are you too tired for your husband's attentions? A continuation of what we started last night is in order, I think."

Celia trembled as the gown parted and his knuckles brushed her skin through the material of the corset and her chemise. "I am not exhausted, my lord. If that is what you are asking."

His chuckle was dark and whispered across her shoulder blades as he bent his head to the task of unlacing the corset. "I am gratified to hear it. I would take you anyway as my body aches for yours, but I am glad you are of a like mind."

Before she knew it, he had loosened everything to the point she could step out of the puddle of material. Once again, she was left wearing only her chemise, stockings, and a pair of elaborately designed heeled slippers of sapphire blue decorated with delicate butterflies of gossamer thin silk.

Gabriel groaned at the sight of them, and Celia's heartbeat increased a hundredfold at the husky sound.

"You are trying to kill me with these damned shoes, aren't you, little witch?"

"No, no, I am most certainly not," Celia stuttered in surprise. "Do you not like them?"

He chuckled again, spinning her back around so that she was staring at his chest. He still wore his evening clothes, although he had removed the formal black coat and tossed it over a nearby chair.

"I like them too much. They are a sinful delight, and I imagine you wearing nothing but these shoes while I'm fucking you."

Celia blushed. She was so relieved that the former topic of her uneasiness was replaced by a discussion of footwear, she did not even mind the wicked nature of his statements.

"You liked it when I did that once before, didn't you?" His question left no room for deception. She could at least tell the truth on this subject.

"Yes," she said softly, her breath catching as a pang of lust rippled through her.

"Sweet little pet. You really are a dream come to life, you know that, right?"

"Yes," she said again, her voice even softer now. There was an element of danger to Gabriel's tone that was not present before.

A darkness of sexuality and possession she both feared and craved. She loved when he spoke with such brutal honesty about his needs and the awakening of her own desires. With this man, she could allow the outside world to fade away, knowing Gabriel would take care of her in his own fashion. Knowing he would break her in the sweetest of ways and then carefully rebuild her.

"I want to see all of you, Celia. Remove your chemise for me. Or would you rather I rip it from your body? Use the remnants as a gag so no one hears your screams?"

Celia tugged her bottom lips between her teeth, biting down hard as a wave of desire weakened her knees.

Ducking her head, she did as he ordered, and he watched with an avarice gleam in his eyes as she wiggled out of her underdrawers. After a moment of hesitation, she pulled the silky chemise up and over her head in a fluid motion and tossed it aside. Now, she was completely bare to his gaze, and Gabriel's eyes roamed over the creamy paleness of her skin with greedy hunger.

He began removing his own clothing as she stood and stared at him, her own eyes wide and dark. First his cravat, then his shirt, his dress boots, and finally the black trousers.

He was as naked as she, with the exception of his cravat which hung loosely from his fingers. He began winding the expensive silk material into a coil. Celia found herself unable to look away from the mesmerizing sight of the white silk wrapping around his large hand.

"Celia, do you have any idea what I want to do to you?"

The question sent a shiver through her body. She swayed toward him as though he'd hypnotized her into a state of willing desperation.

"Something very scandalous, I'm sure," she replied solemnly, her brow furrowing with the slightest hint of anxiety. "Something you've thought a great deal about doing.

Something I may not enjoy at first but possibly will by its end."

Gabriel's smile was tenderly brutal.

"It's difficult containing myself with you when you are so beautifully vulnerable. I'm envisioning several scenarios where you are utterly at my mercy."

Celia swallowed. Gabriel would make sure she enjoyed every second of his form of captivity and punishment.

He trailed a finger over her collarbone, tracing the bones there and moving it down between her breasts, migrating to either side to encircle her aching nipples as they budded tight against his touch and the coolness of the room.

"I will remind you, *ma dragee piquante,* that you are mine in every sense of the word. Your body. Your kisses. Your breasts. Your sweet little quim. It's all mine." His fingertip made a line on her skin, drawing down her abdomen until he reached her belly button. He swirled around it, smiling when she shrank away from him because it tickled, before continuing on until he reached the juncture of her thighs.

He dipped between her swollen lips there, and Celia nearly swooned from the pleasure.

"Gabriel…"

"If claiming you, restraining you, lavishing pleasure upon you until you are hoarse from screaming my name makes me a savage bastard, then we both must accept it for what it is. The truth. And the godawful truth is I enjoy every second of seeing you fall apart at my hands."

His face was stony with resolve, and yet Celia felt the gentleness of his touch. How carefully he handled her and how gently he stroked her flesh until she was gasping for air and melting for him. A wave of love swept over her. It was so strong she nearly claimed it aloud before biting her tongue.

"You are not a bastard," she reminded him. "You are my husband."

A smile touched his lips before he continued.

"Before we begin, you must tell me if I hurt you beyond the point of discomfort," he said, the warning making her eyes close. "You will choose a word, Celia. One you would not normally use during intimate times like this."

Celia's eyes flew open. "Teacakes."

Gabriel grinned. "Teacakes."

"Yes. That is my word." She sounded almost frantic. "I say 'teacakes' and you stop immediately."

"Yes, pet. That is exactly what I will do," he said gently. "You do trust me to stop, don't you, Celia? Because what I've planned for you will not work if that trust does not exist."

"Yes, Gabriel. I trust you. I do."

"Then give me your hands."

Biting her bottom lip, Celia obeyed, watching with increasingly shallow breaths as he expertly wove the cravat in an intricate pattern around her wrists. One tailpiece of the material was left dangling free. It was long enough to bind her to something else.

"Come here." Gabriel tugged her forward, steadying her when she lost her balance. His hands gripped her waist, sure and tight and so hot they might have been burning bits of coal.

Leading her to one of the bedposts at the foot of the bed, Gabriel smiled because her skin was flushing pink with embarrassment. "I'm going to bind you to this post now. And you will give me your tears while I make you come for me. Do you understand?"

Celia hesitated. She wasn't sure how he would go about giving her pleasure, but a bit of pain would accompany the ecstasy she was about to experience.

She nodded slowly, watching as he quickly lashed the free end of his cravat near the top of the post's finial. When he was done, she stood like a filly tethered to a post, the cravat granting a limited range of movement.

"Are you all right?" he whispered against her ear.

Celia moaned, the sound soft and breathy. "Yes." She could feel his muscled chest brushing her back, his cock gliding against the cheeks of her bottom. He was so hard and so big. Everywhere.

"You're such a good girl. Waiting so patiently for me to make you come. Just a bit longer until I show you the stars," he murmured, smoothing his hand over her buttocks. "Christ, I cannot keep my hands off you when you are wearing shoes like this. They scream for me to fuck you so hard we both forget how to breathe."

Celia jolted forward, her belly and the valley between her breasts coming into contact with the fluted column of wood. The coolness of the bedpost's surface made her gasp with awareness. Her nipples puckered even more in reaction. They were now painfully tight. Aching for contact. Aching for Gabriel's mouth. His tongue. His teeth.

"Please…"

The word slipped out. A supplication for more.

"You've been frightened of the dark since I've known you, Celia, and since our marriage, I've realized the severity of your condition is far deeper than just simple fear. Perhaps I can help with this, if you trust me to do what I think is best. Will you allow it, pet? Let me help you?"

Celia's brow creased. Was he trying to cure her of that trauma? How could he? And how did this mesh with the promise of pleasure? It did not seem the two could possibly intertwine.

"I-I don't know."

"Shhh. Let me show you what I mean. You can always use your word and I will stop." He stood beside the bed, his dark eyes burning into hers. His hand smoothed over one of her breasts, tweaking the nipple between thumb and forefinger. When she sucked in a breath and trembled, Gabriel smiled as though he'd just been provided with vital information. "I hope you don't use that word, however. It will please me immensely if you can endure this for even a few moments."

Celia took a deep, ragged breath. She wanted so desperately to please him. Surely, she could do what he wanted for a few seconds. "I'll try. For you, Gabriel."

"Good girl." His approval rumbled through her, leaving her warm and achy all over but especially in the space between her legs. "Wait here. I shall return shortly."

Dropping his hands, he stepped away, and instantly, Celia was cold, her skin pebbling with goosebumps. She hung from the bedpost, listening to the sounds he made while searching for something in the adjoining room which served as a huge wardrobe. It seemed an eternity before he finally returned, and in the soft glow of the lamplight, she saw that Gabriel carried two items in his hands.

A second cravat of black silk and leather riding crop.

CHAPTER 37

Gabriel approached her slowly, using all the caution one might when encountering a wild creature.

Celia tugged against the cravat, dismayed when it did not loosen one bit no matter how she struggled. A sob caught in her throat as fear clawed its way into her soul.

"Shhh," Gabriel shushed. Setting the items down on the bed, he reached out. With a gentle hand, he stroked her hair as it tumbled over her shoulders and down her back in a mass of dark waves. "Calm yourself and listen to me."

"Y-you are going to hurt me," Celia choked out, straining away from her husband and his dark, solemn eyes.

"A little, yes," he replied, his gaze unapologetic. "But, Celia, I swear it is nothing you cannot handle. I believe this will help you. More than you realize, in fact." Gabriel pressed closer, brushing a soft kiss against her trembling lips. "Do you remember your promise to trust me? Believe me, sugarplum, I'd rather stab myself in the heart than cause you harm."

Celia forced herself to stand still and accept the light stroking of his hands down her flanks and over the curve of her buttocks. "Why do you have those things?"

Gabriel moved her hair away from the curve of her neck as he stood behind her. Soft, persuasive kisses were pressed against her skin. Despite herself, Celia's eyes fluttered shut from the pleasure.

"I intend on blindfolding you, pet. And I will use that crop on you in such a way you will experience extreme pleasure. You will associate the darkness, of not being able to see, with unimaginable ecstasy." He murmured his plans in a soothing, singsong voice. The melodic tones were so beautiful and sweet, it was hard for Celia to separate his words from the horror of what he intended.

"If it is a matter of the lamp burning all night that bothers you, I will gladly sleep in the adjoining bedchamber," Celia cried out in desperation.

"Oh, darling. That is not it at all. Your suffering. Your fears. Your nightmares. They pain me because they hurt you. I cannot bear to see you this way night after night. It is killing me. Making me crazy until all I can think about is finding the man who did this to you and snuffing out his life, slowly and with as much torment as possible." Gabriel's hand rose to cup Celia's throat, his fingers spreading wide as he held her immobile so she could not move away. He held her firmly, his cock a hardened steel rod pressing against the softer flesh of her buttocks. Warm breath fanned her ear when he whispered, "I want to destroy that man, but since I have no idea who he is, I must destroy your fears in his place." The tip of his tongue touched her cheek, and with leisurely intent, he licked up one of her tears. "Trust me to help you, Celia. And remember your word that makes all of this stop."

"Tea—" she began, but Gabriel's hand tightened around her throat.

"Think carefully before using that word before we even begin, pet."

Celia swallowed the word. For a long moment, she simply

breathed, taking in all the nuances of her predicament. And Gabriel allowed her to think things through. To rationalize both her fear and her willingness to please him.

And the opportunity to erase your nightmares, her inner voice counseled.

He knew the moment she surrendered, but Celia was not surprised by that fact. Gabriel knew everything about her and used it all to his advantage. He kissed her softly on the nape of her neck, then nipped her there while his fingers still gripped her just beneath her chin.

Celia gasped, the juncture of her thighs growing wetter.

"A bit of pleasure. A bit of pain. They are perfect comple-ments to one another, and I will show you, Celia, how we can use that to erase your fears." As he spoke, he leaned over and picked up the silk cravat from the bed. "I'm going to cover your eyes now. I want you to focus on breathing through every emotion you will undoubtedly experience. Focus on me, Celia, and be stronger than whatever it is you fear in the dark."

He wound the cloth around her head, doubling it so that she could not possibly see through the fabric. By the time he knotted it at the back, she was panting from her panic and frozen with terror.

"Steady, little wife. Steady. I'm still here beside you," Gabriel breathed, his hands moving down her sides as he pushed her more firmly against the bedpost. She instinctively held on to the carved column with her bound hands, fingers digging into the cool wood as though it were the edge of the world and she was in danger of tumbling over.

The next instant, thick, firm fingers swept up between her legs. Celia gasped from the shocking pleasure of Gabriel touching her where she needed it most. She'd not realized how starved she was for it, her legs moving apart of their own accord to allow him greater access. Indeed, it was easy to forget she could not see when he stroked the petals there in a gentle, rubbing motion.

"Yes, there, my darling. Feel my fingers dipping into your quim, spreading your wetness and making your hip buck for more." Gabriel's voice was harsher than before, but he continued the maddening strokes with the same gentleness. "Seven hells. You are so damned lovely like this. Helpless. Wanting. Gasping for me. Wet and needy for me. And so damn brave for me." Sliding a finger inside her, he pumped it in a shallow motion that made Celia see stars behind the blindfold. His thumb teased her clitoris as he said, "Do you like this, pet? Do you like my fingers inside you? *J'effacerai cette peur qui te tient en otage. Va te faire foutre.*"

Even in her dazed state of pleasure, Celia made sense of his words.

I will erase this fear holding you hostage. Fuck it right out of you.

Whenever she felt the panic rising, his fingers moved more insistently, making her forget she could rip the blindfold away with her bound hands. Making her forget she could say the word that would make all of this stop. She could not stop him. Not when she was climbing higher and higher and crumpling for him all at the same time. He was pushing her over the edge, and she couldn't even see the abyss that would swallow her whole.

"Yes, Christ above, *there*. Right there is my sweet girl. My good girl. Come for me, pet. Let the darkness take you and fight back against it. You are stronger than it could ever be. I'll be here to catch you." Gabriel's words became a litany Celia clung to, and when she finally screamed her release, sagging against her bondage at the height of exquisite, pulsing madness, she was jolted anew by the leather crop snapping lightly against one buttock cheek.

The sound was a slap of reality she could not see coming nor anticipate its arrival. A sensation she could only absorb as she helplessly trembled from the climax and shudders rippled through her.

That stinging line of fire was somehow enhanced and tempered when Gabriel's finger was joined by a second digit, both plunging even deeper into her core. She choked on a whimper when the crop struck again without warning. And yet, in this confusing tangle of fear and insanity, her body responded with a jerk of pure lust.

"Again, *ma dragee piquante.* Come for me again." The riding crop bit her flesh several times in a row, and Celia jerked against her restraints with a low wail.

But it was not a cry of pain. It wasn't a cry of terror. It was a plea for more.

More. More. More.

And Gabriel, as always, knew what Celia needed.

The popping sounds of the crop melted into the rhythmic thrusting of his fingers, and Celia sank into the darkness surrounding her. It enveloped her until there was nothing other than her husband's hands on her body. The sting of the riding crop. The burn of her flesh accepting it. She cried for him, cried for herself, tears running down her cheeks in a cathartic, cleansing rush. Washing away the shame, the terror, the pain from before as though it were water swirling down a drain.

This went on for what might have been hours, or maybe only minutes. It was difficult determining the passage of time when pleasure and pain merged into one. But, somehow, the memories of that awful night were being erased. Erased until all that mattered was Gabriel and how he made her feel. Outside of this room, the world did not exist.

He coaxed her again and again into mindless pleasure, and when his cock replaced his fingers, Celia welcomed him by arching her back, allowing him to drive everything from her mind as surely as his body drove into her own.

"Gabriel, my love, my love…" Celia did not even realize she

chanted his name until he abruptly tangled a fist in her hair, turning her head until her lips were accessible. The riding crop clattered to the floor. He kissed the very breath from her as he plunged into her body over and over, the size of his cock burning and stretching her at this angle. Almost painful but divine as well. Two sides of the same coin. The light and the dark melding together into one.

She exploded around him as he groaned in appreciation. When he bit the back of her neck, the sharpness of his teeth was insignificant to the sense of belonging flooding her as he climaxed deep inside her. And when her shaky legs refused to hold her upright, Gabriel was there as he'd promised.

Catching her in the darkness and making her world brighter than the sun.

~

SHE DID NOT REMEMBER Gabriel untying her hands. She did not remember the moment he removed the blindfold from her eyes. One minute she was hanging from the post, the next she was in their bed with Gabriel tending to her so gently she wanted to weep again for reasons she didn't understand.

Her shoes were slipped off her feet, silk stockings rolled down and tossed aside. Gabriel wiped her down with a cool cloth, slipping into the nooks and crannies of her body while she drifted in a pleasant haze. When she began shaking, he wrapped the coverlet around her and held her tight until the tremors passed.

Then he laid her back on the pillows and settled between her thighs.

"I need you again, *mon coeur*," he whispered against her lips. "I'm a monster, but I cannot help myself. I cannot get enough of you."

Celia nodded, too depleted of strength to protest. She

wanted him again as well, even if she could not muster the strength to say so.

Her arms looped around his neck as Gabriel took his cock in his own hand, rubbing against her folds and spreading her moisture over himself before surging inside her.

It feels so right. So good. This is where I'm meant to be. Here. Here with him. Gabriel. My love. My love who dragged me out of the darkness.

"You are mine, Celia. I will keep you safe from anyone and anything who would do you harm." Gabriel's hips tilted, his cock going so deep she moaned. His way was eased by the slickness of her desire, but she felt so full of him it was difficult to breathe. "Do you understand? You. Are. Mine." *Thrust.* "Mine." *Thrust.* "Mine."

Celia cried into his shoulder, her backside burning as the motion of their bodies slid her back and forth on the sheets. It hurt, but she didn't care. She was his, and as he took her with a violence tempered only by his innate gentleness, she accepted that, too.

CHAPTER 38

Gabriel rolled onto his back, throwing a hand over his eyes as memories of the night roared into his head. Beside him, nestled on the pillows with an arm thrown across his midsection, Celia slept soundly. The tracks of dried tears stained her cheeks, a silent recrimination of how brutally he'd abused her the night before. How far beyond the pale he'd taken his plan to release her from the prison of her past.

He'd gone too far.

"Fuck," he muttered.

Perhaps his plan had worked at first. She'd cried, but she'd also accepted what he gave her. She'd not used her special word to stop him. Had not pleaded nor begged for mercy. Miraculously, she'd even slept through the night after he turned the lamps completely down. Slipped into sleep with a faint smile on her face despite the room being in total darkness.

No, his courageous girl accepted everything he'd given her. And he'd masterfully restrained himself until that moment when she'd called him "my love."

Those words, spoken with such desperation, turned him into a wild beast. A feral creature determined to mark his mate.

"Fuck," Gabriel groaned again, recalling how his teeth clamped down on her in the frenzy to stake his claim. She'd been so sweet in his mouth, her taste one of honey. Of sugared fruit. Of all things decadent and inherently sinful.

Then, after all that, he'd taken her again. Knowing she was sore from his cock and the riding crop. Knowing she was coming down from a unique high caused by multiple orgasms, intense pleasure, and the stripes laid across her buttocks as she writhed for him against the damned bedpost. He was worse than his own father could have ever thought of being. He had taken advantage of Celia's weakness. Her innate innocence. Her willingness to please him.

Closing his eyes, Gabriel clenched his fists.

I'm a goddamn monster. Her tear-stained cheeks, the red marks on her wrists from his cravat, and the massive erection between his own legs at that very moment were all irrefutable, damning proof.

"Good morning."

Celia's soft voice snapped Gabriel's eyes open. Turning his head, he encountered the liquid chocolate of her gaze. Her lips curved into a hesitant smile that illuminated the hazy morning light of their room.

Christ, she was so beautiful it made his mouth dry.

"Good morning," he replied, tensing up. Any second now, she would accuse him of violence. Of taking her against her will. Of hurting her, and worse, finding enjoyment in it.

But Celia did none of those things. Instead, she moved closer and pressed a kiss on his mouth. A soft, sweet, shy kiss that surprised Gabriel and did nothing to stem the fire raging through his veins.

"I slept without the lamps, didn't I?"

Her question was not one of accusation. She sounded curious. And proud of herself for the accomplishment

Gabriel nodded.

Celia's fingers twined with his, and the simple act of holding his hand left his heart in utter shambles. The wedding ring on her finger glinted sharply, reflecting the pale light in the room. It reminded Gabriel just how precious this woman was to him.

"Thank you, Gabriel." She brought his hand to her mouth, pressing kisses to his knuckles.

"It will not keep your fears at bay forever, but it is a start." His reply came out in a growl. He sounded like an angry bear when truly he was attempting to behave more gentlemanly.

But, seven hells, how he wanted to fuck his sweet wife into oblivion at that very moment.

She appeared unconcerned by his gruffness. Taking the hand she'd just kissed, she held it to her bosom. Her gaze was calm and steady—so unlike the frightened, anxious woman in his arms last night.

"There is that, at least." Celia smiled again. "I'm willing to try your methods again. If you think it will help me." Her cheeks reddened with embarrassment while Gabriel clenched his teeth to keep himself from rolling her beneath him. Did she even realize she was naked beneath the coverlet? And he was as well?

Did she not know the willpower required to stop from doing everything his body howled for?

"I think, perhaps, I went too far last night. Sugarplum, I do not wish to truly hurt you."

"You haven't and you won't," she stated firmly, her chin tilting up. "I trust you, Gabriel. With all that I am, I trust you."

She moved even closer until the soft scent of roses, lemons, and sex filled Gabriel's nostrils. It was intoxicating enough to make his head swim. "Will you kiss me, Gabriel? And... touch me again?"

Dear God. Celia was not frightened by his methods. She was

not shrinking away from him in horror. She wanted him as badly as he wanted her.

"Yes," he choked out before pulling her into his arms so that she sprawled against his chest. He knew she felt his cock, hard and insistent between their bodies, but she was not intimidated by it. Instead, she rotated a little against him, and he growled in a heated warning.

"Celia, keep moving like that, and I will not be responsible for what happens next. You are driving me crazy with need."

Celia bit her bottom lip, somberly gazing down at him. "I called you my love last night, didn't I? In the height of my pleasure."

"You did. And I loved hearing it from your lips."

"It's true, you know. You are my love. I will do anything for you, Gabriel. Anything you ask of me. To support you. To protect you." There was a tiny quiver of distress in her confession, but Gabriel dismissed it because everything else in that moment meant more.

She loved him.

"I feel the same for you, sweet wife." Gabriel cradled her head in his hands, peering into her chocolatey brown eyes. "I love you with all that I am."

Celia smiled, her head dropping down until her lips met his in a fiery mingling of their souls. They made love then, sweetly, with tenderness and careful attention to each other's needs. And before Celia fell asleep once again, exhausted from his kisses and the force of their passion, Gabriel's arms tightened around her.

"When I say you are my heart, I mean it, Celia." He kissed her temple, nuzzling into her hair. "It cannot beat without you."

"I KNOW I've no need of it, Gabriel, but when might I have a bit of pin money?" Celia asked as Katie finished pulling her hair into a simple updo.

Gabriel grinned while shrugging into his coat. "Right away, little wife. How much do you require?"

Celia's head tilted at his easy reply. Had she expected more of a fight? She must know he would gladly give her his entire fortune if she but asked for it.

"I'm not sure." Celia's brow crinkled as she considered the request she made. "I should have asked Ivy or Sara what is a customary amount. Or even consulted my mother for advice on the subject. I suppose whatever you think is appropriate."

Striding toward her, Gabriel pulled her up from the vanity table's chair and kissed her forehead. "Come to my study when you are done here."

She still looked dismayed, but Gabriel laughed. "We shall figure it out together, Celia. Whatever I have is yours to take. You know that. There's your dowry fund as well that belongs only to you. The barrister is still setting up the account for your use. Come downstairs when you are ready."

Half an hour later, Celia stood in his study staring at the wad of pound notes he'd pressed into her hand.

"It's too much," she said, trying to hand it back.

"You don't know that, sugarplum." He covered her hand with his, closing his fingers so that the money could not be released. "Neither of us has been married before, so your pin money shall be whatever I think necessary."

Celia pursed her lips. "Is this a monthly thing, then?"

Gabriel laughed, the sound rich and melodious. "Weekly. And should you run out of funds before the end of next week, you must inform me immediately so that I may give you more."

Celia thought about that for a moment, then the next thing Gabriel knew, she'd launched herself into his arms. She hugged him so fiercely he thought she might be trying to strangle him in gratitude.

"It's just money, *petite femme.* And since I've more of it than the Devil himself, I won't miss the little bit I give you."

"You are too good to me, Gabriel. Thank you." Her breath was sweet and warm against his neck as she embraced him, then she was turning her head so that their mouths almost touched. "Are you needed anywhere else other than here this morning? Am I delaying you from important business elsewhere or keeping you from seeing important people?"

He wouldn't bore her with the list of tasks he would undertake today. He'd just received the listing of those servants hired since he'd become marquess, and while others might find it tedious and unnecessary, Gabriel wanted to know the people working for him.

"There are matters I must attend to later today, yes." His arms tightened around Celia's waist. "But there is nothing in my life more important than you, sugarplum."

Celia sighed in relief, her eyes dancing with mischievousness. "Then may I show my husband how much I appreciate his kind, generous nature?"

Gabriel grinned, desire roaring to life as it always did when he was near her. Tracing the outline of her mouth with his tongue, he gave her a heated kiss then said with a whisper, "I'm rarely kind, and I'll take your gratitude while I'm seated at my desk. Now, on your knees, pet."

CHAPTER 39

Celia waited until Gabriel was gone before making her way to the stables.

In her pocket was a gold bangle bracelet inlaid with three opals, two ten-pound notes, and a ripe, red apple.

The apple was for Arion, just in case she was questioned about being in the stables.

In the early afternoon hours, the large, sprawling building was a quiet place. The stable boys usually finished their chores well before the noon hour and now caught little naps where they could. The stablemaster was most likely in his office handling the business of paperwork while the grooms and coach drivers gathered in the mews, playing cards while waiting to be summoned to work.

Celia twisted her hands together as she made her way down the long aisleway leading to Arion's stall. It was the spot where Bryan instructed her to meet him, but she was a day early. She wanted to get this over with. Indeed, the quicker the better. Once he had his money and a bit of jewelry, Celia hoped the man would be on his way. Leaving her alone forever.

She nearly screamed when a hand clamped over her mouth

from somewhere behind her. Bryan's fetid, alcohol-laced breath was instantly recognized as his arm wrapped itself around her waist. In this manner, he carried her to a darkened portion of the aisle where a ladder led up to one of the numerous haylofts. There was surprising strength in his thin form, evident in the scrawny muscles that held her hostage as he manhandled her.

Setting Celia down on her feet, Bryan held her close while also pushing her forward until her chin rested on one of the ladder's rough, wooden rungs.

"Climb, milady," he gritted between clenched teeth.

Celia hesitated, but when he squeezed his arm around her until she could barely breathe, and the hand over her mouth clamped down even tighter, tears sprung to her eyes. She nodded the best she could and gulped in great drafts of air when he released her.

Hand over hand, clutching her skirts, she ascended the ladder with Bryan close behind her in case she considered changing her mind. Once in the hayloft, Celia moved as far away as possible. Eventually, she stood before a huge hook at the end of a thick length of rope. It was part of a pulley system, used to swing bales of hay up to that level of the stables.

Bryan followed, his watery blue eyes gleaming in the dust mote-laden dimness. An ugly grin split his features, his teeth yellowed and in need of cleaning. He'd declined so much in the past five years; it was difficult understanding how quickly it had occurred.

"Couldn't wait to see me, could ya?"

Celia shivered. She'd not dressed for the chilly environs of a hayloft. It was much colder up here than it was down below where the horses' body heat kept the stalls warm.

"Once I give you this money, you will leave and never come back," she replied, pulling out the notes. She placed it on a hale bale, then added the bracelet to the small paper pile. "It is all I have," she lied.

Bryan picked up the money, an expression of mistrust twisting his mouth into a scowl. "What's this? I don't want paper. I need gold. Gold sovereigns."

Celia drew up straighter. She would not be afraid of this man. She was stronger than him, no matter that her hands were shaking. "It is more money than you would make in a year on a groom's wage. And the bracelet is pure gold and opals. It is more than enough to buy your silence and give you a reason to go far away from here."

"I don't want paper." He snarled again. "Hard to buy me drink with scraps of paper."

"It is all I have. It is either this or nothing. It's half the pin money the marquess gave me. I cannot give you any more. He will become suspicious of its spending if I've nothing to show for it."

Bryan stared at her, frustration evident in the clenching of his teeth. He stepped closer, and Celia retreated until there was nowhere else to go. She now stood on the edge of the platform with the hard cobblestone floor of the aisleway far below.

"Half, eh?" A calculating glint lit his eyes. "Then you can get more?"

Celia choked on the bolt of panic swelling in her chest. "You must leave, Bryan! Please, I cannot deceive my husband in this manner. I cannot steal from him over and over to pay you. Your blackmail will cost us both our lives. Don't you see that?"

The man moved so quickly, Celia did not realize his intent until he had her by the face, his hand gripping her cheeks and squeezing tight.

Please don't let him leave bruises.

"Either you keep bringing the money I want, or I'll take payment in other forms." He brushed his mouth against hers until Celia gagged. "I've always fancied a tumble with a duchess. But I guess a marchioness will do just fine in your case."

Celia grabbed his hands with hers, pulling hard until his grip loosened. "I-I will bring you money, Bryan. But I cannot do it this week. You must wait until I'm given more pin money."

He released her with a cruel laugh. "I may hang around for a long time with that sort of motivation. But every now and then, milady, I need a bonus. The feel of your sweet cunny on my cock next time you bring me money will do just fine."

Celia nearly vomited, overcome by fear and loathing and terror that Bryan would rape her as he had before.

"You want to keep this all a secret from your fine husband, don't you? Don't want all of London knowing you cuckolded him with the servants. That he married a whore." Bryan sneered, seeing her pale features and delighting in them. "You'll do whatever I say if ya want the bastard marquess to stand with his head higher than everyone else."

"SEBASTIAN AND IVY will arrive in London any day now," Gabriel said over the meal they shared in the enormous dining room. "With Alan and Sara just behind them, no doubt. And if I don't miss my guess, I imagine your brother and mine will appear at some point to assess for themselves how we've both taken to marriage."

Celia smiled wanly while taking a sip of her wine. "It will be lovely to see them."

Gabriel's brow creased with a small frown. "The opening of the season no doubt requires much of our time. I know you are accepting far too many of the invitations you have received. I won't have you exhaust yourself by attending these events, Celia. Not for my sake."

Celia waved a hand in dismissal of his concerns. "I'm always a little weary at the beginning of the Season. It's just how things are."

She knew Gabriel was growing suspicious of her behavior

over the past four days. Ever since she'd left Bryan in the hayloft with her agreement to do as he demanded, she'd been unwell. Nightmares plagued her, returning with such vengeance that Gabriel swore it was all his fault. If he hadn't coerced her into being blindfolded while taking a crop to her backside, she would not be suffering these nightly terrors now, he claimed.

Gabriel reached over, taking her hand in his and squeezing it tight. "I cannot bear to see you like this, Celia. If my presence here is causing this turmoil, then I shall remove myself at once. I will find a townhouse to rent, or perhaps stay in a hotel until you are once again comfortable being with me."

Celia stood up so quickly, the heavy dining room chair tumbled over. "For God's sake, Gabriel! This melancholy of mine is not your fault, and don't you dare leave me when every nuance of your future relies on the *ton* accepting you as the Marquess of Rosenthorne. You will *not* jeopardize this. I won't allow it."

Gabriel's eyes darkened, dangerous glints of gold lighting their depths as he stared at his wife quivering before him. "You will sit down, Celia. You are becoming overwrought, and I won't have you upsetting yourself in this manner. Sit down. Now."

He nodded at one of the footmen. The servant stepped forward, quickly righting Celia's chair so she could sink back into it before retreating to his place along the wall just out of earshot.

"I apologize, my lord. I had no right to shout as I just did," Celia replied woodenly. The urge to cry was welling up inside her, and at any minute, the dam would break. It would spill everywhere. All the ugliness. The shame. The fear. It would destroy and taint everything.

Gabriel stood up from his own chair and approached Celia where she sat. Then, with a heavy sigh, he knelt before her, taking both of her hands within his. Raising them to his lips, he pressed a gentle kiss upon her knuckles while staring into her eyes.

"I *know* something is wrong, Celia. Damned if I can figure it out, however. I will not willingly leave you. I only thought it might help... *Fuck*," he cursed, his head lowering in defeat. "I don't know what to do. Tell me what to do, sugarplum."

Silence stretched between them as Gabriel remained on his knees before her. His broad shoulders slumped as he rubbed a thumb over her knuckles in a soothing manner.

"Make love to me, Gabriel," Celia whispered, her demand snapping Gabriel's head back up. He pinned her with a steely glare as if what she asked was too great a price to pay. He'd not touched her in that way since the morning she'd pleasured him in his study. She thought back to that morning now, clenching her thighs together at the memory of Gabriel's hands holding her head steady while he thrust up into her mouth. The way he'd thrown his head against the high back of his leather chair, emitting a low roar of satisfaction when he exploded into her mouth. She wanted that assurance now. To know that he loved her and needed her as she loved and needed him.

"I cannot. Not when you've suffered some sort of setback at my hands," he said in a tortured voice. "It isn't healthy to revisit such methods."

"It is what I want. It's what I need. Only you can help me, Gabriel. Please." Celia was resolute. She was sure Gabriel's touch could erase the demons chasing her. Her husband could expunge those nightmares as he'd done once before. She needed him to do as she asked because it would give her the strength to face Bryan the next time. "Take me to bed and make love to me. I-I need you inside me."

She knew the instant she broke down his resistance. His eyes darkened and she knew he would do as she asked because he craved her, too.

Much later, after Gabriel held her down and plunged into

her body over and over, his hands squeezing her throat to the point she nearly fainted, his melodic voice crooning in her ear to come for him again and again, Celia lay beside him in the dark and wept against his shoulder.

When he folded her tighter against his body and whispered everything would be all right, Celia realized what she must do to end this nightmare.

Bryan would never leave. Of that, Celia was certain. He would blackmail her over and over, tormenting her until she either wasted away from guilt or Gabriel left her behind in her misery while pursuing his place in society unimpeded. She would become a forgotten, abandoned wife.

As Gabriel's own mother had once been.

Celia dashed the tears from her cheeks. There was only one thing that could be done.

She must eliminate Bryan Flannigan on her own.

CHAPTER 40

Gabriel flipped through the pages of the list he'd ordered of the estate's new employees.

Most had worked at several different places over the years while others were considerably more stable. The ones bouncing around held his attention, however. Those individuals could prove problematic over time, having moved from employer to employer for one reason or another. Some had been sacked while others quit of their own volition.

For that purpose, he'd sent out his contacts into the underbelly of London, finding out as much as possible about the employees on this list. There were eighteen requiring closer scrutiny, and this was Gabriel's first chance to look them over.

Rubbing his brow, Gabriel pondered the reason for his own delay in this task. Neither he nor Celia were sleeping very well. Celia's frequent nightmares, along with her renewed refusals to sleep in the dark, were wearing them both to a frazzle.

It was perplexing, this change in her. Gabriel wondered if the pressure of being a marchioness, of being his wife in particular, contributed to the problem. She was deeply concerned about his acceptance in society, but the fear was unfounded.

There were some who turned up their noses at him, but few dared snub him when faced with his considerable power. Even if they called him a bastard behind his back, Gabriel did not really care. He could deal with that.

It was Celia's nightmares that disturbed him the most.

They occurred over the last few nights without fail. Sometimes, they were full-blown episodes, with Celia shaking and crying out in her sleep. Other times, they were simply a sudden awakening and her sharp, startled gasp of terror.

But whenever Gabriel suggested they return to Rosenthorne Park and the quiet of the countryside, Celia adamantly refused.

"Your place… our place is here in London for now, my lord," she replied with that stubborn tilt to her chin that made him want to both kiss her and turn her over his knee. "And here we shall stay."

The list. Concentrate on that.

Taking a sip from a glass of brandy, Gabriel applied himself to the task he'd put off for several days now.

The section of new groomsmen and the stable personnel contained the highest number of new hires. With his father's bad health and tendency toward reclusiveness the last few years of his life, there'd been little need for stable help before. Gabriel scanned the list, noting the places the different servants had been employed, and came across a name that gave him reason to pause.

Bryan Flannigan.

Gabriel settled back in his chair. He couldn't explain why the name jumped out from all the others, but he quickly perused the man's history. His concern grew when he saw one of the places of Flannigan's previous employment.

For nearly three years, the man worked at Darby Meadows.

Celia's home.

Since leaving that position with Lord Darby, Flannigan bounced from estate to estate over the next five years. He'd worked in London for a short period of time before returning to the countryside and working menial jobs at various inns.

Now, the man was employed here, at Rosenthorne Hall.

Had Flannigan been one of the grooms holding the coach the day they arrived? On the very day Celia fainted? Maybe. Gabriel could not be certain. But the man had definitely approached Celia the night they returned from Lord and Lady Buckholt's dinner party.

Gabriel distinctly remembered the incident. Flannigan had stood disturbingly close to Celia. She had been so pale, blaming the night air for her unease. Her mannerisms were those of someone with a secret to hide.

It was that same night Gabriel tied her up and forced her cathartic episode.

Gabriel's mind swam with questions. What did this all mean? Was it simply a coincidence?

Celia should have recognized Flannigan as being a former employee of her father's. Knowing her love for horses, it seemed impossible she never encountered Flannigan during the three years he worked at Darby Meadows.

"She said not a word that night on the terrace steps. She acted as one would with a stranger," Gabriel pondered aloud. "Only, he cannot possibly be a stranger."

A terrible possibility formed in Gabriel's mind. A scenario too horrible to be true. But prudent as he was, he needed further information before confronting the man. He sure as hell needed more before asking his wife how well she knew Bryan Flannigan.

And if that same man was the reason for her fear of the dark.

IT WAS another two days before Gabriel received word there was additional information regarding Flannigan.

Gabriel agreed he would meet the contact in a tavern just off St. James Street near Brooks, the exclusive gentleman's club.

He thought of having his informant come to him but quickly decided against it. The man was a creature of the back alleys and rougher establishments scattered throughout London. His presence at the Marquess of Rosenthorne's manor in Mayfair would most certainly draw unwanted attention.

Gabriel could not afford losing such a valuable asset on the street, especially now that he was prohibited from these types of underground activities because of his new title. It was frustrating he could no longer do such things with any semblance of anonymity. Just his presence in the tavern would attract notice. For that reason, Gabriel dressed plainly for the meeting, taking a hired cab there after leaving his offices at Parliament.

Consulting his pocket watch as the cab maneuvered the streets of London, Gabriel considered the shortage of time he faced. Sebastian and Ivy had arrived in town just the day before. Their invitation to see the opening night of a popular play at the St. James Theatre, followed by dinner afterward meant he could not take his time in ridding the world of Bryan Flannigan. If it was indeed warranted.

Stepping into The Red Rabbit, Gabriel searched for his man and found him along the back wall in a darkened booth as expected.

Gabriel removed his hat and gloves. Approaching the booth, his expression remained unreadable as Mister Tallard sipped from a mug of ale and waved a hand in his direction.

"O'er here, guvnor."

Gabriel slid onto the pitted wood bench seat. A passing tavern wench placed a full mug in front of him and quickly swiped up the gold crown Gabriel laid on the table. It more than covered the cost of their drinks, so she placed a third tankard down as well.

Mister Tallard pulled that one toward himself and proceeded to gulp it down.

"What news?" Gabriel asked while Mister Tallard swiped his bearded chin clean of sudsy foam. Hopefully, the man would not become too inebriated before he imparted the details Gabriel wished to know.

"That bloke is right bad news, guvnor."

"How so?" Gabriel's scarred brow raised in question. The mere sight of his scar was apparently enough to strike fear into Mister Tallard. The older man swallowed hard and took another fortifying swallow from the tankard.

"Seems he's left a trail of ruined misses 'cross half of England. Once he's had one, he up and leaves 'em. Moves on to the next place. And nothin' is said 'bout what he's done." He squinted at Gabriel. 'Cause what papa wants it known his little girl was tupped by the help?"

Gabriel's heart stilled in its beat, a leaden lump occupying his chest. A dulled roar filled his ears, and without conscious awareness, his hands clenched and unclenched into fists. He gripped his own mug of ale so tight he was in danger of snapping off the handle.

This explained so much of Celia's behavior. Her refusal to marry just any man in her orbit. For weeks now, he had believed the person who so cruelly abused her was a peer of society. A man hiding behind the mask of a gentleman.

How wrong he had been.

His sweet, fiery Celia had been victimized by someone who bore far too much resemblance to himself. A nobody. A commoner. A man of violence. Someone who had taken advantage of a young girl's innocence. A man who returned to torment her even now.

Which begged another question. One Gabriel could not begin to contemplate.

Has that animal touched her again?

"Will you need help gettin' rid of the bugger?" Mister Tallard's question was tinged with a note of hopefulness. "Got me own wee daughter, ya see. Stays with her mother out in Leeds. Any bloke messes with her that way and he won't live to see the next mornin', if you understand my meanin'. Happy to aid ya in this, guvnor. Yessir, more than happy."

The bloodlust rushing through Gabriel's veins could not be ignored. And it certainly would not be denied. The uncivilized side of him, the beastly side always at war with his innate nobility and honesty, surged to the surface. It obliterated any consideration of what a law-abiding citizen would do in this situation. A marquess should not administer judgment and punishment, but then again, he was not a true marquess. Not completely, anyway.

He was Gabriel Rose in this moment, and that was a man who knew death very well. A man who would administer it with stealth and cunning and an exacting level of expertise that was the stuff of nightmares.

What needed to be done would be accomplished by *his* hand. This was something he alone must do. And once the earth was wiped clean of Bryan Flannigan, Gabriel would go about mending his Celia back together again.

"I will not require assistance," Gabriel said, rising from the bench. Tossing a pouch full of coins on the table in front of Mister Talbert, he added ominously, "And if anyone should ever ask, you've never heard of Bryan Flannigan."

CHAPTER 41

elia pulled open the drawer of Gabriel's desk.

She stared at the four-barrel pocket pistol for a long moment before she carefully picked it up. The silver on the inlaid handle gleamed with a dull glow, the wood on the stock polished and smooth beneath her fingertips.

Thank goodness for Tristan's lessons. His instructions were a way of eliminating boredom while growing up on Darby Meadows more than any belief she should learn self-protection, but Celia had been a quick student. Once her brother showed her how to load and unload a firearm, how to mark the sight and steady her aim, it wasn't long before she could hit near the center of the target almost every time.

"Good enough to possibly kill a man," Tristan had cheerfully exclaimed of her skill.

That knowledge in handling the weapon would serve her well now.

With a deep breath, Celia quickly loaded the pistol and slipped it into her pocket. Closing the drawer of the desk, she leaned against the piece of furniture for a moment and considered how much time she had before Gabriel was expected back.

The mantle clock above the fireplace struck the hour of two. Gabriel would not be home until at least five that evening. He would then go about changing clothes for their evening planned with Sebastian and Ivy at the theatre, and Celia hoped she would be in their bedchamber, preparing for the evening as well.

A free woman at last.

"You can do this," Celia whispered to herself. It was possible she could kill a man and then go blissfully on her way. To the theatre. To dinner. She could commit murder then laugh afterward with her friends and kiss her husband, knowing she had done what was necessary to protect herself and Gabriel.

She would do this, and along with the original secret, she would keep the two hidden forever.

Making her way to the stables, Celia could not ignore how heavy the pistol felt in the pocket of her cloak. How it rubbed against the banknotes she also carried. The money was an incentive. Her final attempt at convincing Bryan he must leave and never come back.

And if he refused…

Celia prayed he would not.

After determining the aisleway was indeed deserted, Celia carefully climbed up to the hayloft. The pistol bumped against her leg, weighting her skirts down as she ascended the wooden ladder. She tried not to think about the real possibility of using it.

The moment she was free of the ladder, Bryan grabbed her by the arm. He dragged her away from the loft's edge and shoved her toward the stack of hay bales in the far corner.

"You're late," he sneered.

"Only by a few minutes," Celia replied, rubbing her arm. Even through the cloak and the fabric of her gown, she was sure he left bruises from gripping her so hard. She would need to invent a reasonable excuse to justify the markings when Gabriel discovered them.

"Well? Did you bring what I asked for?"

Celia took a deep, shuddering breath. "I did. And Bryan, once again, I am begging you to take this money and go. Somewhere far away from here. I won't bring you any more money. This is the last time."

"Oh, is it now, Marchioness?" Bryan asked softly, his face twisting into a mask of rage so frightening, Celia's heart began skipping in double time. "You think you get to tell me what to do? Ya do what I say, not the other way around."

Celia pulled the wad of notes from her pocket and thrust it toward him. When he did not take it from her hand, it scattered over the floor of the loft and mixed in with the hay. "Take it. Please take it. It's all the pin money I have. Every bit of it. You could live off this for years, if you are careful with its spending. But you cannot stay here and I cannot bring you more."

A calculating light gleamed in Bryan's cold blue eyes. "Then I suppose I'll be telling everyone I fucked the Marquess of Rosenthorne's new wife. That I had her sweet young cunny long before he tasted her. Do you want them all to know how you begged for me cock and how you cried when I didn't spill inside ya?"

Celia's eyes closed. Her hand found its way into her pocket, her fingers caressing the butt of the pistol.

If I should pull this from my pocket, there is no going back. I will kill him.

"You will not say anything, Bryan. I won't allow it." Her voice trembled, but the thread of resolute strength in it only sent Bryan into a further rage.

"You know what? I think I'll have you and the money. I think I'll take that ring on your finger as well. It'll bring a pretty penny." He advanced on her, ignoring her warning. Ignoring the chance she'd given him.

He'd sealed his death warrant with those words, and she would die before she allowed this animal to take Gabriel's ring from her finger.

The pistol suddenly appeared in her hand, pointed straight at Bryan's chest. For a moment, he appeared surprised, but then he laughed.

"Milady thinks she can shoot me?" He moved forward, daring her to take a shot. "You don't have what it takes to kill a man."

Bryan rushed her then, the shock of his attack freezing Celia in place. The pistol flew out of her hand, skidding across the floor out of reach.

"Knew ya couldn't do it," he mocked just before he backhanded her across the face. His knuckles cut her lip open. Celia flew backward from the force of the blow, a haybale breaking her fall. She rolled away, desperate to reach the pistol, but Bryan landed on top of her. He was so heavy, despite his scrawny form.

"Fight me, milady. I like it better when a woman fights back. Come on, then." He struck her across the face again, laughing when she cried out in pain. "Ya were a lot scrappier back when you were sixteen, ya know that?"

Celia was dazed from the blows, but still, she pushed and shoved at Bryan as he began tearing at her clothes. The rafters above her swirled crazily, but she was able to rake her fingernails down his face.

"You goddamn little bitch. You'll pay for that," Bryan grunted, his hands reaching beneath her gown. He grabbed her thighs, wrenching them apart. "I'm gonna fuck you until you can't walk. Plant my bastard in your belly and stick around long enough to watch you pass it off as your husband's. A bastard for a bastard, eh?"

Celia sobbed as she fought harder. Kicking, scratching,

biting—she was like a wild woman as he tried pinning her down. "I won't let you do this to me again. I won't."

When Bryan fumbled to release his member from his trousers, Celia took that opportunity. Her knee landed in his groin with vicious accuracy and enough strength to drive him backward.

She scrambled out from under him, crawling across the floor to reach the pistol.

Behind her, Bryan wailed in pain. Glancing over her shoulder to see if he followed, Celia saw the way he clutched between his legs.

"I'm gonna kill you when I get my hands on you, ya fuckin' whore." Spittle flew from his mouth as he cursed, his face turning a scarlet hue as he checked himself for injuries. His pale cock now hung between his legs, shriveled and limp as a fallen custard.

A renewed sense of victory surged through Celia with the realization of what she'd accomplished during their struggle. She had hurt him.

I hurt him!

She turned, intent on reaching the pistol and shooting him dead, but instead of the weapon, she encountered a pair of gleaming Hussar boots. They were so shiny; even in the watery, grey light of the hay loft, they reflected her face back to her. Her gaze moved up and up until, at last, she was staring into the stormy visage of her husband. The pistol was in his hand and trained on Bryan.

"I'm here, sugarplum." His voice was soft as he reached down and pulled Celia to her feet with his free hand. He brushed a few pieces of straw from her disheveled hair with a gentle hand. "I'm here now."

His golden-brown eyes flared at seeing her injuries. The bloody lip. The bruises on her face. The rips and tears to her clothes. A cold rage, an expression like nothing Celia had ever witnessed on another human's face crossed Gabriel's features. It was terrifying, and yet, in that moment when her husband might have been the very Devil himself, she was grateful to see him. Even if he learned the truth about her, Celia could not be sorry he had come.

How he'd known she'd be in the stables, Celia did not understand, but he was here now. And that was everything.

"Gabriel," she choked out, sagging against him in relief. "Thank God."

"Shhh, *mon coeur*." He moved her until she stood behind him, his body shielding hers. "Stay here, Celia. Promise me you will stay right here. No matter what." When her head moved in a jerky nod, Gabriel gave her a smile and then turned to Bryan.

"Are you ready to die, Bryan Flannigan?" Gabriel's voice was low, melodic. It was almost soothing, but the violence lacing through it was enough to frighten the strongest of men. "You hurt the woman I love, and I will kill you for touching what is mine. If you are not aware of my reputation, you should know I intend on doing it slowly. I want you to feel the maximum amount of agonizing pain. You will beg me to finish the job before I'm done with you, but those pleas will be in vain."

"She—" Bryan began to say something while stuffing his cock back into his pants.

Gabriel held up a hand.

"Say her name and the first thing I shall take is your tongue. And although I don't want to do that because I am anxious to hear your screams in the next few moments, I cannot abide having my wife's name in your filthy mouth," Gabriel said calmly.

Picking up a forgotten length of rope from the loft's floor, Gabriel tossed it at Bryan. "Tie this around your hands."

Bryan grinned, catching the rope. "Plan on taking me to the bobbies, do ya?"

Gabriel smiled angelically. "Not quite. I know what you've

done to my wife. Both today and in the past when you were at Darby Meadows. I know you took her innocence and left fear behind in its place. The English penal system in general is not prepared to administer the type of punishment you require. This will be my task and one I take quite seriously. As you will soon discover."

Assured his instructions had been followed, Gabriel picked up another bit of rope and approached with the pistol aimed at Bryan's head. "Make one move I don't like and I will watch a bullet split your head open like a ripe melon."

Fashioning the second piece of rope into a noose, he looped it around Bryan's neck and practically dragged him to the hook and pulley system.

The rope was looped around the hook's curved edge.

For the first time, Bryan looked concerned. Celia saw real fear in the man's eyes. Fear and a bit of calculating intelligence. It made her shake with trepidation. Bryan was like a cornered animal. He would chew off his own arm to escape the trap.

No matter his restraints, he was still dangerous.

"Now," Gabriel said with a cold grin as he tucked the pistol into the waistband of his trousers. "*Now*, you and I are ready to begin. Celia, my love? Look away."

CHAPTER 42

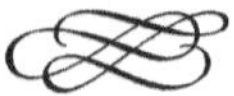

Gabriel's fist connected with Bryan's jaw with a satisfying crack.

He stepped back, shaking out his hand with a slight grimace. It's been a while since he'd punched someone.

Bryan laughed, spitting out blood. "You can't just kill me in your hayloft, yer Lordship. What will the other servants think? You'll not find another groom what to work with ya, I promise you that."

"No one will dare interfere. They are all too afraid of the marquess and what he might do." Gabriel chuckled darkly. "Indeed, the second they saw me entering the stables, every last one of them fled. Perhaps they saw the bloodlust on my face. In my eyes. Perhaps they feared my wrath was intended for one of them."

Gabriel landed a punch in Bryan's midsection and the man groaned.

"Killing me won't erase it, yer Lordship. Won't change how much I liked her squirming when me cock was inside her," Bryan grunted through the pain, then let out an evil laugh. "She thought we was gonna get married or something. That's how I tricked her. But I told her that she better not tell anyone. Told her I wouldn't swing just because she gave it to me like a whore. And I won't swing now. You know that, yer Lordship. You'll let me go. Save yourself the shame of everyone knowing what I done. Just like she tried to do for you."

All of the anger, all of the darkness he'd tamped down, his possessiveness for Celia and the need to keep her safe pooled in Gabriel's center. He'd never felt this way before. Never experienced such desire to end a man's life. To destroy him. To rip him apart.

Bryan Flannigan was an abomination. A feral, disgusting animal who should be removed from society.

As if from a distance, Gabriel became aware of Celia's sobs of terror. Briefly, he wondered who she was more frightened of. Flannigan? Or himself?

He shook off the doubts, allowing the murderous calm to settle over him once more. *This must be done. For Celia. For myself. For us both.*

"I've no intention of letting you go, you bastard," Gabriel growled. "I'm going to rip you apart, limb from limb. Listen to your screams with the greatest of pleasure and watch you die, writhing in pain and begging my wife's forgiveness."

"Aye. She'll be begging all right," Bryan sneered through the blood pooling in his mouth. It was as though he intentionally taunted Gabriel. "Begging me to fuck her again."

With a roar of absolute fury, Gabriel lunged for the man, intending to rip Bryan's tongue from his throat using nothing but his bare hands.

"Stop!" Celia cried out in horror, holding her hands over her ears. "Stop!"

Gabriel half-turned, concern for Celia cutting through the bloodlust. It left him vulnerable for a split second.

It was a stupid mistake. Bryan took immediate advantage of the distraction and Gabriel's closer proximity. With his bound hands, he grabbed the pistol, jerking it free from Gabriel's waistband.

"Gotcha!" Bryan crowed in victory. Laughing maniacally, he waived the pistol at Gabriel.

Cocking the hammer, he pulled the trigger without much forethought into aiming the weapon.

The shot rang out, the bullet embedding in a rafter above them. The loft filled with the acrid smell of gunpowder and hazy smoke. Celia screamed in horror as Gabriel grappled with Bryan, fighting to regain control of the gun now wedged between their bodies.

Another shot. This one winging wide to land in the wall opposite of the hayloft. Below them, horses whinnied in confused fear, stamping their hooves and moving restlessly within their stalls.

Gabriel heard the sound of feet flying across the loft's floorboards. He died a thousand deaths because of her recklessness, but before he could utter anything more than a hoarse "No!" Celia was beside him.

Inserting herself between the bodies of the two men as they fought, Celia shoved Bryan away with a desperate sob.

At the same time, Gabriel grabbed the pistol from Bryan's loosely bound hands. Winding an arm around Celia's waist, he slung her out of harm's way.

"Get away, Celia!" he barked, terror for her safety evident in the violence of his voice.

She landed on her hands and knees a few feet away, dazed by the quickness of Gabriel's actions, her eyes wide as she stared at the two men.

During the struggle, the two men had come dangerously close to the loft's edge. Bryan teetered on the ledge for half a second.

"Help me!" he gasped, his arms flailing for balance.

Determined that Bryan would not escape his brand of

vengeance so easily and painlessly, Gabriel reached for him. But it was too late. The heavy hook over which the noose was looped swung out over the stables with the momentum of Bryan's body.

The snap of his neck was startling. Loud. The creaking of the hook swinging back and forth from the weight of Bryan's body even more so.

Celia let out a muffled scream. Scrambling to her feet, she launched herself at Gabriel.

He crushed her against his chest, his face buried in the wealth of her hair as it tumbled free of its pins. Desperately, he swung her around in an effort to shield her view of the dead man.

"I've got you, my love. *Petite femme.* I've got you. You are safe now. Safe."

It was all Gabriel could say as he held Celia's trembling body. He absorbed her sobs, arms wrapped tight around her as she wept with relief that the nightmare was finally over.

"We've avoided the inquest, thank God," Sebastian said, plopping down on a settee in Rosenthorne Hall's drawing room. The space was full of friends and family who had gathered to celebrate the somber decision delivered by England's highest magistrates that very morning.

Gabriel nodded, taking Celia's hand and squeezing it tight. She smiled at him, then accepted her mother's affectionate kiss on her cheek.

"It was preposterous they attempted charging you with a crime in the first place," Heath chimed in with his customary sardonic grin. "I suppose having friends willing to vouch for your name when it's needed most is a valuable thing. One never knows when a situation might require such influence."

"Obviously, the Rosenthorne title can only do so much on its own," Gabriel replied with a crooked smile. "It took the Duke of Richeforte and the rest of you standing behind me to end this hellish nightmare. Regardless, I was prepared to hang for my part in Flannigan's death. What happened kept Celia safe from further harm."

Celia snuggled closer to him, holding Gabriel's arm tighter. "I would not have allowed it. I would have rescued you from any cell they placed you in, and we would have escaped to a place they would have never found us."

Gabriel chucked his wife underneath her chin. "Coming from my little wife who attempted to stop Flannigan's crime spree without assistance, I believe it."

Celia blushed, but she did not dispute his assertion. Only they knew the full truth of what happened in that hayloft, and it was a secret they would never reveal to another soul. A secret that was buried with Bryan Flannigan in a pauper's grave just three weeks ago.

All of them—Ravenswood, Bentley, Lord Buckholt, Heath, and Celia's family—had banded together and protested Gabriel's imminent incarceration for the crime of murder. But it was Nicholas, the Duke of Richeforte, who'd held the most sway over the proceedings. The man had recently swooped into London, conducted a few secret meetings, then departed just as suddenly. He'd been reluctant to leave his duchess alone for very long, considering the advanced stage of Grace's pregnancy. There was no doubt his actions on Gabriel's behalf resulted in the dismissal of the case.

"Self-defense resulting in accidental death was all they could concoct against you. And even that was tossed based on Flannigan's previous crimes and his activity since coming into your employment," Bentley said, raising a glass of brandy in a celebratory toast. "The man basically hung himself in that loft after stealing God knows how much from you, Rosenthorne.

Everyone knows you could have shot the man several times over for the single crime of holding Celia hostage, never mind the evidence of the money and jewels he'd taken. Who knows how many other estates he worked and used the same tactics?"

"So true," Lady Darby said, holding a hand to her heart. "Thank goodness you thwarted that man's evil plans, Lord Rosenthorne. My daughter is indeed lucky to have married a husband so dedicated to her safety. Her father and I thank you."

"Indeed," Tristan agreed with a kiss on his own wife's hand. "Violet and I are both grateful and proud to call you family."

A round of toasts followed that statement.

When Ivy, the Countess of Ravenswood, leaned in to embrace Celia, Gabriel clearly overheard the lady's amused comment.

"See? You found your prince amongst frogs, after all, Celia."

CHAPTER 43

Celia fell back on the bed in an exhausted heap.

It was late and their guests had all departed, but it wasn't just the festivities from this evening which left Celia so tired. No, the previous few weeks had been a whirlwind of activity. Despite her husband's notoriety, or perhaps because of it, she and Gabriel had attended more parties, balls, and soirees thrown on their behalf than she could count. It seemed everyone wanted the Marquess and Marchioness of Rosenthorne as their guests of honor.

Gabriel was enfolded into society with very little question, despite his unusual inheritance. The news chronicles romanticized him, gave him the moniker of the Hero of Mayfair. They unabashedly celebrated the daring rescue of his wife from a dangerous attacker.

Gabriel leaned over her, tickling her nose with a feather he'd pulled from her coiffure. "Shall I let you sleep, *ma dragee picquante?*"

She still suffered some nights from nightmares, but with Gabriel's love and attention, those events were fading into the past. The knowledge she was safe did much to aid in her heal-ing, and slowly, the memories were being forever erased.

Celia laughed, raising her arms and looping them around Gabriel's corded neck. "Don't you dare, husband. You know full well I've no intention of falling asleep after you kissed me the way you did just now in the corridor."

"You mean how you kissed me, don't you?" he murmured, running the feather down from her nose to the Cupid's bow of her lips. "As if you cannot get enough of my mouth."

Tracing the feather over the outline of her mouth, he moved the delicate instrument even lower. It trailed down her throat and across her collarbone until, finally, he reached the swell of her breasts, rising and falling above the neckline of a lowcut bodice.

Celia squirmed at the ticklish sensation, a giggle catching in her throat when Gabriel's eyebrow lifted high at her response.

"You are ticklish. So sensitive... so responsive. I wonder where else I might touch your body and receive such a reaction?"

"I'm not ticklish," Celia protested, then began laughing uncontrollably as Gabriel dropped the feather and nuzzled his face into the tempting hollow between her breasts. "Stop it, you incorrigible man! Oh!" She giggled harder, grabbing Gabriel's shaggy head between her hands to halt its back-and-forth motion. His own rumble of a laugh vibrated against her chest.

"Cry for mercy, little wife. Cry and I will surely grant it. For the price of a kiss, anyway."

"Yes," Celia breathed in amusement. "A kiss I shall gladly pay."

Gabriel's head rose just enough so that his golden-brown eyes could assess her honesty. "A kiss of my choosing, then." Mischievousness twinkled in the depths of his gaze, and as always, Celia was utterly captivated.

Her breath catching in her throat, she nodded. "Anything you wish, Gabriel. You know that I am yours."

His features softened, eyes smoldering as he ran a thumb over her lips. He encouraged her to open and suck him inside her mouth. "I know. But I love hearing you say the words, anyway."

"I am yours, Gabriel. And I love you," Celia whispered, her tongue caressing him between the words. She was rewarded when his eyes turned darker than the night sky, and a tortured groan escaped his throat as he watched her mouth.

"And I love you, sugarplum. Sometimes, it is more than my soul can contain. It leaves me breathless. Steals my words from me. Lights up the night like a thousand suns. You are everything to me."

Her hand cupped his cheek, loving how its stubbled warmth nestled into her palm and the way his eyes closed with pleasure.

They remained like that for a long moment, then Gabriel said in a husky voice, "I want my kiss in the bathtub, little wife. Will you share it with me?"

Celia nodded eagerly as Gabriel rose from the bed, pulling her up as well and spinning her about so he could begin unbuttoning her gown.

"So many damned buttons," he muttered against the nape of her neck.

With a soft laugh, she ducked her head. "I could say the same of your own garments, Lord Rosenthorne."

"Then we shall engage in a mutual cursing of one another's clothing as we undress," he chuckled. "And then I shall have that kiss."

The next few minutes were filled with breathy sighs and moans of appreciation as they undressed. While Celia removed her shoes and stockings, Gabriel stepped into the bathing room. He filled the tiled rectangular structure with steaming hot water from a spiderweb of pipes on one wall.

"Our bath is ready," he called out from the adjoining room.

Her husband was already in the sunken tub when Celia entered the room. He lay sprawled within it—a dark king waiting for his queen.

Gabriel's whiskey-hued gaze flicked over the thin chemise Celia wore for modesty's sake. A smile lifted the corners of his plush, firm lips. "Remove that. You will present yourself to me, Celia, so I may look my fill."

Celia chewed her bottom lip, tugging it between her teeth and worrying the flesh. She still became nervous when he used that growly voice, but she trusted Gabriel completely. And as always, his roughness, his absolute hunger for her was exciting to the point of madness.

"Perhaps you prefer removing it yourself, my lord," she taunted, shifting her legs so that the chemise fluttered along the tops of her thighs.

Gabriel grinned, teeth flashing white, and crooked a finger in her direction. "Come here, my prickly sugarplum."

When she sidled near, he reached out, grabbing the chemise's hem.

He rubbed the silky material between forefinger and thumb, glancing up at her through his thick eyelashes. "I've no wish to ruin it."

"You shall buy me another." Her voice was breathy with arousal. The way he looked at her sent fire rushing through her veins.

"Very well." Using both hands on the garment's hem, Gabriel ripped it into two halves and it fluttered to the floor.

It happened so quickly, Celia could only gasp in surprise.

"Get into the tub, Celia. Now, lean back opposite of me. Spread your legs and place your heels on the edge."

Gabriel helped arrange her as he liked, a soft curse escaping him as she sat splayed before him. Her breasts bobbed gently in the water, smooth and creamy, and he tweaked both nipples with hard fingers.

"Oh, God," Celia moaned.

Gabriel laughed. "I've told you before. I'm your God when we are like this, pet. And you will do everything I command, won't you?"

"Yes," she choked out. She was already so aroused she almost climaxed just from the way Gabriel called her "pet."

"Good. I want you to caress your breasts. Pinch those pretty, rose-colored nipples while I have that kiss you promised me."

Her hands rose almost of their own accords, doing what he instructed, and then she gulped in surprise as Gabriel's hands cupped her bottom. He lifted her slightly from the tub and moved between her bent knees.

"What are you doing?" she asked, her voice panicked.

"Getting my kiss. Savoring the taste of your quim in my mouth. Feasting on your sweetness." He spread her wet curls, his fingers holding her open as his mouth lowered.

He licked, lapped, and sucked her for what seemed a lifetime. When she hovered on the brink of exploding, Gabriel slowed his actions.

"Wait, Celia. This kiss is for my pleasure so you will not come just yet." He nipped the inside of her thighs to drive the point home.

"Please, Gabriel," she wailed.

"No. Not yet." His voice remained calm. "You won't come until I am inside you." Then he cruelly pushed the point of his tongue into her entrance, spearing her with it as if it were his cock, then sucked her clitoris deep into the furnace of his mouth. "I want to feel you trembling around me."

When her legs began shaking, he finally relented. In a smooth motion, he reclined back, pulling Celia atop of him. Her legs straddled his hips and then, with breathtaking quickness, she was impaled on his cock.

The depth of this position, the control it gave her made Celia nearly combust. She braced herself with her hands on his wide, muscled chest.

"Yes, that's it. My good girl. My good, fucking girl. Ride me, Celia. Ride me and come around me. Don't stop. Don't you dare fucking stop."

Gabriel surged up into her, a hand going to her throat and squeezing as she rocked atop his body.

"Yes," he hissed. "Just like that. Come with me now, Celia. Come with me."

The heavens opened and exploded as Celia reached her climax. She cried out, quivering atop Gabriel as he grunted and squeezed her throat tighter. She felt the warmth of his seed bathing her channel, the world shifting and tilting upon its axis.

Gabriel held her tight through the shuddering climax they shared.

"Mine," he growled, claiming her mouth in a blistering kiss. "My love. My pet. My sweet sugarplum. *Mine*."

"Yes," Celia whispered, kissing Gabriel back with the same fierce intensity. How she loved this man. How she craved his touch. His kisses. "Yours. Always."

"I cannot believe my fortune in having a woman like you love a rogue like me," he whispered, caressing her throat now with gentle fingers.

This was Heaven, Gabriel's arms around her a sanctuary. Her husband was the home she would always have.

She traced the thin scar separating his eyebrow with a gentle finger, her hand drifting lower until it rested against his jaw. Turning his head, his eyes closed as he nuzzled into her palm like a tame lion. His eyes fluttered shut then opened, meeting hers with a blazing intensity that swelled her heart with love. Gabriel brushed her lips with his own, their breaths mingling.

"But you are *my* rogue, Gabriel," Celia whispered before

their mouths fused together once more. "My own darling rogue."

THE END

ACKNOWLEDGMENTS

As always, thank you to my readers for allowing me to go on this amazing journey. Whenever I receive emails, reviews, or notes, I just can't believe how blessed I am. To write, and have others read those words and enjoy them, is a dream come true. So, thank you from the bottom of my heart.

A huge heap of thanks to my amazing editor, Kendra. She spit-shines every word for me. I am so grateful. Special thanks to Dragonfly Ink Graphic Designs for the gorgeous cover. A very special thanks to my PA, Cheryl Maddox for all she does!

Thank you to my sweet husband, James. He understands that when I say I've got to write, that means I've got to write! He's always supportive in helping me accomplish my dreams.

Thanks to the family and friends I can't live without: Alyssa and Trey. Jodi and Tommy. Dad. Danny and Ashley. Dan and Karen. Chris. Ladyne and Gary. Deb and Lance. Winston. Sean. Cecil and LeAnne. You guys make every weekend special, even those weekends we aren't necessarily together.

Special thanks to my friends in the book world. Michelle, Cindi, the ladies in the Historical Harlots Facebook Group. You all mean so much to me. The support, the cheerleading, the commiserating, the sharing, the laughter. All of it helps in this day-to-day world we create as authors. Love you guys.

About April Moran

April enjoys writing both historical and new adult romance

with a generous splash of heat. When not penning tales of passion, she enjoys traveling with her husband, attending rock concerts with friends, and time spent with family. Brainstorming new storylines is best done while riding her horse or during long walks with her German Shepherd. A tumbler of good whiskey helps tie all the details together and brings her characters to life.

BOOKS2READ.COM
https://books2read.com/author/april-moran/subscribe/33016

VISIT APRIL'S WEBSITE
www.aprilmoranbooks.com

SIGN UP FOR NEWSLETTER AND UPDATES
http://bit.ly/AprilMoran_BookUpdates

STALK APRIL EVERYWHERE

https://www.facebook.com/AuthorAprilMoran

https://www.facebook.com/groups/aprilshoneybees/

https://www.bookbub.com/profile/april-moran

https://www.instagram.com/aprilmoranbooks

https://www.goodreads.com/Author-AprilMoran

https://www.pinterest.com/aprilmoranbooks

https://www.tiktok.com/authoraprilmoran